Arthur Collins Maclay

Mito Yashiki, a Tale of old Japan

Being a Feudal Romance Descriptive of the Decline of the Shogunate. Second

Edition

Arthur Collins Maclay

Mito Yashiki, a Tale of old Japan
Being a Feudal Romance Descriptive of the Decline of the Shogunate. Second Edition

ISBN/EAN: 9783744770347

Printed in Europe, USA, Canada, Australia, Japan

Cover: Foto ©Andreas Hilbeck / pixelio.de

More available books at **www.hansebooks.com**

MITO YASHIKI

A TALE OF OLD JAPAN

BEING A FEUDAL ROMANCE DESCRIPTIVE OF THE DECLINE OF
THE SHOGUNATE AND OF THE DOWNFALL OF THE
POWER OF THE TOKUGAWA FAMILY

BY

ARTHUR COLLINS MACLAY, A.M., LL.B.

AUTHOR OF "A BUDGET OF LETTERS FROM JAPAN"

SECOND EDITION

G. P. PUTNAM'S SONS

NEW YORK   LONDON
27 WEST TWENTY-THIRD ST.   27 KING WILLIAM ST., STRAND

The Knickerbocker Press

1890

The Knickerbocker Press, New York

Electrotyped and Printed by

G. P. Putnam's Sons

PREFACE.

In the year 1875, when I was in the service of the Japanese government at Tokio, it chanced that my place of residence was located north of the old Yedo castle grounds, while my office lay to the south of them, thus rendering it necessary for me to pass twice each day through the centre of that vast system of feudal fortification. One stormy day, as I was trudging homeward in company with an inveterate pedestrian,—a young Englishman who persisted in taking "constitutional exercise" in all kinds of weather,—he suddenly halted at the bridge that crossed the broad moat before the Sakurada gateway and exclaimed : " Here is the spot where was enacted the most thrilling episode in modern Japanese history. On a day like this, about fourteen years ago, the *de facto* ruler of the Japanese empire was attacked at the head of this bridge, in the very midst of his guards, by a band of seventeen Mito *ronins*, and was ignominiously beheaded. For adroitness and daring I will match the deed against any found in the annals of any nation." Being deeply interested in his graphic account of the tragedy, I eagerly read up all the narratives of the sanguinary occurrence that could be found, and came to the conclusion that the affair was worthy to be woven into the warp and woof of a romance by some novelist,—little imagining, however, that I myself would ever attempt such a work. For many years the incidents' of this thrilling episode in Japanese history have lain fallow in my mind. After the cordial and flattering reception accorded to my " Bud-

iii

get of Letters " three years ago, I began to seriously consider the matter of writing a Japanese romance based on
this historic fact. While yet undecided as to what course
to pursue in the premises, I happened to read in the
New York Independent an article concerning Japanese
novels, wherein the writer expressed the hope that some
American author would work up this realm of romance,
saying : " There is a vast stock to draw from. Judicious
selections, easy to make, will be gladly received, we are
sure. No small proportion of such stock is historical.
When not entirely that, or when the incidents of the
several tales are woven of truth and fable, facts and
the wildest legends, the inlook it gives us into states of
Japan's national existence, which are fast passing away,
are too valuable to be neglected."

I have accordingly endeavored to picture in this tale
of old Japan the workings of that wonderful system of
espionage that characterized the Tokugawa dynasty
of Shoguns,—a system that covered the empire like
a net, and which was interwoven with innumerable
incidents of the most thrilling interest. I have also
depicted in mild colors the official corruption peculiar
in a marked degree to the *régime* of the later Shoguns. And, finally, I have endeavored to picture the
amazement and bewilderment of keen pagan intellects,
strongly imbued with atheistical ideas, when brought
in contact with the mighty realities of the Christian civilization of the nineteenth century. While freely availing
myself of the license and the latitude accorded to the
novelist, yet in historic and geographical matters I have
striven to lay accurate details before the reader. Through
the meshes of the assassination scene I have woven the
thread of Sir Rutherford Alcock's brilliant description
of that romantic event. In those portions of the book
into which I have incorporated the atheistical objections
of pagan intellects to Christianity I have, two or three
times, found the Japanese ideas on the subject so completely covered by some expressions used in a recent
magazine controversy in the United States between

Christianized intellects, that I have taken those expressions verbatim and have woven them into my text after having enclosed them within quotation marks.

In conclusion, I would state that the title Mito Yashiki means, when liberally rendered into English, "The feudal palace of the Prince of Mito"; and it is pronounced, like all Japanese words, after the Continental method,—*i* having the sound of *e*, and *a* having the broad sound. The accent should be placed on the first syllable of each word, and *o* should be long. Thus, when slowly pronounced, Mito Yashiki = Mē'-tō Yāh'-shĕ-kĕ. When quickly pronounced, as it always is in ordinary conversation, Yashiki sounds as if it contained but two syllables,—thus, Yāsh'-kĕ.

ARTHUR C. MACLAY.

55 LIBERTY ST., NEW YORK CITY
October 1, 1889.

CONTENTS

Contents.

MITO YASHIKI.

CHAPTER I.

THE NAKASHIMA FAMILY.

In the year 1853 of the Christian era, there dwelt in a little hamlet nestled in a sequestered glen at the foot of the Atago Mountains, in the western part of the province of Yamashiro, near to the city of Kioto, in the central part of Japan, an obscure family bearing the name of Nakashima. They traced their ancestry back to the eighth century of our era, to a certain *kugé*, or court noble, attached to the imperial household in Kioto. Those were days of affluence and power for the family ; but as the Mikado was stripped of one prerogative after another, and as successive sources of revenue were cut off, from that time until the seventeenth century, by ambitious and unscrupulous generals, who grasped all the executive and administrative functions pertaining to his office, the imperial household was reduced to great poverty, and was obliged to cast adrift many courtiers, retainers, and descendants of ancient *kugés* through lack of means wherewith to support them.

In the year 1600, Nakashima Isami, one of these *ronin* descendants, enlisted in the service of Tokugawa Iyèyas, and was engaged in many desperate battles under that valiant and victorious warrior, subduing factious chieftains in various parts of the realm. But during the years of profound peace that prevailed throughout the empire subsequent to the founding of the Tokugawa dynasty of Shoguns, the art of war did not require such multitudes of followers ; and, as the Shoguns could not support all who might desire to enlist in their service, it naturally came to pass that those *samurai* who were without money or influence were compelled to resort to peaceful avocations for their livelihood.

Of this luckless number was Nakashima Toyada, one of the descendants of Nakashima Isami. Finding himself politely released from further fealty to the house of Tokugawa, and excused from all further necessity of eating the rice of his recent master, he reluctantly became *ronin,* and drifted from Yedo to Kioto about the middle of the last century. In vain did he seek to attach himself to the service, either of the Mikado or to that of some *kugé ;* for the tide of wealth and of power had set toward Yedo, and gloom and poverty had settled upon the ancient court of the empire.

Seeking in vain for some other employment that should harmonize with his notions of the dignity of a *samurai* and a patrician of the realm, he finally purchased, with what scanty funds he possessed, a small piece of land beside the frothing waters that rushed headlong from their sources in Atago-Yama, and dashed wildly through the glen among the foot-hills a few miles northwest of Kioto. There he built a modest cottage and established his family shrine. Having a thorough knowledge of the native literature,and being no tyro in the art of fencing, he derived a fair living from giving instruction in these branches to the youth of Kioto. He also had a natural talent for sketching and for painting in water-colors, and, although it was considered far beneath the dignity of a *samurai* to earn money like an artisan, yet being endowed with a fair share of good sense (which revealed no reason why the lofty notions of a class that furnished him not a grain of rice should be held precious in his sight), he deemed it best to pocket his dignity and to derive all the revenue possible from ornamenting choice fans and screens with his brush,—the beauty of the surrounding country furnishing many inspired scenes.

Thus employed, he passed the balance of his days in serene contentment. And his son, following his example, gradually accumulated sufficient funds wherewith to purchase adjoining land, and to considerably enhance the value of the estate by careful horticulture.

The present head of the family, grandson of the original settler, Nakashima Yotori by name, was an urbane gentleman of fifty winters. He lived in the old homestead, or rather upon the site of the old homestead, for the original building had been so frequently repaired that there was but little of the former material left in it.

Like all structures in Japan, it was built almost entirely of wood. The roof was tiled ; the gable ends were plastered with lime, the upper story had a balcony along its front side overlooking the garden and the stream ; and along the edge of the balcony railing was a shelf upon which was ranged a row of porcelain flower-pots of various colors and designs, containing chrysanthemums of many brilliant hues, and also containing several sprouts of a species of thick-leaved cactus of dwarfed proportions, from whose broken leaves exuded a thick oil that was used by the ladies as a pomatum for the hair, serving to keep it in shape with its gum-like tenacity. From this balcony a fine view of the glen could be obtained. Along the front and along the back of the lower story of the house, were wide verandas, whose polished floors abundantly testified to the tidiness of the worthy housewife ; and the ends of the house were neatly plastered in white in the spaces between the broad wooden uprights and the cross-beams, thus presenting a unique panelled appearance quite pleasing to the eye.

The rooms in the house were separated, not by partitions, but by *shojees* (sliding doors made of wood and paper), set loosely in grooves so as to render them easily removable in hot weather. The floors were all covered with *tatamis* (thick rush mats). A broad ladder with wide steps instead of rounds gives access to the upper story, which is fitted up in exactly the same manner as the lower one. In order to prevent the rain driving through the house when storms chance to hurl themselves against either of its exposed sides, deep grooves were placed along the outer edges of the balconies and of the verandas into which may be slipped *ahmé* doors ("rain doors" made of light wood). At nighttime these were always brought forth from the closet at the end of each balcony and at the end of each veranda, and were slid into their respective places and bolted there, thus making the house quite dark inside, and serving not only to prevent the pouring in of sudden and violent tempests, but also to obstruct the ingress of all intruders. As a matter of course the house had neither garret nor cellar, as such appurtenances were unknown in the empire.

The road that leaves Kioto toward the northwest, after winding through temple grounds and groves of maple and cherry-trees, continues its devious course through several miles of gradually ascending country until it merges in the foot-hills of Atago-Yama where, when it reaches our hamlet, it passes beside the boxwood hedge that separates the front yard of our homestead from the highway. Through this evergreen barrier, ingress may be obtained by means of a gateway, whose heavy wooden portals stand ajar from daylight until nightfall, giving to passing travellers bright glimpses of the home-life within.

Entering the front yard, we find ourselves facing the veranda where the *O-kami-san* is busily engaged in sweeping off the dust—exemplary housewife as she is. On the right-hand side the yard is separated from that of the next-door neighbor by a hedge of hollyhock shrubbery, while on the left-hand side high copses of camellia bushes ranged together closely in a line before a closely woven bamboo fence served admirably to shut off intrusive inspection in that direction. Upon a bamboo trellis beside this fence there crept a morning-glory vine, while in the middle of the yard a grotesquely trimmed pine tree overshadowed with its spreading branches a large porcelain basin full of water, wherein gold-fishes were sporting amid the shadows cast upon the tiny waves by the clouds and leaves overhead ; and copses of fragrant olea beside the gateway and at the ends of the veranda, that filled the air with delicious perfume during the autumn months, together with clumps of flowering almonds and sweet-scented jessamines, gave forth perpetually their subtle charms, and abundantly testified to the taste and the skill of the inmates of the dwelling. A stately cherry-tree beside the wood-lined well at the end of the house seemed buoyed up with clouds of pink and white blossoms, which sprinkled the grass with showers of petals.

At the back of the house the ground was laid out in a neat garden, where were carefully cultivated long rows of radishes and leeks. A bamboo fence separated this garden from the adjoining one, and also from the girdle of underbrush that skirted the dark woods upon the steep mountain-side that sloped upwards from the fence.

The scenery surrounding the hamlet was subdued and beautiful. From the front balcony of the homestead you gazed upon the slopes down to the glittering sands of the mountain stream. Deep verdure embowered the opposite side of the glen, where cooling cascades among the ravines invited during the hot summer months throngs of pleasure-seekers from the sultry city. Numerous copses of feathery bamboo trees appeared like nodding plumes amid the darker foliage of chestnut, beech, oak and cryptomeria that screened the lairs of the wild boar and the retreats of the deer, which, during the summer and the autumn months, invaded the precincts of the hamlet and devoured more than their fair proportion of the sweet potatoes and the watermelons.

Either up or down the glen the view was circumscribed with deeply wooded hills and with towering crags, which sheltered the place so effectually from the wintry winds that orange-trees grew around the hamlet, and the sago-palm flourished beside the hedges, and the roses, camellias, and chrysanthemums bloomed out-doors in midwinter. The soft mantle of snow which, at rare intervals, descended upon the landscape, faded like a dream before the powerful rays of the midday sun. The stream was never frozen, and the plash of its waves washing the

sands against the pebbles and the boulders in its channel, filled the air with soft whisperings, which the children
likened to the murmurings of vast throngs of monkeys
in mighty convocation amid the secluded forests in the
uplands where they dwelt.

But let us leave the balcony and inspect in detail the
interior arrangements of the house, beginning with the
reception room down stairs.   This large room extends
from the front veranda to the back veranda.   As we
enter it from the front yard, we have on our left hand a
couple of closets in which the bedding has been stowed
away for the day.   A little beyond, on the same side of
the room, is a space raised a few inches above the floor,
allotted to the few ornamental things usually found in
native houses, and which is usually the most picturesque
portion of the interior ; here you will see the handsomely
lacquered sword-rack ; here also is the sombre-looking
lacquered chest containing the suit of armor in which
Nakashima Isami fought at the battle of Sekigahara, two
hundred and fifty-three years ago, and which still shows
upon the massive bronze helmet the long and deep scar
left by the keen sword of some powerful warrior of the
League, whose routed legions were chased by the relentless Tokugawa Iyèyas far into the night, and whose
fierce soldiers frequently turned and stretched low many
an ardent pursuer whose heedless zeal had carried him
away from the supporting body of troops into some fatal
ambuscade.

Above this warlike display is a shelf holding a pair of
blue vases.   Above this again are two brackets whereon
are placed two handsomely lacquered boxes containing
writing utensils, seals, and correspondence.   While yet
higher up, across the top of the space, are little closets
where the ladies keep their best dresses and choice
girdles ; each lady has but one gala suit, which will serve
for many years, fearing nothing from change of style in
a country where styles vary but little in a century.   At
each corner of this space is a post composed of the
trunk of a small tree, the bark of which has not been

removed, and whose knot-holes have been polished until they shine. The charming rusticity of this place is suggestive of the primitive mode of living in primeval times, when saplings and trees propped up the thatch of ancient huts. The wall beyond the closets and the sanctum is decorated with hanging scrolls, upon which are designs of birds, flowers, and mountain scenery, and which, as the breeze plays through the room, gently flutter from the wall like trailing banners, and fall back into position, tapping it with the ivory ends of the sticks on which they are mounted.

On the opposite side of the room, sliding doors separate us from two smaller rooms : the one opening on the front veranda being used during the day as a place for sewing, smoking, and lounging, and during the night as the bedchamber of the three brothers ; and that one which opens on the back veranda being used as the dining-room, and occasionally as a sleeping-room. Beyond these rooms, in a little wing attached to the other end of the house, were the kitchen and the bath-room. In the middle of the floor of each room was sunk a granite block, which had been hollowed out sufficiently to admit a few handfuls of ashes being placed therein to serve as the bed for little heaps of burning charcoal, over which the hands could be warmed in cold weather.

The household comprised the parents, three sons, one daughter, and an old man-servant whose father and grandfather had served the Nakashima family in a similar capacity. When Nakashima Toyada settled at the base of Atago-Yama, he took a fancy to a young wood-chopper who daily passed his gateway in the morning, armed with an axe and a coil of rope, on his way up to the well wooded ravines in the mountains, to gather fagots and fire-wood for the city market ; and in the evening he had always noticed how cheerfully he trudged homeward, with his heavy load of wood tied upon his back ; and, with that knowledge of human nature which his military experience had developed in him, he perceived in this youth qualities of faithfulness and industry which, if they could but be attached to his own interests and to those of his family, would render the boy a valuable auxiliary to his household. Overtures were accordingly made to the young mountain boor, who, in consideration of food, clothing, and wages equivalent to one dollar per month, was induced to abandon his life among the ravines, and take to gardening and light household duties, which avocations proved so congenial to his tastes that old age found him still thus engaged ; and his descendants followed his example, thus making the service hereditary,—an occurrence by no means uncommon during the peaceful times of Old Japan.

The youngest child was O-Hana, a young lass of fifteen summers, who, in addition to being the household pet, possessed a comeliness of person and animation of features that turned the heads of the young bloods from the city to that extent, that the exchequer of the tea booth at the head of the glen testified handsomely to the frequency of their saunterings up the road to catch glimpses of the witch of the hamlet.

Was she handsome ? Not according to your ideas, perhaps, my Caucasian friend. Nevertheless, she was certainly pretty. It is true that her jet-black hair, although done up in a manner that might have met your approval, was glistening with oily juice from the cactus leaves, already described ; but her forehead was full, fair, and shapely ; her heavy eyebrows and sparkling black eyes were surely handsome ; the nose you will call the weak feature of her face, because it is neither Roman, Grecian, nor aquiline in profile, and is rather inclined to flatness at the bridge ; but the rosy dimpled cheeks, the small mirthful mouth, the pearly teeth, and the round plump chin you will admit to be very pretty, and quite sufficient to excuse the pronounced admiration of the Kioto youth, meandering of a summer's eve along the road ; and, finally, you must admit without hesitation that her delicately shaped hands and feet are above criticism. She is only a little over five feet in height ; but her demeanor is that of a refined and courteous

woman. She has ceased to romp through the hamlet
with childish glee, but nothing can stop her chasing the
butterflies through the garden shrubbery.   One gorgeous
butterfly in particular she has nick-named Taiko-Sama,
because of his brilliant colors presenting such a warlike
appearance, resembling an army with many banners.
This martial fellow she chases on every available occasion : no matter what her occupation may be—whether
it be rice-cooking, clothes-mending, or even the formidable attempt to satiate her marvellous appetite with
bowls of steaming rice,—she drops rice, needle, and
chopsticks, and darts off in wild pursuit of Japan's most
famous warrior, until recalled by pangs of appetite, or by
duty.

Nor can lectures on propriety induce her to abandon
her favorite pastime of battledoor and shuttlecock. With
wooden tile in hand, she knocks the shuttlecock over the
hedge to the little lady in the adjoining yard, who merrily sends it back with a hearty stroke until the continued
clicking of the two battledoors against the metallic ball
of the tiny shuttlecock beats with the regularity of clock-
work, to be disturbed only by the exultant laughter of
that one who triumphantly lands the tuft of white
feathers in her adversary's domain.

Our young lady's household duties are not of a very
onerous nature. At daylight, she is up with her mother
helping to slide back the *ahmé* doors.   Then she assists
in the preparation of breakfast : she cuts up the *daikon*
into dainty slices ; she washes out the rice and puts it
into the iron pot over the fire ; she broils a carp over the
glowing coals in the brazier, and, finally, when every
thing has been fully prepared, she helps to serve the
meal.   After breakfast, she sweeps out all the rooms and
washes off the verandas before settling herself down on
the mats for a season of sewing and gossiping with her
mother, at which occupation she will probably be interrupted by the young lady from the next house, who
comes in to compare notes on their recent visit to the
festival at the Gihon temple in the city, when thousands

of people crowded in from the country and thronged the numerous tea booths from morn till eve, feasting on sweetmeats and oranges.   This precious season of amiable discourse will be prolonged until the shortening shadows of the trees and shrubbery announce the approach of high noon, when the session will be adjourned in order to make preparation for dinner.

In the afternoon she employs her time as seems most agreeable to herself.   Perhaps she will call on her young neighbors ; possibly she may stroll up the ravine in search of wild flowers ; or she may help the old servant to trim the bushes and the hedges.   And when the sun begins to approach the summit of Atago-Yama, heralding the speedy return of her father and brothers from the city, she hastens to aid her mother in preparing the evening meal.   And with the closing day, the *ahmé* doors are slid together, and early slumbers settle upon the household.   Thus passed the life of our young lady, like the merry stream coursing through the glen, uneventful and happy like that of her sisters throughout the land.

Our young lady's mother was a kind little body (she was no larger than *neé-san* herself) upon whom forty-five years had pressed but lightly.   Though wrinkled in forehead and face, yet her hair was raven-hued, and the black had but slightly faded from her mild eyes.   It was evident that in her youth she must have borne a strong resemblance to her daughter.   She was the child of a retainer of one of the *kugés* in Kioto.   She had met her destined husband when he gave fencing lessons to her brothers in the large courtyard of her father's house. The daughters of *samurai* in feudal times frequently were instructed in the use of weapons, and you will not feel shocked to know that she also took lessons in the use of the swords (particularly of the short one), and that she learned all the motions of the graceful and pretty spear exercise.   Nor will it much surprise you to be informed that at the age of eighteen she married her instructor and admirer, and followed him to the hamlet among the ravines, where twenty-seven years of wedded life had slipped away quietly and peacefully.

The three sons were hardy young fellows of somewhat diverse temperaments. The youngest one, Kunisaburo, was just entering upon his eighteenth year. He was rather tall and slim, yet agile and muscular in a high degree, being very skilful in fencing and archery. He was gay and vivacious as became his years, but there was no viciousness in his nature. The second son, Junzo, was twenty-one years of age. He was rather low in stature, but he was powerfully built ; and he was as wiry and quick as a cat. He was put together upon the native ideal of a soldier. In fact, in the fencing arena, he had not his equal in Kioto, although some of the long-armed *samurai* from Aidzu, comprising the garrison in the *Shiro*, allowed him to score but few points against them in the bouts. He was his father's favorite assistant in teaching the sword and spear exercises to the youth in Kioto ; for the old gentleman was becoming too old and rheumatic to bend and unbend himself with the great quickness required in delivering the terrific cuts and thrusts. He would, therefore, sit upon the veranda over-looking the combatants, and would give forth a series of lectures composed of principles derived from his many years of experience ; which principles would then be practically illustrated by his son and the pupil, pitted against each other in the courtyard. While the comba-tants rested from their vigorous exertions, he smoked his pipe and discussed the battles of Nobunaga and Hidè-yoshi with the master of the house.

The eldest son, Tomokichi, was twenty-five years of age. Although he was an expert swordsman and frequently aided his father in giving instruction in the use of the foils, nevertheless his tastes did not run in that direction. In build and features he somewhat resembled the second son ; but the resemblance ended there. He was thoughtful, reserved, and studious. He was well read in the history of the empire, in the meagre poetry of the nation, and in the light romance literature descriptive

for the most part of famous duels and feuds between
rival clans in the Yedo *yashikis* or when coming in collision upon the Tokaido. But above every thing he
thirsted for information regarding foreign peoples and
countries,—a thirst, in fact, that was characteristic of a
large number of his countrymen. He diligently ransacked
all the circulating literature in the city for any morsel of
information relating to the unknown regions beyond the
vast waters encircling his native islands.

So ardent was he in his pursuit of knowledge in this
direction, that on one occasion when the Dutch Embassy
passed through Kioto on its return to Nagasaki from
Yedo, where it had been rendering its periodical homage
to the Shogun, he clandestinely visited the hotel where
the Dutchmen and their suite were staying, and took
abundant notes on their personal appearance and peculiarities ; and on the occasion of the next visit, he was
fortunate enough to find one of his father's friends
attached to the guards, and, through his influence he was
able to secure a small chart of the world. This transaction had to be conducted with profound secrecy, for, had
the authorities been aware of what was going on, the head
of our young friend, together with that of his coadjutor,
would speedily have fallen into the same pit.

Hiding the precious document under his garment, he
quietly slipped out of the hotel and hastened homeward
with wild delight, and hid the trophy in his closet
beneath the lacquered chest containing his few worldly
possessions. Whenever he could be quite sure that no
member of the household would come up-stairs, he
would there spread it out on the mats for study. As he
had taken the precaution to mark the principal places in
native characters, he found the map quite intelligible.
By degrees the members of the family were let into the
secret, and their profound agitation was soon merged
into feelings of intense curiosity and delight at the mysterious information conveyed by this colored paper.
From that time the chart became the treasured secret of
the Nakashima family.

Upon another occasion, during one of his rambles among the book-stores, he found in a heap of discarded printed matter a roll of manuscript which appeared to be a translation into Japanese of portions of some work explaining the general principles of some foreign creed. It may have been in the library of some French or Portugese priest in the old days when Xavier and the Jesuits were welcomed to Kioto; or it may have been translated from the books of some Dutchman in Deshima at Nagasaki by some native interpreter, to gratify the curiosity of some inland friend. Eagerly purchasing the document, he took it home and held a family consultation as to its exact purport. It speedily dawned upon them that it was an exposition of the dreaded teachings of the sect designated Christian, against which there had been promulgated by the Shogun, two hundred years before, laws written in blood ; against the introduction of which within the empire the seal of death had been placed ; and against whose God defiance had been hurled and sentence of death had been pronounced in case he should dare to trespass on the sacred soil of the realm.

To keep the document within the family after having arrived at a full comprehension of its meaning, would place the entire household under the ban of death. And, even as the matter stood, it was more than probable that, in case the document were delivered up to the authorities, and an investigation as to its origin were instituted, the frightened bookseller would disclaim ever having had it in his possession, and the burden of accounting for its appearance would thus be shifted upon the melancholy Nakashima family, where it would rest heavily, leading, perchance, to torture and death. The realization of this position staggered the family and cast a deep gloom over their spirits for many days. It was finally decided to keep the matter quiet, to enshrine the luckless document among the treasured secrets of the family, and to relegate it to the secluded chest with the chart. At the same time the members of the family lodged a vehement protest against any further turning

of their peace of mind- upside down in gratifying
thirst for knowledge ; and the head of the house felt
compelled to mildly intimate that, while it was highly
commendable for a young man to cultivate literary tastes,
yet care should be used to select such literature as did
not imperil the lives of his kindred.

Such was the Nakashima family. Although I have
not entered into a detailed description of the worthy
sire, yet I imagine that you are pretty familiar with him
in view of the side lights that have been cast upon him.
He was unusually tall for a native,—lacking but one inch
of six feet. Descended from an ancestry of warriors,
inheriting a strong physique, which he had further
strengthened by many years of vigorous exercise with
the heavy foils, he was a fine specimen of Japanese
manhood. Brought up amid delightful scenery, and living in the beautiful climate of Yamashiro, his temperament was serene and happy.

Delightful indeed was the climate. While upon the
northern slopes of the lofty mountain ranges—not
seventy miles away,—the snow packed six feet deep in
the village streets, and the people shivered beneath
heavy quilts during the violence of the wintry gales that
swept across the Japan Sea from Siberia, here, upon
the southern slopes of this same mountain range, sheltered from the stinging blasts of the north, there reigned
a climate matchless for salubrity and mildness, where
flowers bloomed in midwinter, where the siestas of the
hot summers were cooled by breezes from the Pacific,
where spring clothed the hills and valleys with deepest
verdure, and where autumn was a veritable paradise.
Removed from the pageantry and pomp of court and
camp, he had developed a thoughtful and studious spirit
that had well versed itself in the doctrines of Shinto,
Buddha, and Confucius ; and, though having but little
regard for the precepts contained in any of these creeds,
yet he rather leaned toward Confucianism.

The principle of rigid obedience of children toward
parents, of subordinates toward superiors, of the young

toward the old, exactly suited his military tastes and ideas. Nevertheless he prided himself on being unfettered by any creed, of being a free and bold thinker, and of possessing a rugged and stoical nature. Toward friends he was courteous and obliging; toward enemies he was as unrelenting in his hostility as death itself. While extracting from life all possible enjoyment, yet he held death in supreme and utter contempt. Although he was a kind husband and father, yet he affected an utter indifference for the fair sex, deeming their ensnaring charms beneath the notice of a soldier's mind, and but leading onward to enervation and debauch.

He represented a type of stoics, indeed rare in old Japan, yet a type that really existed even amid the wildest corruptions of feudalism, and which ever served as a sobering influence on the levity and the licentiousness of the times when the carnival of vice prevailed throughout the land. It was a type that was strongly atheistical in all its tendencies. It was a type combining what would seem to us many incongruous elements,—reckless courage, relentless hate, contemptible treachery, fiendish cruelty, unutterable contempt for weakness, supreme veneration for power, unwavering loyalty for friends, amiable condescension toward their families, contempt for violent death, mingled with superstitious dread at the subtle and mysterious encroachments of disease (not above appealing to incantations and exorcisms at the hands of quacks and *bonzes*), vast respect for superior powers, combined with a flat refusal to recognize any moral principle or law in the universe that could bind them against their inclinations ; abstemious in diet, yet indulging unhesitatingly in mad revels when occasion required ; while honestly intending to cultivate rigid and austere virtues, yet never considering themselves bound by any scruples of conscience when it became expedient to cast aside integrity and principle ;—verily, a queer combination of physical bravery and moral cowardice.

Does not this type remind you of a house built on shifting sands ? It was capable under favorable circumstances of performing many grand deeds ; but under adverse conditions the moral and ethical structure that it had raised would be shown to be without foundation. Ah ! Quietly and gently flowed the stream among the sequestered glens and remote villages of the empire, but turbid and troubled were the waves amid the contaminating influences of great centres of population. Such was Nakashima Yotori—a genial and amiable pagan.

CHAPTER II.

IN the year 1853 Kioto was probably the most secluded capital city in the world. Situated in a lovely valley near the southern end of Lake Biwa, in the heart of the main island of the Japan group, it was screened from the gaze of America by five thousand miles of ocean billows, from the scrutiny of Asia by tempestuous seas and rock-bound coasts, and from the commercial enterprise of Europe by intervening continents and by many thousand leagues of waves ; and, in coalition with these formidable barriers of nature, there brooded within the council chambers of the Yedo castle the fierce spirit of the Tokugawa House that had hurled defiance at humanity, and sealed with blood, two centuries before, the gates of the empire against the universe. Far removed from the great highways of commerce, the profound repose of Kioto was not even disturbed by the appearance at rare intervals of ill-starred barks that tempests chanced to drive upon those inhospitable shores.

But, as present conditions are best understood in the light of past events, let us change the scene and go back twenty-five centuries, to the time when native history begins. The first vision that rises to our view is sylvan in its aspect. I see a vast woodland—a virgin forest—covering the entire province of Yamashiro, clothing the mountain ranges to their very summits, and stretching many hundred miles away to the distant waves of the encompassing seas. Here in the valley of Yamashiro grow the pine, the oak, the beech, the camphor tree, the lordly cryptomeria, and the mighty *kayaki*, whose colos-

17

sal trunk is destined to form in coming centuries a stately
pillar in some vast temple. Here the climbing vines of
wild wistaria drape the boughs with lavender-colored
festoons, and the copses of feathery bamboos grow beside
the pools and the damp margin of the stream.

From its sources in the northern range, the Kamogawa (River of the Wild Ducks) pours its torrents
through the underbrush southward toward the sea. Here
dwell the aboriginal Ainos, the heavily-bearded savages
whose ancestors came from the far north and had spread
themselves southward over all the islands in sparsely
peopled settlements.

Along the course of the stream, wherever long and
wide stretches of sandy soil appear, and also in the
woods where natural clearings occur, and upon the hills
and mountain slopes where springs gush forth from their
rocky fastnesses,—there cluster the huts and the wigwams
of the Ainos. Simple structures indeed are they,—fragile
frames of saplings, covered with bark, with skins of wild
animals, and with coarse thatch plucked among the
sedges. With barbed flint they spear the carp and the
trout in the shoals of the river ; with clubs, stones,
arrows, and sharpened poles they hunt the bear, the
wolf, the badger, the deer, the wild boar, the fox, and
the monkey ; while with the sacred spark, brought perchance from some volcano, the busy squaws send the
curling smoke above the tree-tops to warn the absent
Nimrods of the approach of the evening meal. Ah ! in
those days the centuries passed as if they had been but
decades. The years sped along unregistered and un-
chronicled. Spring was known by the budding of leaves,
autumn was known by the gorgeous colors of the forests,
and winter was heralded by the snow-capped mountain
peaks and by the myriads of wild ducks coming from the
northern shores. Immured in forest solitudes, living on
the spoils of the chase, almost entirely ignorant of agriculture,—so lived unknown generations of aborigines.

But the scene fades away. Fifteen centuries have
fled. And, lo ! the second vision rises to our view. I

see the surface of the land covered with well tilled fields, with villages, with groves, and with shrines. I see beside the shoals of the Kamogawa the white walls and the heavily tiled roof of the imperial palace, surrounded by a city whose dimensions attain unto a full square league. What has wrought this change ? A race of nut-brown warriors from the archipelago beneath the tropics, borne to the southern shores of the Japan islands on the mighty current of the Black Stream, overran the land and drove the aborigines northward. They cleared the country, and then *Inari*, the mythical fox-god, brought in his mouth from China a tuft of the rice-plant, which the people planted in their fields, and filled the land with abundant crops ; and the picturesque shrines scattered through the groves have been erected in his honor ; there is he venerated and worshipped ; and when in the gloaming his flitting form is seen threading the narrow causeways through the rice-fields, he is believed to be bent upon some errand of mercy, as when in days of yore he left the portals of Cathay and skimmed the sea-girt isles, bearing his priceless gift between his teeth.

Thus the people were enabled to derive their sustenance from the ground, and were no longer bound down to a mere animal existence by the uncertainties of a livelihood dependent on the chase. Agriculture and horticulture made rapid progress. Architecture was speedily developed. These favorable conditions gave birth to literature ; the classics of Confucius were introduced from China, and were extensively studied ; pottery, woven fabrics, and paper were manufactured ; and cutlery and bronze ware were most skilfully made. And finally, in the year 793 A.D., the Emperor Kwammu abandoned Nara, and selected the little village of Uda, at the foot of the hills on the east side of the Kamogawa, and founded Kioto.

And now, in the year 1853 of the Christian Era, a thousand years after its foundation, we have before us the romantic city of Kioto. The primeval woodland has disappeared from valley and from mountain slope. Well

trimmed forests cover the mountains ; and innumerable
groves of maple and cherry-trees are scattered over the
foot-hills and among the glens, gardens, and parks surrounding the city ; while the rose, the lily, the lotus, the
chrysanthemum, and the wistaria fill every yard with
beauty and fragrance. The Kamogawa, no longer encumbered with driftwood, nor harassed with impeding
underbrush entangling its shores, has spread itself on
either side beyond its ancient limits, until it has become
a broad, shallow river, requiring five long wooden bridges
to span its shores   During heavy rains it becomes a
deep and rapid stream, rushing through the city with
tremendous velocity ; but during the summer it becomes
so shallow and peaceable that mats are spread upon its
sands and low platforms are built over its shallow waves,
and the entire leisure element of the city turns out to sit
cross-legged in the bed of the stream, to make merry and
to enjoy the cool breezes that surge up and down the
channel. The stream runs due north and south, and fully
three quarters of the city will be found upon the western
bank where the level ground stretches away for seven or
eight miles before reaching broken ground ; while upon
the eastern bank but a few minutes of walking will lead
to foot-hills.

The city is laid out in a very regular manner. The
streets cross each other at right angles, running east and
west by north and south. They are not paved ; they are
wide and clean, and the system of drainage is entirely
above ground, in gutters that line each side of the highway. The houses are but two stories high, and are all
built of wood. The suburbs, the foot-hills, and the surrounding mountains are filled with vast temples, superb
monasteries, parks, gardens, and villas,—a girdle of romantic beauty and magnificence such as no other city in
the world can boast of.

In and around this city of four hundred thousand inhabitants there arc no less than four thousand temples
and monasteries, mostly Buddhist.   If we calculate that
upon an average there are twenty-five priests attached to

each temple and to each monastery, then there must be
fully one hundred thousand of these shaven gentlemen in
Kioto. And they seem to have cast over the entire population such a spell of lassitude and indifference to worldly
occupations that the reputation of the citizens for pride,
laziness, and dilettanteism stands unmatched throughout
the empire. There are, however, extensive industries
carried on in a leisurely manner. The usual trades and
mercantile occupations find free scope to act ; and the
special manufactures of silk, bronze, porcelain, and embroidery are justly and widely celebrated for their exquisite and unsurpassed workmanship. Yet time is
considered of no consequence to anybody, and the
artisans are notoriously slow in executing orders for
work, as they are perpetually running off on some picnic
or celebrating some one of the innumerable fête days at
the neighboring temples.

Since the laying of the foundation of the city marvellous changes have marked the history of the world. The
Normans conquered England ; the Crusades convulsed
Christendom ; Columbus discovered America ; hardy
mariners circumnavigated the globe ; a mighty nation
sprang into existence in the North American wilderness,—
but what cared the Kioto people for all that ? Did not
the Mikado, the descendant of the sun-goddess, dwell in
their lovely city ? And were not they all the descendants of the gods, and therefore inherently superior to the
rest of mankind, who had probably descended from in-
ferior deities, or from beasts ? Why should the vulgar
bickerings of outside barbarians in any way interest the
Japanese ? Smoke your pipe, quaff your tea, loiter away
whole days in the theatre ; frequent the wrestling
matches ; don your gala dress and drink *saké* whenever
the temple in your district has a fête day ; revel in
carousal and debauch as far as your means will allow ;
take but languid interest in public affairs ; demolish
strangers with refined *hauteur* and cultured repartee,—and
occasionally work. That was the correct style in Kioto
in 1853. With a licentious court and a lazy, sensual

priesthood, the people surely did not have much to elevate them.

In the northern part of the city, a few hundred yards
west of the shoals of the river, stood the Gosho, the
palace of the Mikado. It comprised a collection of
structures in the midst of parks and gardens that covered
twenty-six acres of land. The entire place was enclosed
within rectangular walls pierced by six gates, one of
which opened on the north, one on the east, one on the
south, and three on the west. These walls were quite
unique. They were about ten feet high, were very broad,
and were heavily tiled. They sloped inward slightly
from base to roof. The framework of the walls was composed of wood, and the large rectangular spaces between
the uprights and the cross-beams were plastered so as to
present the singular appearance of an unpainted wooden
wall having large white panels and a black cap. As a
defence they were comparatively useless ; but to the ob-
servant mind the well grained wood and the dazzling
plaster told the history of the Mikado's fortunes, and bespoke the simplicity of the primitive court.

The Shogun and the Daimios surrounded themselves
with thrice-moated castles, whose ramparts were of hewn
stone and sodded embankments ; but the Gosho required
no moat, because its style of architecture antedated the
age of stone by many centuries, and went back to the
patriarchal days when the Mikado lived among his people in his simple rustic residence. Did not the islands of
Dai-Nippon and the denizens thereof even now belong to
the descendant of the sun-goddess ? Why, then, should
he abandon the simplicity of his ancestors and imitate the
innovations of the Shogun, who might well dread the
people because of his cruelty and tyranny ? The wigwam
of the sachem, unmoated, stood beside the shoals of the
Kamogawa free of access to the tattooed savages ; the
thatched cottages of his descendants, unmoated, stood
for many centuries amid the groves and the gardens of
Yamato, unmolested ; therefore, it became the ancient
dynasty, as its imperial power has been wrested away by

usurping servants, to screen itself within the simple wooden barriers of the Gosho, until the time should come to fling open the gates and to go forth to resume the sway of empire. Aye! keep the gates closed. Let not the world cast its vulgar gaze upon the humiliation of the ancient dynasty.

Many palaces have stood within the precincts of the Gosho. The first one was built about 793 A.D. In 1177 it was destroyed by fire. The second one was destroyed in a similar manner in the year 1249. The third one was destroyed a few years later. And during the seventeenth and eighteenth centuries five successive palaces were thus destroyed. These conflagrations were sometimes occasioned by the carelesness of people within the palace, and sometimes they were started by warring factions in the city during their fierce struggles for supremacy. These fires, when once started among the thousands of tinder-boxes outside the palace walls, speedily gathered great headway, and would roll their vast waves of flame to the uttermost limits of the city, overleaping every obstruction and storming every barrier with fiery assault.

Within the walls of the Gosho you will find considerable massive architecture and some pretty garden landscape. The buildings are all of wood. They are but one story high, and have immensely heavy roofs as a protection against being thrown down by the jarring tremors of earthquakes. In the southern part of the enclosed quadrangle stands the Secluded Purple Hall, a building about one hundred feet long by sixty feet deep, and facing the southern side of the enclosure. Within its lofty chambers important ceremonies are held. Here the Mikados are enthroned, and here they grant audiences on New Year's Day.

Northeast of this hall a corridor will lead you to a smaller building, where is kept a copy of the sacred mirror, with which the sun-goddess was enticed from her cave at some remote cycle of time, and which she bestowed upon the Mikado's ancestor, together with a sword and a stone as insignia of authority. Northwest of the Purple Hall stands the Pure and Cool Hall (so christened because of a stream of water that bubbles beneath its steps), a building about sixty feet by forty, and facing eastward, wherein levees were held, and also wherein were performed on great fête days the sacred rites connected with Shintoism. Northeast of this chastely christened hall stands the Lesser Palace, a building about seventy feet by forty, and also facing eastward, and looking out upon a pretty garden filled with evergreen shrubbery, and containing a miniature lake. Within its handsome audience chambers his Majesty receives the high officials of his court and the priests of Shinto and of Buddha.

North of this stands the August Study, a building of nearly the same dimensions as the Lesser Palace, and also facing eastward. In this beautiful suite of apartments, the Mikado and his court listen to lectures on Chinese literature, to dissertations on poetry and music, and to instruction upon whatever subject he may desire information. Northward again we find a building about fifty feet by thirty, wherein are held theatrical performances for the amusement of the court. Northward again we find the imperial palace, wherein the Mikado resides. It is a laige building (ninety feet by seventy-four) facing the east,—the source of light and the quarter whence came the imperial dynasty.

This palace contains eleven rooms. The middle one on the east side was his Majesty's sitting-room ; and directly behind it was his bedroom ; while on all sides he was surrounded by suites of rooms filled with attendants, so that he was guarded from all intrusion. In a closet near the imperial chambers were the mystic stone and a copy of the sword forming part of the insignia of the imperial authority. Near the northern end of the palace were two pleasure pavilions, where tea could be served, poetry could be composed, the miniature landscape of the garden could be enjoyed, or where, perchance, a longing gaze could be cast upon the hazy blue of the distant mountains. The palace of the Empress was quite distant from that of the Mikado. It was reached by a long corridor that led by the imperial bath-rooms and the suite of the heir-apparent. It was a large building facing the east, and it contained a splendid suite of rooms.

Such was the Gosho in 1853. Although the buildings were massive, although the paintings on the screens and the panels had been executed by the best native artists, yet an air of extreme simplicity distinguished the entire place. As far as possible, paint had been ignored, and the natural graining of the wood highly polished ap-peared in all the woodwork. The bare condition of rafters, posts, pillars, planks, steps, and railings bespoke the chaste simplicity of the ancient régime. There was no display of magnificent furniture, plate-glass mirrors, stately equipage, costly carpets, priceless gems, and silver dinner services. All the floors were covered with simple rush mats, or *tatamis;* everybody sat, ate, and slept on the floors, using square embroidered cushions for seats, low lacquered stands for tables, and heavy silken quilts for beds ; everybody patronized chopsticks and porcelain dishes ; horses and carriages were un-known throughout the empire ; and jewelry, in our sense of the term, was almost an unknown quantity, because the ladies never disfigured themselves with ear-rings, the gentlemen knew nothing of gold watches and chains, and the court never possessed massive diadems and costly sceptres requiring a fortress and a regiment of troops to guard them. A few finger-rings, perchance a score of bracelets for a few fair wrists, some highly ornamented sword hilts and scabbards, and a few simple ornaments for the ladies' hair, comprised about all that could be designated as jewelry.

The places where decoration and ornamentation cen-tred were the elaborate screens and the panels of the sliding doors. Here the efforts of the most skilful artists had exquisitely reproduced nature in her varied moods. Cherry blossoms, chrysanthemums, pine trees of grotesque shapes, flocks of wild geese, bamboo trees

dripping with rain, stately maples, fishes frolicking amid
waves, rainbows arching the hills, glades, and woods,—
these were a few of the designs around the walls of the
stately apartments, poor substitutes, indeed, for the beauteous realities of the outside world.

In this vicinity, then, had dwelt the Mikados for over
a thousand years.   To the outside world they appeared
to be shrouded in profoundest mystery.   Popular rumor
pictured them as objects of deepest reverence.   Nobody
approached them, except on bended knees,—even the
Shoguns being obliged to conform to this regulation.
Their feet never touched the ground, but trod upon
cloths, so that the sacred person might not be defiled by
contact with the earth.   They must sit motionless upon
the throne for a certain number of hours each day, in
order that the empire might have peace.   Their persons
were so sacred that nobody was permitted to lay hands
thereon ; therefore their hair and nails might have grown
to an unseemly length, had they not been clandestinely
trimmed during sleeping hours.   The dishes from which
they had partaken of food were forthwith dashed in
pieces, in order that nobody else might ever use them.
And the very rice that they ate was picked over kernel
by kernel, in order that no broken or imperfect grain
might find lodgment within the imperial stomach.

Such was the halo of majesty thrown about the person
of the Mikado.   In such light did the court wire-pullers
present the imperial puppet to the outside world.   But
to the inmates of the palace these profoundly mysterious
personages appeared as amiable gentlemen of languid
temperaments, much given to pleasure of every description, and quite unconventional in their deportment.
Stripped of all political power, they spent their time in
diversions almost childish in their nature, and in traffick-
ing in honorary titles that the Shogun and his minions
could not purchase from any other source.

While the Aidzu *samurai*, stationed in the moated
castle a mile or so southwest of the Gosho, seemed to be
standing guard in behalf of the Tokugawa House over a

mere family of dilettanti and imbeciles, yet there dwelt
within those whitened walls the germs of sovereignty
that were destined speedily to expand and regain their
pristine power; and the idle warriors who loitered
around the imperial portals, carelessly guarding the helpless creatures within, little dreamed of the wild scenes of
carnage and turmoil destined speedily to rage around
that quiet place, and rouse the whole empire from its
profound repose of two centuries. As to the traveller's
eye the inky clouds drifting over the summits of the
distant mountain ranges bespeak the black storm gathering behind those mighty peaks, so the mutterings of
Mito and of Satsuma ominously heralded to the political
leaders of the realm an era of profound agitation and
social upheaval not far distant.

CHAPTER III.

In the month of July, 1853, the Nakashima family became the guests, for a few days, of Mr. Yamada, a retainer of a *kugé* in Kioto. Leaving their house in charge of their faithful servant, they journeyed in the cool of the morning toward the city, the ladies travelling in *kagos*, while the gentlemen leisurely strolled down the shady glen, through the groves and gardens environing the suburbs, and, after threading the dusty streets, found themselves before the massive gateway of their host in the vicinity of the Gosho, where the obsequious gatekeeper received them with profuse salutation. Escorting them into his little lodge beside the gateway, he brought a basin and a bucket of water wherewith to wash their feet. Their dusty sandals were speedily exchanged for socks and neat straw slippers, wherein they made their way across the courtyard to their host's house, where they were warmly welcomed by the members of the Yamada family. Etiquette prescribed that the house of the Japanese gentleman should be set somewhat back from the public street, and that it should be approached through stately portals and spacious courtyards; and that the humble domicile of the laborer and of the artisan should open directly on the public thoroughfares.

The Yamada mansion was built upon the sandy soil that stretched some distance back from the west bank of the river. It was a double-storied wooden structure. Wide verandas screened its lower story on all sides, and airy balconies, freighted with flowering shrubs, were perched at various points around the upper one. The

grounds all around the house were tastefully and beautifully laid out with gravelly walks, boxwood hedges,
bamboo copses, and pine trees trimmed into grotesque
forms representing turtles and storks; while a trellis-
work that arched the doorway was weighted down with
blossoming wistaria and morning-glories. Heaps of
white pebbles from the river-bed, resembling banks of
snow, were placed at the angles of the flower-beds, amid
cushions of velvety moss; while between the crevices
of the stones there sprouted feathery ferns that nodded
all day long, coquetting with the zephyrs. At one end
of the house an orange-tree cast its shadows upon the
veranda, and almost tendered its golden fruit to persons
standing there. The back yard was shaded by a stately
camphor tree. Beside the party-fence stood a couple
of cherry-trees, and scattered at various points were
peach-trees and quince-trees that contributed their share
of blossoms and shade for the premises.

Our friends were duly ushered upstairs, where all of
the *shojees* had been removed, thus making the entire
story a cool pavilion, open on all sides to the breezes.
After the usual salutations and enquiries had been exhausted, tea and tobacco were duly discussed for half an
hour or so; after which, the conversation beginning to
diverge upon subjects of special interest to each sex,
the gentlemen naturally drifted over to one balcony,
while the ladies drifted over to another one, where poli-
tics and household matters were respectively discussed.

"It is a matter of regret to me, honorable sirs," remarked Mr. Yamada, "that I can furnish no male companions for your entertainment on these occasions, when
you honor me so greatly with your visits. But, as you
well know, the gods have frowned on me and no male
offspring have been given to me; so that to-day I am
without an heir to burn incense at my tomb and to transmit my unworthy name to another generation,—for my
two daughters cannot be of service in such matters."

"Have no regret in this matter so far as we are concerned, honorable sir," replied the Nakashimas; "the

wide scope and the great suggestiveness of your conver-
sational powers require no supplementing. Our minds
are indeed busy from the moment of our entry to the
time of our departure from your residence. When one
has a well occupied mind, what other pleasure can he
desire ? "

" You exalt my powers too highly. Nevertheless, in
order that we may have abundance of company, we will
spend this evening in one of the picnic booths on the
Kamogawa shoals. There we shall be surrounded with
company and shall discuss unreservedly the public matters of our country."

The greater part of the morning was spent in alternately smoking their tiny pipes and sipping hot tea from
diminutive cups ; occasionally, however, their conversa-
tional fusillade of flattery, condolence, and gossip would
be varied with a game of chess. At midday dinner
was served upstairs. The natives took their meals in
whatever room they pleased ; although, as a matter of
convenience, meals were generally served in the room
nearest to the kitchen, yet, as tables and chairs were unknown, the food could be served in any part of the house.

The duty of reinvigorating the inner man devolved
upon the Misses Yamada, two amiable damsels aged
respectively sixteen years and fourteen years. Pretty,
did you inquire? Well, yes ; decidedly so as to the
general expression of good nature that animated their
features, and somewhat so as to the qualities of each
feature. Do you admire jet-black hair and sparkling black
eyes, offset by rosy cheeks and ruby lips, that enshrine
the whitest of teeth and the merriest of smiles? Do
you admire respectful demeanor and obliging ways ?
Do you admire perfect hands and feet, and a clear,
though dark complexion ?

Either of these young ladies, I imagine, will find
grace in your eyes. Miss Masago, the elder one, is
rather tall for a Japanese lady, being somewhat over
five feet high ; her form is slender and lithe ; her manners are supremely lady-like, according to the unwritten

code that prevails among all peoples possessing any degree of culture ; and her grave countenance is sweet
and refined in expression. Miss Seisho, the younger
one, is short, plump, and merry, being a fair sample of
her sisters throughout the empire ; her face is cheerful
and pretty, and she well knows how and when to subdue
her blithesome temperament, and to assume a dignified yet winning bearing. According to Japanese ideas
these ladies are well educated. They read and write the
native language, and also have a fair knowledge of the
Chinese characters ; they can compose poetry according to
the stiff rules of the times, and can hum a few melodies
of native production ; and, above all, they are well-
versed in those supremely important duties that pertain
to the household. As to geography, arithmetic, foreign
history, chemistry, or philosophy, they do not possess
even a schoolboy's ideas.

The tub heaped full of steaming rice was duly brought
upstairs ; the tiny lacquered stands, containing various
pieces of vegetables and raw carp sliced into small bits
and accompanied by *soy*, were duly placed before each
person ; then all gathered around the collation in a
circle, decorously sitting on their heels, while Madam
Yamada dipped forth with a small wooden shovel the
steaming rice into beautiful porcelain bowls, which she
duly handed around to guests and family, and which
speedily disappeared before the steady assaults of chopsticks and teeth. The hungry ones were able to dispose
of three or four bowls. At the end of the meal, clear tea
was passed around in small cups, for the natives were
not accustomed to drink during their meals. Right
daintily has her ladyship performed her duties ; and
now, while the recipients of her bounty are scattered
around on the *tatamis*, leisurely indulging in tea and tobacco, she tarries at the bowl finishing her repast. Her
face is but slightly wrinkled, her hair is still raven-hued,
and the lustre has but slightly faded from her black eyes.
Her teeth sparkle like bits of jet, with the hideous cor-
rosive coating that matrons put thereon after marriage.

This upper story made a very picturesque dining-room. To the northward were the parks and the white walls of the Gosho ; to the eastward, seen through the foliage of the camphor tree, were the mountain ranges that formed the barrier for that side of the valley ; to the southward lay the gray roofs, the white gable ends, and the green gardens of the city ; while to the westward, beyond the limits of the city, stood another range of lofty mountains. Every passing breeze was caught. Here our friends spent the greater part of the afternoon in smoking and chatting.

Toward evening the party prinked up somewhat and strolled toward the river, where they arrived at dusk. Stepping from platform to platform, and walking along narrow planks, they finally reached a couple of booths, quite in the middle of the stream. These they rented for the evening, and at once prepared to make themselves comfortable. There were hundreds of these booths built upon the shoals and out into the stream ; and thousands of people frequented them during the hot summer evenings, picnicking and feasting to their hearts' content. Each booth was about ten feet square, and was constructed in a very simple manner. Four stout posts, one at each corner, were driven deep into the sands ; crosspieces were then tied on ; boards were then duly laid across until there had been constructed a platform about one foot above the sand or the water—as the case might be ; and finally mats were spread over the platforms, thus making delightful little places for recreation. The posts extended about five feet above the platform, and cords were stretched from tip to tip, along which paper lanterns of varied colors were strung for use on nights when the moon was not shining.

Vendors of fruit, *saké*, and melons were on the bank, and their couriers threaded the maze of booths, receiving and executing orders with energy and boundless suavity. Waiter-girls were buzzing around like butterflies from booth to booth, in response to clapping hands—the universal hailing signal of the country. Thousands of peo-

ple were spread over the mats enjoying themselves by
drinking *saké*, eating fruit, sipping tea, smoking tobacco,
or dabbling hands or feet in the cool waters of the stream.
The murmur of their voices could be heard some distance away. The view from the wooden bridge that
spanned the stream below was grotesque and weird,—as
if the water-elfs had turned out to feast beneath the moonbeams.

Our friends had wended their way to the outermost
limits, and had selected a couple of booths on the channel of the stream, where the construction of scaffolding
had ceased, and thus had secured private boxes,—so to
speak. Here they spread themselves over the mats, and
luxuriated in the cooling breezes that surged down the
channel freighted with cool mountain air. Sitting upon
the edge of the platform, they dipped their dusty feet
into the waters that flowed beneath, after which ablution
they put on neat straw slippers, and tying their wooden
clogs in a bunch, hung them up on one of the posts to
await departure for home.

Every thing was now ready for feasting and gossiping.
Clapping his hands, Mr. Yamada summoned a waiter-
girl, through whom he ordered vermicelli, lotus-root
(sugared), raw carp and *soy*, *saké*, melons, and tea ; which
articles having been speedily produced, serious inroads
were at once made into them. The young ladies amused
themselves by taking the quarter sections of melon
rinds and rigging them up as boats, with chopsticks for
masts and paper napkins for sails ; which clumsy crafts
they would then launch upon the stream, and would
wager melon seeds upon the length of time that they
would keep afloat.

After an hour or so of gossiping, nibbling, and smoking,
the ladies, in accordance with the laws of natural selection—so to speak,—monopolized one booth, while the
gentlemen occupied the other ; and from that time diver-
gent tides of conversation flowed onward far into the night.

It was indeed a superb night for picnics. The full
moon hovered over the mountain tops and suffused the

valley of the Mountain-Castle with its bright rays, giving
to the wimpling waters of the river the sheen of silver.
But our gentlemen friends had become so absorbed in
conversation that they took but little notice of their surroundings. The buzz and the hum of conversation went
up on all sides ; the ladies laughed and talked and threw
crumbs to the fishes that glided up within the shadow of
the booths ; a steady stream of travel rumbled unceasingly over the bridge ;—but they heeded nothing,—not
even the solemn tones of the monastery bells that filled
the valley with their booming vibrations ever and anon.

" Nay, sir, but the latest rumors that have drifted down
from Yedo are of a very disturbing nature," Mr. Yamada
was saying in a low voice, as if fearful of being overheard ; " and no one is able to foretell what possible complications may arise in the near future. Through
my connection with the Gosho as retainer of a *kugé* I am
in a position to obtain much important information of a
profoundly secret nature. You will remember that the
present Emperor, Osa-hito, ascended the throne six
years ago at the age of sixteen, and although even now
he is a young man, yet he possesses much tenacity of
purpose and considerable political sagacity. Although he
is shut up within a few acres of enclosed ground, presumably having no contact with the outside world, yet
he keeps himself better informed about public affairs
than is generally supposed. His spies in Yedo furnish
him with much accurate information, and occasionally
he sends special spies to particular Daimiates to pick up
whatever news may be available.

" This underground service, as you well know, is an
extremely dangerous one, because the secret emissaries
of the Shogun are as thickly strewn over the land as ants
over a bowl of rice ; they penetrate everywhere, and
mercilessly assassinate any one whom they presume to be
acting as spies against their master. We have lost some
valuable men during the last five years ; one was found
hacked to pieces in the purlieus of Shinagawa, the southern suburb of Yedo,—officially reported to have been

slain in a drunken brawl with *ronins* (*but we know better*) ; another one was slain on the Nakasendo, near a mountain village in Shinano, by a cut from behind that slashed its way between his ribs and split through the backbone, causing instant death,—officially reported to have been slain by robbers (*but we know better*) ; and the last one was murdered near Hikoné, on Lake Biwa, only eight months ago, on his way back from Yedo with highly valuable verbal information, as we subsequently were told ; he fought like a demon, and slew four of his adversaries and wounded several others, but finally fell beneath a spear thrust in his throat,—officially reported to have been the victim of some long-standing vendetta (*but we know better*).

"A spy is a double-edged sword in your hands. He may be bribed by your adversary to transmit false information to you, or to suppress important details, or even to act as a spy against yourself. Great care is required in selecting your man. Our master never employs strangers. He usually finds some faithful retainer connected in some capacity with some one of the one hundred and fifty *kugé* families here in Kioto. But since the recent information lately transmitted to us from Yedo, the Shogun has issued orders to the commandant of the Castle here in Kioto to increase the rigor of his surveillance over the members and the kindred of the imperial household, in order that their whereabouts may be located on very short notice.

" In compliance with this stringent order they have increased their guards, and have surrounded us with a web of espionage, so complete in all its details that we hardly dare to open our mouths for fear of being reported, through some obscure channel, to the Shogun as being the utterer of seditious sentiments. I do not doubt but what at this moment some sneaking cur has reported my departure from my house in company with yourself, and that our families are in for an evening's carouse on the Kamogawa shoals, and that interesting piece of information has been probably discussed ere this by the officers within the council-chambers at the Castle, and a memorandum has doubtless been duly noted opposite my name on the tabulated list that they keep of all *kugés*, of all *kugés'* retainers and servants, and of everybody having intercourse with said *kugés*. In fact, I dared not communicate to you at my own house the important information that I wish to convey, because I knew not what *shojee* or what *tatami* had ears. So I brought you out here under the screen of jollification and good-fellowship, and I think that I have given the spies the slip for this evening, at least, for I do not see in our vicinity the glitter of watchful eyes."

"Your words, honored sir, agitate me exceedingly," said Mr. Nakashima ; "your language sounds like that of a romance of the Ashikaga period. Though I have been intimate with you during these many years, yet have I never been aware of these facts that you have just been divulging. It is not unlikely, then, that your long absence from home during last spring was caused by your being engaged in one of these dangerous expeditions in behalf of Osa-hito." [1]

"Your surmise is entirely correct," replied Mr. Yamada, " and as that expedition forms but a prelude to the information that I am about to impart to you, I shall now give a brief account of it. Early this year, vague rumors floated up from Nagasaki to the effect that it had been reported by the Dutch in the island of Deshima that some barbarian power contemplated sending an expedition to our shores. These rumors failed to specify when the expedition would appear ; also whether it would be of a hostile nature, or merely a friendly visit. I was delegated to find out further details relating to this matter. Knowing that the Dutch Embassy was about to leave Yedo on its return to Nagasaki, I determined to

---

[1] Komei-Tenno, the 122d Mikado in descent from the first Mikado, Jimmu-Tenno (660–585 B.C.), ascended the Imperial throne in 1847, and died in 1867. His reign of twenty years thus covered the most momentous period in Japanese history. It is with this period that this book has to deal. Prior to his death Komei-Tenno was called Osa-hito, in accordance with ancient custom.

fall in with it on some part of its route, and pick up what information I could.

"I accordingly shaved my head and disguised myself as a mendicant monk, and slipped out of my house one night, after leaving word with my family that business in Osaca required my attention for a number of days. Instead of going there, however, I made my way to Lake Biwa, and then followed the Tokaido until I came to Nagoya, about three days' journey from Kioto. I there changed my garb and assumed that of a blind shampooer, who also shaves his head like a priest. I then began journeying back slowly over the same road to Kioto. I travelled generally in the dusk of evening,—for what does a blind man care for daylight? Thus I avoided scrutiny. And I strengthened the part that I was acting by blowing my whistle continually along the road and by groping along with my long staff. Arriving at some wayside inn late in the evening, I would solicit the privilege of plying my vocation upon the travellers sojourning there, and would generally make enough by shampooing and rubbing the tired muscles in their backs and legs to pay for a night's lodging. The daytime I spent in loitering between stations.

"The great difficulty with which I was obliged to contend, was to disguise my eyes so as to make them harmonize with the part that I was acting. There are various kinds of blindness. Those who are born blind have bleared eyes, pitifully expressionless and vacant. Then you have those over whose eyes whitish films and cataracts have grown ; these people go about with dead-fish eyes. Then you have those who have gone blind from ophthalmia and other diseases ; their eyes in many cases appear to have entirely sloughed away, causing the shrivelled lids to contract and close up tightly over the empty sockets.

"Now, this last form of blindness I could simulate fairly well by tightly closing my eyes (naturally deep-set in their sockets) and keeping up a twitching of my eyelids, as if afflicted with nervous disorders. A slight touch of dark coloring applied to the outside of my lids aided the disguise by giving a diseased appearance to those members. But I could not keep up the unnatural motions for any great length of time ; therefore I left the main road and spent the daytime loitering among the woods and groves beside the thoroughfare, where I, unobserved, could watch the passing travellers. When dusk came on I would resume the main road, and would walk on to the next convenient resting-place for the night, where it would not be necessary to practise blindness for over an hour or so. Thus I went slowly back over the road toward Kioto, waiting to be overtaken by the Embassy, and I was kept waiting a number of days.

" One day, as I was in a grove of scrub-pines near the highway, I saw a cavalcade of horsemen and *norimons* approaching from the direction of Nagoya. There must have been twenty horses loaded down with bundles, baskets, and boxes. To my surprise several of these *norimons* were without occupants ; this curious fact, however, was speedily explained by seeing a group of strangely dressed people walking along the road some distance behind, and attended by about a dozen *samurai*.[1]

" There were four foreigners. Two of them had hair like bleached hemp, light-blue eyes, and very white skins ; both of these were tall and powerfully built men, and one of them carried at his waist a fragile sword that could have been severed with one blow of my sword. The third foreigner had brown hair, brown eyes, and white skin ; and he was somewhat shorter in stature, but was very thick-set and powerful in his build. The fourth man was slender in structure, yet he was taller

---

[1] This word is used either in the singular or the plural number. These are the double-sworded gentlemen that we see so often represented in Japanese pictures. They were the retainers of the Daimios. They were bound (in theory) body and soul to the interests of their respective lords. They were to gird them around with a living wall, standing between them and every danger. In return for such service they were to receive annual pensions of rice. They formed the military caste of Japan. They were the aristocrats of the realm. Their swords were typical of their genteel and chivalrous breeding.

than the average Japanese ; his hair was jet-black, his eyes were also black, and his complexion was considerably darker than that of the other gentlemen. Such a mixture of color and features amazed me immeasurably.

" I was also astonished at the freedom allowed to these barbarians by the guards in attendance ; but I presume that the matter had been settled upon a money basis satisfactory to all parties concerned. While we Japanese suppose that these foreigners are being duly escorted in closed *norimons* through our country, yet, as a matter of fact, they are spying out every thing.

" These fellows came sauntering down the road, talking and laughing like boon companions. Occasionally they would stop and gather flowers, herbs, specimens of soil, and stones, which were carefully done up in small parcels, then placed in small lacquered boxes, and finally hid away in the *norimons* as if they were articles of great value. What, in the name of Kobu-Daishi, did they do that for, do you suppose ?

" My feelings against these barbarians were those of anger and disgust. I was angry because such people were allowed so great freedom in examining our country ; and I was disgusted because my countrymen deigned to affiliate with such uncouth and graceless people upon terms of such intimacy. ' A fine report I shall make of you to my master ! ' said I in my sleeve. I remained in seclusion until they had gone a full league down the road ; then I came forth and followed them slowly until near sunset, when they stopped at an inn.

" After dusk I strolled into the town blowing my whistle and groping along with my staff, at the same time making enquiries for hotels ; and I was referred to the only one in the place, where I duly made application for a night's lodging. At first I was peremptorily ordered off by a rude officer, who informed me that the place was filled with the guards and the attendants of the foreign embassy, but, upon its appearing that I was a helpless, blind shampooer in quest of trade, permission

was granted for me to take up my quarters with the servants in the kitchen.

"My evening meal was quickly served; after which I
humbly begged to be allowed to ply my vocation upon
the weary limbs of the travellers in the inn ; to which
reasonable request no objection was raised by the
fatigued members of the suite, upon many of whom I
plied my trade, and soon had worked myself into their
very best graces. It was finally suggested by some one
that the foreigners in the back-room upstairs might be
refreshed with a course of rubbing. This suggestion gave
rise to a heated controversy, some urging that such a
thing would be unprecedented, while others urged that
it would come within the letter of their instructions to
escort the foreigners carefully and to keep them in good
health during the journey.

"At this juncture my simple enquiry as to whether the
foreign gentlemen were not human beings constructed
like ourselves, and likely to be benefited with similar treatment, provoked great laughter, and was pronounced to
be a shrewd bid for fresh custom. Nevertheless the observation put everybody into good humor, so that it was
finally settled that I should shampoo the foreign gentlemen, receiving from the treasurer the customary fee of two
rin, while I was instructed by that urbane and upright
gentleman to charge the foreigners themselves a *bu*
apiece—nearly thirty times more than I received.

"This financial basis appearing satisfactory to the downstairs party, I was ushered upstairs into a large apartment opening toward the back on a veranda. I was
duly introduced, and was then left quite alone with
those strange creatures, to perform whatever rubbing
they might call for. The room was but dimly lighted
with an *andon* (paper lantern).

"I began upon the captain of the company, who lay
stretched on the *tatamis* in one corner of the room. As
I was now compelled to simulate blindness to the utmost
of my capacity, I could observe nothing for several minutes. While rubbing and squeezing the muscles of his

arms, neck, and shoulders, I kept up a perpetual winking. I was amazed to find him shaped in every way like ourselves. When I rolled him over on his face and began to operate upon the muscles of his back and legs, I was further amazed to find how heavily he was built. He was as heavy and as massive as one of our gigantic wrestlers. Why so powerfully constructed a gentleman should be contented with twirling a puny little sword, like a girl dallying with a needle, was beyond my comprehension.

"As I rubbed and thumped his back, I took sly glances around the room. The black-haired barbarian lay upon his stomach beside the *andon* and appeared to be writing in a small book which he would hastily slip into his pocket whenever footsteps approached the room. The wretch was doubtless entering his observations on the country made during the day. I felt like drawing forth my short sword from beneath my clothes and pinning him to the floor. The brown-haired fellow was lying on some silk cushions and was busily engaged in talking to the yellow-haired beast, who sat on the veranda smoking a pipe of vast dimensions and occasionally ejecting from between his lips some muddy fluid into a flower-pot beside him.

"Truly they were a strange set of fellows ! Their voices were strong and coarse, and came up from their very stomachs, for when I was rubbing the back of the big fellow he coughed and spoke to the black-haired fellow, whereupon my hand fairly trembled with the deeply intoned vibrations beneath ; and when he laughed at my tickling his ribs during the process of punching and pinching, I felt as if I were handling an earthquake, because of the suppressed gurglings within the caverns of his breast. After finishing him up, the brown-haired fellow came to me, and was duly kneaded and thumped. He was not so large as the captain, but he was wonderfully well knit and tough. He was exceedingly ticklish, and laughed immoderately whenever I touched his ribs. It did not take me long to finish him up.

Then I went to work on the other yellow-haired fellow. He was exceedingly large-boned, but he was as limp and as flabby as a baby, and smelt like a mangy dog. He did not have enough vitality to laugh when I made special efforts to tickle his ribs, but he dozed and grunted, and grunted and dozed, like an immense pig.

"Having finished with him, I sat waiting for the black-haired man to come and take his turn; in the meantime I blinked at the light like an owl, and furtively watched him between the blinks. Suddenly he looked up from his writing and, beckoning me, said in a low and musical voice : 'Come over here, Mr. Shampooer. and work on me near the veranda ; the air is fresher here.' Like a simpleton, I coolly went over to him and began to talk, when it came over me like a thunder-clap that I was supposed to be blind, and that the foreigners were supposed to be ignorant of our language ; yet so smooth and so natural had been his speech that I was drawn to his side like a charmed bird. 1 was overwhelmed with confusion and fear at my indiscretion, for if my action had been observed by anybody watching my movements, my head would soon have parted company with my shoulders."

"Excuse my interruption, sir," exclaimed Mr. Nakashima in an undertone, "but did you just now feel a tremor of this platform whereon we are sitting ? "

"I did not, sir. Daughters, are you shaking the booth ? "

"No, sir ; we are quietly listening to the account of the latest freaks of the demon of the Maruyama cascades," replied his daughters.

"Yet I felt a decided tremor," said Mr. Nakashima ; "The people in the adjacent booths all appear to be quietly enjoying themselves. My son, will you kindly step over into the water and carefully look beneath the platform and see if any one is there listening to our conversation ? "

His youngest son, who was sitting on the edge of the booth, accordingly slipped down into the water, and gazed beneath. The bright moonlight revealed nothing but the rippling waves and the sandy shoals as far as he could see. A heavy piece of drift-wood, however, had been borne by the current against one of the posts, and this appeared to be the cause of their agitation. But the party now became aware of the possibility of some one creeping beneath them and thus catching the drift of their conversation.

The young men therefore agreed to take turns in look- ing over the side of the booth every few minutes or so, and occasionally stepping into the water and thoroughly inspecting the shoals beneath the flooring of the booth. Such was the system of espionage prevailing in those days that the people never knew when they were being watched.

" I trust you will excuse my interruption, sir," said Mr. Nakashima.

" Nay, sir, mention it not. I am under boundless obli- gation to you for your caution," replied Mr. Yamada. " With the bright moonlight overhead, and with a clear sweep for the eyes on all sides of us, it never occurred to me that those sneaking Tokugawa reptiles could creep beneath us. Never fear now. Let them come on if they wish to taste this steel that I shall thrust between the chinks in this flooring just as soon as I hear a sound below. But let me see ; I was at the point where I was outwitted by that black-haired devil of a Hollander. Well, to continue, I was feeling extremely uncomfortable. I determined, however, to put a bold face on the matter, and to make the best of it ; for I perceived that no one appeared to notice this by-play, and that the matter lay entirely between the black-haired Hollander and myself. ' Mr. Shampooer,' said he, in a soft voice, ' you do not appear to be totally blind, nor am I totally dumb as regards your language. You have exposed yourself as well as I have done. Therefore we must both be fast friends and keep each other's secrets, or we shall both come to grief. Now, we are over here near the veranda · where we cannot be heard, and I wish to hold friendly

converse with you for a few moments. You are no more
of a blind shampooer than I am. I was impressed by the
cast of your countenance when you came into the room,
and being the doctor of the Dutch settlement in Deshima
at Nagasaki, I have become very familiar with the various forms of eye diseases prevailing in this country.
In fact, I know more of such subjects than your people
know. Therefore when you began to pound and to
thump your first victim, I opened the door of this
andon here, punched a hole through the paper, and, thus
screened as to my head, took profound interest in your
performances from that time onward. Oh, you are a
wonderful shampooer, my friend ! You handled that
last victim about as delicately as a wild boar would
manipulate a sweet potato ! '

" ' However, I don't care any thing about your history.
All I wish from you is direct answers to a few questions
about the customs and features of the country around
Kioto and Lake Biwa. You of course know that we
Hollanders are not allowed to learn your language under
penalty of banishment from your shores. Nevertheless,
I have obtained—never mind how—a pretty fair mastery of the common language of your people. I do
not use it, however, to your country's detriment, but
only to secure geographical and scientific matter pertaining to your country for my own information and
pleasure.'

" Thus he talked. His pronunciation was strangely
accurate. And his language, though not couched in the
exact forms of our own people, yet was wonderfully
clear, comprehensive, and thoughtful. And he had a
capacity for getting at facts and at ideas (even through
the medium of imperfect expression) that was perfectly
amazing. The exactness with which our minds came in
contact almost convinced me that he was a native of
Japan. How could the mind of a being whose ancestors
never had any connection or communication with mine,
and who, instead of being descended from the gods, had
descended from beasts, thus commune with my mind and

exchange ideas so similar to my own—yea, even superior to my own ? How do you explain such things ? "
" I do not know how to account for it," said Mr. Nakashima, " unless upon the supposition that we have been misinformed about these barbarians, and also about our own country. There is a mystery about this entire subject that grows deeper all the time. We live in a strange period of Japanese history."
" However that may be," replied Mr. Yamada, " of one thing I am certain, that if there be many men like that black-haired doctor in foreign countries, then we will have much to learn from outside barbarians. That man elicited all the information that I had to convey about the city of Kioto, its history, its temples, its religions, its theatres, and about its silk and porcelain manufactures ; and he probed for a vast amount of information concerning adjoining provinces that I knew nothing about. Truly, I was amazed at the depth of my ignorance concerning Japan outside of my native province of Yamashiro. Pray, what do we folks here know about what is transpiring in Satsuma, or in Nambu, or in Musashi, or even in so near a place as Kaga ? Verily, our ignorance and narrow-mindedness in such things are abominable ; like frogs in a well, we see nothing but the sky directly overhead. Pray, what do you or I know about what is happening just beyond these mountains surrounding us, over in the adjoining provinces of Tamba, Omi, or Yamato ? Truly, our ignorance is deplorable in the extreme ! "
" I am sure, sir," replied Mr. Nakashima, " that I know no more about the features of Nambu or Awomori than I know about the uttermost bounds of barbarism. I know a little about Satsuma through rumor, but nothing definite. Verily, we Japanese are profoundly ignorant about what is transpiring within the four seas environing our own country. My knowledge of Japan is limited by these mountains here. And the scope of my general information seems to be circumscribed by a series of original lectures on the art of thrusting, parry-

ing, and smiting with bamboo foils. With what else am
I conversant? I know absolutely nothing about foreign
countries, and I know but little of my own country beyond the mountain walls of Yamashiro. This is truly
a shameful state of affairs. And yet I am reputed to
be an educated Japanese gentleman! Truly, Yamashiro
is a well, and I am a frog living therein! Pray, sir,
what else did that black-haired gentleman inquire
about?"

"Well, he wished to know what kind of fish lived in
Lake Biwa. Who knows? He then inquired as to the
varieties of fish found in the waters of Osaca Bay and
off-shore along the coast. Do you know? Ha! ha! I
thought it quite likely that you were not familiar with
that morsel of information. Then he wished to know
the names of the various animals, insects, trees, herbs,
and flowers, that grew in our province; concerning
which, I am pleased to say, I was able to give some information.

"Then he desired to know the amount of rain that fell
in Yamashiro and in the adjoining provinces during the
year. How would you answer such a question as that?
You hesitate! Well, I am not surprised. And finally,
he wanted details about the history of Kioto and of the
imperial family, concerning which I gave him considerable information very reluctantly, because it seemed to
me that he was trespassing beyond the limit of legitimate inquiry. I began to garble facts and to suppress
details; but he corrected my false statements at once
with utmost precision to my great confusion and amazement. Verily, the fellow had read up our country's
history from some source or other with most commendable accuracy.

"During a half hour of shampooing he compelled me
to disgorge an amount of information that I did not
know was in my possession, and an amount quite sufficient to take off my head. Once or twice the *shojee* was
slid back by the interpreter, who looked in to see how
my work was progressing, but the doctor informed him

that his sore back and legs required special rubbing to ease them. I heard the interpreter translate this to the officer of the guard. I suspected that the interpreter and the doctor were upon very familiar terms, for there was a sly chuckle in his voice as he made his inquiries. At last my work was completed, and I was led out into my kitchen quarters, where I spent a somewhat uneasy night.

" In the early dawn I left the hotel and had gone well on my way before sunrise. By midday I had reached a convenient clump of trees where I tarried until nightfall, thus allowing the embassy to precede me into Kioto. Then I came quietly into the city, and slipped into my house unobserved.

" During the weeks that I was waiting for my hair to grow again, I compared notes with the spies who had been delegated to watch other portions of the embassy's route. My report, compiled from these sources, was duly submitted to the Emperor and to his councillors.

" It therein appeared that the embassy left Nagasaki about six weeks before the end of the year, and travelled overland nearly two hundred miles to the Shimonosèki Straits. Embarking there in boats, they came through the Inland Sea to Osaca, a distance of about two hundred and fifty miles. Thence they passed overland by way of Nagoya and the Tokaido to Yedo, where they tarried until after the commencement of the new year. On New Year's Day they called on the Shogun, and were allowed to do him homage. After that event they returned to Nagasaki by the same route that they came. It seemed that the foreigners were kept closely guarded on the upward journey, but that on the return journey they were allowed more liberty in consideration of their gracious reception by the Shogun. It also appeared that I was the only spy who had obtained personal access to the foreigners. My information was pronounced varied and instructive.

" Nothing of importance had been gleaned at Nagasaki or on the upward journey. At Yedo, however, there were various rumors set afloat by the foreigners to the effect that some barbarian naval expedition would soon appear off the coast of Japan. These rumors excited considerable fear and conjecture in the metropolis as to the object of such an expedition. Such were the main features of our report. A few days ago, however, a secret messenger came through the inland mountain roads from Yedo, bearing to us the important information that a foreign fleet had put in its appearance in the bay a few miles south of Yedo, creating great consternation in that region. Our spies in Yedo also notified us that they needed two or three assistants to render aid in the work of securing information. You well know that our emperors have long been treated like puppets by the Shoguns, and that our present Emperor has long chafed at the undignified and degrading position in which he has been placed. You also know that Satsuma and the southwestern Daimios have long been bitterly hostile to the encroachments of the Tokugawa Shoguns, and that they are carefully watching for a favorable opportunity to overturn the Yedo tyrant ; therefore, it is of vital importance to our cause that we keep well posted on all matters of a public nature, in order to know how to act. If we can create such violent discontent among the provinces as to create a revolution, whereby the house of Tokugawa may be overthrown, who knows but what our Emperor may regain his prestige and ancient power ?

"I do not imagine that the southwestern Daimios have any special love or admiration for our imperial master, nor do I think that they would worry themselves much about him under ordinary circumstances ; but their hatred for the house of Tokugawa, dating from the time when Tokugawa Iyèyas routed the legions of the league and stormed the castle of Osaca, where perished the only son of Hidèyoshi, cherished friend and ally of Satsuma, has become of late years so very pronounced that the Shogun hardly dares to cast his eyes in their direction. And, in order to gratify their spite against the house of Tokugawa, who knows but what our Emperor may form a coalition with the southwestern Daimios for allies, and thus regain his former power ?"

" Aye, who knows ?" exclaimed the Nakashimas.

For a while they all sat musing over the strange ideas suggested by the extraordinary narration of Mr. Yamada ; which, though told in a few concise words in this chapter, yet occupied a long time when interspersed with abundant gestures, frequent explanatory comments, and answers to queries from the attentive listeners, together with alternate smoking of pipes and sipping of tea. It was drawing well on toward the middle watches of the night as timed by the deep-toned mournful notes of the massive bells of the temples. Mr. Nakashima was gazing dreamily across the river upon the sombre groves that covered the mountain sides, in whose sylvan depths the booming vibrations announced the presence of monasteries embowered there.

"Sir," said Mr. Yamada, abruptly, addressing Mr. Nakashima, "what say you to allowing your sons to assist me in this matter of collecting information for our common master, the Emperor? I know that this proposition is a sudden one, and that, from the danger connected therewith, it must shock you somewhat. I have cast my eyes around for assistants, and I can find no one so well suited for the Yedo circuit as your sons. The fact that their ancestors were retainers of Tokugawa Iyèyas will aid them immensely in attaching themselves to the retinue of some Tokugawa lord in Yedo ; while their blood relationship to the imperial family—remote though it be—insures their loyalty to our cause. I have long considered this plan, and my prime object in bringing you down here this evening was to submit it to you in confidence. I can well see that your sons are eager for the service, and need no urging to enter upon the dangerous career of imperial spies ; but at the same time I can well understand the solicitude of your paternal heart, and I therefore do not urge upon you an immediate answer. You may consider this matter at your leisure, and notify me in due time of your decision."

"Honorable sir," replied Mr. Nakashima, "I cannot feel otherwise than highly honored at the supreme confidence you repose in me and in my sons. My loyalty and zeal for our imperial master will ever remain steadfast; and my friendship for the house of Tokugawa surely cannot be very strong after the shabby treatment our family has received at their hands. Yet, as your proposition is an important one, requiring serious and careful consideration, I will duly weigh it in consultation with my sons, and you will have our reply at an early day."

Our friends now wended their way homeward, where they indulged in a brief siesta upon the balconies, and then the master ordered the servant to slip the *shojees* into the grooves in the middle of the room, and to spread out the bedding on the *tatamis* on both sides of this extemporized partition. Gentle slumbers, like a soft mist, then settled down upon their busy brains, and dreams of flashing blades and mangled bodies reflected the gory recitals of the host.

CHAPTER IV.

In the gray dawn of a morning in August a courier
stood beside the western gateway of the Shogun's castle
in Yedo. It was beside the outermost moat, at a place
where the flat lands surrounding the waters of the bay
abruptly merged into the rolling hill country that undu-
lated far away in all directions to the distant mountains.
The broad ditch that had closely clung to the grassy
ramparts in all their twists and turns on the low lands
now found itself confronted with a high hill, through
which it had to pierce its way. On either side of the
mighty cutting the swarded embankments sloped upward
in graceful curves of living green, opening up a sweet
vista of deeply shaded waters, upon whose placid bosom
the gorgeous lotus plants unfolded their broad leaves to
catch the rosy petals of their glorious blossoms ; along
whose margin the reeds and lilies grew beneath the
shadows of the dwarfed pines that stretched forth their
grotesque branches upon frail bamboo trellises ; and
where the poky little wild ducks from far northern lakes
floated in myriad squadrons during the winter months,
giving to the landscape an appearance that cannot be
otherwise described than as *Japanesque.* A fragile
wooden bridge crossed the moat below the cutting, and
a wide causeway gradually curved up the hillside toward
the portals of the massive gateway that stood at the top
of the cutting.

This gateway was a massive double-storied tower of
rectangular proportions. It was constructed of wood,
plaster, and tiles. The beams and the planks were of

immense size, and were plated with thick sheets of iron. The heavy wooden gates were also heavily plated with iron, and were thickly studded with massive iron nails. When the massive wings swung inward on their grating hinges they swept nearly all the space beneath the second story.   There was, however, a small room on either hand for the accommodation of the guards who opened the gates at sunrise, and who opened the little wicket gate (inlaid within one of the wings) to duly accredited persons demanding entrance after sunset.   The upper story was one immense room, pierced on all sides with heavily barred windows for archers and matchlock-men to discharge their missiles upon assaulting ranks beneath.

The gates had not yet been opened for the day, and the guards slumbered in the lower rooms of the tower. Outside of the gateway, leaning against its massive posts, stood the courier, awaiting the delivery of the despatch that he had been notified to call for at daybreak.   He was a tall muscular fellow, tanned from head to heels in a manner quite sufficient to have excited the envy of some professional athlete.   On his feet were straw sandals ; around his loins was a scanty rag ; around his shoulders was flung a dark-blue cotton tunic as a precaution against cold during inaction ; upon his head was a broad-brimmed coolie hat woven out of bamboo strips ; and in his hand he held a coarse cotton handkerchief, with which he industriously brushed off the mosquitoes that seemed inclined to breakfast on his bare legs.

But the despatch was delayed.   If you will follow the road inside the gateway for half a mile or so over the brow of the hill, past the barracks and past the mansions of the gentry, to that stately *yashiki*[1] near the innermost

---

[1] " A *yashiki* was a style of feudal architecture peculiar to Yedo. The central feature was a palace of vast proportions.   Around this, on all sides, were gardens, lawns, and courtyards, covering frequently many acres of ground.   All this was then hemmed in with an unbroken line of barracks arranged in a quadrangle and having heavily barred windows and iron-bound gates of massive proportions.   Each

A Courier Despatch. 53

moat, you will find the lights still glimmering in the council-chamber of the presiding officer of the *Gorojio*.[1] There had been a stormy night session of that body. It was long past midnight before the Daimios in council had summoned their respective escorts and had been borne in their *norimons* to their respective *yashikis*. There had been much wild and fierce discussion over the answer that should be given to the letter of Millard Fillmore, the President of the United States of North America, which had been delivered by a powerful fleet of vessels a fortnight before to the Shogun's envoy about twenty miles below Yedo.

The contents of the letter were friendly enough, but they proposed to invade the policy of two centuries and to inaugurate changes whose momentous consequences could not be foreseen. No conclusion had been arrived at except to speedily summon an experienced interpreter from Nagasaki and to instruct the governor of that city to collect whatsoever information he could from the Dutch merchants in Deshima concerning the history and the characteristics of this strange nation beyond the seas. The presiding officer has just put the official seal to his communications to the governor of Nagasaki, and his secretary is now placing the despatches in a long lacquered box, something like a lady's glove-box ; and now, after tying that up carefully and placing it within a square box of larger dimensions attached to a long stick, he locks the lid carefully with a duplicate key and gives it to his servant to carry in haste to the courier waiting

Daimio had his *yashiki* in Yedo, wherein he and his army of retainers resided during their long visits under the Tokugawa *régime*. But few of these grand structures remain ; many were burnt during the Revolution, and some of the finest, having been turned into government offices, were set on fire and destroyed by stoves improperly set up therein."—" A Budget of Letters from Japan," page 132, note.

[1] " The Shogun was assisted in his deliberations and executive functions by the *Gorojio*, or council of smaller Daimios ; and as the Shogun was oftener a puppet than not, the government of Japan came at last to be practically vested in the president of this council—a man, under ordinary circumstances, of comparatively low rank."— *Blackwood's Magazine*, vol. 101, p. 430.

at the western gateway. With flying feet he speeds by the gardens and the barracks and reaches the gateway just as the drowsy guards are awaking the echoes of the place with stentorian yawns. At sight of the lacquered chest, stamped with the gilded crests of the Tokugawas, they prostrate themselves upon the *tatamis* and receive it with reverential hands. The doors are flung back and the expectant courier is ushered in to receive his burden. Making profound obeisance, he proceeds with trembling hands to wrap the chest carefully in oil-paper to protect it during its long journey overland to the western gates of the empire. Then drawing forth his jade-stone monogram from his tobacco-pouch, he stamps with nervous hand his signature to the receipt, that states that on that day he duly received from the proper officer a government despatch contained in box number 200 for transmission to the next station on the *Nakasendo* (Inland Road), twelve miles from Yedo. Then fastening his tunic to one end of the pole, he swings the chest over his shoulder, and rushes down the causeway just as the morning sun, rising from the broad bosom of the Pacific, is tinting with its beams the shores of the sea-girt isles.

The courier is now fully under way, and very rapidly does he speed westward over the hills. After a sharp trot of about an hour and a half he rushed panting into a village where the first relay was stationed. The post-office was an ordinary native house, in front of which stood several coolies and pack-horses. In one of the large front rooms that served as an office were the relay couriers lying around upon the *tatamis*, smoking pipes and sipping tea. As soon as it was announced that a despatch from Yedo was on its way up the street, a tall, muscular fellow at once sprang up and stripped himself for work. So quick was he in his preparation that, ere the glittering body of the approaching courier had swung past the gateway, he stood in the street ready for the despatch. The box was instantly seized by the post-master, its number and alleged contents quickly noted in the register, a receipt duly given therefor, and, after a delay of barely five minutes, it was again speeding along the road toward its destination.

Thus it sped onward all day long with fresh couriers at intervals of ten or twelve miles. At night it was nearly one hundred miles from Yedo, upon the verge of the mighty mountain regions of the interior. It was carefully guarded at the village post-office until daylight, when it was again on its way up into the grand mountains of central Japan, where it sped onward all day long over mountain passes thousands of feet high ; deep down into valleys well shaded with forests of maple, cryptomeria, beech, and oak ; past the base of the volcano Asamayama, that lifted its smoking head eight thousand feet above sea level ; past engroved temples and villages tucked away amid gulches and ravines, where monkeys and deer abounded, and where bears and panthers waged war against the wild boars ; past hot mineral springs, and past hamlets embowered in bamboo groves ; over lofty mountains whence could be seen mighty Fujisan on the eastern coast, and massive Hakusan that linked the corners of five provinces on the western coast ; through vales that were filled with the rustlings of mountain torrents freighted with the melted snows of a past winter ; through some of the grandest and most picturesque mountain scenery in the world. Yet the couriers heeded none of these things, but, with bated breath and bowed heads, sped over passes, through vales, and across torrents, bearing onward yet deeper into the mountain fastnesses the message of the Shogun. The nut-brown, glistening hounds chased the parting day with hurried feet, for the sun sets early in these deep valleys, and they must at all hazards make their eighty miles of journey. Late in the evening the last courier rushed down into the sweet valley of Agematsu and deposited his burden with the village postmaster. Thus has it come one hundred and eighty miles on its way.

At daylight on the third day it was again on its way over mountains that gradually merged into foot-hills until the courier leaped forth upon the plains of Mino among wheat fields, rice fields, and groves of mulberry-trees. By dusk the despatch had been borne quite across the province of Mino near to the mountain barriers of Lake Biwa. And on the fourth day it had skirted the lovely hill country encircling the eastern and southern shores of Lake Biwa, had passed over the northern barrier of Yamashiro into Kioto, and thence had gone onward to Osaca on the shores of the Inland Sea, thus making nearly four hundred miles in four days.

Here the scene changed. Instead of continuing the journey by following the road along the shores of the Inland Sea, the despatch finds a large and swift boat with two sets of oarsmen ready to receive it. Eight lusty scullers—four standing on each side of the stern— plied the long narrow blades with such skill and power that the trembling craft rushed through the blue waters with such tremendous speed that, ere the first day's sun had set, its sharp prow had cut through nearly eighty miles of waves, and was threading the channels of the inland archipelago. Late at night the crew turned the prow toward the lights of a village on the shores of a hilly islet. Shooting the boat high up on the sandy beach, the weary crew bivouacked in its immediate vicinity, while the officer in charge of the despatch conveyed it to the house of the mayor, where he was hospitably entertained during the night. While dawn was yet tarrying in the east, the boat had been shot down into the waves ; and the chanting and the tramping of the scullers, as they simultaneously threw themselves inward and then outward over the gunwales, kept up a monotonous rhythm of motion and of song that could be heard for a great distance over the peaceful waters. All day long it sped through the maze of channels. The *yakunin* (officer) lolled upon a *tatami* amidships, smoking and dozing. At high noon they lunched at a fishing village ensconced upon the shores of a picturesque island. And the evening shades found them camping on the shores of a little inlet midway through the channel. The next day, having shaken themselves clear of the maze of islands,

they came into wider water, where they hugged the shore
of the mainland. And on the following day they reached
Shimonosèki Straits, the gateway to the open sea.

Here, instead of sending the despatch to Nagasaki by
the land route, it was found that the orders directed
them to proceed there by sea. Accordingly the oarsmen
were changed and a stock of provisions was taken aboard.
Then they went outside and crept for three days along
the sea-coast, sometimes among clusters of islands quite
as picturesque as the inland archipelago. And on the
evening of the third day they slipped between the headlands of Nagasaki harbor and went skimming along
toward the landing, where the adventurous box, after a
journey of nearly one thousand miles, was duly delivered;
and it was soon on its way to the palace of the governor,
who received it, and was soon deeply buried in the contents thereof.

Early on the morning of the following day, a messenger
hurried from the gateway of the palace down to the edge
of the harbor, where had been filled in about half an acre
of land, upon which were built the warehouses and the
residences of the Dutch merchants, constituting what has
become known to the world as Deshima. Coming to the
solitary bridge that spanned the broad canal cutting the
island from the mainland, our messenger was challenged
by the guard stationed there, who, upon a careful examination of the governor's passport, at once ushered the
bearer thereof over the bridge to the gateway leading
into the walled compound of Deshima, where he was
challenged by another guard, who took the passport with
profound obeisance and examined it on bended knees.
Passing muster here also, the heavy gates were swung
open, and our messenger stepped beyond the threshold of ·
the "compound" that had served as a mercantile prison
for over two centuries. The place was shaped like that
part of a spreading fan upon which paper is usually
pasted, and it measured six hundred feet across its face,
and two hundred and forty feet across its sides. At each
corner stood a guard-house. A broad promenade

bounded it along the water's edge. Two well-gravelled
walks meeting at right angles in the centre divided the
enclosure into four nearly equal parts, that contained the
warehouses, residences, gardens, and flower-beds of the
"factory." In the right-hand corner near the gateway,
enclosed by a high bamboo fence, stood the house of the
Dutch Resident, in a pretty garden filled with shrubbery
and flowers. It was a double-storied house, built after
the native style. In front of it stood the tall flag-pole,
from whose top floated the flag of Holland.

Our messenger was duly ushered upstairs into the
presence of the Resident, who, loosely attired in a Japanese robe, was sipping his morning cup of coffee on the
veranda. He received the governor's messenger with
profound obeisance, and, while the interpreter was being
summoned, he ordered up refreshments for his guest.
There was great curiosity in the community to know
what might be the purport of this early communication
from the governor; but the interpreter promptly put in
an appearance, and the message was found to be tanta-
lizingly brief and characteristically peremptory : "The
Resident is commanded by the governor of Nagasaki to
appear without delay at the palace." It was useless to
inquire as to the nature of the business, for the astute
messenger had profoundly bowed himself out of the
house as soon as the order had been communicated. The
Resident hastily dressed himself, and, summoning his
norimon, went to the palace with the interpreter. After
being regaled with tea and cakes in an anteroom, he was
ushered into the august presence of the governor, before
whom he prostrated himself in abject salutation. A long
list of questions was then put to him through the interpreter. He was requested to give all the information he
could concerning the population, productions, manufactures, and general resources of the United States of
North America. What was its power in war? What
were its weak points? What were its capacity and its
facilities for waging foreign war? Was it on good terms
with the nations of Europe? What was the present con-

dition of its army and navy? How many days would it require to navigate a fleet from those shores? The answers to these and to a multitude of similar questions were duly recorded by the secretaries. After a couple of hours thus spent, a short intermission was allowed, and tea and tobacco were passed around. After that, a few general questions, that appeared to have subsequently suggested themselves, were then put. Then the Resident was requested to send to the governor all the maps, charts, atlases, and books descriptive of the United States and of Europe that he could spare, and also to release immediately from his employ the senior interpreter attached to the "factory," to be sent to Yedo for an indefinite period. The interview was then terminated, and the Resident was forthwith escorted back to his home.

The office of the governor presented a busy scene far into the night. The literature and the atlases that the Resident had sent up with his compliments, were duly wrapped up in oil-paper, and were carefully packed in a stout lacquered box, which was duly locked and sealed. The busy fingers of the secretaries were many hours at work on the despatches. At daybreak the last item had been transcribed, and box number 200 was filled with voluminous despatches. It was then locked with the duplicate key, and was duly delivered, together with the box of books, to servants who at once hastened to the beach with them, and before sunrise the swift boat bearing the interpreter and the *yakunin* in charge of the boxes was gliding between the headlands of the bay on its way back to Osaca through the Inland Sea. On the eighth day after its departure from Nagasaki, it entered the mouth of the river on which Osaca is situated. Without delay the despatch box was sent flying overland on the shoulders of couriers toward Yedo, where it arrived within four days at the *yashiki* of him who held the duplicate key thereof.

But the books and the interpreter not being adapted to such rapid means of conveyance, were transferred to a long, flat-bottomed river-boat in charge of a *yakunin* who had been delegated to escort our friend to Yedo by the Tokaido (overland shore road) as rapidly as might be consistent with comfort. All night long the boatmen alternately sculled, towed, and punted their shallow craft against the swift current of the Kamogawa up toward Kioto. They arrived there at daylight. Here the overland journey was to commence. It was decided, however, at the suggestion of the interpreter, to tarry in Kioto for a couple of days in order to make necessary preparations for the long journey before them. But back of this delay was a subtle cause unperceived by the bluff old *yakunin*, but the undercurrent of which will appear in the next chapter.

CHAPTER V.

ON the morning of the day when our friend Konishi, the interpreter, arrived in Kioto, he set out with his companion ostensibly for a ramble around the city. His elderly friend, however, soon became wearied with sight-seeing, and suggested that a day be made of it in one of the fine theatres in the vicinity of Gihon-machi. Here the bluff *yakunin's* attention was rapturously absorbed in a sanguinary plot of the thirteenth century transacted at Kamakura, the capital of the Ashikaga Shoguns. In fact, so carried away was he with the wild horrors of the scene, that he repeatedly roared forth his approval and shouted forth his name (in accordance with native usage) from the gallery-box where he was ensconced, so that the actors might know whose approbation their meritorious performance had brought down.

Toward noon he ordered up a repast of rice, fish, and *saké* from a neighboring restaurant, and, under the influence of the exhilarating beverage, became so uproarious when the play was resumed in the afternoon, that Konishi was vexed and mortified beyond measure, for it was not considered very good form for knightly gentlemen to be seen in such places. Finding that his friend was in for a tempestuous gale for the balance of the afternoon, Konishi left him in charge of a couple of friends whom he had invited to the theatre, and excusing himself on the plea of illness, he slipped out of the building. Having thus shaken off his shadow, his movements were by no means uncertain, but showed themselves to be in accordance with a well studied plan. He

61

rapidly crossed over to the other side of the city, and
was soon wending his way among hedgerows and groves,
following the road toward the mountains that formed the
western barriers of Yamashiro.   When in doubt as to his
route, a few polite inquiries at wayside cottages always
set him in motion toward the place that he seemed
desirous of reaching.

At last he entered the sequestered glen at the foot of
Atago-Yama.   Following the road up toward the hamlet,
he halted before the Nakashima gateway, as if in doubt
about his bearings.   Perceiving Madame Nakashima
demurely sewing upon the veranda, he clattered across
the yard upon his clumsy wooden clogs, and inquired of
her whether a gentleman named Nakashima Tomokichi
dwelt anywhere in the vicinity.   His voice speedily
brought from upstairs the gentleman in question, together with his father and brothers.   It soon became
manifest that the arrival of Konishi had been expected,
and that he and Tomokichi were old friends.   Profuse
and profound salutations were exchanged, and Konishi
was speedily refreshed with tea and tobacco, and he was
ceremoniously introduced by Tomokichi to the other
members of the family as Konishi Yèyoshi, vassal of the
Daimio of Mito, temporarily detached from the service
of said clan and in the employ of the Dutch Resident at
Deshima as senior interpreter, and a dear friend of his
excellency the governor of Nagasaki, but now promoted
to be an adviser to the *Bakufu*[1] in matters pertaining to
foreign affairs, because of his scholarly familiarity with
foreign literature.

After much general conversation the gentlemen retired
upstairs, and the old lady was left below to keep watch
on the gateway and to announce the approach of
strangers.   In the back-room upstairs there were spread
upon the floor the wonderful chart and a large map of

[1] *Baku* is a curtain such as the Japanese used in war to enclose the
part of the camp occupied by the general, and, in peace, by picnic
parties.   The curtain was emblematical of the military power, and
hence the office from which the country was administered by the military vassal was called *bakufu, i. e.,* curtain office.—E. SATOW.

Japan. Evidently some route was being marked out. The gentlemen seated themselves around the map, and at once plunged into an earnest conversation that clearly showed that the subject-matter thereof had long been carefully under consideration by each one of them.

"The hotel boy brought your message this morning," said Tomokichi, "and I was beginning to fear that some unforeseen event had intervened to prevent your promised visit. I was delighted beyond expression to hear the familiar sound of your voice downstairs."

"Yes, I was delayed by that stupid old idiot who has been delegated to shadow me to Yedo," replied Konishi, "and if a kindly bottle of *saké* had not come to my rescue I would yet be wilting in the close atmosphere of the Gihon-machi theatre. If that old fool be not rollicking drunk by night time and ready to turn the theatre upside down, I shall be very much mistaken in my estimate of his capacity for working iniquity. I was fortunate in being able to leave him in the keeping of a couple of Aidzu *samurai*, whose acquaintance I made last year here in Kioto, and I would not be surprised if they had their hands full by night, for I left the *saké* bottle filled with some of the headiest stuff that I could find, and if he be not lively enough to make the Kamogawa run up hill when the play ends, it will not be my fault. I told him that I wanted fresh air for my headache, and excused myself for the balance of the day."

"We are immeasurably gratified at the success of your stratagem, and we are deeply mindful of the honor that you have conferred upon us by your presence," replied Mr. Nakashima.

"Sir, you honor me too highly," responded Konishi.

"Father," said Tomokichi, "would it not be best for us to hasten with the matter we have under discussion, and to arrive at some conclusion before it becomes necessary for our friend Konishi to return to his hotel? Kindly lay before him our plans, and solicit his advice in this matter that so deeply concerns our family and our Emperor's honor."

"Your words are wisely spoken, my son. We must, indeed, hasten with our discussion. Know, then, honored sir, that we desire your friendly assistance in a matter of profound interest to ourselves. Some time ago it was suggested to me that I should allow my sons to engage in the secret service of our imperial master. You well know the great danger that accompanies such service, and you can well appreciate the great kindness of our master who, although sorely in need of such aid, yet has waited many weeks for our answer to the proposal, in order that we may well consider the matter, and that we may do nothing that shall grieve our paternal heart in the future. I have this day given my consent that my sons may engage in this enterprise. They have been appointed to the Yedo circuit. Now it has occurred to my eldest son that our ancient vassalage to Tokugawa Iyèyas might be of great use to us in the present emergency. You are from the Mito branch of that house. Why could not my two eldest sons attach themselves to that clan through your influence, and then be located in the Mito Yashiki in Yedo as retainers of the Daimio of Mito? Can we not have shadows at the Shogun's gateway, and ears within his moats? Who can be more anxious to check the boundless arrogance of Tokugawa than your lord?[1] Pray be frank, and let us hear your candid views on the subject."

"The honor that you bestow upon me by reposing such confidence in my judgment is indeed flattering," replied Konishi, bowing his head downward until his forehead touched the *tatamis*, "but the matter that you lay before me requires delicate handling and careful deliberation. It is indeed well that we have so secluded

[1] Many years prior to the advent of Perry's fleet in the waters of Yedo Bay, it had been notorious that the leaders of the Mito clan were hostile to the Shogunate. They not only cherished a bitter dislike of that system of government, but they were the patrons of a school of thought that advocated the abolishing of the Shogunate and the reinstatement of the Mikado as sole hereditary Emperor of the Japanese Empire.

and so well guarded a place wherein to carry on our discussion. It is now well known to you that I have long
carried on a secret correspondence with your eldest son
during my residence at Deshima as interpreter. I made
his acquaintance several years ago here in Kioto when I
was accompanying the Dutch Embassy to Yedo, and I
was then much attracted by his intense interest in all
matters relating to foreign countries. I risked my head
in smuggling him into the hotel to see the foreigners one evening, when the members of our escort were
scattered over the town on business or on pleasure.

"Since that time I have sent him many letters by
friends journeying from Nagasaki to Yedo, wherein was
much information about foreign countries, furnished to
me by the Dutch doctor in Deshima in return for information I gave him about our country and language.
This doctor was indeed a profound and insatiable
scholar, and had many books pertaining to foreign
science, history, and religion, which he allowed me to
examine freely in return for secret instruction in our
language. It was my duty to report myself at his house
in the morning. During the delightful days of spring,
summer, and autumn, we sat upon the balcony overlooking
the peaceful waters of the beautiful harbor, and would
watch the fishing boats skimming over its deep blue
waves. We spent our days in leisurely study and conversation. The maps were spread upon the *tatamis*, the
books were laid upon the table, the servants brought in
tea and tobacco every hour or so, and we lounged around
alternately upon the chairs while conning over the books,
and upon the *tatamis* while consulting the charts and
maps. Sometimes patients from the city were ordered
in by the governor for treatment by the foreign doctor.
And at other times we spent many hours in examining
specimens of stones, herbs, flowers, and soil collected
during our excursions among the hills and around the
bay.

"If you were to consult my letters during that period
—not only to your son, but also to members of my clan

in secret correspondence with myself—you would find therein a faithful transcript of many curious ideas and observations. If I were to endeavor to give you an account of all the information that I have secured about foreign countries, I would hardly know where to begin. Our conceit about the progress of our own country is unbounded. We are many centuries behind the world. We must radically change our institutions or speedily find ourselves at the mercy of some unscrupulous but shrewd foreign power. I am convinced that the system of government by proxy in our country is injurious. The Shogunate stands in the way of our national development. It must be abolished. But we must proceed circumspectly and slowly. I am heartily in favor of your scheme of becoming conversant with matters at Yedo. By so doing we can be in a position to take instant advantage of a favorable turn in the tide of public affairs, and thus restore unity to our sadly divided nation, and in this way take the first step forward. Honored sir, I tender my humble services with extreme pleasure. Whatever I can do to aid your sons in their dangerous enterprise shall be cheerfully done. Kindly explain somewhat more fully your scheme as thus far developed."

"Our plan, sir, is almost matured," replied Mr. Nakashima. "When you reach Yedo, fifteen days hence, you can suggest to your lord that a friend of yours, an ancient vassal of the Tokugawa family (now living near Kioto) is desirous of resuming his allegiance, and that his two sons being your dear friends are naturally desirous of connecting themselves with the Mito branch of that family and to be retained as knights-in-waiting at the Mito Yashiki in Yedo. It is our supposition that all of the Daimios will now be desirous of swelling their ranks in view of the rumored approach of a foreign fleet in the spring. Having secured your lord's permission, my two eldest sons can then depart from here for Yedo about the commencement of next month, and can arrive there in about a fortnight thereafter in good season to commence observations. This simple plan is contingent

on your good services and is subject to any amendment
that may appear to be necessary."

"I have no amendment to offer, sir," replied Mr.
Konishi. "The plan is good, but the difficulty will come
in attempting to carry it out. However, we will not
worry over that now. The compact between us, then, is
that I shall journey on to Yedo and secure for your sons
two appointments as knights-in-waiting at the Mito
Yashiki, under my lord the Daimio; that they are, within
a reasonable time thereafter, to report themselves at the
Yashiki; and that they are then to use their best efforts
to ferret out all information they can to benefit our great
cause. It is agreed that absolute secrecy and good faith
are to characterize all of our proceedings. It does not
take very long to state the agreement, does it? Our
minds having thus met, I would suggest that the compact
be reduced to writing and be duly executed in knightly
fashion by the parties thereto. Your youngest son can be
preparing duplicate copies of the compact while we are
waiting. I must soon return to my hotel, for I see that
the sun is not far from the mountain top. The shorter
my absence from head-quarters, the better will it be."

"Fortunately our evening meal is now ready and I will
order it up so that you may have some refreshment
before undertaking another long walk," said Mr. Nakashima. And here he clapped his hands together several
times as a signal for the ladies downstairs to bring up the
tub of steaming rice, the broiled carp, the bean-paste, the
soy, the tea, and the *saké*. The ladies spread the repast
on the floor, prostrated themselves on the *tatamis* in
salutation of their guest (who returned the salute with
obeisance equally profound), and then retired below,
leaving the company to continue their discussion in
seclusion.

"It will be necessary, sir," said Konishi, as he reached
forward and pinched out a delicate morsel of carp with his
deft chopsticks, and then thrust it into a mouthful of hot
rice, through which his half-swallowed words managed in
some way to creep outward to the attentive ears of his

eager listeners,—"it will be necessary for your sons to draw up a formal letter, over their signatures, addressed to me, wherein they express a desire to become knights in attendance on my lord the Daimio of Mito, and wherein they request me to exert my influence in their behalf in the matter. You, honored sir, as head of the family must then endorse thereon your approval under signet. This document I will take with me to Yedo, and will there lay it before my father, who as head of our family, will endorse thereon his approval of the application, and we will then lay the matter before our lord, who, after due consultation with the head men of our clan, will probably express himself in favor of adding such skilful swordsmen to his retinue. The proper officer will then billet you in the barracks of the Mito Yashiki, and will send you through the proper channels a notification of your appointment duly *viséd* by the *Bakufu*, and will order you to report immediately at Yedo for duty. You must be very careful not to lose this document, for it will be your passport at the Hakoné Gate.[1]

Unless you can produce it there, endless trouble will ensue. After passing that spot you will find your course again unimpeded until you approach Yedo, when you

[1] The great roads that led to Yedo from the southwest, the west, and the north converged toward a semicircle of mighty mountain barriers that fringed the rolling hill-country surrounding that city at a distance of from seventy to ninety miles. Amid these rugged passes the *Bakufu* had laid its iron grip upon the throat of every road. Everybody going to or from Yedo was compelled to be examined at guarded gates built across their path. After the Tokaido had left behind it the garden-like slopes of mighty Fujisan, it plunged into the wild defiles of the Hakoné Mountains. At a point near Hakoné Lake, at an elevation of nearly three thousand feet above the Pacific rolling but a few miles below, stood the famous Hakoné Gate, through which millions of vassals had trooped for over two hundred years. The haughtiest Daimios within the realm had here unbent their pride, while the Shoguns' emissaries examined their retinues to see that no female hostages were being smuggled from the Yedo Yashikis. Entrenched in Yedo with the boundless billows of the Pacific Ocean at their backs and with a mighty mountain wall in front of them, the Tokugawas bid defiance to the empire and wrung tithes and homage from nearly two hundred principalities.

must be prepared at any moment to produce your passport. When you enter Shinagawa, the southern suburb of that city, you will find yourselves under close observation from many quarters and your words must be judicious and your actions must be circumspect. Any thing unusual either in your demeanor or in your language will be at once reported by spies to the *Bakufu.* You cannot be too prudent from the time you come within sight of Yedo, for the very gate-posts seem to have ears, and the very *hebachis* over which you bend when whispering into a friend's ear seem to be able to transmit information to head-quarters. Even after you have entered the gates of our Yashiki you must continue your caution and be ever on the alert to avoid dropping any word to indicate the real purpose of your appearance there. Accustomed to the secluded life of these serene mountains, you can have but faint conception of the duplicity and the treachery that exist in our great metropolis."

Thus they conversed in subdued tones, while the nimble chopsticks furnished periods to the discourse by tucking away liberal supplies of hot rice. The lengthening shadows of the cherry-trees in the yard betokened the speedy approach of eventide. The soft notes of the vesper bells could be faintly heard throbbing in the groves near Kioto. And as the meal drew towards its conclusion the copies of the designated documents were duly completed and ready for signature. It required but a few moments for the papers to be executed and for the parties thereto to pledge their knightly honor to the faithful fulfilment of the terms thereof. Konishi carefully wrapped in paper the letter and his copy of the compact, and then hid the packet away in his flowing sleeve. He then quaffed the farewell cup, smoked the parting pipe, and took respectful leave of his friends, and hurried downstairs, where he put on his clogs and then shuffled across the yard toward the gateway, where his friends bid him a final adieu with endless bowing and scraping.

Down the road, beside the frothing stream, down where the enshrined gods gazed stupidly upon the misty waters tumbling amid boulders at the rugged throat of the glen, out among the maple groves and the yellow fields of rape-seed, went our young friend, until in the dusky gloaming he entered the quiet streets of the sub- urbs. Over on his left hand the white walls of the imperial palace, plumed with nodding trees, stood out serenely in the moonbeams. He soon found himself in the courtyard of his hotel, where he was warmly greeted by the landlord and his fair lady, who congratu- lated him on his having had so fine a day for seeing the far-famed sights of Kioto. Giving orders for his evening meal to be served upstairs, he proceeded to the bath- room, where he soon found himself up to his chin boil- ing in a huge tub of water. Stepping forth from this caul- dron, he hastily dashed a bucketful of cold water over his person (partly with the idea of cleansing himself more effectually after having bathed in water already used by a score or so of persons, and partly with an idea of closing up the pores, in order to prevent catching cold), he proceeded to dry himself with a coarse cotton cloth that bore but the faintest resemblance to a towel, and then, in accordance with the free and easy manners of the country, sauntered airily upstairs, where he leisurely dressed himself.

He was not at all surprised to find his companion buried in a profound slumber, from which he did not appear likely to emerge before next noon. From the attendant in charge of the room Konishi gathered a vivid and picturesque description of the afternoon's debauch. It appeared that after he had left his "shadow" to the gentle and attentive guardianship of his Aidzu friends, matters had become steadily worse (as might have been expected). As the play progressed, the tragic scenes crowded each other with ever-increas- ing interest, and the enraptured house rose to the excite- ment of the occasion with ever-increasing demonstra- tions of approbation. The "shadow," very naturally, was equal to the situation, and with each potation his approbation rose to loftier heights, until his companions began to wish themselves at home.

Finally, toward the close of the day, the plot reached a point where the hero of the day was to become the victim of a long-standing vendetta. When the luckless hero was set upon by the crowd of assassins beside the gateway of his mansion, the "shadow" roared forth his disapproval in no uncertain tones ; and when the villains began to mar the beauty of that manly form with a profusion of highly scientific cuts and thrusts delivered with the express intent of prolonging the agony, his actions became so wild that confusion prevailed throughout the house. His companions were finally constrained to coax him into the street. Before they had enticed him beyond the vestibule, however, he succeeded in breaking away from them and then rushed back to the box, where he drew his long sword, and, bestriding the railing of the gallery, as if mounted on some fiery charger, began to deliver a series of frightful slashes into the air and in the direction of the actors, until the vicinity fairly gleamed with the sheen of flashing steel.

With much difficulty his companions induced him to sheathe his formidable blade and to accompany them into the street. Once outside in the cool air, away from the excitement, and the reaction set in ; and the erstwhile pugnacious "shadow" ambled along about as one might imagine a blind horse would come down stairs. At one moment he would bend forward between his supporting friends, as if he were trying to emulate Samson between the pillars of the temple ; then he would list over heavily to larboard, taking his friends along with him into the side of a house ; then he would appear to rebound diagonally across the street, ignobly trailing one guardian in the dust and rudely sitting down upon the other one after having rolled him into the gutter. On one or two occasions he grasped frantically for his sword at the sight of a dog. As the cool air began to operate upon his blood, he rapidly became drowsy, and

by the time the hotel had been reached he had to be
carried upstairs. Our friend, therefore, found himself
obliged to take his evening meal alone, chatting with the
amiable waiter-girl, who dipped forth the steaming rice
in response to repeated calls thereon.

On the morrow the "shadow" did not rise until late
in the afternoon, so that Konishi had abundant time to
see a few sights and to make whatever preparations
were necessary for the next day's journey. At daylight
two pack-horses were ready at the gate of the hotel to
receive their loads, which were quickly tied on with
ropes. Konishi then mounted one beast and sat cross-
legged thereon, while the "shadow" did likewise with
the other one, and they started on their long journey for
Yedo. For the purposes of this chapter it will suffice to
say that they arrived safely at their destination, after a
pleasant and uneventful journey of a fortnight.

CHAPTER VI.

THE PLOT THICKENS.

NEARLY a month after the events narrated in the last chapter, the commandant of the Shiro [1] in Kioto, gave an entertainment in the audience chamber of his palace within the moats. The invited guests assembled about the middle of the afternoon, for, in a land where gas and petroleum were unknown, business and pleasure were alike sandwiched in between sunrise and sunset. The elegant *shojees* around the audience-chamber were removed, so that the guests arranged around the sides of the room could gaze upon the beauties of the garden, where musicians concealed amid the shrubbery doled forth at intervals weird strains of monotonous music, and where upon an extemporized stage the *geisha* girls alternately danced and acted pantomimes. Course followed course with deliberate precision, until forty covers had been served. *Saké* flowed like a steady stream ; and by nightfall the revelry had run so high that the captain of

[1] In the western part of the city of Kioto, about a mile southwest of the Gosho, stood the castle of Ni-jo built by Tokugawa Iyèyas in the year 1601. It was always designated in ordinary conversation as the Shiro (Castle). It covered many acres of ground and was a fine specimen of feudal architecture. Ostensibly it was intended as a stopping place for the Shoguns when they came to Kioto to render homage to the Emperor—(an event that occurred only about once in a century) ; but, as a matter of fact, its moated embankments and grotesque towers held a powerful garrison of zealous Aidzu *samurai*, who while professing to be acting merely as a guard of honor to the Emperor, yet, in reality, instituted over him a respectful but most unrelenting surveillance. Their sentinels lounged at the very gateways of the Gosho. Thus did the Tokugawas hold within their iron grip the imperial seal.

73

the garrison confused his identity with that of the pretty dancers on the stage, and made several futile attempts to .perform the fan jig to the unbounded amusement of the assembled company. It was rumored that the commandant himself made no less than three passes with his chopsticks for the dish of honeyed lotus-root before he succeeded in picking up a morsel of that delicious edible,—and he was then heard to enquire what kind of fish it was! As the guests were all inmates of the Shiro, they tarried at the feast long after the moon had risen and kept up their songs and laughter well into the night.

On the morning following this convivial gathering, the commandant very naturally slept late. Several hours after the sun had risen he was awakened by a commotion outside of his apartments. In accordance with the usage of the country his silken quilts had been spead upon the *tatamis* so that, with his ear to the floor sounds from distant parts of the palace could be transmitted to that organ with remarkable facility. Rousing himself, he slipped on his loose robe and stepped out upon the polished floor of the wide veranda where he clapped his hands and summoned his servant and enquired of him the cause of the recent disturbance. He was informed that a courier had just rushed in with a despatch from the *Bakufu* for the commandant of the Shiro at Kioto.

"Shades of Kobu-Daishi! What can be the meaning of that? My regular communication from that quarter is not due for ten days," muttered the commandant, confusedly. "Bring me the despatch at once," said he, addressing the servant.

In a few minutes the obsequious attendant entered the apartment with the lacquered despatch box in his hands, and, kneeling down with it lifted up reverentially to his forehead, he bent forward low upon the *tatamis* and laid it at his master's feet. Then he retired into an adjacent apartment to await orders. With eager hands the box was unlocked and the despatch from the *Bakufu* was read in fear and trembling. After perusing it carefully, he laid it down in his lap with a sigh of relief. Clapping his hands, he ordered the attendant to bring in his breakfast, and he then picked up the despatch and proceeded to read it over again.

"It seems to me," murmured he to himself, slowly tapping his forehead with his fingers, "that this name Nakashima Yotori herein mentioned, has a familiar sound. Where have I heard it? Has it not recently been brought to my attention in some connection or other? Will you kindly request Mr. Murata, the captain of the guards, to come here at once?"—said he, suddenly addressing the attendant who had just laid down the tray containing the breakfast. That worthy dignitary received the summons to report to his commanding officer with considerable trepidation, as his recollection of the feast on the preceding evening contained a vague impression that there was something worthy of censure connected therewith. With faltering step and sheepish demeanor, he entered the dread presence of the commandant.

"Ah! Murata, where is your fan?" said that officer, jocosely. "You will have to take some private lessons before you can get the proper swing to that jig step."

Murata bowed down to the *tatamis* in response, and then, folding his hands in his lap, resignedly prepared himself for a reprimand.

"By the way, Murata," continued the commandant, "that is not what I wanted you for. I have received an order from Yedo to notify the two eldest sons of Nakashima Yotori, living at the foot of Atago-Yama, that they have been appointed as knights in attendance at the Mito Yashiki in Yedo, and that they are to report at once for duty. I am instructed to hand them these two passports and to tender them whatever assistance they may need in starting on their journey. Now, there is a strangely familiar ring about this name, and there lingers in my memory a flavor of suspicion in connection therewith. I cannot account for this vague impression. Can you help me out in the matter?"

"Most assuredly I can," quickly replied Mr. Murata.

" That is the family of the fencing master. Don't you
remember that his sons last spring participated in the
fencing tournament here on the parade ground ? Don't
you remember the remarkable dexterity of his youngest
son in fencing with the foils ? Am I not rated as one of
the flowers of Aidzu in that knightly accomplishment,
and did not that presuming youngster adroitly whack me
thrice over the head in a single bout? Yes, sir, I have a
very vivid recollection of that name."

"Your memory, sir, is excellent," replied the commandant with a smile. " I do remember something about
the unexpected outcome of your bout. But has not that
name come up in some other connection here recently ? "

"Oh ! yes, I remember now," said Mr. Murata, drawing forth a small pocket-book from his sleeve. "I have
a memorandum here to the effect that they are apparently
on very intimate terms with that foxy scamp Yamada.
I have also another memorandum to the effect that they
spent an evening with the family of that fellow in a picnic booth on the Kamogawa shoals. Neither of these
entries, however, shows any thing against the Nakashimas. But the actions of that old fox, as reported by
our spies, have been so mysterious during the last year
that we have put his name upon our black list as that of
a person to be watched with the closest scrutiny. As
yet we have nothing against him except the fact of his
protracted absence from home on two or three occasions
to parts unknown to us. He may be all right, but we
deem it advisable to keep our eyes on him. And, very
naturally, as we have him under such close scrutiny, we
look with more or less suspicion on all of his intimate
acquaintances. We have absolutely nothing against the
Nakashimas, but we have placed their names on our red
list as being persons whose general movements should
be under observation. This is all that I know about the
matter, sir."

"You have cleared up my mind entirely, sir," replied
the commandant ; "that is precisely the flavor of suspicion that I was groping after. Well, these young men

are in luck, anyhow. It would be advisable to remove their names from your list, as they are now on our side. It appears that their ancestors were ancient vassals of Tokugawa ; and the recent prayer of the present head of the family for renewal of this ancient allegiance has been granted. You will please send these passports to them together with my congratulations. At the same time, tender to them my humble services in whatsoever they may choose to command." Thus speaking, he bowed low and dismissed the captain of the guards.

As the Nakashimas were at their noon-day meal, a courtly *samurai* entered their gateway, and approached the veranda. His noble mien, his silken garments, and his costly swords betokened a gentleman of high rank.

"Does Mr. Nakashima reside here ? " inquired the stranger.

" He does," was the reply.

"I am the secretary of the commandant of the Shiro in Kioto, and I have the honor to be the bearer of a message from him. Know, then, that we this morning received a notification from the *Bakufu* to the effect that your eldest sons have been appointed knights in attendance at the Mito Yashiki, in Yedo, and that they are to report there at once for duty. My master, the commandant, tenders his hearty congratulations, and begs that you will condescend to accept of whatever assistance he may be able to render in connection with your journey. Honored sirs, be pleased to accept these passports. Command my humble services." Saying this, he bowed low upon the *tatamis* and reverently handed the documents to Mr. Nakashima, who bowed down and then reverently raised them to his forehead, while he drew a long breath between his lips, expressive of his supreme gratification at the honor thus bestowed upon him.

Ten minutes or so were then spent in introductions and profuse salutations. Pipes were smoked, tea was quaffed, and then the courtly secretary took respectful leave of the family and departed. Trained from in-

fancy to conceal his emotions, the *samurai* is cool and
self-possessed to an astonishing degree. The Nakashimas
expressed neither surprise nor pleasure at this unexpected visit. They deliberately resumed their meal and
discussed, in a business-like way, the arrangements for
their journey. It was decided that the young men
should start within two days. They were to travel the
entire distance on foot, consequently they could carry
nothing but their swords, their wallets, and a change of
raiment tied up in a large silken cloth.

The night before their departure was one of conflicting
emotions. Human nature asserted itself at times, and
rueful countenances bespoke sad thoughts of the morrow. In the evening the old gentleman and his sons
strolled high up the glen to a picturesque tea-booth.
It was near a beautiful cascade that fell like a mist down
the black face of a crag into a deep pool, where gold-
fishes nibbled rice and cake-crumbs that had been
thrown to them by jolly picnickers in the afternoon, and
where the shadowy minnows sported amid the long grass
that lined its margin. The volume of the waters of the
pool was further augmented by the waters of a spring
that gushed forth from a fissure in the face of the crag
just behind the sheet of descending spray, and whose
stream being conducted through a dragon's mouth
carved in stone, poured forth a jet that descended into
the middle of the rocky basin.

In primeval ages the spot had doubtless been the
favorite camping-place of some Aino chieftain ; and, in
later ages, a Shinto shrine had been built upon a
mossy mound at the water's edge to receive the humble
offerings of rice, fish, and game, of the simple-minded
mountain dwellers who came thither to propitiate the
unseen powers that controlled nature. But, with the advent of Buddhism in the sixth century of our era, the
adroit priests of that creed discovered that the locality
was sacred to the memory of Kwannon, the goddess of
mercy. The dreamy fancies of the primeval settlers were
brushed aside, and, while their thatched shrine was

allowed to stand beside the bubbling waters, a stately temple was erected upon a grassy plateau near a grove of maples, somewhat to the left of the crag. There the neatly matted floors, the tastefully lacquered *shojees*, and the well polished floors of the broad verandas bespoke the abundance of the contributions that flowed in from the pilgrims of Yamashiro and Tamba.

The shrewd priests, with an eye to working the locality to its utmost capacity, announced that it would be well also to propitiate those unseen influences of the neighborhood that had been from time immemorial accustomed to the Shinto method of treatment. This adroit diplomacy secured the adherence of the small faction that still clung to the ancient faith, and brought in a steady stream of contributions from the conservative fogies of the neighborhood, whereby the shrine had been kept in a fair state of repair and the dividends of the institution had been much increased. At some remote time, tradition said, a sick person had bathed in the waters of the pool and had become cured of his maladies. Forthwith the ancient monks declared that whoever bathed in a similar fashion would enjoy perfect health for one year (provided the bathing was accompanied with a suitable offering). For many centuries, therefore, the cooling streams pouring into the flinty basin had been utilized by myriads of ailing humanity. In the gray dawn, at high noon, under the sheen of the shimmering moon, you were liable to see some nude form troubling the waters of the pool.

As our friends came upon the plateau after their long climb up the mountain side, they saw two persons drenching themselves beneath the moon-lit spray of the cascade. A priest before the shrine of the temple was chanting in deep monotones some weird liturgy for the exorcism of lurking maladies, and, judging from the vigor of his incantations, the mother and daughter in the pool must have contributed most liberally toward the temple funds. For the space of fully half an hour he continued to clap his hands, to ring his bell, and to bow his head with the most unremitting devotion. With graceful indifference our friends passed on to the picnic booth and, leaving their heavy wooden clogs ranged in a row upon the veranda, walked across to the rear balcony overlooking the ravine, where they seated themselves upon the *tatamis* and ordered from an attendant in waiting there some tea and tobacco.

The view from the balcony extended down the steep mountain side over groves of pine, beech, and maple, far down to where the brook rushed through thickets of whispering bamboo. The moon was shining with unusual brilliancy, lighting up the mountain with great clearness. A light breeze, with the faintest suggestion of a chill about it, played through the rooms of the booth, and rendered useless the fans that our friends had tucked in their girdle when they left the house. Demurely they sat beside the low rustic railing of the balcony gazing out upon the beautiful scenery, and quaffing tea at intervals. They seemed to be buried in profound thought, and spoke but little, occasionally alluding to the delightful coolness of the evening and the drowsy humming of the priest. After the lapse of about half an hour they espied a *samurai* slowly ascending the last steep ascent in the road leading up to the plateau. From their keen interest in the approach of this gentleman it at once became manifest that they were expecting the arrival of some such gentleman.

" It is he ! " exclaimed they in subdued tones, when he had finally reached the plateau. " Our message reached him at midday, and he has contrived in some way to give the Shiro hounds the slip."

Mr. Yamada—for it was he—slowly approached the booth and profoundly saluted the Nakashimas, who thrice bowed down upon the *tatamis* in response thereto. He was soon seated beside the balcony railing, busily occupied with jauntily whiffing off half-a-dozen pipes of tobacco, and in vigorously tapping the bronze pipe-bowl on the brazen edge of the *hebachi*.[1]

[1] In old Japan stoves were unknown. The only heating apparatus was the *hebachi*. This was a portable brazier, shaped very much like

"Honored sirs, ' said Mr. Yamada, daintily pressing a pellet of tobacco into the delicate bowl of his pipe, "since my picnic on the Kamogawa shoals last summer I have been obliged to be exceedingly circumspect in all my movements. The glitter of watchful eyes follows me everywhere. It is manifest that I have been blacklisted at the Shiro. I will wager that you cannot guess how I eluded the ' shadows ' this evening. Will you not even venture a suggestion? Well, I dressed myself up with my best garments, as you see me here. I put the finest touches on my entire toilette, and then sallied boldly out of my front gate in broad daylight. The natural conclusion to be drawn from my appearance would be that I was either out for a call on some friend or out for a harmless stroll, for I did not appear to be dressed for mischief ; and it did not take me very long to see that nobody was following me.

"After making one or two calls I gradually edged off

---

a large broad-rimmed flower-pot. It was filled with soft gray ashes, upon which was placed a shovelful of burning charcoal, giving forth intense heat. The hands were warmed over these coals ; the teapot, mounted on an iron tripod, merrily boiled on them ; and pipes were lit and relit there from morning till night. Sometimes these *hebachis* were stationary, being cut out of a block of stone and sunk in the middle of the floors of every room. Even in midwinter no other heating appliance was known in Japan. In some portions of the northern part of Hondo, and along its western coast, and in Yesso, during the terrible blizzards that came over from Siberia, the people suffered terribly from the cold. Malignant catarrh, influenzas, rheumatism, and consumption were common maladies. During these Siberian gales a square frame was placed over the *hebachi*, and then several heavily wadded quilts were laid over the frame so as to confine the heat thereunder. The family would then crawl beneath these coverlids and keep very comfortable, so long as they kept their heads outside where fresh air could be obtained. So comfortless and cheerless was existence in the far north that the island of Yesso, beyond its southernmost coasts, was a wilderness peopled by a few tribes of Ainos ; and, during the cold weather, thousands of people passed in junks from Yesso southward across Tsugaru Straits to Hondo, to escape what seemed to them to be intolerable winter. Yet the climate of Yesso is about the same as that of New York State. But just fancy what it would be to pass a winter on the shores of Lake Ontario with merely a *hebachi* in a fragile Japanese house, through whose *shojees* the air filters like water through a sieve !

toward the outskirts of the city, as if merely on pleasure bent, and by dusk I was under full headway through the fields and hedgerows for Atago-Yama. So far as I have been able to see, my bold front has completely bluffed my 'shadow,' for I cannot see that any particular notice has been taken of my movements since leaving home. Well, well, I did not come here to discuss myself. There are weightier subjects to be considered. The matter of your commission from the Emperor has been fully adjusted. Of course nothing is in writing. Although the imperial person may be sacred, yet, if the Bakufu were to receive tangible evidence of intrigue against their power, they would subject the feelings of our master to many resentful indignities. And documents, even under the seal of heaven itself, would not protect your luckless persons from the vengeance of those Yedo upstarts.

"Yesterday morning I went, in company with the *kugé*, whose retainer I am, to the western gateway of the Gosho. Those Aidzu guards (insolent beasts !) admitted us within the sacred enclosure after duly inspecting the imperial passport. As we approached the imperial palace through the shrubbery, we saw several persons playing foot-ball in the imperial garden. The ball was made from some kind of skin, and was about as large as an infant's head. It was lacquered in white and was decorated with chrysanthemums lacquered in natural colors. They were kicking it along right vigorously, and were shouting and laughing so merrily that we halted for a moment to watch them. One of the young ladies in the party finally succeeded in kicking it into a fish-pond, and, judging from the hand-clapping and merriment that ensued, that spot must have been the adversary's goal. An attendant quickly fished it out, however, and in a moment the ball was flying along the gravelly path in our direction. A tall, slim young man was bowling it along with great vigor, evidently bent on sending it into the little pond on our side of the garden. He was closely pursued by an eager group of young men and comely women, who vainly strove to head him off from what was evidently their goal. They rushed past us through the shrubbery, too intent on the game to pay us the slightest notice. Although they were all plainly dressed, yet from their silken raiment and refined features I at once perceived that we had before us the imperial household, and I recognized in the tall, slim young man the Emperor himself."

"Surely, sir," exclaimed Mr. Nakashima, voicing the mute amazement of the listeners, "you do not mean to say that Tenshi (the son of heaven) would indulge in such riotous proceedings! We have always understood that his feet never touched the ground, that whenever he went out for an airing in the gardens there were cloths spread over the ground for him to tread upon."

In reply to this Mr. Yamada laughed softly, and then dreamily smoked his pipe and demurely cast a thoughtful glance down the moon-lit glen. In the deep silence of the evening the voice of the torrent far below was borne upward on the still air, and seemed to echo his subdued mirth. Suddenly rousing himself from his revery, he briskly smote his pipe on the rim of the *hebachi*, and said : "Yes, I am well aware that the popular idea enshrines our master as if he were a Buddhist god upon a pedestal of lotos leaves. But, as a matter of fact, we who are admitted within the sacred precincts of the Gosho know that he is very much like ordinary mortals. I was amused at the rude shock that this popular delusion just now received. It did not occur to me that you were entirely ignorant of all matters pertaining to the inner life of the palace. However, it would be well to bear in mind that our master, although proud of his ancestry of ten thousand ages,[1] and haughty in

[1] According to Japanese cosmos as set forth in their ancient books, the universe was originally like a fowl's egg. Then the yellow part separated from the white, and the one became the sky and the other the earth. Then a long reed sprang out of the earth and grew up into the sky, and became a *kami*, or god. From this god a multitude of other *kamis* sprang, and thereby peopled heaven. Then, after countless ages, a pair of *kamis*, male and female, stood one day upon "the bridge of heaven" (whatever that may mean) and gazed down upon

his bearing toward strangers, yet in his domestic life he is merely a courteous and intelligent Japanese gentleman.

"Well, when we had satisfied ourselves with watching the foot-ball game, we made our way through the shrubbery to the western end of the palace. We went up close to the side of the superb veranda, and waited for some of the court ladies to appear. But not a living being could we see within the deep shade of the magnificent chambers. It was evident that the inmates had either joined the Emperor in his sport or were watching the game. My companion then respectfully announced, in a deep voice, that visitors were awaiting an interview. This served to awake a beautiful little *chin* dog that had been sleeping on an embroidered square of dark blue silk. He bounced around the room in a state of frantic excitement, barking vigorously at us all the time. This disturbance speedily brought one of the ladies from a distant wing of the building. She came tripping along noiselessly over the superb *tatamis,* twirling in her hand a spray of *olea fragrans.* As she approached we recognized her as the niece of my companion. She graciously invited us to enter the audience-chamber and state our message.

"You must bear in mind that, in accordance with ancient usage, communications delivered at the palace are transmitted through the court ladies. Clapping her hands, she speedily summoned an attendant from an inner chamber and ordered tea and tobacco to be set before us. My companion then stated that we had come to seek a private interview with the Emperor in reference to a matter that would be fully explained by the sealed letter now delivered to her for transmission. Taking the

the troubled waters that covered the earth. Querying as to the depths of those waters, they plunged their tridents deep beneath the surging billows, and when they drew them up again the ocean's muddy ooze that slipped off the points became the islands of Japan— Dai-Nippon. The land being goodly, the godly pair came down and settled there thousands of centuries ago. And the Mikado and the Japanese people descended from them. Hence the Emperor speaks of his dynasty as having ruled for "ten thousand ages."

envelope and lifting it to her forehead she hastened to deliver it to the Emperor.   After a delay of nearly an hour she returned and announced that an audience had been granted, and that if we would follow her into the sitting-room on the eastern side of the palace that we could have a personal interview."

Here Mr. Yamada again laughed softly to himself, and tapped his pipe vigorously on the rim of the brazier. "I clearly see," continued he, "that you do not comprehend such simplicity in an imperial reception, and such utter absence of ceremony.   But you must bear in mind that, while pomp and ceremony always characterize the Shogun's court, on the other hand, the Emperor's court is based upon the primitive simplicity of an era that dates back more than ten thousand years.   While the Shogun delights to make Daimios tremble and creep into his presence with downcast faces, amid hushed throngs of attendant courtiers, on the other hand the Emperor scorns pomposity (except on those exceedingly rare occasions when the Shogun comes down to Kioto to render him humble homage), and affably receives those who are entitled to access to his presence.   You must also bear in mind that the boundless rapacity of the Bakufu has absorbed the revenues of the entire realm in a most heartless manner, and that the pittance which has been set aside for maintaining the imperial court is but grudgingly given, and comes to hand with extreme tardiness. And the stipulated allowance credited to us at the start becomes sadly shrunk in dimensions before it gets inside the imperial moats, owing to a vicious and shameful usage of shaving by commissions indulged in by those officers of the Shogun through whose hands it passes ; so that, even were our master inclined to be ceremonious, those unconscionable rascals at Yedo and at the Shiro see well to it that he shall not possess the means to indulge any such tastes."

Here the speaker lapsed into profound meditation for several minutes ; but the furious energy with which he puffed his pipe and smote the rim of the brazier therewith in quick succession between the refillings, bespoke his suppressed indignation at the humiliation heaped upon his imperial master. And the Nakashimas gazed at him in silent and respectful wonder, as if stupefied with amazement at such strange revelations.

" Well," resumed he, " we followed her ladyship through some stately apartments, until we entered a lofty chamber that opened on a broad veranda looking eastward. In one corner, near the spacious veranda, were some superb folding screens that enclosed a space equal to about ten *tatamis.* As we approached this spot, a *kugé* (whom I recognized as the adviser and secretary of the Emperor) stepped forth and received us most graciously. He then escorted us behind the screens into the imperial presence, where we humbly prostrated ourselves upon the *tatamis* until bidden by his Majesty to rise. Truly he is a most gracious and refined gentleman! Instead of transmitting his conversation through his secretary, he communicated with us directly. He was seated upon a magnificent tiger-skin near the veranda, where a grand view of Hiyeisan could be obtained as it towered above the blue mountains that loomed up beyond the wooden ramparts. His silken robes were in subdued colors. He discarded head-gear, and his hair was arranged like that of any gentleman of rank. His recent exercise had given a color to his face and a sparkle to his eyes that rendered his countenance comely and animated. At his right hand were his symbols of sovereignty—the stone, the sword, and the mirror.

" The admirable simplicity of every thing rendered the reception exceedingly impressive. His Majesty enquired kindly as to our health, and expressed the hope that my recent exploits in shadowing the Dutch Embassy from Nagoya·to Kioto had not reacted injuriously on me in any way. I disavowed any special credit for that performance, and expressed the sincere hope that my feeble efforts in the future might be productive of more pronounced benefit to the great cause. By degrees, the conversation gradually drifted to the subject-matter of our interview. My companion stated that I had at last come under the strict scrutiny of the Shiro people, and that as a natural consequence my usefulness had become sadly circumscribed ; that I had, after long negotiations, finally secured the services of two young men, remotely connected with the imperial family through an ancient *kugé,* to act in Yedo as spies ; and that I had now come to make full report about the matter and to secure the imperial commission for the enterprise.

" This led to a long talk about your pedigree, acquirements, and loyalty. Your former connection with Tokugawa was deemed a most fortunate circumstance. His Majesty was particularly pleased with the strategy whereby you had succeeded in resuming your allegiance. And he highly approved of your determination to proceed at once to Yedo. He has received your names as subjects worthy of future reward in case our cause be substantially aided by meritorious conduct on your part, and he has duly commissioned you as his secret emissaries at the court of the Shogun. In witness whereof I am authorized to hand to you a tiny signet. The design is a chrysanthemum flower. It is engraved upon an exceedingly small stone ; and after the first impression on this peculiar paper and with this yellow ink, several petals will disappear, so that the signet will thereafter be forever useless. Therefore, you can use it but once.

" In some great emergency when it becomes necessary to communicate directly with the Emperor, or to indicate to some member of his household that you are in his special employ, and therefore entitled to a personal interview, you must write your request together with your names on this paper and place the signet stamp beneath. When you have done this then will you be entitled to immediate attention. This becomes the imperial commission. Then crush the signet to atoms. In the meantime, however, keep it with the utmost care. It is now packed in silk in the hollow end of this bronze pen-and-ink holder, a gift to you from his Majesty. No amount of jarring can disturb it. Nothing indicates its presence there. And when you wish to use it, take your short sword and cut off the little plate soldered on the end here. The paper is rolled up in this little side compartment. The yellow ink is now caked in this little block here beside the pens, and can be easily dug out with your sheath-knife point and prepared for use when the time comes for you to utilize the signet. I now have the pleasure, honorable sirs, to deliver into your hands the commission from our master for your perilous enterprise."

And so saying, he lifted the little box to his forehead, and, bowing low down on the *tatamis*, handed it to Tomokichi, who, bowing equally low, reverently took it in his hands and lifted it thrice to his forehead, violently sucking in his breath through his teeth between times as a token of his profound appreciation of the honor conferred.

"Bear in mind, sirs," said Mr. Yamada, "that all ordinary communications are to be addressed to me. It is only when some extraordinary emergency arises that you are to directly communicate with the Emperor ; and after that occurrence you must be supplied with a new signet. Therefore use great care and judgment as to when it shall be necessary to go over my head."

A long and earnest conversation then ensued regarding the details of the eventful journey to be commenced on the morrow. Yashiki life in Yedo was also discussed. And when the party broke up and strolled down the mountain side, they were questioning among themselves as to what would be the outcome of the next visit of the foreign fleet to Yedo in the spring. And when they parted company in the shadow of the gateway, Mr. Yamada bid them an almost affectionate farewell and a warm-hearted god-speed.

CHAPTER VII.

AT daybreak on the following morning the Nakashima household was astir. The rain-doors were duly slid back, and preparations for an early breakfast were at once begun. The old lady carefully spread upon the floor two large square pieces of drab-colored silk. Upon each one of these she placed a black suit of silk clothing, a couple of white cotton tunics, two pairs of black socks, and a broad silken girdle striped gray, white, and black. Then carefully gathering up the four corners of each cloth, she securely knotted each dainty parcel for carrying by hand. This simple operation completed the packing of the boys' clothing for the journey. She then hastened to the kitchen to aid her daughter in making ready the early meal.

It was one of those delicious autumnal mornings for which Kioto is so justly celebrated. The clear and bracing air was freighted with the odor of jessamines and *olea fragrans*, and the gauzy shreds of mist that hung along the mountain sides, as if entwined amid the deep foliage of the lofty trees, made haste to flee before the warm touch of the morning sun. The young men were up quite as early as the active ladies, and busied themselves with collecting their few treasures into small bundles, to be placed within the capacious silken cloths. The chart and the ancient documents were carefully folded up in white paper, and were hidden away in the depth of Tomokichi's package. Breakfast was then duly despatched, and the family made ready for the departure. The ladies were to remain in charge of the house while the gentlemen were to journey on to Otsu, a town about ten miles distant, at the southern extremity of Lake Biwa, where they were to spend the night, and where in the morning they were to part company. The gentlemen sat on the edge of the veranda and tied straw sandals on their feet. Then they tucked their frocks up around their waists, thrust their swords into their girdles, grasped their bundles, and were ready for the journey. Around the gateway were grouped the neighbors who had assembled to bid them farewell, and very picturesque they appeared as they stood there in the bright sunlight of that bracing autumn morning. There stood the fond mother holding the child by the hand, while over her shoulders peeped the bright eyes of the baby tied on her back. There stood the village misses with their rosy cheeks, black hair, and bright eyes. They were chattering like so many magpies over so momentous an epoch in the serene history of the peaceful hamlet as the departure of any of its inhabitants for a camp-like *yashiki* in Yedo. They had heard that Mito was the most warlike of all the clans ;—could that be possible ? How terrible to think of entering a place where glittering swords were as common as chopsticks !

As the Nakashimas came through the gateway into the road, they were saluted with profound bows and respectful ejaculations expressive of wishes for a happy journey, which greetings were duly returned with gracious courtesy and with profuse farewells. Then the entire family went down the road as far as the place where the foothills merge into the fields and meadows, and there the mother and the daughter took a sorrowful farewell in that undemonstrative manner peculiar to the country. There were no embracings, no handshakings, no kissing, no gush of emotional sentiment,—such exhibitions were unknown in that strange land. There was merely a profound bow, a parting gift of silken girdles from mother to son, and of soft black socks from sister to brother, a parting adjuration to bring honor upon the family name, another bow accompanied with motherly

advice about avoiding undue exposure to heat and cold,
—and then two ladies stood alone in the middle of the
road (occasionally brushing away their tears with their
sleeves), watching a group of gentlemen disappearing
around the bend.

"Come, mother," finally exclaimed the daughter, "let
us cheer up and go back to the house. The separation
is not as bad as it might be. Father and Kunisaburo
will be back to-morrow, and we can now pride ourselves
on having two gallant knights at Mito Yashiki in Yedo.
How gay! How delightful to be able now to receive
regular news from that quarter!"—Thus does the joyousness of youth cast off sorrow in all lands. And then
they trudged back home to their daily duties, little
dreaming of the serious nature of the boys' mission at the
distant *yashiki,*—for all information of that nature had
been carefully and considerately withheld.

Around the bend, through fields and temple groves,
across the northern suburbs of Kioto, straight to the
other side of the valley toward the base of Hiyei-san
where the Tokaido enters the foothills, strode the four
pedestrians on that glorious morning. Long before midday they entered the hills and had commenced to climb
the range of low mountains that separated Yamashiro
from Omï and Lake Biwa. The sun was now shining
with great power, and the deep shade of the forests that
covered the slopes was delightfully cool and refreshing.
Tarrying for an hour or so at a tea-house picturesquely
located beside a mountain torrent, they soon scaled the
pass and saw through the trees lovely Lake Biwa stretching away to the northward, among the lofty ranges that
clasped it round about. It did not take long to descend
the reverse slope into Otsu. There they secured an
upstairs room overlooking the blue waters of the lake,
and ordered dinner to be brought up as soon as they had
bathed and dressed themselves. As a matter of course,
they ordered for a side dish the famous raw carp fished
from the lake and served up with *soy* while the flesh yet
quivered with life. The balance of the day was spent in

strolling about the town and in resting, smoking, and conversing together.

On the following morning they all went some distance down the stately avenue of pine trees that shaded the greater part of the Tokaido in its devious course over plain and mountain to Yedo. At the first tea-booth they quaffed the farewell cup and parted company. " Bear in mind, my sons," was the father's parting behest, " that death must always come before dishonor. Death ends every thing, but dishonor lives to afflict friends and kindred. An insult must always be avenged with blood unless due apology be made therefor. Never abandon the pursuit of an enemy. Follow him, if necessary, with smiles and cajoleries ; follow him for years if need be ; but, at the supreme moment, smite him with curses and with death. Be candid with your friends, but wear a mask in the presence of strangers. Spare no means to induce an enemy to believe the contrary of what you really intend. And, in carrying out a purpose, hesitate at nothing that you may deem expedient."

High noon found the father and son entering the gateway of the homestead at Atago-Yama, and it found his two eldest sons striding along the avenue ten miles or so beyond the point where the parting message had been given.

The Tokaido was a broad avenue (along which two teams could easily drive abreast) stretching from Kioto to Yedo, a distance of three hundred and twenty miles. At distances of every five miles were tea-booths where refreshments were served to tired travellers. At distances of every ten miles or so were villages and large towns. Therefore it would not be inapt to describe this superb highway as a magnificent avenue, stretching over plain and mountain, and beaded along its entire length with tea-booths, villages, towns, and cities strung along at regular intervals. Between the cities and the towns the highway was a stately avenue of tall pine trees winding across fields, over hills, and among mountains. The road-bed was well gravelled and hardened ; on each side was a well swarded embankment upon whose green slopes the wearied travellers could recline ; and, at many places, streams of water bubbled along the edge of the road for miles. In its sinuous course the road passed through a number of Daimiates, and it devolved upon each Daimio to keep that portion of it which lay within his domain, in thorough repair. As there were no lumbering teams and no trains of artillery ever passing along, the turnpike was never cut up, so that in the rainiest weather it was always in a condition fit for travel.

The Tokaido was a fair sample of a magnificent system of highways that covered the entire island of Hondo,— and, as for that matter, the islands of Kiushiu and Shikoku also. All the great roads in Hondo finally led to Nihon-bashi, a bridge in the heart of Yedo. The great northern turnpike commenced at the extreme northern end of the island on the Tsugaru Straits, and then seeking the milder climate that prevailed on the eastern slopes of the mighty mountain spine of Hondo, it went southward for five hundred miles over mountain, hill, valley, river, and plain, through the long straggling provinces of Nambu, Sendai, and Mito, until it reached the muddy stream bridged by the Nihon-bashi. The great northwestern turnpike commenced at Niigata over on the west coast, and, after crossing the rice flats and the hemp fields of the Daimiate of Echigo, wound through the magnificent mountain range that extends from one end of the island to the other, and was finally merged in Yedo. The great inland road (Nakasendo), along which our fleet-footed courier so recently sped, began at Kioto, skirted the eastern slopes of the watershed that borders the eastern shores of Lake Biwa, then, turning eastward, traversed the fields of the Daimiate of Mino, then plunged into the magnificent mountain system of central Hondo, whence it finally emerged into the beautiful plains surrounding Yedo. And the Tokaido, also commencing at Kioto, shrank from the rugged mountains of Shinano and sought the seashore and reached Yedo by that circuitous route.

In addition to these four great roads, others almost equally grand left Kioto on its other side and passed south to Osaca, and then went westward along the shores of the matchless Inland Sea for two hundred miles to Shimonosèki Straits. Upon the west coast a long, straggling road ran through the length of the provinces that line the Japan Sea. And a perfect network of minor roads covered the entire empire. All of these highways were in constant use. Along the grand-trunk roads, the traffic and the pageantry of the empire streamed at all seasons.

Let us soar like the falcon far above the central peak of Asamayama, and take a bird's-eye view of the realm. Far toward the north you can see the long retinue of some Daimio, pouring down the length of the island betwixt 'shore and mountain. Far away in the south you can see the cavalcades of Tosa and Choshiu meandering along the shores of the Pacific Ocean. Toward the west the retainers of Echizen stream through the defiles and over the superb passes of Shinano. And among the by-roads that cover the realm like a cobweb, you can see a multitude of pack-horses and coolies freighted with the produce of the waters and of the fields. Not a steam-whistle, not a rumbling train, not a wagon anywhere in sight! The carriers of burdens are human beings, and vicious little nags!

Yonder where that rugged promontory so boldly ploughs the blue Pacific, and where a fishing hamlet nestles beneath the cliffs, you can see a long line of pack-horses ladened with salted fish captured but a few days ago by the venturesome boats whose white wings now bespeck the distant blue of the mighty deep in pursuit of fresh booty. That caravan will journey along the sandy beach, up through rice fields and forests deep into the mountain, until it shall reach an inland city, where it will unload, and will take back to the seashore hamlet a cargo of rice, charcoal, and *sakè*. That caravan toiling so laboriously over those mountains toward the south is freighted with an inland cargo of salt and edible sea-weed ; while that one passing it is outward bound with a mighty cargo of earthenware, ironware, and cotton fabrics. That long dark line to the eastward, winding across the Yedo plains, is the mighty retinue of the Daimio of Kaga, leaving Yedo on a visit home to the west coast. Twenty thousand retainers swell the train. Five thousand coolies grunt and sweat under boxes, *kagos*, and *norimons*. The head of the column has reached the mountains before the tail has straggled out of the gates of the Kaga *yashiki*.

Let us descend from our lofty station and stand beside the avenue at the point where it merges in the foothills, in order that we may closely inspect the stately procession: First comes a group of horsemen clad in ancient armor, and carrying spears and fluttering ensigns, emblazoned with the heraldic crests of their mighty lord, whose approach is thus announced, and whose right of way is thus secured. Woe betide those who turn not aside ! Then—oh ! for miles and miles—streams an endless train of coolies, carrying lacquered boxes containing the princely paraphernalia. Then comes a long line of straggling *samurai* leisurely sauntering along enjoying the shade and the scenery. Then more horsemen follow. After that comes a squad of banner-bearers, pacing along with dignified deliberation. Close upon this comes a multitude of *kagos*, bearing the ladies and gentlemen in attendance on his Grace. Then a vast throng of *samurai* appear. Following them comes a myriad of coolies, carrying innumerable baskets and boxes loaded with the paraphernalia and the impedimenta of this army of retainers. After which, come a vast throng of spearmen and archers, a long cavalcade of gallant knights in armor, preceding a long line of *norimons*, bearing his lordship's household, and swarms of elegantly dressed *samurai*. A gap of half a mile or so now intervenes, and then we see a stately procession of swordsmen, spearmen, bowmen, and banner-bearers escorting a superb *norimon* borne slowly along upon the shoulders of eight stout men. Here we have before us the lord of Kaga, reclining upon cushions and enjoying the scenery from his latticed window. And this is but the middle of the procession ! For two days the straggling column of coolies and warriors steadily pours over this lofty mountain pass into the mighty ranges beyond. And upon some portion of the network of highways covering the empire you will see at all times some such host streaming either homeward or Yedo-ward. Such pageantry has covered these roads for two hundred and fifty years.

We are travelling in a country whose history extenas back for twenty-five hundred years, to a period when an unbroken wilderness covered the American continents, when England was covered with forests and marshes sparsely peopled by tattooed savages living in caves and fens, when Europe was a vast solitude within whose gloomy depths roamed tribes fiercer and more dangerous than the wild beasts that swarmed there, and when Rome was but a village of banditti. Two hundred and fifty years have barely elapsed since the Jesuits were driven forth with such terrible slaughter from the island of Kiushiu ; and at every cross-road, at every bridge-head, at the entrance to every village, and in the streets of every city, we still have staring us in the face the blasphemous language of the following proclamation, which the enraged Tokugawas posted up all over the empire at the time when they sealed the gates of the country with blood, and hurled defiance at humanity and at the universe : "*So long as the sun shall warm the earth, let no Christian be so bold as to come to Japan ; and let all know that the king of Spain himself, or the Christian's god, or the great god of all, if he violate this command, shall pay for it with his head.*"

The empire thus closed, comprised nearly four thousand islands, scattered along the eastern coast of Asia, and trending from Formosa on the south up in a northeasterly direction toward the peninsula of Kamtchatka. It was an empire nearly two thousand miles long, but not over two hundred miles wide in its widest part. From one extreme to the other this archipelago is grandly mountainous, and is diversified with varied and exquisite scenery. Among the islands of the extreme north you will find the seal, the otter, the fox, the wolf, and other fur-bearing animals that thrive in those bleak and wild regions that have been almost deserted by human beings. At the extreme south, among the Loo-Choo islands, you will find the verdure and the climate of the tropics,—a region where, in the language of the poet,

" Droops the heavy-blossomed bower, hangs the heavy-fruited tree,—
Summer isles of Eden, lying in dark-purple spheres of sea."

   And the climate of the islands of Dai-Nippon (grouped in the middle of the archipelago) is a delightful com-bination of both extremes,—that of Yesso much resem-bling that of New York State, and that of Kiushiu being decidedly sub-tropical ; while that of Hondo, the main island in the middle of the group, owing to a combina-tion of circumstances which I shall now briefly explain, is most wonderfully varied. This long and narrow island (upon which we are now travelling) is shaped like an obtuse angle with its apex pointing eastward into the warm Pacific Ocean, while its long arms stretching northward and southwesterly—five hundred miles in each direction—embrace the chilly Japan Sea on the west. Thus'the black stream from the equator washes its eastern shores, while the frigid waters of the Sea of Okotsk, flowing southward in a steady stream between the Japanese archipelago and the Asiatic continent, washes its western shores.

   In addition to this a mighty range of mountains ex-tends from one end of the island to the other, divid-ing it into two nearly equal halves facing east and west. Consequently the climate of the western half is much more severe than that of the eastern half, inas-much as the blizzards coming from Siberia, heavily charged with the vapors of the Japan Sea, are caught by this mighty scoop-net of mountain ranges, and are forced to precipitate their snowy freight back among the valleys and upon the rice flats of the west coast.

While the western slopes of these mountains are buried deep in snow, the eastern slope is comparatively free from it, and the southeastern slope has a climate as balmy as that of Sicily; and along the shores of the Inland Sea you have one of the choice climates of earth, where flourish the orange and the fig.

Although Japan is a land of sunshine and of flowers, yet there is abundance of rain there. It has been estimated that in England the number of overcast and rainy days during the year exceeds the number of sunshiny ones. In Japan the ratio is about ten sunshiny days to three rainy and overcast days. Yet the amount of rainfall in Japan is three times as great as it is in England. When it does rain in Japan, it does so with a vengeance. With its numerous lofty mountain summits towering many thousands of feet above the surrounding waters, every current of moist air landward bound is speedily chilled, and is compelled to pour down its liquid freight on valley and field. Japan is, therefore, a land of small rivers, but of sudden and mighty torrents; a land of deep verdure, of well-wooded hills and mountains; and it is a land of lovely lakes and cascades.

Of course there is abundance of beautiful and magnificent scenery in all parts of the world Every country has its natural glories. The Yosemite Valley is matchless. The Falls of Niagara are peerless. The White Mountains are exceedingly beautiful. The lake regions of Switzerland and of Northern Italy are of surpassing loveliness. The Vale of Cashmere and the valleys of the Lydder and the Scinde branching therefrom into the mighty ranges of the Himalayahs, are unparalleled in beauty and in magnificence. Yet, take it all in all, the empire of Japan, with its superb volcanic cones and rugged shores, its majestic mountain ranges sloping seaward and ocean-ward, its bold promontories ploughing the mighty deep, its exquisite lakes mirrored among lofty mountain crests thousands of feet above sea-level, its bays, inlets, and inland archipelago (comprising three thousand islets scattered broadcast through an inland sea), its garden-like fields and embowered villages, its picturesque hamlets and engroved monasteries,—is truly the most beautiful country on the face of the globe ; and it possesses a combination of ocean, mountain, lake, and temple scenery, which, by coining an adjective, we may justly describe as *Japanesque*.

But we must now hasten with our journey. As in the study of campaigns, it.becomes necessary to obtain in advance a correct idea of the theatre of war, so in this tale of Old Japan it seemed expedient at this juncture to introduce a brief description of the theatre of coming action. The operations will be confined entirely to the island of Hondo, as around this island cluster the romance and the historic events of the empire. Here you will find the bulk of the population ; here are located Kioto, Yedo, Nagoya, and other great cities ; and here we have the grandest and the most beautiful scenery.

Our enterprising knights are well on toward the end of their first day's journey. They have followed the stately avenue all day through a level sandy country. As evening comes on they tarry at a village in the vicinity of some well wooded hills. The hot-water bath speedily relaxes their contracted muscles and puts them in condition to make short work of their evening meal.

On the following morning they were off at an hour that would correspond to seven o'clock by our method of measuring time. The road led over a well wooded country for many miles, and then, toward midday, wound up among picturesque hills, amid whose cooling shades and embowered hamlets it twisted, until late in the afternoon it finally descended the reverse slopes of the range, and led through a deeply shaded valley into the rice fields of the ancient province of Isè. Spending the night at the village of Seki, they continued their journey on the morrow through a long stretch of level country toward the waters of Owari Bay. During the afternoon they were much delayed by meeting the extensive train of one of the southern Daimios, for which they were obliged repeatedly to turn aside. On this day they covered but eighteen miles. On the following day, however, by diligent walking they were able to reach the city of Nagoya, near the head of Owari Bay, where they decided to spend a day for rest, as they had completed the first hundred miles of their journey. It was also decided that the remaining two hundred and twenty miles were to be walked more leisurely,—averaging about twenty miles per day. Nagoya was a city of about half a million souls, and was the capital of the Daimio of Owari, whose superb castle and parks covered many acres of commanding slopes on the northern boundary of the city.

After due rest, the journey was resumed along the windings of the stately Tokaido. For two days they travelled through the hilly country bordering that deep inlet constituting the Bay of Owari. Occasionally they met the trains of Daimios. On the third day, toward midday, as they reached the crest of a range of hills, they espied through the trees the deep-blue waters of the mighty Pacific spread out before them. The distant roar of the thundering surf could be distinctly heard as they descended the slopes toward the beach. Following the sandy shore for some distance, they finally came to a deep arm of the sea, over which it was necessary to cross by boat to the opposite headland. Here, hemmed in on all sides, they were confronted with the first Tokugawa barrier, where they were obliged to hand their passports to the Bakufu officials for inspection. Everything proving satisfactory, they were allowed to embark in a small fishing boat, and were sculled three miles across to the town of Maizaka, situated on a long sandy spit. Here they decided to spend the night. They secured a room that overlooked the roaring breakers and the mighty expanse of waters as well.

In the night a violent storm arose, and raged along the coast for two days with such fury as to keep our young friends weather-bound during its continuance. Toward evening of the second day the wind subsided and the

steady deluge abated. The masses of sombre clouds
rushed inland toward some lofty crest, like hostile hosts
gathering around some standard. Then the mighty
ocean, that had been so mercilessly badgered by the hurricane, arose in majestic wrath and came landward in
stupendous billows, and smote the shore with such terrible blows that the hotel fairly trembled with the shocks.
Late in the evening the moon shone forth on a scene of
terrific grandeur. As far as the eye could reach were
raging white-crested waves that massed themselves in
tremendous billows, which thundered so impetuously on
the beach that the hissing waves frothed up the white
sand nearly to the balcony, where our awe-stricken
friends were looking forth upon the wild scene. The
wake of the storm, consisting of gauzy shreds of clouds,
was flying inland to the cool embrace of some lofty
mountain summit. A fishing smack, that had outridden
the tempest, was tumbling shoreward in a very demoralized fashion, creating the impression that it was trying
to probe the ocean's bed alternately with prow and stern.
A multitude of little red crabs fled up the beach to escape such trip-hammer thumping as was being inflicted
thereon, and sought refuge in the hotel yard and in the
village street, where they proved themselves to be an endless nuisance to the kind-hearted natives, who could not
bear to tread on them, fearing, forsooth (devout Buddhists as they were), lest by crushing the little creatures
they might inadvertently break in upon the cycle of existence of some spirit working its way to human shape.
High upon the beach, beyond the reach of the rushing
waters, stretched a long line of fishing boats, with their
long, narrow prows pointing down toward the heaps
of kelp and sea-weed washed up by the angry waves.
Occasionally a well-bronzed fisherman would come down
to the shore and contemplatively puff his pipe while gazing seaward to diagnose what the atmospheric conditions
might indicate for the weather on the morrow, as his last
catch of fish had gone inland several days before, and his
supply was running very low. The sea-birds that had

been driven from the storm-swept waters now began, on timorous wing, to venture on the deep in search of food.

Our young friends studied the tempestuous scene for long hours. The landlady had closed all of the rain-doors for the night, but had left open the balcony to accommodate the gentlemanly young travellers from Kioto.

" How far does your chart represent this water as extending ? " enquired Junzo of his brother.

" It extends fully five thousand miles in the direction of the rising sun, and it extends fully ten thousand miles from north to south," was the reply.

" And on the other side rises a mighty continent, beyond which lies another body of water almost equally as large as this one, I understand you to say," said Junzo ; " and then, beyond that, yet mightier continents, upon whose remotest borders lie the islands of Dai-Nippon."

" Precisely so," replied Tomokichi.

" That much I clearly understand," said Junzo ; " but how this vast body of land and water can be of a circular shape, I cannot understand at all. I think that you did not clearly understand what your Nagasaki friend said in his letters. The face of your chart is surely flat enough, and does not indicate roundness at all, so far as I can see."

" Well, I must confess that I cannot explain the matter to even my own satisfaction," replied Tomokichi ; " but the letter clearly states that this earth is a round body of land and water. I am going to probe this matter deeper when I reach Yedo. But, if the earth be flat, why cannot you see the land looming up on the other side ? "

" Because," replied Junzo, " our eyes are not made to see so far, perhaps. Beyond a certain point, things become invisible to us. With proper eyesight we might see the mountains over there on the other continent, I suppose."

" It may be so—it may be so," replied his brother slowly, as he dreamily watched the shimmering foam on the beach ; " I am free to confess that the stupendousness of the mystery enshrouding the entire subject quite appalls me. We, who slumbered and dreamed amid the profound repose of our mountain nest, find ourselves unable to think fast enough when brought for the first time face to face with such colossal subjects as now confront us ; and, in our dazed amazement, we seek refuge in bewildered speculations."

The next morning broke with an atmosphere as clear and as serene as crystal. The only vestige of the hurricane was the sonorous voice of the disturbed ocean, still complaining of the rough treatment that it had received. Oh ! how matchlessly pure and cool was the air as our young travellers continued their journey along the avenue that now wound for three days among hamlets, pine-clad hillocks, and well-wooded ridges in the rear of a broad promontory that pushed its bold cliffs far into the deep. On the afternoon of the third day after leaving Maizaka, they were walking along the ridge of a series of high hills when they espied, down the long vista ahead of them, the snow-capped cone of Fujisan looming up magnificently in the clear air, far above the mighty ranges that intervened like colossal billows of adamant. They tarried a full half hour at a tea-booth, to enjoy the beauty of this far-famed cone. Then they descended into the exquisite hill country environing Shidzuoka.

This city contained a population of about forty thousand inhabitants, and in ancient times was the capital of Tokugawa Iyèyas, who spent many years of his life there and died there. Its castle ranked next to that of Yedo as to size and impregnability, and it was occupied by a prince of the house of Tokugawa, with a powerful garrison. Our friends found themselves in streets filled with a bustling crowd of citizens and *samurai*, where they were subjected to many a polite stare as being strangers in the place. Hardly had they set foot within their hotel before word was passed up to their rooms that two officials desired an interview with them. These formidable gentlemen were then duly ushered in by the willing landlord, who fairly bent to the ground each time these sublime personages opened their mouths to address him or even when they cast glances in his direction. After a mutual exchange of profound salutations, the visitors excused their intrusion on the ground that it was their duty to keep track of all strangers coming to town, and, it having been reported to them that two gentlemen of distinguished mien had arrived, it devolved on them to call and examine their credentials and make report to the castle in order that the official record there might be regular, so that no blame could at any future time be charged by the government against the commanding officer. With apparent reluctance and humility they then proceeded to examine and to copy the two passports willingly handed over to them by our young friends.

"Honored sirs," enquired the officers, "in what manner have you prosecuted your journey hitherto?"

"We unworthy creatures have journeyed altogether on foot," was the modest reply.

"Verily, you have selected a gallant and knightly method of travelling, honored sirs," responded the officers quickly. "May the balance of your journey be equally prosperous. And may you enjoy a long and happy service with the lord of Mito. Sirs, we humbly return your papers as being in all respects satisfactory. May the subtle influences of air, fire, and water be in your favor. Farewell."

On the next morning the streets were filled with the retainers of the Daimio of Satsuma, sweeping southward to their distant home in Kiushiu. All day long the endless throng poured steadily through the city. Late in the afternoon the princely *norimon* came slowly along amid hushed throngs of attendants, and was followed by a multitude of *samurai*. Our friends decided not to continue their journey until the following day, in order to avoid meeting the reckless and quarrelsome members of that most warlike clan. All next day, as they continued their journey, they met detached groups of attendants, men-at-arms, carriers, and *kagos*, streaming southward in the wake of the stately column of their lord. At one of the wayside tea-booths, a low-grade

Satsuma *samurai,* who had been imbibing too freely of *saké,* sallied forth into the road munching a boiled sweet potato of huge dimensions, which he very rudely hurled at the head of Junzo, who chanced to be passing along at that moment. Luckily, however, his unsteady arm failed to communicate the proper bias to the missile, and it missed its mark and spread itself out like a big plaster on the bare back of a *kago*-bearer, who roared lustily, supposing that a sword or an arrow had gone off by accident upon that unprotected region.

Now, as a matter of fact, no insult could have been more pointed than to hurl a common edible that had been touched to the mouth at the person of a *samurai* with the deliberate intention of hitting him therewith ; but, from a diplomatic standpoint, a person engaged on an important mission should have been looking in an opposite direction and thus, as the missile failed to reach him, have been able to waive with becoming dignity the insult, and thus to avoid a disturbance. But Junzo was inexperienced. He took notice of the insult. Therefore but one course was available. He was bound by the code of feudal etiquette to resent it at once. The hot blood mounted his face, and, uttering an imprecation, he turned upon the aggressor with his drawn sword, and he would soon have been involved in a mortal combat had not the companions of the drunken fellow intervened and offered suitable apology for his beastly conduct,—for the true *samurai* admired bravery and was quick to make amends for unjustifiable wrongs done to fellow *samurai.* The expression of supreme relief that came over the *kago*-bearer's countenance when he ascertained the true nature of the assault upon his person, and the sight of the red disc upon his broad back as he turned around with a contented grunt to resume his journey down the avenue, threw everybody into fits of laughter and restored general good-nature. Nothing of note occurred during the balance of the day to annoy them, and they journeyed peacefully along the shores of the "deep-sounding sea."

On the next morning the journey was continued around the shores of Suruga bay, amid most magnificent scenery. On the right hand lay the crescent-shaped bay, whose encompassing headlands ploughed the deep half-way to the horizon with their sylvan crests and ridges. The surf bathed the shores with eternal foam. On the left hand rose the mighty cone of Fujisan,—a glorious and magnificent sight,—fields, forests, and cinders sloping upward for thirty miles from shore to summit. In the latter part of the day, deep forests along the shore shut out the sea-view, but occasional glimpses of the superb cone still flashed through the woods.

All next day the road led behind the base line of Idzu promontory until it reached at night the shores of Odawara bay. This day's journey was one of great magnificence and beauty. At first the road led through garden-like fields around the base of Fujisan. Then it entered the gorges of the colossal ranges of the Hakonè Mountains, among which it writhed and twisted for several hours until it came out at the famous Barrier at the top of the pass near the southern end of Hakonè Lake ; then it descended through mountain scenery of the grandest description until it reached the castle town of Odawara on the shores of the bay. From this point our young friends continued their journey next day along the shores of this lovely inlet, and stopped for the night at Fujisawa. Again diverging from the shore, they, on the following day, continued their course along the base-line of Uraga promontory, through picturesque hills and glades until they reached Kanagawa, on the shores of Yedo Bay. Here they took their midday meal, and then they journeyed along the shores of the bay to Kawasaki, just twelve miles south of Nihon-Bashi. Here they were delayed a day by the Daimio of Kii-shiu, going south-ward. And on the following day they reached their hotel in Yedo, where they decided to tarry until their arrival had been communicated to Konishi at Mito Yas-hiki.—And thus ended the overland journey.

CHAPTER VIII.

EARLY on the morning of the day following the events narrated in the last chapter, a large brown rat was nibbling the grains of rice that lay at the door of a government warehouse on the banks of the Sumida River in Yedo. From the balcony of the hotel on the opposite side of the broad canal which, at that point, made junction with the river, our friend Junzo watched him with amused interest. The dusky rodent leisurely disposed of the stray grains, and then followed the scattered trail down to the plank gangway that led from the shore to the side of a large junk that had brought the grain as the tribute from some southern Daimio, and from which coolies had been unloading it on the previous day.

Here the animal paused to study the ground before proceeding further. He sat upon his haunches and meditatively pointed his nose into the fresh breeze that came through the rigging of the vessel, as if he might be scenting the gale for indications of lurking danger,— for, at that early hour, the drowsy sailors had not yet shaken off their slumbers. Hearing no sound, and gathering fresh courage from the arrival of auxiliaries in the shape of four other rats, the rapacious plunderer led the way along the plank, nibbling the white grains that had been trailed along the entire length, until he came to the gunwales. Here it was deemed judicious to order a reconnoissance, and the inquisitive eyes of the five depredators peered over the side of the junk into the mysterious depths of the cabin. Emboldened by the silence that prevailed, they ventured in various directions about the decks, tasting, touching, and handling every thing eatable that fell in their way. At length, when successive reinforcements had swelled the invading forces to nearly three-score rats, the ceaseless pattering of so many feet finally caused the captain and the steward simultaneously to arise to a full comprehension of the situation, and they promptly hurled four pairs of wooden clogs into the midst of the bandits, thereby causing a violent stampede along the plank, during which retrogade movement several of them fell overboard and were well soaked before they could swim ashore.

The Sumida River, on whose banks the above scene was transacted, was a shallow and rapid stream, whose waters came from the distant mountains on the north. It flowed through the eastern part of Yedo from north to south, and emptied its turbid flood into the blue waves of the bay. The banks of the southern portion of the river were lined with fire-proof *godowns*, hotels, and tea-houses. The banks of the northern portion were lined with gardens, parks, groves, and *yashikis*. Numerous canals branched off from the stream into all parts of the city, bearing cargoes to the *godowns* scattered everywhere along their banks. Loads of fish, vegetables, and fruit came up the river and were borne along these water-courses to the great market beside Nihon-Bashi, in the very heart of the city. Five long wooden bridges spanned the stream and connected the eastern with the western portion of the city. The eastern portion was built upon the level stretch of country that extended around the head of the bay. Although this part of the city covered much ground, yet the population was by no means dense, inasmuch as large sections were occupied by the *yashikis* of Daimios and by the extensive grounds of wealthy merchants, who sought this quarter of the city to escape the rolling seas of flame that periodically swept the transpontine city from moat to bay. In the upper part of this section were the Mukojima gardens, that stretched along the river bank for a mile or so, embowering it with cloud-like masses of cherry blossoms during the spring. Here picnicked the citizens amid gardens filled with fragrant shrubs and screened by bamboo and box-wood copses. During the spring and summer multitudes of pleasure-seekers came hither in boats that floated up on the waters of the Sumida, and were moored beneath the overarching trees.

Crossing now over to the western portion of the city we find before us a long strip of flat country, about two miles wide and stretching many miles northward and southward. This section of Yedo was densely packed with the stores and houses of the mercantile classes. These structures were low, double-storied affairs, built entirely of wood and covered with tiles. A network of canals extended up to the very moat of the castle, forming, in fact, a connecting link between it and the waters of the river and bay. Through the streets poured an incessant stream of commerce and of military pageantry. The principal thoroughfare ran north and south. It commenced where the Tokaido merged in Shinagawa, the southern suburb of the city, where congregated the brothels, the hotels of ill-repute, and the abodes of the poor,—the lowest slums of Yedo. Passing northward three or four miles, this great thoroughfare reached the wealthy section of the city, and went through two or three miles of broad and well kept streets, until it finally led through the temple grounds and the parks of the northern suburbs into the Oshiukaido, the great northern highway. In all portions were incessant bustle and activity. At regular intervals along the various streets were heavy wooden barriers that could have been speedily thrown across the road to stop travel in times of sudden tumult or alarm. Guards of *samurai* were scattered everywhere to secure order, and to be available in sudden emergencies. Whenever a fire broke out in any part of the city, a member of the guard would climb a tall ladder, and, after locating the conflagration, would sound the alarm on a large bell suspended there between high poles.

The sanitary condition of Yedo was very poor. All

the drainage was above ground in shallow gutters along the sides of the street. In every back-yard was a garbage heap whereon rats, crows, and dogs operated as scavengers, busily dodging fresh accumulations hurled from the kitchen door or window. But for their services and the natural excellence of the climate, pestilence would have spread sad havoc in the city. As it was, however, small-pox was the regular winter epidemic. " Dirt can not be unhealthy, else how can the Heratee live ? " exclaims the traveller in Herat. The magnificent climate of that portion of Afghanistan alone keeps the population above ground. You might have said the same thing about Yedo. The flushing of the numerous canals with the regular ebb and flow of tides, aided greatly in keeping the city healthy, for vast quantities of filth daily found its way into the bay through those well-washed water-courses.

We now come to the castle, the centre-piece of Yedo. In the year 1853, Yedo was emphatically a city of warriors, and it was fitting that the massive castle of the Tokugawas should have formed its grand central feature. Out of a population numbering about fifteen hundred thousand souls, fully half a million of them filled the numerous *yashikis* scattered over all parts of the city. While the commercial part of the metropolis was built upon the flat lands bordering the bay, the aristocratic portion was built upon the summit and at the base of the commanding semicircle of bluffs that swept around the western and the northern sides of the citizens' quarters. These bluffs rolled away toward the north, the west, and the south, into the undulating hill country constituting the Yedo plains.

The castle was built partly upon the bluffs and partly upon the lowlands, and it covered a vast extent of territory. Its general plan was a triple system of circumvallation, one inside the other. The innermost system comprised the citadel, which formed the heart of this entire fortress. It was a moated enclosure, a few hundred yards in circumference, located on the edge of the

bluffs, about two miles from the waters of the bay. It
was surrounded by a precipitous and well swarded embankment, that rose to a great height, and whose summit
was crowned with ramparts, composed of a foundation of
small rough-hewn granite blocks, fifteen feet high, surmounted by white plastered walls about ten feet high,
with several square, double-storied towers at the various
angles. This enclosure was entered by a wooden bridge
thrown over a deep ravine. The second system of circumvallation was much more extensive, and enclosed
within its moats and swarded embankments three or four
miles of territory—the western half encircling a great expanse of bluffs, and the eastern half descending to the
lowlands and embracing a large portion thereof within
the waters of its deep, broad moats. At every angle, and
at every gateway, was a massive, square, double-storied
tower, built with immense timbers, and plastered in white.
Along the top of the ramparted embankments were pine
trees, that stretched their grotesque branches over the
murky waters at various points, thus beautifying the forbidding aspect of the martial surroundings.

The third system of circumvallation was eleven miles
in circumference ! Commencing on the northeast at the
Sumida River, about one mile below the cherry groves
of Mukojima, it went due west for a mile or so over the
lowlands, and then pierced the bluffs and continued on
in the same straight line through some tremendous cuttings in the hills, until it arrived at a point about two
miles northwest of the citadel ; it then turned sharply
southwest, and then southward, following the hills for
several miles, until it arrived at a point about two miles
southwest of the citadel, where it turned due east and
descended into the lowlands, and finally reached a point
near the bay ; here the moat abandoned the rampart
and, merging into devious canals, came out on the bay
below the mouth of the Sumida, nearly five miles south
of the point whence it started.

If you will draw a line due north and south through
the city, just beneath the eastern ramparts of the citadel,

you will divide this immense system of fortification into
two nearly equal parts. You will find the western portion to be almost entirely upon the bluffs, and to be filled
with *yashikis*, government offices, and the residences of
the aristocracy ; and you will find the eastern portion to
be entirely upon the lowlands, and filled with the marts
of trade and with the residences of the mercantile classes.
You will readily perceive that the term " castle " is mis-
leading, and that we have before us something like the
fortified cities of modern Europe. A large part of the
city is built within the second and the third system of
moats, although it was not the intention of the government to defend the commercial quarter at all in time of
war, but to wipe it away by fire when the enemy approached near enough to render it probable that they
might seek shelter therein. The citadel and the aristocratic quarters, however, were rendered almost impregnable against feudal assaults.

Let us now take a glimpse at the *yashikis.* There
were over two hundred of these feudal structures, varying in size from a walled enclosure of fifteen acres to
immense " compounds " of more than two hundred acres.
They were scattered in various parts of the city, but the
majority were to be found along the summit and at the
base of the bluffs. The proud and wealthy Daimio
sought the highlands that circled around the bay, or ensconced himself at their base, while the noble of mod-
erate income sought the flatlands and the grassy meadows that sloped gently down to the sandy shoals of the
Sumida. Upon the hills north of the castle stretched the
superb grounds of Kaga Yashiki, whose lord was the
wealthiest nobleman in the realm. To the west of this,
just beyond the northwestern angle of the castle, lay the
beautiful and stately grounds of Mito Yashiki. Among
the hills bordering the western side of the castle were the
vast grounds of Owari Yashiki ; and, rolling away from
the southwestern angle of the castle, extended the immense enclosure of Kii-shiu Yashiki.

The three Daimios of Mito, Owari, and Kii were the

heads of the most illustrious families in the realm. These families were founded by the three youngest sons of Tokugawa Iyèyas, who endowed them with the wealthy provinces bearing the above names. Kii-shiu was the bold and massive promontory that jutted into the Pacific Ocean about one hundred and thirty miles south of Kioto. It was an exceedingly choice Daimiate. The province of Owari lay at the head of Owari Bay, along whose shores we so recently journeyed. And the province of Mito lay on the shores of the Pacific Ocean, about seventy miles northeast of Yedo (Mito was, properly speaking, the capital of Hitachi province, but in popular parlance the name of the capital city became synonymous with that of the province). These three families were known as the Gosankè (three illustrious families). They were permitted to wear the same heraldic crest that the Shogun wore—three inverted mallow leaves trefoiled in a circle. And, in default of direct issue in the Tokugawa line, an heir to the feudal throne must be chosen from the Gosankè.

From the year 1603 A.D. to the year 1716, the first seven Tokugawa Shoguns were direct descendants of Iyèyas. The direct issue then becoming extinct, the Kii family was called upon six successive times to furnish a Shogun ; or, expressing the idea in political parlance, the succession having once gotten into that family, the influential head men of that powerful clan took exceedingly good care that it should continue to revolve within the ring. The year 1853 found the sixth member of that clan just seated on the throne of the Tokugawas. Thus had Mito and Owari been utterly neglected in the matter of succession. Mito had long felt sore on this point. The *yashikis* of these three mighty princes formed a cordon that guarded the castle most effectually on the western side. In the other sections of the city were the *yashikis* of minor nobles,—equally grand, although covering less ground than those of the Gosankè and of Kaga. Within these immense " compounds " were groves, orchards, landscape gardens, lawns, artificial ponds, gravelled walks, and acres of shrubbery and of bamboo copses. Every thing was laid out on the most munificent scale.

The climate of this region was very fine. The winters were mild and open. Snow appeared once or twice during the season and usually disappeared before midday under the powerful rays of the sun. Shrubs and flowers lived and bloomed outdoors in the coldest months, and many kinds of vegetables and several varieties of grain were cultivated in midwinter. The spring season, though occasionally very windy, was delightfully balmy. The summer, though hot, was cooled at all times with delicious breezes. And the autumnal months were perfection.

Such was Yedo in the year 1853 ; a city of enterprise, bustle, and excitement. Merchandise from all parts of the empire streamed into it at all seasons. Junks, loaded with the products of the seashore provinces, swarmed up the bay and poured into the Sumida, where they emptied their cargoes into the warehouses along its banks. Numberless caravans from the inland provinces converged here and jostled each other in the streets. Between sunrise and sunset all creation seemed to be outdoors enjoying the warm sunshine and the balmy air. The falcon that soared above on passing wing, looked down on twenty-eight square miles of tiled roofs, waving groves, emerald lawns, embowered parks and temples, vast gardens, and white towers, and well shaded ramparts. Truly a strange and a unique sight ! It would seem as if a people who had lived twenty-five centuries all by themselves possessed many intensely human traits of character. Have not the feudal times of Europe been reproduced with startling exactness in this remote corner of the earth ? How homelike the moat, the tower, the heraldic crest, and the mounted knights ! Can you think of Tokugawa lording it over the Daïmios, and not think of Charlemagne reducing the Frankish dukes and barons to subjection ?

CHAPTER IX.

THE month of October, 1853, was drawing to a close, and all the arrangements had been completed for the reception of Tomokichi and Junzo in their new home at Mito Yashiki. One bright sunshiny morning they donned their best clothes and were duly escorted by their friend Konishi to the princely residence of their liege lord, four miles away. Leaving the hotel, they sauntered slowly through the citizens' quarter, until they came to the bridge that led within the second moat. Here they were duly challenged by the guard, and, upon Konishi's countersign, were admitted within the massive gateway.

Here they followed the broad, well gravelled road for a long distance in its devious course between the white walls of feudal "compounds," through vast parade grounds, beside the deep waters of the innermost moat, and finally emerged at the Kiji-Bashi (Pheasants' Bridge) into the *yashiki* region, that stretched on from that point northward to the third moat. They walked leisurely through long, wide, well kept avenues, that were flanked on either side by glistening lines of barrack-like walls, in whose heavily barred windows and in whose massive gateways loitered groups of *samurai*, enjoying the sunshine and the delicious air while taking in the outer world. At length they crossed the outermost moat by the Suido-Bashi (Aqueduct Bridge) and found themselves in the beautiful hill country that lay to the north of the castle.

Near this bridge, the large square wooden tube of the Kanda aqueduct crossed the moat into the castle and thence into the city, bearing the pure water of the Kanda region to the people of the metropolis. Beneath the ooze of the moat at this point formerly was situated the renowned well from whose crystal springs bubbled forth waters so delicious that the Shoguns for many generations were accustomed to steep their tea therein, so that the immediate locality became known as " the Waters of the August Tea." Upon the right hand, the moat was carried through the hills by the largest cutting in the entire circuit. It was designated as " the Cutting of Weeping Sendai," because, according to the legends, an ancient Daimio of Sendai was compelled to cut it at his own expense, by order of the Shogun, either as a penalty for some political offence, or to keep him from squandering his patrimony in profligate carousals within the brothels of Yoshiwara. Our friends tarried long here to take in the rugged beauty of the scenery and to locate the points of historic interest.

Leaving Suido-Bashi, turning sharply to the left and following the moat for a short distance, they soon found themselves in front of Mito Yashiki, which overlooked the moat at its northwestern angle,—a location of rare beauty and excellence, commanding on the eastern side a fine view of the result of the labors of sorrowful Sendai, and on the southwestern side looking down a long vista of moat, stretching through the hills toward beautiful Owari Yashiki. Along this stretch of peaceful waters the gorgeous petals of the pink lotus bloomed in midsummer, and myriads of wild ducks skimmed in midwinter.

The approach of our company was not announced by couriers and blare of trumpet. They were but humble retainers of Mito, and feudal etiquette required no ceremony when they presented themselves for duty at the mansion of their master. No grand reception awaited the vassal who fell into the ranks of his lord. The white walls basked serenely in the sunshine, and

groups of *samurai* were passing in and out of the massive
gateway that faced the moat. The shape of this stately
yashiki was almost quadrangular. The southern side
was somewhat longer than the northern one, so that it
would not be inapt to compare its general shape to that
portion of an unfolded fan whereon the paper is pasted.
The entire "compound" was surrounded with a high
plastered wall covered with tiles and pierced with a
massive gateway on each face. To the right and to the
left of each gateway the walls were enlarged into long
lines of stately barracks, erected on massive stone
foundations, and constructed of mighty uprights and
crossbeams, surmounted with an exceedingly heavy tile
roof.

These barracks must have been nearly forty feet deep.
The outside was plastered in white, and was pierced at
intervals of every ten yards or so with large windows
protected with heavy bars of wood painted in gloomy
black. The inner side of the barracks opened out freely
on the beauties of the grounds within. In order to carry
out the idea of a castle, a miniature dry moat ran along
outside of the foundations. The massive gateways were
edifices in themselves. They were double-storied, and
were built of immensely heavy timbers, and were covered
with exceedingly heavy tiled roofs. They were square
in shape. Through the lower story passed the entrance.
The great doors were plated with iron, and were studded
with heavy iron knobs. They swung inward on creaking pin-hinges that revolved in deep holes sunk in the
mighty beams above and below. At night-time they
were barred with square plated posts slipped into immense iron staples. Upon each side of the entrance
were the rooms of the guard. The upper story was one
vast room intended for archers to ply their shafts through
barred windows upon enemies trying to force the gateway ; but, as there had been a profound peace of two
centuries throughout the empire, the room was only used
on those grand occasions when the coming of the lord
of Mito filled to overflowing the accommodations of the

yashiki, and rendered it necessary to crowd the retainers upstairs.

Now let us approach the main gateway with our friends. Entering the shadows of the portal, they were received with great cordiality by the *samurai* on guard, who ushered them into the reception room on the left, where they were invited to slip off their clogs and to brush the dust from their clothing. Tea and tobacco were then set before them, while word was sent within to the private apartments of the captain of the gate that some gentlemen awaited his pleasure. After the lapse of a few-minutes, they were ushered through a suite of well matted rooms occupied by the gentlemen of the guard, until they came to the private apartments of the captain of the gate. The floor of his reception room, or office, was covered with *tatamis* of exquisite whiteness and softness, edged with broad bindings of brocaded silk. The heavily barred windows to the south looked out upon the moated ramparts of the castle. The warm rays of the sun shone in upon a superb porcelain flower-pot that had been placed in the deep recess of the window, and which contained an extremely fragrant bulbous plant, bearing clusters of beautiful pink blossoms that contrasted well with the glorious Ming Blue of the enamelling. The *shojees* were of cream-colored paper, and were set in narrow frames lacquered in glistening black. The designs thereon were from nature, and represented flowers, birds, mountains, and cascades. The ceiling was in panels of highly polished woods without any decoration except the finely developed graining.

The room was quite bare of furniture. On one side stood an elegantly lacquered sword-rack, and upon the other side loomed up a tall and narrow Dutch clock, which the indulgence of the Bakufu had allowed some former lord of Mito to import through the Hollanders at Deshima. The *shojees* on the north side of the room had been removed, and you could look out upon a broad veranda and upon the luxuriant acres of the vast enclosure. Upon the edge of the veranda were several exquisite porcelain flower-pots of large dimensions. One was broad-brimmed, of a square shape, of a deep-blue color stamped with the gilded crest of Tokugawa on each face, and contained a small Ningpo orange shrub that was loaded down with the peculiar egg-shaped fruit of that variety of orange. Another pot was hexagonal in shape, and was tall like a jar. The groundwork of the enamelling was pure white, variegated with a delicate spray of wistaria in natural colors entwined on its glossy surface. It contained some variety of the iris, whose light-blue blossoms contrasted beautifully with the lavender-colored buds of the wistaria. Another pot was shaped like a boat, and contained a rare species of dwarfed pine that had been so skilfully trimmed that it resembled the masts and sails of a boat under full sail.

A broad road, whitened with pulverized shells and mixed with soft fine sand, led from the southern gateway, bearing to the left, around toward the western portal, thence up toward the northern one, where it met a similar road that had started from the same point on the south, and had borne around by the right toward the eastern gateway, and thence to the northern one. A third road led up through lawns and groves toward the palace of the lord. Its stately roof could be seen among the trees on the higher and more commanding ground at the northern end of the "compound." Groves, shrines, target-ranges, fish-ponds, deep wells, hillocks, artificial landscapes, and gardens were scattered in all parts of the extensive *yashiki* grounds.

Near the palace were many acres devoted to a magnificent grove of rare and beautiful trees, and a beautiful garden containing rare and costly plants, many of which had been imported through the Dutch and Chinese merchants in Nagasaki. Just in the rear of the barracks were extensive gardens of exquisite beauty, filled with shrubbery, flower-beds, and even vegetable-beds. A beautiful hedge of boxwood and hollyhock enclosed the ground back of the various barracks, thus shutting off the road and ensuring privacy. These large tracts of land were laid out with sanded walks, landscape scenery, clumps of bamboos, miniature fish-ponds, and flower-beds. Beside the various gates, that led through the hedgerows into the road, were the picturesque lodges of the gardeners. Throughout the gardens were stately jars and flower-pots containing rare and beautiful plants. Sea-shells and white pebbles lined the walks, and were occasionally piled up in grotesque little rockeries tufted with moss and ferns.

Such was the scene that spread out like a scroll through the *shojees* opening out upon the veranda. In a few minutes the captain made his appearance. He was a tall, stately gentleman, about forty years of age. As he entered the room the rustling of his silken *hakama* (frock) sounded like the breeze among the leaves. All four gentlemen prostrated themselves upon the *tatamis* in profound salutation—the humbler in rank doing reverence to the superior officer, while the superior in rank (lest he be deemed haughty and ignorant of etiquette) bowed equally low in response to the obeisances. "Honored sir," said Konishi, when the oft-repeated compliments had been duly exchanged, "the gentlemen from Yamashiro, whom you ordered me to bring into your worshipful presence, are now with me praying for an interview with you in reference to their connecting themselves with the service of our most august master, the lord of Mito. You will remember that in your interview with my unworthy self yesterday that you appointed this hour for the ceremony of an introduction."

"You indeed state the case most truly," replied Captain Matsuda, bowing low, "and I now most respectfully welcome these worthy gentlemen to the service of our august master. Honored sirs, have you been long on the way from Kioto?"

"Your unworthy servants have been nearly twenty-two days on the journey," replied the young men.

"And in what way did you travel?" continued the officer, fastening his clear brown eyes upon their features with a kindly yet keen gaze.

"We insignificant youths travelled entirely on foot," they replied.

"Truly a most soldierly method of journeying!" exclaimed the captain.

Here the captain clapped his hands for an attendant in the adjoining room to bring in tea and tobacco. The party now became very sociable, and discussed at considerable length the incidents of the overland trip and the features of life in the great metropolis.

"Most estimable sirs," said Captain Matsuda, taking up his pen and preparing to make entries in a large book that lay open in his lap, "it has been arranged that for the present you shall be attached to the guard of this southern gate, under my direct command; and I may truly say that two more soldierly gentlemen have rarely come under my orders. All that Mr. Konishi has urged in your favor, I find to be entirely accurate. If you will now kindly favor me with your full names, the place of your birth, your respective ages, and a few items about your family history, I will enter them in this ledger, and will then see to it that they are duly transcribed to the great register of our clan.

"You are perhaps aware that our clan has been without its proper head for the space of nearly thirteen years. Our noble lord had become imbued with the scholastic distinction between the Emperor and the Shogun, and urged the Bakufu to surrender their usurped prerogatives into the imperial hands, whence Tokugawa had snatched them two centuries ago. But, very naturally, the Bakufu failed to see the matter in that light, and notified him to abstain from his wild schemes. But he persisted in his efforts to arouse public sentiment in favor of a reinstatement of the Emperor in his ancient power. He even went so far as to melt down the monastery bells into cannon in order to wage war against the Shogun. When matters had been carried to that extreme, the Bakufu bestirred themselves and promptly quashed the revolt, and ordered him into close confinement, where he has remained until the present time. The son who has represented him during these years is now in Mito, so that there is no prince at present in our *yashiki.* Some of the members of the family, however, and some of the ladies of the household, are up at the palace ; but they have little control over affairs here. Practically, the command-ant of the *yashiki*, Mr. Hattori, is managing matters in the absence of our liege lord. We will therefore report ourselves to him this afternoon.

" Mr. Konishi, although in the employ of the Bakufu as interpreter of barbarian documents, is yet a sojourner within our gates, and occupies an apartment with his father in the picturesque lodge west of the palace. He has requested me to allow you to occupy an apartment adjoining his. As a member of my guard you should be quartered in one of the rooms in this line of barracks, but I see no objection to your reaping the advantage of having a friend at court, and so long as you report promptly for duty at midday, I see no reason why you should not stay with him. And now, gentlemen, as I have finished my clerical duties, if you will honor me with your presence at my humble midday meal, we will, after that, go around the barracks and the grounds, and will report for duty at the office of the commandant."

So saying, Mr. Matsuda clapped his hands for an at-tendant to bring in the repast. Throughout the empire the meals of all classes were substantially the same on all ordinary occasions. Boiled rice constituted fully ninety per cent. of every meal year in and year out. The only difference between the meals of the wealthy and those of the poor lay in the variety of the little side dishes. Where the lower classes could only afford a few morsels of broiled fish or of salt radish, the upper classes would have four or five little side dishes containing bean-paste, salted shrimps, sea-weed, poached eggs, brook trout, pickled fruits, and vegetables of various descrip-tions. Centuries of Buddhism had practically abolished a meat diet. As a matter of course, state dinners were very elaborate, and comprised forty or fifty courses, drawing on sea, air, and land for materials.

The meal now being served was quite martial in its
simplicity. Before each guest was placed a tiny lacquered stand, whereon stood little bowls containing
string-bean emulsion somewhat resembling soup, tiny
clams boiled in *soy*, and delicate morsels of boiled
chicken. Little bottles of warm *saké* were also provided.
The attendant dished out the steaming rice quite as
daintily as any lady would have done. The conversation
grew quite animated under the influence of the warm
beverage, and a great variety of topics rotated rapidly
under discussion, for the natives were always exceedingly
talkative while eating.

Soon after the repast, Mr. Matsuda took his long sword
from the rack, and, thrusting it into his girdle, led the
way on the tour of inspection. Reaching the gateway,
he pointed out the first chamber as the one to be used
by them as an office when on duty. Just back of the
gateway, upon the right hand and upon the left hand,
stood massive, square, deep-blue porcelain flower-pots,
containing small orange-trees, whose glossy dark green
leaves and whose golden fruit rustled and nodded with
every passing breeze. Strolling leisurely to the right
hand, they passed the hedgerows that enclosed the gardens which lay behind the barracks. After that they
took no particular course, but rambled leisurely along,
enjoying the delicious sunshine and the balmy air. They
frequently met squads of *samurai*, who bowed half-way
to the ground in salutation of the captain. Around the
lawns were spruce pines and boxwood shrubs that had
been trimmed to represent herons, storks, turtles, stags,
and junks under full sail.

In one place our party halted in the shadows of a
stately grove to watch some gorgeous pheasants that
were being reared by the prince. In another part of the
grounds they watched with great interest the majestic
peacocks and the speckled guinea-fowls that some former
prince had imported through the Dutch. In one place
where the greensward sloped toward the warm and sunny
south, there had been constructed quite a menagerie.

There were monkeys tied to posts ; there were myriads
of birds of numerous varieties, singing and chattering
away in wire cages ; there were little spaniels known as
"chins"; and there was a small black bear from Yesso
shut up in an iron cage, and looking very hungrily at
some deer roaming about the park. In another place
mounted archers were riding at full speed down a long
avenue, and delivering blunted arrows at sundry luckless
curs chained at regular intervals along the route. The
snarling and the howling of the luckless brutes abundantly testified to their hearty disapprobation of the proceedings.

Just before turning their steps toward the lodge of
their friend, they sauntered through the choicest part of
the grounds,—the far-famed botanical gardens of the
lord of Mito. This was the costliest and the most beautiful collection of trees, shrubs, and plants to be found
within the empire, and they covered many acres of
ground. No money had been spared by the princes of
Mito in making this collection. Rare and beautiful productions from all parts of the empire had been gathered
there. Shrubs and plants from China, from Batavia, and
from Loo-Choo had been imported regardless of expense. The place was a veritable paradise, and our
friends lingered long amid the shade and the sunshine
of the enrapturing locality, until the lengthening shadows
of the stately camphor-trees warned them of the speedy
approach of eventide.

Then they extricated themselvelves from the labyrinth
of flowers and trees, and turned their steps toward that
wing of the palace where the commandant had his head-
quarters. The building was surrounded on all sides
with exquisite gardens and waving trees. A hedge of
dense boxwood, trimmed square, kept intrusion at a
respectable distance from the precincts of the palace. A
long covered way led from the wicket-gate in the hedge
up toward the main entrance of the magnificent structure.
The roof of this shed was covered with thin sheets of
bronze, and it was sustained by immense square columns

of *kayaké* wood carved with chaste arabesque designs. Its farther end merged in a stately vestibule, from which numerous doors opened into the grand chambers of the palace.   This edifice, like all similar structures in Japan, was but one story in height ; but that single lofty story, when surmounted by an exceedingly massive roof, caused the white gable ends to loom far above the trees.

The entire underlying idea of a *yashiki* was that of a camp.   Every thing was presumed to be characterized by military simplicity.   Of course, those who could afford it, made every thing as elaborate as possible ; but, even then, the air of simplicity that characterized every thing was most noticeable to the eye of the foreigner. The immense structure was surrounded by a broad veranda, with floors so highly polished that every bit of graining stood out with utmost clearness.   The many suites of lofty chambers that opened from the verandas into the great building were uniformly matted with soft white *tatamis* well bound with silken borders.   The *shojees* were magnificent works of art, and were set in wide lacquered frames that slid in metallic grooves above and below.   Yet the rooms were comparatively destitute of furniture.   Some chaste and costly pieces of bronzes, some superb specimens of porcelain, and some exquisite articles of lacquer-ware were scattered tastefully about in various nooks and corners, either upon little ebony stands or upon the floor.   An occasional rug or fur-skin would trip you up with its clumsy folds.   In the innumerable closets was a vast assortment of books, silken garments, bedding, and general household effects.   On all sides the rooms looked out upon beautiful gardens filled with shrubbery, flower-beds, and weird spruce-pine and boxwood figures of birds, fishes, and animals. From the ceiling of the lofty veranda there dangled threads of copper wire suspending bird-cages containing the mournful-voiced nightingales of Awomori, and the sweet-toned larks of Nambu.   Half a dozen *chins* romped around the verandas, barking shrilly at every fancied intrusion.

Our friends entered the vestibule, and were ushered

into a suite of apartments on the left-hand side, where dwelt the commandant of Mito Yashiki with his family. It was only the favored few that were allowed to, bring their families from home. And as the *samurai* were thus compelled to leave their families in their native provinces, the result was that the multitudes of retainers in the various *yashikis* were leading the lives of gay and merry bachelors—each one being a law unto himself, and doing that which seemed right in his own eyes.

The attendant ushered our party into a large and airy chamber, where sat a pretty young lady busily working on a piece of embroidery. She was sitting on the floor, and a low wooden frame held the drab-colored piece of silk that she was embroidering. She greeted the gentlemen with dignified obeisances, and hastened to communicate their message to her father, who was busily at work in his private office. In a moment she returned with the request that the gentlemen be ushered into his presence. It was an airy room that opened out upon the garden, and it was littered up with books and documents lying about on the floor, whereon he was sitting before a small lacquered stand utilized as a desk. He saluted his guests with old-time courtesy and heartiness, and expressed great pleasure at the safe arrival of our auxiliaries from Kioto, whom he keenly but politely scanned during the intervals of the conversation that ensued. He duly entered their names in his register, and confirmed their appointment as guardsmen of the southern gateway under the direct command of Captain Matsuda ; and he further informed them that for the present the stipend that had been assigned to them would be five *rios* per month apiece, which would be duly transmitted to them on the last day of each month through their captain.

This sum, by the way, equalled about five dollars per month ; but it possessed a purchasing capacity in that. country equal to the purchasing capacity of fifty dollars in the United States, so that our young friends were provided with incomes about equal to those allowed by the

United States government to the West Point cadets,—a sum amply sufficient to keep them comfortably. With great pleasure he granted permission for them to take up their quarters in the Konishi lodge. Then, for half an hour or so, the conversation branched out upon general topics of interest, and was brought to a close by the visitors excusing themselves on the ground of the lateness of the hour.

Leaving the palace, they went toward the western part of the "compound" and finally reached the picturesque little house occupied by Mr. Konishi. It was on a commanding spot and was surrounded by a beautiful garden hedged in by boxwood shrubbery. The elder Konishi, his son, a servant, and a gardener were the only occupants. At this point the kindly captain took a polite leave of his companions and hastened back to his post. A well gravelled walk led up to the house. It was single-storied and contained four rooms surrounded by a veranda. A little extension at the back contained the kitchen and the room for the two servants. Two rooms faced to the warm southern exposure. One of them was occupied by the Konishis, and the other was allotted to the two brothers The two rooms behind these were used as a dining-room and as a reception room. It did not take long for our friends to make themselves quite at home. The greeting of Mr. Konishi was most cordial and fatherly ; the little bundles had already been sent up from the hotel ; the contents thereof were speedily unpacked and stowed away in the little closets ; and then came the evening meal and a long evening of gossiping relaxation. And here, having seen to it that our friends have been comfortably settled in Mito Yashiki, let us bid them good-night.

CHAPTER X.

ON the morning following the events chronicled in the last chapter, Tomokichi was up bright and early. He slid back the *shojee* and stepped out on the veranda. The air was clear and delightfully cool ; and, although the trees were placed so as to shade that side of the house from the powerful rays of the sun, yet through the leaves there was a view that stretched beyond moat, rampart, and hill, and took within its scope the snowy crest of Fujisan eighty miles to the southward. The rosy dawn stole stealthily upon the scene and speedily merged the pinkish hues of opening day in the glorious blue of full-blown morn. There was no sound to break the stillness of what was really a Sabbath morning ; but in that land no such day had ever been known, for the native calendar had been copied after that of China, which began each year upon some newly selected day in February and divided it into twelve months, thus utterly ignoring the weekly division of time. For over two thousand years the months had rolled in and out without the slightest suggestion of a Sabbath-day.

Soon the mournful blare of a large Chinese horn awoke the echoes of the place and notified the guards to fling back the gates and to commence the duties of the day. Breakfast was served at seven o'clock, and, after that, the younger Konishi hastened off to his duties at the Bakufu, while the elder Konishi volunteered to escort his young guests to the chrysanthemum show at Sugamo, a village of florists about a mile or so among the hills northwest of the *yashiki*. Strolling out through

128

the western gateway, they leisurely rambled through lanes, cherry groves, orchards, and gardens until they reached the floral exhibition of the beautiful village. Everybody appeared to have turned florist as if infected with the horticultural passion of the Mito princes. On every side were long rows of gorgeous chrysanthemums blooming in pink, white, red, violet, orange, blue, purple, yellow, and lavender. How gay and inspiring the scene! Every yard bloomed with the varied glories of the imperial crest. Busy gardeners zealously trimmed the plants and carefully plucked the dead leaves and twigs. Mothers, with babies tied on their backs, blithely flitted about sprinkling water from tiny watering-pots. Children, chickens, and puppies tumbled about the grassy streets in high glee under the warm sunshine, and earning well merited rebukes when they romped dangerously near the treasured flowers.

It was still a long time before noon when our sight-seers had finished their inspection of these floral beauties, and it was decided to return by a roundabout route that would lead through the magnificent grounds of some celebrated Buddhist monasteries. Fully two hours were spent in this delightful ramble through temple parks. As they strolled slowly homeward they passed a hill which Mr. Konishi designated as Kirishitan-zaka (Christian slope), a name that at once excited the interest of Tomokichi.

"What is the origin of so extraordinary a name?" inquired he of his guide.

"Oh! perhaps that name does sound very strange to you Yamashiro folks," was the reply.

"I will explain the matter, for there is quite a history connected with this place. Know, then, that many years after the extirpation of the foul and dangerous sect of Kirishitans (Christians) by our matchless Iyèyas there came to the southernmost shores of our empire several priests of that proscribed sect. They desired to secure renown and martyrdom by attempting to re-establish their accursed creed on our sacred soil. They came from the south on some foreign ship, and, when near the coast, they embarked in a small boat and were put ashore. The ship then spread its broad wings and fled southward, leaving the reckless voyagers to their fate. Had these fellows landed in the days of Iyèyas, they would certainly have been slain without mercy. But the lapse of several generations of profound peace had cooled the fierce passions of the government to that extent that they were not adverse to quietly gratifying their curiosity about this strange religion and about the people among whom it prevailed, so long as there appeared no danger of a revival of Christianity. They accordingly sent word to the southern Daimio, who was holding the prisoners subject to the government's decision, to select two or three of the most intelligent of these foreigners and to forward them in closed cages under strong guard to Yedo, but to behead the other prisoners at once, and to make public proclamation of the execution in order that the people might know that those who trifled with the terrors of the law could not do so with impunity.

"Thus the government played a double game—on the one hand striking a wholesome terror into the people, and on the other hand clandestinely securing some intelligent and well informed foreigners to catechise at leisure in regard to their religion, customs, language, and history. Upon the arrival of these priests at Yedo they were taken to this hill and were subjected to a long and careful examination upon all matters relating to foreign countries. Many days and months were devoted to these enquiries and the results were noted down accurately and were subsequently published in several volumes for circulation among government officials. There is a set of this work in my possession, which, as you appear interested in the subject, I will place at your disposal on my return home. The responses of these learned foreigners gave such satisfaction, and they appeared so full of valuable information, that the government gave them a house on the slope of this hill and allowed them to live there many years in the quiet enjoyment of their peculiar religious practices until the various dates of their natural death, which occurred about one hundred and fifty years ago. They were buried in the grounds of the Buddhist cemetery just behind us. This is a strange history. It is said that in their room they had a large red cross painted upon the *shojee*, and that they would kneel daily before it and chant mysterious incantations and prayers. Oh! sirs, it was indeed a strange creed, and the people greatly feared their magic spells and shady arts. They appear, however, to have led just and pure lives and to have died amid general regrets."

"Did these priests leave any writings, or books, or doctrinal essays?" inquired Tomokichi.

"I believe there were a few religious books and some manuscripts found in their possession," replied Mr. Konishi.

"Do you remember what became of these documents?" was the eager inquiry.

"I understand that the Bakufu, according to their custom, pounced upon every thing just as soon as the breath had gone out of their bodies, and put every thing under seal subject to future inspection," was the reply. "After the burial, an investigating committee was appointed by the Shogun to look over the things, and to destroy whatever they might consider useless or dangerous. These gentlemen worried over the documents for several months, and finally admitted that the matter therein contained quite surpassed their comprehension, and recommended that the whole matter be referred to the noted scholars of Mito, who were very fond of all kinds of learning. This was accordingly done, and the matter has been left in that position ever since."

"What has become of the documents, sir?" inquired Tomokichi.

"I think that they must be somewhere in the archives of our clan," replied Mr. Konishi. "In fact, I now remember that the custodian of our books and documents brought them recently from Mito to our *yashiki* at the request of my son, in order that he might consult them in reference to certain points about foreign religions, that arose during the course of his translation of foreign documents at the Bakufu's office. They must be either in the palace or at the lodge."

" Would it be possible for me to have access to them, from time to time, in connection with my studies of foreign subjects ? " timidly ventured Tomokichi.

" I do not think that there will be any objection raised to that," was the reply. " My son has spoken to me about your great interest in such matters. The thing can be so arranged as to give you abundance of opportunity to examine these documents at our lodge. Our clan has always been allowed much freedom in such matters, and the Bakufu is now giving every encouragement to students in foreign literature."

They arrived at the lodge in time for the midday meal. After that the two brothers sauntered down to the southern gateway to report for duty. Captain Matsuda received them cordially, and introduced them to the ten other gentlemen who were to act with them as guardians of the portal. Six of the gentlemen occupied the office on one side of the gateway, and six of them that on the other side. The young fellows were all about of the same age, and made very congenial companions. Their duties were very light, indeed, being merely to keep track of every one who came in or who went out of the gate, and at sunset to bar the doors, leaving the little wicket-gate in charge of a relieving guard. They were allowed to smoke, read, play chess, or do any thing else that did not conflict with the discharge of their simple duties. Groups of *samurai*, bent on business or on pleasure, were passing in and out all the time. Occasionally a retainer—somewhat the worse for *saké*—would be skilfully piloted home by his comrades in the spree,—for life in Yedo meant a gay round of pleasure and dissipation for the thousands of retainers in the *yashiki*.

Late in the afternoon, as the gentlemen of the guard

were stretched around on the *tatamis*, variously occupied, a messenger from the Bakufu hastened up to the gateway , with a despatch from Konishi to the commandant. This event caused quite a breeze, which became quite a gale when it became noised abroad through the *yashiki* that the Bakufu had decided to release the old ex-Daimio of Mito from his long confinement. This step was prob- ably taken in view of the intense excitement that had been caused by the arrival of the American fleet during the summer. The government probably felt that it needed to secure every ally available, and that it could not afford to lose the support of any member of the Tokugawa family.

" I presume, sir," said Junzo, addressing Mr. Taka- hashi, a bright young fellow-guardsman, " that this event will bring the young prince of Mito down to Yedo at a very early date."

" Without any doubt," replied his companion. " It is my opinion that before another moon has waned we shall have this *yashiki* filled to overflowing. We shall then have abundance of old-fashioned splendor and pageantry. Ah ! sir, those were grand times when thirty thousand men filled these grounds. The old prince, in his day, was a great power in the land, I can assure you. The young prince, since his father's incar- ceration, has filled his place as well as could be expected, but the cold frown of the Bakufu has rested like a chilly shadow upon our entire clan, quite dampen- ing our animation and loyalty. Of course the young prince will still be the head of our clan, but the hand of his father will control his policy, and will make things lively and highly interesting before long. Of course you are aware that it is by no means an uncommon occur- rence for a Daimio to be deposed, either by government order or by his own voluntary action. In such an event the heir steps in and rules the clan, but he is always mindful of filial duty as expounded by the Chinese sages, and gives implicit obedience to his father's com- mands. The father being thus freed from official trammels, has far greater freedom of action and no less effectually shapes the policy of the clan."

" What do you consider the true inwardness of this matter ? " inquired Tomokichi.

" Oh ! well, as to that, my private opinion is that it is a shrewd piece of diplomacy on the part of the new Gotairo (Prince Regent). You will remember that just after the departure of the barbarian fleet last summer, the Shogun suddenly died under circumstances that were, to say the least, somewhat indicative of foul play on the part of the anti-barbarian faction. However that may be, he was at once succeeded by the present Shogun, Iyèsada. Great excitement and panic prevailed throughout the city and along the shore provinces, because of the appearance of the smoking ships of the foreigners. The new Shogun selected for his right-hand man the lord of Hikonè, the head of the *fudai* (direct vassals of the Shogun), whom he made the Gotairo. This man has extraordinary capacity for both virtue and iniquity, and is really the ruler of the empire, although nominally mere prime-minister. Now, it is always in order for the incoming Shogun to grant pardons for political offences occurring during the *reign* of his predecessor. Taking advantage of this fact, the shrewd Gotairo has released the old prince of Mito, with the evident intention of thereby securing his friendship and of conciliating our entire clan. We shall see whether his little game will work,—whether twelve years of insult can be thus wiped out with a stroke of the pen. Little does the foxy Gotairo dream of the nature of the despatch that we received from the imperial court yesterday. Perhaps, if he were to see it, he would feel disposed to tighten his grip on Mito instead of loosening it."

" What do you mean ? " exclaimed several of the listeners, in almost the same breath.

" Oh ! you are all interested, are you ? Well, I get my information from responsible parties, and as the matter vitally concerns our clan, I shall let you have the benefit thereof. Know, then, that when the news of the intrusion of these barbarian ships flew overland to Kioto last summer, it very naturally excited much comment, and the Emperor sent messengers to the shrines of his ancestors at Isè ordering the Shinto priests there to pray to the gods to drive away the intruders. But as the summer wore away and it became manifest that the Bakufu meant to parley with the barbarians, the *kugés* and the imperial councillors met and made an indignant protest against the action of the Shogun. This they submitted to the Emperor, who at once seized the opportunity to regain his political importance within the realm, and he sent an order to the old prince of Mito to aid the Bakufu with his advice, and to help in quieting the public excitement, and thus to restore peace to the imperial bosom. Of course none of you gentlemen are so blind but what you are able clearly to perceive the political significance of this suggestive commission from the Gosho.

"Now, I apprehend that the Bakufu does not dislike the barbarian any more than the Emperor does, but the former realizes most unpleasantly that the barbarian has power which cannot be ignored. Of course the Emperor through "underground channels" is tolerably well posted, and comprehends in a general way that the new-comers are disagreeable people to handle, but he rather laughs in his sleeve at that melancholy circumstance, inasmuch as the handling happens to devolve on the Bakufu. Our imperial sovereign can afford to crowd his tongue into his cheek, loudly call on the Shogun to keep the people quiet, and then calmly await further developments. Do you gentlemen fully grasp the grim humor of the situation ? The Emperor, on the one hand, while urging the Shogun to restore peace to the imperial bosom by keeping peace within the realm, can, on the other hand, complacently watch the increasing anger of the people at foreign intrusion, and wait with diplomatic serenity for a favorable opportunity to step into the political arena with a powerful following of angry Daimios quite ready to sweep away the Shogunate and to re-

establish his own sway.   Then, if he finds that the barbarians are creatures not to be tampered with, he can
gracefully tolerate them within the realm upon some
pretext or other that may suggest itself.   Gentlemen, I
consider the situation to be as instructive and interesting
as any that has arisen within two centuries."

This narrative of "inside facts" provoked a long discussion, that had not terminated when the setting sun
proclaimed the hour for closing the gates.   The relieving guard found the party apparently inclined to spend
the night there.   When our friends discussed the matter
over their evening meal at the lodge they found that
young Konishi had heard rumors to the same effect at
the castle that morning—rumors that had come through
"underground channels" from Kioto, for the Gotairo
was also an adept at political undermining, and he had
his spies at work everywhere.   Nothing escaped their
keen scent.   Konishi said that the Gotairo appeared to
bother himself very little about the matter, evidently
looking on Mito as a spoilt child of Tokugawa that must
always be pouting about something or other,—a child
that always had been troublesome and probably always
would be troublesome, but which he would handle with
a rough hand when too demonstrative.   That night the
message from Kioto was the great theme of conversation
throughout Mito Yashiki.

On the following morning Tomokichi busily occupied
himself with reading the documents connected with the
ancient exiles on Kirishitan-zaka, while Junzo spent the
morning in the target range practising with bows and
arrows.   In the afternoon, they again did duty as guardsmen at the gate.   And the evening was spent in reading
and in gossiping at the lodge.   And so passed many delightful days of the beautiful month of November.   The
young men from Yamashiro grew daily in favor with
comrades and officers because of the modesty of their
bearing, their faithful discharge of duty, and their high
proficiency in warlike arts.   Within a fortnight after their
arrival at the *yashiki* they were listed for a grand fen-

cing bout that came off on the parade ground. On that occasion our young friends quite distinguished themselves. Inheriting from their ancestors a peculiar aptitude for fencing, and having developed the precise muscles needed for quick action in cutting and parrying, and also having learned under their father's careful tuition all of the intricate possibilities of the double-handed sword, their wonderful expertness now became very conspicuous when contrasted with the savage chopping of the careless, pleasure-loving fellows who had learned the art in the slip-shod fashion characteristic of the military dilettanteism that always prevails during centuries of profound peace.

So pleased was the commandant with their display of skill, not only with the sword but also with the spear, that he at once promoted them to the staff of instructors to assist in drilling the young *samurai* in the *yashiki*. This promotion from guardsmen to "professors" entailed an agreeable increase of income from five *rios* to ten *rios* per month apiece. This arrangement gave them much more time to themselves and enabled them to adjust their hours to suit themselves. On some days they drilled their classes early in the morning ; on other days they drilled them late in the afternoon ; and, on other days, at midday. This arrangement gave them abundance of time to ramble over the city and the suburbs, for purposes of sight-seeing. Very naturally this work of instruction much increased their circle of acquaintances, so that many evenings were spent with acquaintances in different parts of the *yashiki*. On these occasions our Kioto friends were thoroughly informed as to the history of the Mito clan, and as to the history of the great metropolis. It did not take long for the fact to leak out that Tomokichi was in possession of much interesting information concerning foreign countries, a discovery which added much to his popularity.

But, as all roads tended toward Nihon-bashi, so every conversation drifted into the all-absorbing question of the day : " What shall we do with the barbarian when he returns in the spring for an answer to his letter of last summer ?" This subject was discussed from every conceivable standpoint. The prevailing sentiment was strongly against permitting any intercourse whatsoever with the interlopers. Yet there were some who hesitated to take this view upon the ground that the time could not be far distant when the shell of exclusiveness would be broken anyhow by some foreign nation endeavoring to conquer the country, and that, when the time came, it would be very convenient to have a few foreign allies to assist in keeping the aggressor in check. It was generally conceded, however, that the *samurai* could receive no possible benefit from the opening of the country to outsiders. This last sentiment prevailed in all the *yashikis* throughout Yedo, and was in fact the sentiment of the Bakufu. But in those quarters where the Bakufu was hated more than the barbarian, there was a sly hope that the savage foreigner would intrude himself sufficiently within the country to create an uprising against that hated oligarchy, leading ultimately to the abolishing of the Shogunate. The excitement that prevailed was subdued but intense. The fires that were soon to break forth and consume the political institutions of centuries' duration were smouldering in the Yedo *yashikis.*

And so the smiling month of November slipped away amid scenes that enraptured the imaginations of our Kioto lads. So utterly different from any previous experience ! So like the glowing pages of the romances that they used to read at Atago-yama ! And the old ex-Daimio and his son were soon to arrive at the *yashiki,* and then what rejoicing and merry-making would there be ! Already the long train of retainers had left the triple-moated castle beside the Pacific seventy miles to the northeast, and was winding leisurely down the grand avenue toward the metropolis. Early one bright morning in December a courier breathlessly dashed up to the northern gateway and announced that the princely cortege was on the Oshiu-kaido, but a few miles distant, and that it might be expected by midday. Oh ! what hurrying and scurrying to complete the arrangements for the reception, what rushing of messengers, what marshalling of soldiers, what haste to spread the emblazoned banners before the gates, and to screen the long hedgerows with heraldic panoply ! A large body of horsemen hurried off northward to meet the long-exiled lord, and every steed within the stables was brought forth to be mounted by knights in full armor, who drew up in squadrons around the gateway. Long rows of *samurai* lined the road outside of the gate, and a multitude of them were marshalled within the gates to receive their master. Hundreds of servants and attendants lined the road near the palace to make obeisance to their lord, as their ancestors had done for centuries before. Everybody and every thing were in gala dress. The ladies of the household crowded the garden walks and stood upon the verandas, with their heads so bedecked with flowers and wearing embroidered raiment of such gorgeous hues, that one might well have been pardoned for taking them for a flower show.

In a short while the vanguard of the procession came in sight, and was received most cordially with endless waves of obeisance, after which it entered the gate and swung into place among the bowing ranks within. There was neither shouting nor cheering, merely the most profuse bowing. Profound decorum and dignity characterized every thing. The loud brazen yells of Saxon races would have been entirely out of place there. For two hours a long train of baggage, retainers, horsemen, servants, and *kagos* came pelting into the *yashiki* from the north, and were all received with utmost cordiality. At length, when the dial in the garden indicated high noon, a long line of *norimons* bearing the ladies of the princely family came into view, and were received with obeisances even more profound and impressive, until it seemed as if there was a vast wheatfield around the gateway waving in continued billows to the whispering winds, to which sound the sucking inhalations of the vast multitude might well have been likened. Then came the squadron of horsemen that had sallied out of the gateway that morning ; and then the crowd knew that the Prince was approaching. Not a sound was made as the gorgeous *norimons*, conveying the princely son and father, approached. The vast throng knelt upon the ground and bowed down until the train had passed. The subdued murmurs of welcome and the hissing breath of the vassals within the gates, as they welcomed the master and his sire, were far more impressive than cheers or shouts could ever have been. The massive and beautiful doors of the superb vestibule, used only on such occasions, were thrown wide open, and the lord was at home.

For hours afterwards straggling squads of *samurai* and coolies came rambling down the road into the *yashiki*. But the crowds and the pageantry dispersed as soon as the mournful horns and the croupy drums announced that the Daimio of Mito had entered the palace. Then was there grand jollification, not only for that day, but also for three days thereafter. Feasting, fireworks, and tournaments ran riot. The fencers banged each other most unmercifully ; the spearmen prodded each other most unceremoniously; and the archers pounded away at the yelping curs, until those persecuted brutes lapsed into a condition of silent despair, mechanically turning their flanks to the whizzing shafts without indulging in useless comments. Old friends bivouacked in the barracks, and, over their *saké* cups, revived past events to their heart's content. Groups of officers were continually going to the palace to present homage and congratulations. On this great occasion nearly thirty thousand men were crowded within the walls of the *yashiki*, and every available *tatami* on the premises was occupied. In a few days, however, large numbers of the retainers returned to Mito to attend to the routine of provincial duties, and then everybody was able to settle down comfortably.

CHAPTER XI.

SIX or seven weeks after the events narrated in the previous chapter, the people inhabiting the region surrounding the magnificent bay of Yedo stood, metaphorically speaking, on the tiptoe of expectation at the prospect of the promised return of the American squadron. The month of January was well on its last half, and, although it was midwinter, yet the powerful rays of the sun were making the winter vegetation quicken with fresh verdure, and caused the leaves and the blossoms of the oncoming spring to swell in their green buds preparatory to their début three or four weeks later on. The Nakashimas had just finished their breakfast, and were preparing to start out to the parade ground to give a new class of valorous warriors some instruction as to what constituted the art of correct swordsmanship. At that juncture, a messenger from the commandant was announced by the servant. Being duly ushered into their presence, he communicated an order from the said commandant to appear at his office as soon as convenient. They at once hurried off at the very heels of the messenger, and duly reported themselves at the office of said dignitary. They were informed by that urbane gentleman that the old Prince desired to have an interview with them upon a matter of much importance. To their reply that they were at that moment due on the parade ground to instruct their regular classes, he made speedy answer by despatching a messenger there with notice that the instructors were otherwise engaged, and that the classes must adjourn until the following day.

Having adjusted that matter, the commandant led the young men through several suites of magnificent apartments out upon the broad veranda, along which they slowly walked until they came to the stately suite of chambers along the eastern side occupied by the old Prince. It was winter time, and all the *shojees* were in place, so that the rooms were well shut in. The commandant now slowly called out his name in a sonorous voice, whereupon an attendant slid back a *shojee* and ushered his party into a stately room, where they were requested to wait a few minutes until their message had been communicated to his Grace. They were not kept waiting very long, for the attendant speedily returned with orders to at once usher them into the audience-room. Here they found themselves quite alone. But they were informed that his Grace would join them as soon as he had finished some writing upon which he was engaged. *Hebachis* heaped up with glowing charcoals were set before them to warm their chilled hands. Tobacco and tea were also brought in for their refreshment.

The lofty chamber was finished off with the highest native skill. Royal tigers crouched upon the gilded panels of the *shojees*, and the impassioned hues of the lovely lotus flower gleamed amid the imperial ponds. The square panels of the ceiling were emblazoned with gorgeous phœnixes and dragons. The room was utterly destitute of upholstered furniture, for nothing of that sort existed within the four seas of Dai-Nippon. A huge bronze figure representing the thunder-fiend, and a half-dozen exquisite porcelain vases and *jardinières* completed the furnishing of the room. Four handsome rugs of foreign manufacture were arranged around the *hebachis*, ready for the expected occupants. Window glass was unknown, but abundance of light filtered through the translucent paper panes, and flooded the stately apartment with a mellowed, dreamy light.

After the lapse of nearly half an hour the old Prince entered the audience-chamber and, graciously responding to the profound salutations of his guests, proceeded to occupy one of the rugs, and invited them to occupy the others. He was an urbane yet vigorous gentleman, who possessed many striking characteristics. That he was scholarly and energetic even his enemies did not attempt to deny. It was also generally admitted that he possessed executive abilities of a high order. His temper when roused was violent and ungovernable. And he was a daring schemer and recklessly brave in the carrying out of his projects. But, perhaps, you would not have detected these qualities beneath his genial and polished exterior.

As he sat there in his modest silken garments you might well have been excused in not suspecting that beneath those rustling folds there dwelt the spirit of the bloodthirsty beasts upon the gleaming *shojees*. He was glossy and sleek until the time came for the spring, and then he bristled up hideously. His Grace possessed a remarkably large family. According to native usage, he had taken unto himself not only a wife but, in addition thereto, a large number of concubines, so that he was able to boast of eighteen sons and twenty-five daughters. But family cares and state affairs had borne lightly upon him, and he appeared in the eyes of our young friends as an exceedingly gracious old gentleman, in hale and hearty condition. Before closing our brief description of this extraordinary old gentleman, it should be stated that there were two characteristics in his nature that loomed above all others, and were conspicuous from their terrible intensity. The first of these was his bitter and unmitigated hatred of the Shoguns and the Bakufu, and the second was his merciless contempt toward foreigners. It is true that he had supreme respect for the literature of the Chinese, but this was the only consideration that he was known to show in an animosity as sweeping as the universe.

"I have obeyed your orders, most worshipful sir," said the commandant, "and have brought to you the two young gentlemen from Yamashiro whom you desired to see. We await your orders."

"Your promptness is indeed highly commendable," replied the Prince. "I have been informed," continued he, addressing the young men, "that you have recently resumed your ancient alliance with the Tokugawa family, and I am pleased to welcome you personally within the gates of our *yashiki.* At the time your ancestors connected themselves with Iyèyas, the barbarian beasts from Portugal had created grievous disturbances within the realm, which finally terminated in dreadful sedition and civil war. It is indeed curious ¬that now, when you resume your allegiance with us after a lapse of two hundred years, our nation should be again pestered by these red-haired dogs. Let us hope that this reunion may prove a good augury of success in our present efforts to drive off these abortions of beasts. Curse their monkey-faces!"

It was manifest that the old gentleman was rapidly working himself up into a foaming passion over the complicated foreign question ; but, as his listeners obsequiously bowed assent to every sentiment that he uttered, his ire speedily subsided and he soon plunged into the subject concerning which he had desired to interview them.

"You are well aware, gentlemen," continued he, after having blown off the surplus steam that appeared to have been pent up in his mind, "that, whatever may be our dislike for these interloping curs, we must deal with them cautiously until we have ascertained their precise strength. Now, the Bakufu appears to be overwhelmed with a supreme fear of their prowess. I do not know the grounds of this fear. I do not even know whether it be real or assumed. If the Shogun, whose ancestor drove forth the barbarians, be now disposed to allow their return, we of Mito must know something about these fellows in order that we may be prepared to act intelligently. We, of course, have no special love for the Shogun, although having sprung from the same ancestor. Mito has always been a cipher under the Shoguns, and, in view of the fact that we have always upheld the authority of the Emperor and have opposed the usurping of imperial power by the Bakufu, will probably always remain so."

To all of these observations a ready assent was breathed by the absorbed listeners. The impetuous old Daimio now allowed a few minutes' intermission for sipping tea and whiffing pipes. He then resumed the thread of his conversation (if so one-sided a discourse had not better be termed a harangue) : "We wish to know something about these barbarians from personal observations ; that is to say, from observations made by trusted members of our own clan. Public rumor is very unsatisfactory. The meagre accounts that filter through the Bakufu screens and lattices are not to be relied on at all. Who knows but what the barbarians are but a weak lot that could be brushed aside with a puff of breath, but whom the Bakufu exaggerate into fierce and powerful creatures, so as to inveigle us dissatisfied Daimios into open revolt, with the secret intention of crushing us unmercifully? On the other hand, the intruders may be indeed powerful, and it may be the sly game of the crafty Gotairo to lead us on into some personal collision with them, in order to afford him the delightful opportunity of standing by and exultingly witnessing our humiliation. Now, we wish to escape from this dilemma. We must know for ourselves about these people. As you already know, the ships of these barbarians will be due here at any time during the coming month. You two young gentlemen have been reported to me as persons full of energy and discreet intelligence. Will you undertake to watch the ships on their arrival and secure whatever information you can concerning these strange intruders?"

The brothers bowed down low in profound acknowledgment of the honor thus conferred on them, and replied as follows : "Your unworthy servants are duly mindful of the supreme confidence that you have reposed in them. We are willing to undertake whatever you may command, but we deem it proper to inform you that we are exceedingly inexperienced in matters of this description, as we have lived all our lives in a remote part of the empire, secluded and screened from matters and affairs of importance. We therefore humbly doubt our ability to conduct a matter of such magnitude."

"Your points have been modestly taken," replied the Prince, "but, under existing circumstances, they must be waived. Your recent journey overland from Yamashiro demonstrates that you are not mere children, and your bearing since entering my employ clearly shows that you possess both skill and intelligence. If you will carefully consider this matter you will perhaps decide to venture on the undertaking."

"We, your humble servants," replied they, "offer freely our insignificant services in whatever enterprise your supreme excellency may desire. We will gladly undertake this matter now that we have plainly stated our meagre abilities. Command, and we will obey."

"Well spoken!" exclaimed the Prince, gayly, as he clapped his hands for an attendant to bring in a map of the country surrounding the bay of Yedo. This he spread out upon the floor and then proceeded to explain the plan of the campaign. "The ships will undoubtedly be here within a month. They will enter the bay between these two bold promontories, and will come up the western side of the harbor, and will cast anchor probably in the same place where they did on the occasion of their previous visit. Now, two plans suggest themselves. Either you can secure quarters in some village on the eastern side of the bay, or you can secure accommodations of a similar description on the western side of the bay, and can watch for the incoming of the vessels. When the vessels arrive you can secure a boat and can go out and inspect them. The advantage of operating from the eastern side of the harbor is that less suspicion will attach to your appearance there, because of the great distance across the waters to the ships. On the other hand, the proximity of the western shore to the probable anchorage of the vessels is a point to be carefully considered. But all of these matters of detail you must discuss with the commandant, inasmuch as he is well acquainted with the region on both sides of the bay."

"I will endeavor to assist the gentlemen to the utmost," modestly murmured the commandant.

"By the way," exclaimed the Prince, "I had well-nigh forgotten about the financial part of this business. You must have plenty of funds, for you will find it very convenient at times to have money wherewith to unlock doors that would otherwise be closed. In other words, you will frequently be obliged to bribe your way among the Bakufu officials. You will find this out later on. Therefore, to provide for this contingency, I will give you this written order on the commandant to furnish you with whatever money you may need for your expenses."

After this the conversation continued for a while on general topics, and was finally brought to a close by the attendant bringing word that some gentlemen were waiting to see the Prince by previous appointment. Our friends then bowed themselves out of his presence and retired to the commandant's office to discuss the details of their projected expedition. That practical officer speedily brought forth a chart and a globe of the earth to assist in his investigations.

"What is this?" inquired Tomokichi, examining the globe with great interest. "It appears to me like a spherical chart."

"So it is," was the reply of the commandant. "It represents the actual appearance of the earth."

"It is round, then!" exclaimed both of the brothers in a breath.

"So the Dutch scholar, from whom I purchased it through young Konishi, alleges," was the reply.

"We had heard from Konishi," replied they, "that such was the case. But we cannot understand the matter at all. How can it possibly be round? This fact is contrary to the universal and unalterable experience of our countrymen. It is also contrary to our reason. How can we believe that, which we cannot understand, to be true? Can you explain this matter unto us so that we may understand it?"

"Ah! my young friends," replied he, "I fear that I do not understand the matter any better than you do. Nevertheless I believe the earth to be round."

"What! Do you then believe that which you cannot understand?" was the astonished rejoinder.

"Yes, my young friends," replied he, "I am prepared to make even that admission. I do not allege that my intellect is any keener than yours, but I have lived about twice as long on this earth (be it round or flat) as you have, and I have learned two very stubborn facts, which, on sundry occasions, quite paralyze my reason and make me very distrustful thereof. In the first place I have learned that I am compelled to believe many things that I cannot understand at all,—and not only to believe them, but also adapt myself and my plans just as if I did fully understand those inscrutable things. Let me illustrate with a few examples this first fact. Our province you know is a long and narrow strip of territory stretching along the shores of the ocean. Our capital city, Mito, is not over seven or eight miles from these waters.

"During my boyhood I spent the summer in my father's villa near the shore. It did not take long for me to find out that during certain hours the long strip of sandy beach in front of our house was covered with water, and that during other hours it was quite free from water. Very naturally I adapted my sports to the emergency of the case,—romping there at low tide and absconding when the mighty waves rushed shoreward. And I soon found that all the shore dwellers adapted themselves to the emergency of the same circumstance, —that every fisherman pulled his boat and spread his nets far above high-water mark, that every hamlet stood far back of the line of sea-weed and drift-wood, and that even my father had built his villa beyond the reach of the restless waves. I never understood why those waters rose and fell at regular intervals during the day and night. Even now I fail to comprehend the cause of this great phenomenon. Yet I have never ceased to believe that those waters *did* rise and fall at regular intervals along the entire sea-coast, and if I were to build a villa to-day on any part of the coast of Dai-Nippon, I would build it above high-water mark, even though I am unable to understand why there should be any high-water mark at all. I must *believe* the stubborn *fact* although I fail to understand it.

"Here is another example. I do not understand how the eating of food sustains life in my body, yet I believe that it does sustain life in me, and accordingly I gracefully accept and adapt myself to this stubborn fact. *Again,* I do not understand the process whereby I lift my arm. I fail to understand the subtile power that moves the various muscles of my body. I fail to understand the mysterious connection between my will and the tissues of my body, whereby I act and move. Yet I fully believe that I can act and move whenever I choose to make volition. Will either of you gentlemen in the midst of a fierce fencing bout fail to believe that a descending foil will smite you on the head because you do not understand the muscular process whereby that foil got there? I apprehend that you will indulge in a masterly parry even though you fail to understand any better the theory of muscular action than you do the theory of the earth's rotundity. In short, gentlemen, I could multiply examples indefinitely, but it will be time wasted. The longer you gentlemen live the more will you become convinced that you believe multitudes of things that you do not understand.

"Then the second stubborn fact that I have found out is that the standard of my reason is very fluctuating. Many things appeared reasonable to me as a boy that appeared ridiculous to me as a young man. And many things that appeared quite consistent to me as a young man became laughable when I grew older. Things that appeared reasonable to me ten years ago—yea, even si::

months ago—I cannot now reconcile with my reason. One year ago the reasoning mind of Dai-Nippon would have laughed to scorn anybody who had alleged that a ship could sail against wind and tide ; yet last summer the barbarian fleet came up Yedo bay in the teeth of a gale and against the bosom of an ebb tide ! What is your reason good for? Pray, what is the standard of human reason ? The Dutch report that when their ambassador told the king of Siam that water in Holland sometimes became quite solid like stone, he scoffed at him and said that such could not be the fact, because it would be contrary to the reason and the universal and unalterable experience of all Siam. Yet we know that water even here in Yedo sometimes becomes solid, and that up north it becomes solid and remains so for many months. Pray, what kind of a test is human reason when it fluctuates perpetually, so that what our ancestors deemed reasonable succeeding generations laughed to scorn, what we deemed reasonable in youth we sneer at in maturer years, and what in our old age we deem reasonable our children will scoff at within a decade of our death? It is the course of wisdom to hold in abeyance those matters not demanding immediate action, and which we do not understand. It is silly to repudiate any statement merely because we fail to understand it.

" But, young gentlemen, while all this may be very entertaining, it is not business. Let me see, here is a map of Yedo bay, together with the adjoining provinces. Let us proceed to map out your course. Now I think that the western side of the bay will be the best one for our operations, but the great question is how to get there. The Bakufu sentinels swarm between here and Uraga. It will be useless for us to try to slip you through them, for we would probably have your two heads adorning our gateposts as a warning against future attempts at such an offence. Nor can you very well skirt the eastern shore of the bay, for the sentinels are almost as numerous there. If we can only land you on the beach near Yokoska, far down the western side of the bay, then you can hide away in some hamlet or fishing village and assume but little risk. But how shall we set you down at that spot? That is a very difficult question to answer."

And, indeed, it so proved itself, for they puzzled over it nearly all day. His Grace, the ex-Daimio, when he spread out the map and grandly pointed with his fan to the course to be pursued, probably realized the difficulty of the situation as little as did the Czar of Russia in the matter where he drew a straight line from St. Petersbürg to Moscow, and bade his engineers construct a railway accordingly. It was finally decided that the young men should go up to Mito ostensibly on business, and should embark in a fishing boat at that point some night, and slyly steal down the coast to the eastern promontory of Yedo bay, and then cut across to the western shore under cover of darkness and find some good hiding-place around Yokoska, where they were to wait until the fleet had made its appearance and had taken permanent anchorage, when they were to spy out all they could until the departure of the ships. Then they were to steal back by the same route by which they had gone.

As the route was very circuitous, and might, in case of tempestuous weather, involve many weeks, it was decided that the journey should commence on the very next day.

CHAPTER XII.

A CHANGE OF SCENE.

ACCORDINGLY, at dawn of the next day, two horses duly caparisoned were led forth by the *bettôs* from the stables of Mito Yashiki, and were taken to the northern gateway to await the arrival of their riders. These *bettôs* were wiry little grooms, who invariably trotted alongside of the horses from one end of the journey to the other. Of course the horses did not go at full speed. They ambled along leisurely at the rate of about twenty-five miles per day, and were carefully cared for by their *bettôs* at each resting-place. Rapid riding was a rare thing in that country. When Julius Cæsar left Rome to place himself at the head of his legions on the farther slope of the Alps, he is said to have taken but eight days in riding that great distance. With the same relays of horses he could have covered the same distance on the highways of Japan, but he would have shaken off his *bettôs* very soon, and he would have shaken up the sorry nags of the empire worse than he shook up the Helvetii, and in a manner quite sufficient to have gained their eternal enmity.

Just before sunrise the commandant, together with the two brothers, slowly approached the gateway. The young men purported to be the bearers of official messages to the castle at Mito. But why should messengers have so much gold and silver coin tied about their waists beneath their clothing? And how happened it that the alleged messages never found their way within the Mito moats, but were carefully burnt by their bearers on the night of their arrival in Mito? But we must not anticipate events. "When you reach Mito," said the commandant, as they neared the horses, "turn off from the street that leads to the castle, and follow the one to the right hand and go out toward the suburbs, where my father's house is situated, and, after having communicated my message to him, journey on in the night toward our sea-side villa. Next day he will join you there, and will assist you in securing a boat suitable for your purposes. Then, on the very first favorable day, embark on your 'fishing excursion.' Every thing else connected with this expedition will be left to your natural good-sense. May great success crown your journey!"

So saying, he bade them farewell, and riders and grooms trotted out of the gateway along the broad road that wound among the green hills environing the northern suburbs of Yedo. Long before midday they had reached the Mito-kaido, and were journeying through the vast rice fields that stretched away to the northeast. By leisurely trotting, they reached the low, sandy banks of the broad and rapid Tonégawa—twenty-seven miles on their way—late in the afternoon. On the opposite shore, among the trees, stood an inviting village. It was decided to spend the night there. Accordingly, a long flat-bottomed boat was engaged, the horses, after considerable "moral suasion," were finally induced to embark, and the ferry-men poled the craft across to the other side.

On the following day the party started bright and early, and trudged through twenty-seven miles of rice-fields, moorlands, and marshy lagoons, until, at nightfall, they entered the town of Inayoshi, situated near the western end of a large lake, which the retreating waters of the Pacific Ocean had left as a footprint a thousand years or so before that time. This lake had a circuit of nearly ninety miles. Its shores were low and well wooded. And it was filled with islets of most picturesque beauty, one of them being of sufficient size to support a population of sixteen hundred people. Dining on broiled eels, for which this section of Hitachi was celebrated, our friends fortified themselves for the last day's journey of

twenty-six miles, which furnished scenery somewhat similar to that already described, and which brought them
late in the evening to the southwestern suburb of Mito.
They rode down the broad, clean street that traversed
the lower town from one extremity to the other. Above
them, on the left-hand side, rose the lofty, swarded embankments of the castle, draped with magnificent trees,
and surmounted with white walls and turrets that glistened weirdly in the moonlight. Passing beyond the mer-'
cantile quarters, they came to the region where the
small *yashikis* of retainers were spread out on either side
of the great thoroughfare. They speedily found the
particular one of which they were in quest, and duly announced themselves at the wicket gate. After a short
delay, an elderly gentleman emerged and announced
himself to be the person whom they were seeking.
Tomokichi at once dismounted, and, after the inter-
change of the profoundest of salutations, quietly communicated to him the message from his son, the commandant of Mito Yashiki. Very naturally, the abrupt-
ness of the proceedings created considerable surprise,
with, at first, a mild flavoring of•incredulity ; but Tomokichi produced tangible evidence that at once put all
suspicions to rest. The courteous old gentleman at once
ordered a servant to guide the visitors to his villa at the
sea-shore, and to make them as comfortable as possible
until his own arrival there next day.

Journeying now with accelerated speed, our belated
travellers followed the road that went winding among
hills, whose picturesque beauty was made highly conspicuous by the bright moonlight. Finally, reaching some
rising ground, they halted several minutes to survey the
magnificent scenery that spread out on all sides. Behind
them glimmered the lights of the upper town on the high
hills north of the castle. The citadel, crowning the crest
of the loftiest ridge, loomed up grandly in the shimmering light, with its white battlements gleaming like silver
against a dark background of majestic trees. In their
immediate front were sighing pine groves, that fell rapidly

away into dunes and sand-drifts, which met the mighty waves of the thundering ocean that rolled away in awful grandeur to the distant horizon, where the queenly moon paled the stars with her brilliancy. The high wind was blowing the spray from the foaming surf far inland, and the gauzy mists sped whispering through the foliage of the groves,—"*the voice of the ocean, in accents disconsolate, answered the wail of the forest.*"

Resuming their romantic course, the party soon reached the beach, and, after following its stately sweep for a considerable distance, they finally reached the villa, a neat and pretty Japanese house, surrounded by a beautiful garden. It was apparently deserted. But a few loud knocks at the front door speedily brought the family that had been left in charge to the scene of disturbance. The door was slid back, and a very much demoralized top-knot was thrust out upon the scene. This represented the major-general of the premises. As the tone of the conversation outside became reassuring, there appeared a head of dishevelled hair, a set of glittering black teeth, and a smiling, inquisitive face, slipping out upon the veranda beside the major-general. This second personage was the captain of the household forces—the beloved spouse. Then there gradually glided out from unknown quarters sundry infants, who cautiously marshalled themselves in line with their parents, and timidly clung together when any thing in the strangers' manner or speech startled them. And a very picturesque group they made there in the moonlight !

When the inmates had fully comprehended the situation, they hustled around with the most commendable amiability and efficiency. The best room was at once placed at the disposal of the guests. A blazing *hebachi* was speedily brought in, for the weather was yet chilly and the high wind that had been blowing for two days sent its piercing breath through every crevice of the frail structure. Refreshments were then placed before the guests, and they ravenously partook thereof while the heavy bedding was being spread out on the floor. Then,

undressing themselves, our party resigned themselves to
that sweet and mysterious influence whose subtle spell
we all acknowledge even though we fail to comprehend
how the drowsy torpor creeps over our being.

They all slept late into the following morning. When
they finally roused themselves they found that the lady
of the house had prepared a hot bath for them in order
that they might enjoy their breakfast better after having
relaxed their sore muscles and stiff joints. After breakfast they found that the wind had gone down, and that
the day was one of those deliciously balmy ones so common at that season. They sat on the veranda and
smoked their pipes while enjoying the warm sunshine
and gazing upon the roaring surf. Toward midday a
norimon appeared on the beach. As it approached the
house the young men correctly surmised that their host
was within it. When he arrived he most cordially
greeted them and entered with immense zest into their
schemes. He sent the horses and the grooms back to
his *yashiki*, to be there kept until the return of the young
adventurers. He then despatched his attendant down
to the fishing hamlets along the shore to make enquiries
as to what boats were available. As the water was too
rough for any thing to be attempted on that day, the gentlemen spent the time in talking over matters of general
interest. Late in the afternoon the attendant reported
that there were three boats from which a selection could
be made. Accordingly, on the following morning, the
party strolled along the beach to inspect the crafts. One
of them was too small. Another one seemed too much
weather-beaten. But the third one seemed quite well
adapted for the purpose in view. It was comparatively
new and contained sufficient room for ten people. It
carried a single mast, with a square sail. On each side
of the stern was room for two scullers. The boat was
forthwith hired for one month.

On the following day the water was so quiet that our
young adventurers decided to start. Accordingly they
began to load the boat as it lay on the beach. A man

climbed on deck and caught the bundles that were tossed up to him. Then the passengers and the crew went aboard. In the stern there was a little cabin large enough for three or four Japanese to sit in comfortably. In the bow of the boat there was quite a forecastle where five or six men could pack themselves away and sleep. Orders were given for abundance of warm bedding to be brought down from the villa and to be placed in the after-cabin, and for an abundant supply of provisions to be stowed away in a deep hold beneath the plankings amidship. When every thing was ready for the start, a large number of fishermen placed their shoulders to the graceful craft and slid her down the soft sand into the tumbling surf, giving her such momentum that she glided far out into smoother water beyond danger of capsizing. The scullers soon turned her prow southward, and the journey was well under way.

The crew comprised ten stout fishermen. Four of them were to work the sculls, two of them were to keep the vessel in trim, and the other four were to constitute a relay of scullers. The distance down the coast to the destined point in Yedo bay was fully two hundred miles, —a journey that would take ten days of very leisurely travelling. Frequent stops were to be made along the coast, and the nights were to be spent at anchor. The morning and the evening meals were to be cooked ashore. It had been announced to the crew that the two *samurai* were seeking recreation and desired to take a fishing excursion along the coast. The black-eyed fellows blandly accepted the statement without comment ; but they shrewdly drew their own conclusion that, inasmuch as the gentry were not addicted to risking themselves in that fashion on the tempestuous deep for a few cheap fishes that could be purchased ashore, the young gentlemen had probably gotten into some political scrape and were going boating until the affair had blown over. But who they were, or what their schemes might be, was none of their business. They were well paid for their services, and they well understood that an impassable barrier lay between them and the *samurai* class, so that they were not at liberty to pry into any thing pertaining to their affairs.

As the wind was favorable they spread the sail and soon drew away from the shore, bound for a hamlet twenty miles down the coast, where they intended to spend the night. The boat tossed about a good deal, and the young men soon began to experience those well-defined sensations familiar to all who have been sea-sick. At first they were quite alarmed, not knowing what might be the matter. They fought valiantly against the overpowering qualmishness, turned deathly white, and then precipitately rushed to the side of the boat and balanced themselves as gracefully as they could over the gunwales, while " the voice of deep answered unto deep." This uncouth position mortified them exceedingly, but they were constrained to adopt it as no other alternative appeared available. The captain of the crew, however, speedily assured them that there need be no occasion for alarm, and suggested a swallow of salt water and a re-tirement to their cabin, where they could lie down. The good-hearted fellow nursed them quite tenderly for several hours, and, when they drew near to the hamlet, he ran the boat into smooth water and pulled down the sail, ordering the men to scull the balance of the distance.

There was a secluded cove, locked in with well-wooded hills, near the hamlet. Toward this point the boat was steered and anchored close to the wide, sandy beach,—so close, in fact, that the men easily stepped overboard and waded ashore, where they set to work in a sheltered spot to prepare the evening meal. When the rice was cooked and the fresh mackerel, procured from the neighboring hamlet, was duly broiled, the meal was handed over the side of the boat, and was regularly discussed by the hungry crew. The captain, acting in the capacity of steward, personally waited on his cabin passengers, and served them bountifully on the quarter-deck. The morning meal was prepared and served in a similar fashion. The boat then started on her cruise. There

was a light northerly breeze, and she stood out well from
the shore to take full advantage of it. This day was far
more enjoyable than the preceding one had been, inasmuch as the qualmish sensations were barely felt. After
having sailed nearly thirty miles, they put inshore and
began leisurely sculling along in search of a quiet spot
for spending the night. This part of the coast was low,
sandy, and well covered with scrub pines. There were
but few coves and inlets. However, late in the afternoon, they found a small inlet where they moored their
boat and spent the night. On the following day they
rounded a bold promontory, and changed their course so
as to point southwesterly. They could now see the dim
outlines of Fuji-yama standing out faintly against the
rosy tints of the evening sky.

Thus they continued their delightful journey down the
coast, avoiding as far as possible the habitations of men,
and occasionally throwing out their fishing tackle with
varying success. The weather was fine during the entire
trip, so that none of the anticipated delays from tempestuous weather were experienced. On the evening of the
ninth day they stole quietly around the bold promontory into the bay of Yedo. It now became necessary for
them to be very circumspect in their movements, because
the vigilant shore guards were on every commanding
eminence, watching for the arrival of the expected ships.
They glided quietly across the bay and cast anchor in a
secluded bight until the dawn was sufficiently advanced
to enable them to select a favorable location for beach-
ing the boat. Creeping along the lovely shores in the
gray dawn, they finally came upon a secluded fishing
hamlet on an exquisite inlet. A beautiful range of hills
crowded the fishermen's cottages quite close upon the
broad beach and shut off the place from the gaze of the
world. It was not near any great thoroughfare, and the
only exit to the country behind was a steep foot-path
that zigzagged up the cliff to the summit, and then went
twisting through miles of woods and fields to a distant
village. Our young voyagers accordingly gave orders

for landing. The boat was pulled high and dry up on the sand in line with several other fishing-boats of almost precisely similar appearance, so that nothing but a special enquiry would have revealed the fact that there had been a new arrival at the hamlet.

CHAPTER XIII.

As a matter of exact history, Tomokichi and Junzo
had reached their destination many days prior to the
arrival of the fleet of Commodore Perry, so that they had
abundance of time wherein to survey the vicinity of the
locality where they had decided to establish their head-
quarters. Giving strict orders to the crew to make no
mention of whence they had come (but to reply, when
interrogated by the fishermen in the hamlets, that they
had been sent down by the Bakufu from Yedo to watch
for the expected arrival of the barbarian ships and to
watch their movements after arrival), the young spies
proceeded to engage a desirable room in one of the
cottages. The fact that they wore the Tokugawa crest
(which, as vassals of Mito, they were entitled to wear)
rendered their story exceedingly plausible ; and, so long
as their crew kept aloof from the inhabitants of the place
(which they were under orders to do), there was hardly
any possibility of there being any discovery as to their
true character. And there was no danger of the timorous fishermen plying them with any improper questions,
for they had been brought up to dread the *samurai*.
The house that our young spies selected was that of
the headman of the hamlet. It faced the wide entrance
to the inlet and gave a splendid view of the waters of the
bay. The roof was deeply thatched with straw ; and in
a long trough along the ridge-pole there were planted
lilies, irises, and azaleas, which bloomed in their seasons
and gave a wonderfully jaunty air to the roof. There
was but one story, and that was surrounded by a broad

veranda on all sides. The large room opening out on the front veranda was the one selected ; and the *shojees* at the back, that shut it off from the rest of the house, were as effective in keeping out intrusion as walls of adamant would have been,—for the timid members of the family shrank out of sight and kept themselves in the remotest chambers at the rear. The meals were always prepared by the crew as before, and were served by the captain in the front room. All the land about the cottage (and there was considerable) was given up to gardening. At the back were long rows of garlic, radishes, and *taro*. At the front were flowers and shrubs arranged in a manner that would have done credit to Mito Yashiki itself. A hedge of hollyhock and square-trimmed cedar bushes surrounded the place. Camellias, flowering almonds, and cherry blossoms were in full bloom, as the sheltered locality and the powerful sun made all vegetation very forward.

The climate of this promontory was balmy and de-licious, like that of all those along the southern shores of the empire, jutting so boldly into the warm waters of the Pacific. All of the cottages, in fact, were quite as tastefully arranged as this one. No matter how poor a Japanese was, yet he delighted in his garden, and would cultivate a plot of ground only a few feet square with as much assiduity as if it were a farm. In the cliff back of the hamlet was a deep and wide fissure that had probably been cleft through the black rocks during some earth-quake. Shrubs and bushes had sprung out of the numerous crevices in its walls, thus giving the place the appearance of a beautiful grotto.

A spring of cold water, as clear as crystal, gushed from the farther end and emptied itself into a capacious granite basin, over whose sides it poured in a steady stream that gurgled down the rocks and flowed across the sands until it mingled with the briny waters that lapped the beach. At various points along the course of the stream were deep and wide pools that had been scooped out and then walled in with pebbles so as to form basins where clothing could be washed and where fishes and vegetables could be cleaned. Far back in the fissure stood a little Shinto shrine, upon a rocky ledge among the bushes. A bowlful of rice, a fish's head, and a small jar of *saké* stood before the latticed doors. The thrifty Buddhist priests had evidently not considered this secluded nook worth the tilling, and had left the simple denizens undisturbed in the exercise of the religion of their remotest progenitors, who chased the wild-boar and the deer through the primeval forests that covered the land as with a garment. In short, our friends could hardly have found a lovelier or a more sheltered spot wherein to spend a few weeks.

It was a dreamy kind of existence that they led for the next week or so. The denizens of the hamlet were usually astir at daybreak. The women-folk had breakfast ready in a very short space of time, and by sunrise the fishermen had slid their boats into the water and were under bellying sails down the bay. Sometimes they went out to sea for their prey; sometimes they fished in the deep waters at the mouth of the bay; and sometimes they angled in the still waters along the coast. Generally, however, the waters of the bay provided all that they needed, and, by about the middle of the afternoon, they took advantage of the sea-breeze and came scudding home with great éclat. Between four and five o'clock every afternoon the waters of the bay presented a beautiful sight, with multitudes of white sails scattered about in every direction.

From the top of some one of the hills surrounding the shores, you could have watched the on-coming fleets dashing along in the glorious sunshine, and slipping away like shadows into the numerous inlets about the enchanting shores. Sometimes the boats would glide out on moonlight nights and sweep, ghost-like, over the still waves in quest of those denizens of the deep that love to sport in the moonbeams. And sometimes they would venture out on dark nights and kindle torches to allure their victims into the vicinity of the boats, where the meshes of the cruel nets could be cast about them. Weird and spectre-like seemed the bay on those occasions, with jets of flame dancing all over its surface as far as the eye could reach, while the subdued tones of the fishermen could be heard chanting some monotonous measure, whose mystic rhythm was supposed to be freighted with spells that charmed and allured the scaly dwellers of the deep.

Oh ! a hardy and a cheerful set of fellows were those fishermen along the shores of Dai-Nippon. Their vocation had been hereditary for so many, many centuries, that each rising generation literally took to the water from infancy, for the little toddlers were able to swim nearly as soon as they could walk. After having received merely the rudiments of an exceedingly primitive education, the little fellows accompanied their fathers on their fishing expeditions. They grew up to be densely ignorant, but jolly and hearty men, and very expert in whatever pertained to their particular occupation. These simple people, dimly realizing that behind the phenomena of nature there dwelt some unknown power, endeavored to propitiate it with the traditionary rites and ceremonies of Shinto, the indigenous fetich of the primeval savages that fished and hunted by forest and stream so many centuries before. And they had, indeed, developed into a superstitious and timid set of amiable boors, knowing nothing of the literature of their country, and knowing next to nothing about what was transpiring beyond the hills back of their hamlet. So long as they caught their regular supply of fish and could sell it at a fair price,— what cared they for court and rabble ? So far as they themselves were concerned, the Shoguns might usurp the imperial authority for myriads of years, and the emasculated Daimios might make childish faces at each other until the stars grew pale over the scene. The sparkling waves, the bracing air, and the thrilling expectancy of the fisherman's life were quite sufficient to satisfy their humble ambition.

After two or three days of rest the order was given to

the Mito men to go out on a fishing excursion. The greater part of the day was spent just inside of the promontory that formed the western side of the bay. Good luck attended their exertions and they spent the next two days in cleaning, salting, and drying their haul. Whenever the young spies accompanied the boat they took good care to keep themselves well secluded in the cabin, lest prying eyes on shore might detect their presence and institute disagreeable investigations. By thus keeping their men occupied they succeeded in killing time and in preventing that promiscuous familiarity with the natives which leisure and idleness would surely have engendered.

February was nearly half gone when one day our young friends were lying on the *tatamis* enjoying the delightful prospect over the blue waters of the bay. Their boat had been gone several hours on an excursion down the bay, and they were languidly sucking their pipes and querying as to whether it was not nearly time for it to put in an appearance. It was a kind of shore-day for many of the natives, some of whom were drying their nets on the broad white sands, while others were busily engaged in curing their last catch of fish. The children made the place vocal with their romping mirth in the gardens and along the shore, for their terror of the two *samurai* had worn off sufficiently to permit of this much of boisterous fun. The little urchins took good care, however, to keep out of the garden where the strange visitors could see them.

" I am beginning to get tired of this kind of life," Junzo was saying.

" So am I," was Tomokichi's hearty response. " It is all very well to live thus for a few days, but the excitement soon dies away under such tame surroundings. These simple people stimulate no thought and exchange no ideas beyond the merest commonplace sentiments. The sense of danger has entirely disappeared in this atmosphere of peaceful security."

" Yes," replied Junzo, as he slowly picked the glossy

orange leaves from a twig that he held in his hand,
" these surroundings are certainly very dull. I am going
to lie down here on the *tatami* and take a nap. By the
way, did any of the native boats accompany our boat to-
day ? "

" I believe two of them did," replied his brother.

" I do not much like our men becoming so familiar
with these natives," continued Junzo, " but I suppose it
cannot be helped. I fear something may leak out.—
Well, here I go for a nap ; I cannot allow my mind
to become too heavily burdened with care."

So saying, he spread himself out on the floor and lay
quietly for several minutes. Suddenly he lifted his head
and exclaimed, " What is that throbbing noise ? "

" I hear nothing," replied his brother.

" Neither do I now that I am sitting up," said Junzo.
" Nevertheless, when recumbent I heard such a sound
most distinctly. There must be some water in my ear. I
splashed about tremendously in the bath this morning."
So saying, he again lay down. But he soon arose and exclaimed in a tone of growing interest :

" Surely I cannot be mistaken this time for I certainly
did hear a long-continued and regular throbbing louder
than before. I am positive that the water that may be in
my ear has absolutely nothing to do with the sound.
There ! I hear it again just as soon as I place my ear to
the floor. I am *not* mistaken. Just put your ear to the
floor and listen."

Tomokichi, with considerable interest in the matter,
did as his brother requested, and, placing his ear to the
floor, listened attentively. " Surely there is a throbbing
of a most peculiar nature," he at last replied with ill-
suppressed excitement. " I wonder what it can be. Let
us listen for a long time and see if it will grow any
louder."

Accordingly they both lay down and eagerly listened
to the strange sounds. Steadily and rapidly the pulsa-
tions beat upon their ears as if coming up from the
ground. Yet, when they compared notes, they decided

that the throbbing did not proceed from the ground at all,
but from some remote distance on land or on water.
And, strange to say, the noise became continually louder !

"Well!" finally exclaimed Junzo, "I give this matter
up ; it is beyond my comprehension. As we are in a
region where we are not familiar with the natural phenomena, it would be well to consult with the headman of
the village as to what this thing portends. Who knows
but what it may be the precursor of an earthquake or of
a cyclone. Let us call him in to listen."

Accordingly the individual in question was duly summoned. He approached with humble manner, and,
kneeling down, awaited their announcement as to the
object of the summons.

"I presume," said Junzo, "that you have lived in this
hamlet all of the years of your life and are familiar with
all of the features of the locality. Is this not so ? "

"You have spoken truly," was the modest reply. "Not
only I, but my father, and his father, and unknown generations of my ancestors have lived here. I am tolerably
familiar with the locality, but I am an ignorant fellow
and do not have the full knowledge that should be possessed on such matters."

"Will you place your ear close to the *tatami* and
explain to us the meaning of those throbbing sounds,"
said Junzo, rather anxious to get at the gist of the matter
without further delay.

The fisherman looked up much perplexed at so abrupt
and extraordinary a request. He had heard terrible tales
of playful *samurai* hacking up common folk just to try
their blades. Was this extraordinary request but a
pretext for getting his head into a convenient position for
some clever stroke of practice ? He hesitated to comply,
and glanced furtively aside to see if the veranda was
clear. But the laugh of his visitors reassured him, and he
followed their example and placed his ear close to the
floor as requested.

"Truly a strange sound !" he soon exclaimed. "The
gentlemen were indeed not jesting. I beg ten thousand

pardons for doubting their sincerity." Again he listened attentively for several minutes. "Yea! a most wonderful sound. And it grows louder!"

"Does it portend an earthquake or a cyclone?" enquired Tomokichi.

"I do not think that it portends either the one or the other," he replied.

"What do you think it can be?" enquired Junzo.

"I think," replied he, meditatively scratching his head, "that it must be some kind of fish in the bay beating the water with its tail. Many years ago I heard my father say that fishes sometimes can produce sounds like thunder by deep rumblings and bellowings in their bellies. There must be some new variety of fish in the bay. I will enquire of the other men and see if these sounds can be heard on every *tatami* in the hamlet."

"There!" exclaimed Junzo in great excitement, "you can now hear the sounds without placing your ear to the floor. Let us stand on the veranda and listen." ·

Accordingly they went and stood there, and found that they could hear the throbbing with great distinctness. Perplexed and amazed, they pondered and queried for several minutes. The headman went around among the houses calling out everybody to listen. They all crowded to the beach and closely noted the sounds, that seemed to be growing louder by the minute. Thus they listened and speculated for fully half an hour, when they observed numerous fleets of boats hurrying landward. Presently a multitude of demoralized crafts—like a shoal of fishes flying before some monster of the deep— shot around the headland and rushed northward in great haste, while the crews seemed by their excited gesticulations and frantic yells to be in great agitation. This scene continued for half an hour or so, creating great uneasiness among the people on the beach, who were naturally at a great loss to account for such unprecedented conduct. Finally three boats dashed around the headland and rushed into the inlet as fast as the panting scullers could drive the trembling keels through

the water. It was at once perceived that these boats belonged to the hamlet. "The ships! The barbarian
ships!" yelled the boatmen when they came within earshot. "They are coming up the bay! They are close
behind us!"

This announcement created great excitement and consternation. But the agitation speedily subsided when it
was remembered that the Bakufu was prepared to punish
the bold intruders this time for their temerity. The
Mito men, in reply to the eager questionings of their
masters, described the ships as being like immense
whales with volcanoes on their backs. Everybody now
crowded down the beach to watch them pass up the bay.
The throbbing of the mighty paddle-wheels increased in
volume every minute. The timorous crowd now listened in silence to those strange sounds,—the children
clinging to their parents in abject terror while the women
huddled together in the middle of the crowd.

"Look there! Look there!" exclaimed several voices
at once as a large black object pushed around the headland. Sure enough! It was the bow of a mighty steamer.
It rapidly came into full view, and the frightened crowd
(not knowing whether to stand or fly) seemed glued to
the spot, as if spellbound in fascination of the hideous
object. There it went trailing the blackness of night
from its sable funnel and warning off the Bakufu guard-
boats with shrill howls and terrific roars from its huge
steam-whistle, while the spray dashed up by the revolv-
ing wheels fell from the paddle-box like charming cascades. Then came another black monster around the
headland! And another! And another! Until seven
huge leviathans passed up into the broad waters of the
upper bay. Surely, no such sight had ever been witnessed by the people of Dai-Nippon! Then came, for
the space of fully half an hour, mighty billows breaking
upon the beach in an almost unbroken roar, as if they,
too, were flying in terror from the unwelcome visitors.
As soon as the monsters had passed beyond the hamlet's
field of vision, the crowd broke for the hills, and from

their summits watched the majestic line of vessels slowly advancing up the bay, and finally casting anchor in the bight subsequently called Mississippi Bay in honor of the flagship of the squadron. Late into the evening, little groups would climb up to gaze upon the distant lights that gleamed from rigging and port-hole out upon the quiet waters, as if a city had been anchored there by some supernatural influence.

CHAPTER XIV.

FOR several days after the arrival of the steamers and frigates, the Mito boatmen regularly went on their fishing excursions down the bay ; while our young friends as regularly climbed the hills and viewed the fleet. After several days they gave orders to change the direction of the excursions and to fish along the shores of the bay in the direction of the barbarian ships. These trips they accompanied, and, from the seclusion of their cabin, they took note of many matters of interest as their boat crept nearer and nearer toward the black leviathans each day. After eight or ten days of this distant inspection, they came to the conclusion that they had obtained about all the information possible under such conditions, and that, unless they could by some means get within the cordon of Bakufu guard-boats and obtain a closer view of the foreigners, there was not much use in their assuming the risk of a more protracted stay.

They pondered long as to how they could secure a nearer inspection of the vessels. There did not appear to be more than two courses available. Either they must slip through the cordon unobserved some dark night, or they must bribe the officers commanding one of the guard-boats to allow them to pass through under cover of darkness. It was finally decided to adopt the latter plan. Accordingly, about nine o'clock, one night, the boat was quietly slid down the beach, and they embarked for this new venture in espionage. Noiselessly the craft slipped out of the inlet into the still waters of the sombre bay, where they headed their prow toward the dim lights that faintly glimmered across the wide expanse of waters that lay between them and the American fleet. Rapidly they skimmed through the gloom, until first the lofty masts and then the massive hulls of the ships loomed up in the uncertain light. The vessels lay several cable-lengths from shore, and were marshalled in line of battle with broadsides shoreward. Formidable and forbidding enough they appeared there, shooting forth from many port-holes baleful gleams of warning light. At a respectful distance, a circle of Bakufu guard-boats surrounded the fleet with a cautious but vigilant embrace.

As the Mito boat drew near, they were suddenly challenged by a craft that seemed to rise up from the waves at their bow : " Halt ! What is the nature of your business here ? Do you not know that this is prohibited territory ? "

" Some *samurai* on board of our boat desire to communicate a message to the officer in command of your boat," was the answer that went softly back from the Mito boat in response to the challenge.

" Remain where you are until we come alongside," was the prompt order that came back through the night from the Bakufu boat.

The young spies were now thoroughly committed to their hazardous undertaking, and their hearts beat quickly as they realized that they were prisoners in the hands of the merciless Bakufu and were about to be subjected to a searching inspection. The guard-boat quickly came up and laid itself alongside,—prow to prow and stern to stern. A dozen hands reached forth and grasped the gunwales of the Mito boat and firmly held it against the side of the Bakufu boat. A tall Yakunin then stepped over the side and began looking around the decks for whatever might indicate the true character of the craft. Seeing merely a harmless fishing-boat with a cowering crew of timid fishermen, he haughtily walked aft and presented himself before the two *samurai* and critically surveyed them in the dim light furnished by the paper lanterns that the guards were holding up over the sides of the boat. The young men were standing on the quarter-deck. They had donned their best clothes for the occasion, well knowing the respect that an elegant attire always inspired among their countrymen,—especially among the mercenary and venal Bakufu officials. Their features were most effectually disguised by the customary black dominos worn in winter-time throughout the country, thus exposing merely their eyes, noses, and mouths. The haughty stare of the Yakunin, as he glanced at their intelligent faces and aristocratic raiment, relaxed into an expression of respect, which became one of downright amiability when he caught sight of the glittering ornaments on their sword-hilts.

" I perceive," said he, slowly, in the polite and conciliatory language with which *samurai* invariably address members of their own class, " that the gentlemen are travelling *nébon*." [1]

" We are, honorable sir," was the respectful and fearless reply.

" May I enquire," continued their inquisitor, perceiving from their tones and accent that they were *samurai* of no ordinary stamp, " what business has brought you out at such an unseasonable hour ? "

" Most certainly, honorable sir," replied Tomokichi. " We are from one of the Yedo *yashikis,* and you, as a fellow-samurai (profoundly bowing), will readily comprehend our reason for not designating it. Being much

---

[1] The word incognito does not fully express the meaning conveyed in the word *nébon.* To travel *nébon* was one of the peculiar privileges granted to Japanese of the very highest rank. The party thus travelling adopted some sort of disguise and went forth into the world to see the sights. By a refinement of fiction he became turned into the character of his disguise, leaving his proper and correct self behind, to be resumed when the wandering character should return. To everybody he must be known merely as *nébon,*—even though recognized. He had left behind every particle of his former self ! Even emperors are reported to have travelled *nébon.* Consequently every Japanese accorded instinctive courtesy to everybody thus travelling.

interested in these barbarian ships, concerning which
there have been innumerable wild rumors afloat in Yedo
for many days past, we became consumed with a desire
to examine them for ourselves in order to gratify that
overpowering curiosity and that thirst for accurate information for which we *samurai* have always been
famous.   Perceiving that our government had received
the strangers in a friendly manner, we very naturally
came to the conclusion that there could not be any
reasonable objection to our visiting this place and seeing
what we could.   Therefore we hired a fishing-boat this
morning and came down the bay to carry out our
purpose."

  "That which you have just spoken is indeed reasonable," replied the Yakunin in gracious accents, " and, so
far as I am personally concerned, there would not be the
slightest objection to your seeing every thing.   But, as
you gentlemen well know, we are under strict orders
from the Bakufu to prevent all intrusion within this
cordon of boats about the ships.   It would be highly
presumptuous for me to attempt to instruct you gentlemen regarding the duty that devolves on a subordinate
to obey the orders of his superiors.   What can I do but
inform you that this is prohibited territory ? "

  " Well and honorably spoken, most dutiful officer," replied Tomokichi, readily inferring from that most dutiful
officer's tone and manner that much method lurked beneath his overwhelming sense of duty ; " but orders, as
you and I well know, in times of peace are not made of
stone, but admit of much judicious bending.   Had we
come before it was manifest that the barbarians meant
no harm to our country, then would we be guilty of supreme contempt of knightly honor in trying to induce
you to violate the letter of your instructions.   But your
orders were given many days ago when hostilities appeared imminent.   When every thing showed the peaceful nature of the intruders, you should have received
modified orders.   This matter has doubtless been overlooked. Undoubtedly you will receive less stringent

orders within a few days. However that may be, you undoubtedly feel convinced that your 'stone orders' need not be harshly and inflexibly applied under existing circumstances. Of course we will obey if you give the order to turn back ; but we cannot help thinking that the case is one of those rare emergencies where induce-ments may be legitimately offered and received. The night is dark and the other guard-boats will not see us,— or, if they do, they will take us for you, owing to the great similarity of our boats. We can prowl around the ships for a little while and then come out by this way. What think you, sir, of our suggestion ? "

" It is cleverly put, noble sirs," replied the dutiful official, fully comprehending the covert meaning of the broad suggestion, " but in a matter of such importance I must consult with my colleagues in the boat. If you will remain here a little while I will soon report our decision in the matter." So saying, he turned around and walked toward the gunwales and stepped over into his boat, where three *samurai* were standing on the quarter-deck waiting to hear the result of the interview.

"Who are the gentlemen ? " exclaimed they, addressing the Yakunin.

" Two *samurai* from Yedo," was the reply. " They are exceedingly anxious to see these barbarian ships and are travelling *nébon* in a fishing-boat that they hired in Yedo this morning."

" So far, so good," said a thick-set fellow whose coarse features and bleared eyes bespoke the voluptuary and the debauchee louder than words could have done, " but of course you notified them that this was pro-hibited territory. Furthermore, if your good sense did not forsake you, they were duly notified that it would cost them just four *rios* to get out of this pretty scrape into which their unbridled inquisitiveness had lured them. Eh ? "

" For shame, Yamagata ! " exclaimed a tall, genteel young man, whose reproachful countenance betokened his nobler nature. " Remember that we are dealing with *samurai* and not with vulgar fishermen. Courteous and knightly behavior is now in order."

"Well!" exclaimed Yamagata, utterly unabashed at his companion's rebuke, "you can't expect us fellows to mount guard these blustering nights without any prospect of a little fun when we go ashore. Even though they be *samurai*, they have no business to be prowling around here, and we are under strict orders to make things very disagreeable for such as they. Judging from their dress, it looks as if they could well afford to pay four *rios* for their little spree. That sum, you know, means one *rio* apiece for us ; and a *rio* means a night of very respectable and comfortable carouse in the Yoshiwara."

"While you two extremists are quarrelling," put in the third *samurai*, a plump morsel of sleek humanity who had not yet spoken, "I shall proceed to business by inquiring what our distinguished prisoners intend doing about this scrape ? They must take the initiative in the matter and offer some suggestion. Of course we must bear in mind the fact that they are knightly gentlemen and treat them accordingly ; but so doing does not imply that we should forego the perquisites of our position. They must be presumed to have come into this matter with open eyes. Unless they can show that they have just come from their cups they cannot expect us to endure our hardships for nothing. Truly a night in the Yoshiwara would be a fitting solace for some of our bleak vigils ! What word do they send to us, Sir Yakunin ?"

"They wish to say that, as the barbarian ships have shown a friendly spirit, and are upon good terms with the Bakufu, that there can be no reason why our 'stone orders' should not be made flexible for respectable *samurai* desirous of securing information, and they think that this is one of those rare occasions where inducements for us to waive a strict application of our instructions can be legitimately offered by them."

The student of human nature would surely have been edified at the variety of effects produced by this simple announcement. Yamagata's bleared eyes fairly glowed

with excitement, and he licked his heavy chops in anticipation of the forthcoming *rios.* " Ha ! ha ! " he exclaimed, in hoarse, guttural tones, " the question then
merely resolves itself into one of ' how much?' Four
rios to let them out of the scrape, and ten *rios* to let them
inspect the ships, is what I should say."

" I say the whole matter is too disreputable for us to
handle," said the genteel man, in disgusted tones. " I
move that we order them back home, with notice of
arrest in case they come again."

" Now don't you spoil our fun with your country
ideas," exclaimed the plump morsel of sleek humanity.
" When you have lived in Aidzu Yashiki another six
months, I promise you that it will not be my fault if you
be so squeamish. How can it be expected of *samurai* to
bear up under the hardships of their position without
occasional relaxation ? I vote to make the price ten *rios*
for release, and twenty-five *rios* for permission to inspect
the ships."

A long series of gurgling chuckles from the direction
of Yamagata announced that the hearty approval of that
gentleman was given to the amendment.

" It seems to me," said the Yakunin, in thoughtful
tones, " that you gentlemen have lost your heads over the
question of spoils. Perhaps these gentlemen are Bakufu
officials, trying to see whether we are faithfully fulfilling
orders. Their language and bearing indicate that they
are not ordinary *samurai.* And when the wind blew
open the folds of their sleeves, I perceived the Tokugawa
crest stamped thereon. They certainly are either government officials in disguise, or they belong to the
Gosanké. In the former case, we must warn them off.
In the latter case, we may negotiate for ' inducements,'
to permit an inspection of the ships. The way they
spoke about fresh orders coming from Yedo to relax the
severity of our surveillance, rather makes me fear that
they are government officials in disguise."

Again would the student of human nature have been
amused at the variety of effects produced by this last

announcement. The blear-eyed man muttered a fierce imprecation against the god of luck, and looked very much as if on the verge of a fit.

The genteel young man smiled resignedly.

The plump young man wore a most doleful countenance, and looked as if he were being dunned for a bill.

" In order to help us to decide this matter," continued the Yakunin, " I will call these two gentlemen over into our boat, and we will cautiously feel our way and arrive at some definite conclusion." So saying, he went over and brought them back.

" Honorable sirs," said the Yakunin, " you spoke of having come from Yedo this morning. Have you heard what the Gotairo intends doing in reference to these barbarian demands for a treaty ? "

" We regret our inability to give you the information that you seek," replied Tomokichi. " Although we live in Yedo, yet, being in no way connected with the government, we have no means of hearing of any thing new until such time as the government may choose to inform the public at large,—an occurrence that may not transpire for many days subsequent to an event."

This welcome intelligence produced a fresh cast of features among the four gentlemen. The Yakunin looked immensely relieved. The blear-eyed man burst into smiles. The genteel man looked very much interested. The plump morsel of humanity coughed significantly.

The ground now being open for negotiations, the Yakunin continued as follows : " Did I understand you gentlemen correctly when you spoke of certain inducements being offered for certain permission to inspect certain ships ? "

" You most certainly did so understand us," replied Tomokichi.

" Are you aware that you are tempting government officers to violate their duty ? " slyly suggested the plump young man in measured tones.

Tomokichi, who at once understood the tone and the shuffling gesture that accompanied it, turned to the

speaker, and replied : " I do not think that the government will care so much about your duty since the barbarians have conducted themselves in so friendly a
manner.   Besides this, you well know that ' inducements '
are winked at by the government, when their interests are
not jeopardized.   And how can it possibly jeopardize
government interests to allow two harmless *samurai* to
gratify their curiosity by inspecting barbarian ships on a
dark night ? "

Sure enough, how could it ?   That was a new idea for
them to consider.

" Never mind that matter," exclaimed the blear-eyed
man impatiently.   " Of course you know that you are in
our power for daring to approach as near as you have
done already.   Now what 's your price for our letting
you off ? "

" Oh ! We care nothing either about arrest or being
let off.   We do not care to offer inducements for matters
that are immaterial to us.   But we will do handsomely
by you if you will allow us to inspect the ships, for we do
care about that matter very much indeed."

This cool reply astonished and pleased the four officers
immeasurably.   After a short whispered consultation,
the Yakunin said :   " Well, if we allow your boat to
inspect the ships, you must not object to our boat following you at a short distance.   This is a very necessary
precaution."

" We shall have no objection to that," was the prompt
response.

" What say you to twenty-five *rios* for this extraordinary privilege that we are granting you ? " suggested the
plump young man.

" Of course, that is a very large sum of money,"
replied Tomokichi (who, by the way, had come prepared
to pay double and triple that sum if necessary), " but we
can meet you there."

" Call it twenty-five *rios* then," said the blear-eyed
man, nearly bursting with ill-suppressed emotion at
the prospect of an entire week's debauch in the Yoshi-

wara. "Pay the amount over to our commanding officer."

Accordingly the young spies accompanied the Yakunin to the cabin, where, by the light of a paper lantern, the gold coin was duly counted out and paid over. After this ceremony they were escorted with supreme respect to their own boat. The Bakufu boatmen then released their grip on the gunwales, the lanterns were put out, and the two boats (within easy hailing distance of each other) plunged into the gloom. The fleet comprised three ma-jestic steamers and four sailing vessels. The Mito boat went flitting around among the latter craft, and the young men inspected them to their hearts' content. These sailing frigates did not present, however, as many points of interest as the steamships. Accordingly our friends decided to spend the most of their time in examining the latter.

Their boat was therefore headed toward the mighty flagship of the squadron, the stately *Mississippi,* whose lofty masts and massive spars were destined nine years later to crumble into ashes while lighting up the dark waters of its namesake at Port Hudson. It stood out in the darkness like a magician's palace. Brilliant lights were swinging aloft amid the meshes of the rigging; the grim guns were trimmed for immediate action and thrust forth their iron mouths threateningly into the night ; long rows of port-holes shot forth shafts of light that fell glimmering and twinkling on the waves ; steam was being kept up, and clouds blacker than the hues of night rolled lazily out of the gloomy smoke-stack, and, mingling with the hissing steam, trailed seaward on the wings of the wind ; the shadowy guards were carelessly pacing the deck, and the uneasy wheels (as if trying to keep in practice) occasionally churned the waves with their broad blades ; while the vast hull, like some pant-ing thing of life,—some weird creation of the fancy,— fitfully rolled from larboard to starboard in the restless ground swell. The scene was indeed awe-inspiring, and the wonder-stricken fishermen hesitated to draw nigh unto the sleeping "volcano on the whale's back." So they prowled around in the deep shade abaft the stern. Being urged to advance closer, they finally slipped noiselessly and unobserved beneath the projecting quarter-deck and halted for a reconnoissance. Upon the planks overhead they heard the tramp, tramp, tramp, of the tireless watch ; beside them the colossal rudder creaked and moaned most dismally, as it helplessly writhed in the surging waves created by the swaying of the vessel from side to side ; and within the cavernous sides of the black monster they heard the boisterous merriment of some late convivial gathering.

Leaving the stern and creeping along the sides of the leviathan, they finally came to the frothing wheel and they were obliged to make a slight détour in order to pass that uneasy fin. Then they came to a square hole in the side of the vessel that had been left open for the purpose of allowing fresh air to pour into the stokers' room. The shutter opened outward, so that the captain of the boat was able to have a convenient place where to hold fast while he stood on tiptoe and gazed down into what seemed to him to be the mouth of hell and the portals to dens of iniquitous sorcery. He could not have been more amazed if he had been gazing down a square tunnel into the bowels of the earth.

Within there was a vast chamber lit up with the crackling, seething flames of perdition, such as the Buddhist temples in Mito pictured on their walls ! Huge black devils were firing up the furnaces for some carnival of horrible torment ! The gigantic fellows had monstrous bandanna hankerchiefs tied around their woolly heads, and the glaring ends of the cloths were knotted in front so as to stand out like glaring horns. Their white eyes rolled horribly, and their glistening teeth shone hideously, as they conversed in savage tones over their hellish work. Their bodies above and below the waist were bare, and the black skin glistened with streams of perspiration as they bent to their fearful task, gleefully swinging back the clanging doors of massive iron, and exultingly shovelling vast quantities of black stones into the fiery throats of gigantic furnaces that glowed so fiercely that the terrified fisherman would willingly have closed his eyes but for the absorbing fascination of the horrible scene. " This, then, is the root of the volcano ! " he muttered to himself, as he made way for his young masters, who long gazed in awe-stricken wonder and mute silence upon the weird scene, where the playful negroes were dancing and howling around the lurid furnaces in boisterous merriment over their work. Truly, the scene was one quite sufficient to have suggested demons revelling over some carnival of anguish in Hades ! Tomokichi finally drew a long breath and murmured : " I understand ! "

" What is it ? " whispered Junzo, as they crept onward toward the bow of the steamer.

" It is connected in some way with the making of watery vapor for moving the ship through the water. There is a scientific work at Mito Yashiki that fully explains the matter. But I do not understand the subject fully enough to go into details. How supremely hideous those black devils appeared ! Can it be possible that such beings exist in foreign countries ? "

The boat had now reached the bow of the flagship and was headed for the next steamer in the line. The fore-castle watch sighted them as they slipped away, but as they appeared to be moving off it was not deemed necessary to challenge what was considered to be a party of harmless sight-seers. The same tactics were followed when the next steamer was reached,—slipping under the stern and creeping along the side. Here they found one of the cabin port-holes open so that they could look into the stateroom of one of the officers.

Now that particular officer happened to be the second lieutenant, who had a very peculiar and inveterate habit of always washing his hands with scented soap just before retiring to rest for the night. Precisely what hygienic principle lurked beneath this idiosyncrasy no one had ever been able to ascertain,—not even after a purloined cake of the soap had been subjected to a chemical analysis. He had been twitted and teased most unmercifully by his messmates about his peculiar habit, but to no purpose except to make him sensitive and irritable. They had nicknamed him Pontius Pilate, not merely because he washed his hands at unseasonable hours, but because they intended to ungenerously intimate that his nightly fetich signified that he washed his hands of the daily iniquities of his sinful messmates. Now, it happened on this particular evening that this particularly particular young gentleman was engaged in his ablutions just as the grinning head of the Mito captain peered into the port-hole of his stateroom. He was standing in his night-dress before the tin wash-bowl from whose foaming suds he had just lifted his dripping hands in order to dry them on the towel. Looking up and turning around, he beheld the smiling features in the port-hole. Without stopping to think, he at once surmised this intrusion to be another trick of his tormentors, and immediately resented the insult by dashing the contents of the basin into the face of the intruder. The soapy emulsion went into the eyes of the luckless fisherman, causing him to howl and to drop with great noise from the ratlines down into the boat. This disturbance roused the deck watch to a realizing sense of their duty. And then was enacted the second scene of the comedy.

It seemed that the vessels of the fleet had frequently been annoyed by sight-seers prowling around at night. Uncouth heads had frequently appeared at port-holes and windows, causing annoyance to the officers, and amusement to the sailors. On several occasions, venturesome spies had even climbed up the chains to the deck, in order to view things more fully. Consequently, strict orders had been given to keep all boats off at a respectful distance, but to inflict no injury (if possible to avoid doing so). The precise methods to be employed in carrying out these orders had been left pretty much to the discretion of the crew. The American tar, when left to his own resources, rarely displays any lack of ingenuity, and invariably rises quite equal to any situation requiring diplomatic *finesse.* In the China ports, the favorite method employed had been to hurl lumps of coal and sundry superannuated eggs, accompanied by potatoes in advanced stages of dissolution, upon the heads of the thieving Chinamen prowling about the vessels.

But such heroic treatment was deemed too harsh for the amiable natives of Dai-Nippon. Jack, however, did not long puzzle his head over what specific to employ for the case in hand. During the daytime he found that a shake of his tatooed fist was quite sufficient to head off the most venturesome intruder. But at nighttime he found that such mild treatment was of no avail. Accordingly, he would clandestinely fill up during the day half-a-dozen or so of buckets with swill, collected from the galley barrel, and secrete them in divers nooks and corners about the forecastle. This unofficial proceeding, of course, defrauded the swine of their just allowance of rations, for the crafty tars filled up the barrel with water, and thus foisted on the helpless porkers some highly diluted diet. Well, well, all that is neither here nor there. Suffice it to say that when the disturbance occurred on this particular evening the boat had sped forward and was below the forecastle chains when the grinning faces of the forward watch peered over the sides of the vessel to view the situation. "Lay 'em aboard, my hearties!" was the laconic order overhead. Then down came a deluge such as our cheerful fishermen had never experienced in all of their years of battling with the elements, and it was a deluge that well-nigh swamped the boat.

Pure, undiluted swill, such as the hearts and the stomachs of the aforesaid hogs had been yearning after, constituted the prime ingredient of that downpour. Masses of soaked bread, huge lumps of hardtack, and disgustingly mushy biscuits formed a few of the interesting items. Yards upon yards of potato peelings, hosts of cabbage leaves, muddy coffee-grounds by the jugful, and the prosaic odds and ends of hash, puddings, and pies, were a few other articles that served to eliminate the last vestige of romance from the situation. The decks of the boat betwixt the after cabin and the forecastle was turned into a condition of nameless horror much resembling a pig trough,—a scene that would have rendered the luckless swine frantic with resentment at such prodigal waste of their food. Tomokichi, Junzo, and the four scullers were but slightly spattered with this avalanche, as they happened to be astern. But the remainder of the crew came in for full dividends.

The gleeful chucklings from above grew rapidly fainter as the unhappy fishermen fled in wild haste. This mirth was not appreciated nor in any way entered into by the crew until they began to unwind long festoons of potato peelings entwined about their necks, and to skate around on the decks on oranges and quarter loaves of bread. Then the humor of the situation dawned upon all of them (especially those astern), and they indulged in immoderate laughter. They soon met the guard-boat, and were duly escorted beyond the cordon of boats. Then they rushed homeward. The crew whiled away the time by removing the débris from the decks, and in picking dough and mush out of hair, eyes, and ears. On the whole, they voted it a very jolly thing to shadow the barbarian ships in the dusky night,—but they unanimously hoped that there might not be another such an expedition very soon. On the morrow they were kept very busy cleaning the boat and in bailing out the swill that had flowed into the cabin, the forecastle, and the storeroom amidships. Many of the articles fished out of the boat created much lively comment, and Tomokichi was constrained to confess that no scientific work at Mito Yashiki, so far as he knew, could throw any light on their nomenclature.

CHAPTER XV.

AFTER the events narrated in the last chapter our young friends began to consider the advisability of turning the prow of their boat homeward. They had acquired about all the information possible to be gathered under the conditions whereunder they were conducting their investigations ; yet they were loath to quit the waters of the bay, and they lingered day after day, as if fascinated by the novelty and by the danger of their surroundings. They did not again attempt to make a close inspection of the vessels ; but hardly a day passed without their boat being seen hovering about outside of the cordon of guard-boats watching with profoundest interest the minutest manœuvres of fleet and crew,—for the experiences of that night of shadowing had filled their bosoms with the sincerest respect for every thing pertaining to the foreigners and their mysterious vessels. After a week thus spent they reluctantly came to the conclusion that no adequate reason existed for any further delay, and that both duty and prudence required their speedy departure from the place. Accordingly, they issued orders to have the boat put in readiness for the return voyage.

On the afternoon of the day preceding that of their intended departure, Tomokichi was busily engaged in entering in his little book copious notes and comments concerning the " barbarians," and, as he appeared to be settled down for several hours of steady work, Junzo decided to stroll up the path that zigzagged up the cliff and to walk along the tops of the hills and to take a last

look at the stately squadron riding at anchor to the northward. The day was warm and bright, and, after taking
another look at the boat to see if the preparations for
departure had been properly made, he leisurely followed
the cliff path in its windings through underbrush and
thicket until it finally emerged at the summit. There he
tarried awhile to gaze upon the picturesque hamlet nest-
ling peacefully on the white sands, and to sweep with his
eyes the broad expanse of blue waves that stretched away
to the distant shores. Then, resuming his course, he
took the path through the woods and finally emerged at
a clearing on a hill-top which overlooked that portion of
the bay where the ships lay uneasily champing at the
cables that fretted their iron mouths. The site was covered with grass and was ornamented with a little wooden
shrine in honor of *Ebisu*, the ubiquitous god of fishermen. The little fat fellow was peeping out from behind
some wooden bars, and was gazing stupidly on the beautiful scene with eyes begrimed with the smoking incense
that many decades of votaries had placed beneath his
very nostrils. The shrine belonged to the circuit of a
large Buddhist monastery situated many miles back
among the hills, and whose priests came hither on fête-
days to perform ceremonies and to receive the offerings
of the simple-minded denizens of the coast.

On this particular afternoon there was nobody there.
The only visitor that day had been an old woman from
some hamlet along the shore, who had journeyed thither
to burn incense and to beseech good-natured *Ebisu* to
bring back her son who had been too long away on a
fishing excursion. The place was indeed too lovely for
any thing but peace and happiness. Yet inexorable fate
had marked it for the scene of a tragedy to be speedily
enacted thereon.

That very day, a *samurai*, wearing on his sleeves the
Tokugawa crest, had left a fishing hamlet some miles
northward, and had been diligently making a tour of
every fishing village and hamlet that lay in his way as he
journeyed southward. At each place visited he sought

out the headman of the village or hamlet, and imperi-
ously demanded whether there were any strangers
within his jurisdiction, or whether any had recently been
there. He had received various replies to his enquiries,
but in no case did he seem to secure the information
which he desired. It was not until he came to the hamlet just to the north of the one where our friends were
sojourning that his eyes brightened as he was informed
that there were several strangers in the next hamlet, and
that among them were two gentlemen who appeared to
be *samurai.* When he was informed that these gentlemen claimed to be Bakufu officials acting as shore-
guards, he drew forth from his sleeve a book that he
spent several minutes in thoughtfully consulting. Then,
with the eagerness of a bloodhound that has caught the
scent, he tapped his forehead and hastily continued his
journey along the shore.

The path soon left the beach and wound up through
woods to the top of the hill where stuffy old *Ebisu* held
his dreary vigil. Junzo had been there nearly two hours
and was just beginning to think about returning to his
quarters in the hamlet, when he heard somebody coming
through the thickets near where he was sitting on a grassy
knoll. His first impulse was to slip behind the shrine
and hide himself from view. But long immunity from
alarm had rendered him somewhat reckless, and he
furthermore reflected that it might be only a fisherman
coming to worship at the shrine, and that it would be
very undignified for a *samurai* to be found skulking behind it. He therefore boldly held his ground and fearlessly awaited the approach of the stranger.

There was a swaying of the bushes, a few labored puffs
for breath, the crackling of twigs, and the falling of loose
stones down the steep hill—and then the climber
emerged panting from the woods and stood facing Junzo
Nakashima. A hasty glance at each other's faces, and
the recognition was mutual and instantaneous. Junzo
had met this stalwart *samurai* on several occasions hovering around the precincts of Mito Yashiki during the

winter, and knew him to be the most adroit, the most fearless, and the most merciless bloodhound in the secret service of the Shogun's government. He was the most successful and the most dreaded of all the swarms of spies that flitted like bats and owls around the latticed windows of every suspected Yashiki in Yedo. This man had dared to enter Satsuma on the heels of a score of other spies, who had perished there, and had returned alive ! Junzo's heart stood still. The very blood in his veins seemed turning to ice. He required no sooth-sayer to tell him that this dreaded sleuth-hound had been on his track and had finally hunted him down. While his physical powers seemed benumbed with mortal fear, his mental powers worked with unwonted activity, and there flashed through his brain within the space of but a moment of time a course of action that will take long for my slow pen to describe and which his quick brain would have but slowly evolved under ordinary circumstances. It is at such supreme crises that noble spirits soar above physical frailties and seem to imbibe inspired powers from mysterious sources in the very atmosphere.

From remotest times in the history of mankind, there has been but one fate reserved for the detected spy,— *death !* Junzo fully realized that he was caught in the very act. He well knew that this dreaded fellow had doubtless been on his track for many months, had noted his absence from Mito Yashiki, and had probably been delegated to run him down. He well knew that from the native standpoint his guilt was clearly proven ; that while the gentleman before him might smile and affably greet him in friendly conversation (which he seemed quite disposed to do), yet that on the return of his brother and himself to Yedo, their bodies would be de-manded by the terrible Gotairo in the name of the Sho-gun, and would be put to terrible torture in order to force the disclosure of presumed accomplices, and would finally be subjected to ignominious and horrible muti-lation.

Unlucky Junzo well knew that both he and his brother

were in the dread power of this terrible man who stood there with unruffled features and serene countenance as if ready to enter upon a most amicable interview. Then there rushed over him the shame and the humiliation of having failed in a grand enterprise almost consummated. He seemed to see the sorrowful and the reproachful countenances of his Mito friends. And there rose the vision of a hamlet in a glen and a bereaved family mourning over two sons cut down on the threshold of life and perishing in ignominy and shame. It was then that the numbness left his arms, that the chill fled from his veins, that the heart leaped and bore on its angry floods up to the ready brain a fierce, a desperate, a murderous resolve. The Bakufu spy must die then and there! Spy had met spy, and war to the death must ensue! No mercy! No quarter! This was his only salvation! There would be no witnesses to the scene. Escape for the Bakufu spy was impossible, as he could not fly through the tangled woods without exposing his back to his adversary's deadly blade, nor could he leap over the cliff without meeting with sure death. He was completely entrapped, and must fight out the issue in a lonely spot far away from human habitations.

Even in such an emergency the true *samurai* abides by his notions of chivalric honor and does things in accordance with prescribed rules and ceremony. Instead of drawing his sword at once on his adversary so as to take him unawares, Junzo quietly threw his loose garments back first from his right shoulder and then from his left shoulder, thus leaving his body bare down to the waist. Then deliberately drawing his long, sharp sword and pointing it downward into the green turf, he looked steadily into the eyes of his adversary.

His enemy knew full well the meaning of this action, and the color left his cheeks an instant as he realized that he must now try the mortal issue with a person whom he already knew to be the most expert swordsman in Mito Yashiki. He glanced furtively around to see if any avenue of escape remained open. He saw that he was completely shut in. But why fear this young man ? True he was very expert with the sword, but were not experience and endurance on his side ? And was he not also an adept in the use of the blade ? Had he not slain twenty men in his venturesome career ? Had he not met at a hotel in Satsuma three of the deadliest swordsmen in that clan, and had he not dashed out the light when they attacked him, and knelt upon the *tatamis*, and cut them all down while groping about the room in the dark, sweeping the air over his head with their swords ? Had he not met single-handed some of the best blades in the Yedo *yashikis* during his various adventures, and had he not come off victor ? Why then fear this country-bred youth from Atago-Yama, now about to engage in his first mortal combat, and who probably would fight in strict accordance with the ceremonious methods drilled into him by his punctilious father, and who would probably not resort to the tricky methods so well known and so unscrupulously employed by himself ?

Thus bracing himself up with a *résumé* of his deeds of valor, and remembering the many tight places out of which he had adroitly crawled during his extraordinary career, he proceeded not only to throw off his upper garments, but also his lower ones, and stood forth with merely a clout about his loins and sandals on his feet. This was his first unfair trick, for, when Junzo began to make motions as if to disrobe himself in a similar fashion in order to secure agility equal to that of his wily antagonist, the sly scoundrel at once advanced to the attack and compelled him to fight with his lower limbs hampered with frock-like *hakamas*. Junzo deftly parried his adversary's blow, and, kicking off his wooden clogs, fought in his stockings. Truly it was a weird sight ! The nervous tremor that falls upon the hands for the first time raised to destroy the life of a fellow-being had completely fled, and the small hands of our young friend closed upon the hilt of his weapon with a firm and dextrous grip, while the steady fire in his eyes bespoke his deadly purpose and dauntless courage in language far more effective than reams of Homeric verses could have done. With his shaven head and jet-black top-knot, together with his clumsy petticoats, you might well have taken him for some heathen goddess pirouetting over the greensward with some savage partner,—for the brown body of the spy, glistening like that of an eel in the sunlight, twisted itself into all manner of shapes as he whirled around his adversary delivering cuts with the rapidity of lightning.

It was about four o'clock in the afternoon and the western sun was in a position to greatly annoy that swordsman who had to face it. It is needless to say that the cunning spy speedily noted this fact and got into a position where his back was toward it. Matters thus opened very inauspiciously for our young friend. He advanced, however, undaunted to the attack, and by a few quick and skilful passes soon compelled his enemy to abandon his vantage-ground and to turn sideways toward the sun ; and from that time onward to the close of the combat they shifted their positions all over the greensward, so that each one took his turn in facing the sun.

For the first ten minutes, neither party gained any decided advantage. The spy was indeed a powerful and a skillful swordsman, and in the opening attacks it required all of Junzo's agility and skill to ward off the terrible blows that poured down like hail. He had resolved to let his antagonist do all of the fighting at first, in order that he might study his style of fencing, and also to allow him to become tired with his tremendous exertions and thus neutralize the agility derived from his nude condition. For the next ten minutes, however, he pressed the fighting more vigorously and followed the spy all over the grounds.

Then came a quarter of an hour of exceedingly bitter and vigorous fencing, wherein each combatant displayed wonderful skill and power. It now became manifest that the younger man had thoroughly mastered the elder one's style, so that victory could only come to the latter either from the exhaustion of his adversary or from some accident befalling him. Then came a period of slower and more cautious warfare, for Junzo had perceived that his adversary was continually edging over to the path by which he had climbed up, and it was manifest that his intention was to seize a favorable opportunity and leap to one side and rush down the hill, where his escape would be very easy, inasmuch as his youthful foe's long flowing garments would catch in the underbrush and check most effectually his pursuit. It required no small amount of skill and patience to guard against this contingency.

Then came an incident that well-nigh brought the fight to an abrupt and unexpected termination. The spy, despairing of slipping out of the fatal arena, suddenly picked up one of the heavy wooden clogs that his adversary had kicked off at the commencement of hostilities, and hurled it most unexpectedly into his face, striking him heavily on the forehead therewith. He followed up this unfair advantage with a terrific onslaught. For a moment it seemed as if the game was up for our brave young friend. He staggered back and nearly fell down on the slippery grass. That backward movement, however, saved his life, for the blows that followed up his demoralization all fell short of the mark and wounded him but slightly in the leg and on the shoulder ; and, before the treacherous knave could follow up his advantage, his antagonist had recovered from the effect of the stunning blow.

But it is a long lane that has no turn. The combatants had now been fighting for nearly an hour, and the advantage seemed to be with the Bakufu man. He had, however, in his violent efforts to force the fighting, nearly exhausted himself, and, although he had inflicted two wounds on his adversary, they were of so slight a character as to be quite harmless. On the other hand, he had awakened a spirit of savage vindictiveness in his adversary that seemed to add fresh strength to his youthful arms and to intensify the vigor of his attacks. He made one more attempt to escape by the path, and then edged over slowly toward a large stone, which he hoped to be able to pick up and to repeat therewith his previous tactics. But his design was frustrated by his wiry antagonist, who now seemed transformed into a perfect demon, and who fought with a ferocity and an energy incredible. Hereditary aptitude and a lifetime of training were fused together in white heat, and blow followed blow with bewildering celerity until the ringing of the blades made one continued clangor. The spy retreated slowly to the middle of the open space near the shrine, and fought on the strict defensive for several minutes. Then there was a sudden cessation of turmoil, and the stalwart Bakufu man threw up his arms and fell backward. Junzo's blade had at last reached solid flesh, and had cut through his foeman's abdomen from right to left, severing the great veins and arteries of that region at one fell stroke. It was his favorite cut, and it was one that he had been holding in reserve to use at an unexpected moment.

There are six cuts and one thrust known to Japanese fencers. Cut straight down for the head ; cut obliquely at the left shoulder ; cut across the left side, bending your right knee in order to give delivery thereto : *recover position ;* cut again for the head ; cut obliquely at the right shoulder ; cut across the right side, bending the left knee : *recover position ;* draw the hilt of the sword close up to your chest and lunge forward with both hands at the breast. These cuts, like the rules of war, are certainly simple enough ; but in their combinations and application there is room for boundless skill and complexity. The right-handed man will naturally cut across his adversary's abdomen from left to right with far more readiness than from right to left. But Junzo had learned to cut from either direction with equal celerity. In this fight he had continually delivered the stroke from left to right, in order to lead his adversary to suppose that he could not deliver the reverse cut from right to left with equal skill. And when the supreme moment had, in his opinion, arrived, he feinted as if to deliver his regular left-side abdominal cut, and then with marvellous dexterity reversed the stroke and came in upon the unguarded right side of his enemy with the full sweep of a powerful cut delivered with both hands upon the soft tissues of a bare body. The result was horrible. The hideous gash reached across the body, and the contents of the abdominal cavity gushed forth through the ghastly fissure. The stalwart warrior survived but a moment. The grass became deluged with blood, the hands stretched out convulsively for the fallen sword, the feet were spasmodically drawn up, and the gurglings in the throat announced that the end had come, and that the secrets locked up in his bosom would never disturb his adversary.

Junzo stood for several minutes as if spellbound with horror gazing on his dead enemy. Then he proceeded to a little spring near the shrine and washed the blood from his blade and carefully sheathed it. He then grasped his enemy by the heels and dragged him far into the thickets. The sword and the clothes he hid away carefully in the underbrush, after having removed from the grass every possible trace of the bloody fray. Then he washed off his own wounds and proceeded to dress himself. It was quite dusk when he found his way back into the hamlet, where his brother with great anxiety awaited his return. It did not take long to explain matters to him. His admiration and astonishment were unbounded. His brother's prowess had indeed saved their lives, for the spy never trusted any matter to paper nor to third parties, so that the results of his investigations since leaving Yedo died with him, and they could slip back to Yedo long before any discovery could possibly be made (if any ever were made) as to his fate, for it was always expected that when these creatures started out on their secret tours they would take their own time and adopt whatever methods seemed best to them. And then who would ever think of connecting their purported absence in Mito with a murderous combat down on Yedo Bay?

But no time was to be lost ! They must be off that very evening. Calling their boatmen, they at once issued orders to embark, saying that an accidental tumble down the cliff path had rendered it necessary for Junzo to consult medical advisers in Mito,—a statement which appeared plausible enough when his lumpy forehead and limping gait were considered. Hastily settling up their accounts with the village people, they started off in the dark and had gone well up the coast before daylight. Junzo lay quite ill for two days. The feverish reaction, however, was soon blown away by the southwest monsoon before which they were gayly scudding homeward. So fair was the breeze, and so steadily did the crew keep to their work, that they took but five days to make the trip back to Mito ; and when the keel of their boat slid up the sands near the villa, our young adventurers looked none the worse for their experience. Hurrying on to the stables, they hastily mounted the nags that awaited them there, and were back in Mito Yashiki safe and sound on the evening of the fourth day after leaving the sea-shore villa.

CHAPTER XVI.

A CONVOCATION AT THE CITADEL.

Soon after the return of our young friends to Mito Yashiki, there was a grand convocation of the Daimios, called by the Gotairo in the name of his master, the Shogun Iyésada. They were convened to discuss the ratification of the great treaty made with Commodore Perry, whereby certain commercial privileges were to be granted to the Americans, and wherein it was stipulated that two seaports were to be thrown open to the vessels of that country. The council-chambers of the Shogun's palace, within the innermost moat, had been placed in readiness to receive the assembly, and special guards of honor had been placed at all the gates of the castle to receive with due ceremony the pompous trains of lords, who flocked from all parts of Yedo to participate in the momentous debate. The very cherry blossoms that bloomed in myriad clusters throughout the royal gardens appeared to be in a flutter of excitement, and profusely showered their snowy petals upon the well gravelled avenues and over the velvety lawns. The council-chambers opened out upon the beautiful gardens, and a host of servants in their best attire were flitting about perfecting the arrangements for receiving their master's guests with the befitting and comforting " pomp and circumstance " of tea and tobacco, in order that the debate might be alternately stimulated and soothed. The great terror that had seized upon the city when the fleet first appeared, had subsided as soon as the amicable disposition of the strangers had become manifest. But there yet pervaded both *yashiki* and mart a feeling of subdued but most intense excitement. A political volcano indeed slumbered beneath the very feet of the people.

At about ten o'clock in the morning, the various retinues began to sally forth from the gateways of the various *yashikis*, and to wend their way toward the citadel. At the second moat the lords were obliged to alight from their *norimons*, and to enter the citadel enclosure with but a few personal attendants, who escorted them to the commodious anterooms to await the signal that should announce to them the fact that they were to be ushered into the council-chambers. Every thing was done with utmost decorum and with the utmost deliberation. There was an utter absence of turmoil and confusion, and the groups of dignitaries were silently ushered in by the attendants, who glided about like well-oiled machines, manipulating the preliminaries of some state funeral. No salutes were fired, no trumpets gave tongue to their inspiring notes, no cheers from the spectators awoke the drowsy proceedings. Each Daimio was courteously received at the gateway of the palace by an attendant, who slowly walked ahead of him down the long corridor, while a page, carrying his lordship's sword (hilt upward), brought up the rear. Like shadows they looked as triplet after triplet steadily and stealthily followed each other with noiseless tread down the long corridors toward the waiting-rooms, where each lord silently knelt upon the cushion assigned to him, while his page stood behind him with upheld sword.

Toward midday the anterooms had become well filled with a silent and expectant throng, that awaited the Gotairo's arrival with meek quiescence and decorous patience. As yet that important personage had not left his *yashiki* near the western entrance to the Shogun's parks. He tarried there with his councillors, worrying over some diplomatic point involved in the treaty. At last light broke upon their perplexity, and the order was given for the *norimon* to be brought to the door, and for his Lordship's retinue to be in readiness for immediate departure. Finally his Lordship emerged from the massive doorway of his mansion ; his bearers prostrated themselves in the dust at his feet ; his retainers did unto him profound obeisance ; and, entering his elegantly lacquered vehicle, he gave the command to start. Slowly the train moved across the courtyard and out through the main gateway, upon the broad road that skirted the moat. Following it for a short distance to the left, they came to the Hanzo Gate that led within the Shogun's park. They were not to enter here, but were to turn to the right, and follow the edge of the moat down the hill until they came to the Sakurada Gate.

It will therefore appear that the main gateway of the Gotairo's *yashiki* stood nearly opposite to the upper gate that furnished ingress to the royal park. In ancient times this entire locality was the crown of a hill ; but when the castle was constructed it was deemed best to carry the second system of circumvallation right through the hill. Accordingly the indefatigable architects dug their way through the very foundations of the bluff, leaving only a narrow causeway in front of the gate, thus making one of those mighty cuttings for which Yedo Castle was so justly famous, and leaving the two gateways to ogle each other across the intervening ravine. The precipitous sides of this cutting were well swarded, and the deep, broad waters of the moat beneath were filled with water-lilies and lotus-flowers, amid which the wild fowl from northern lakes sported unmolested during the winter months. The opposite side of the steep embankment was fringed along its top with stone ramparts, upon which were planted pine-trees, whose green boughs showered needle-leaves and long resinous cones upon hillside and water, startling the wayward teal with their rustlings and splashings as they slid down into the waves.

The long retinue of Nawosŭké, Lord of Hikoné, turned aside from the lofty causeway and marched leisurely down the hill and entered the Sakurada Gate by means of a fragile wooden bridge thrown across the moat at that point. The procession was not a very imposing one, for his Lordship was a man of simple habits, loving decisive action above all things, and having but little regard for pompous display. At the head of his procession stalked a retainer who bore aloft on a long pole the black tufted tassel that betokened the rank of a Daimio of the realm. Then came other retainers bearing aloft the heraldic insignia that betokened the approach of the Lord of Hikoné, whom it had pleased the Shogun to constitute the Gotairo (or Prince Regent, as foreigners were accustomed to designate him). Then came some mailed warriors on horseback, followed by some spearmen and archers. Then came the *norimon* of his Highness, borne on the shoulders of eight coolies, and surrounded by a body-guard of stately *samurai* in full regalia costume. And the rear was brought up by a score of armed horsemen.

The entire procession did not comprise over two hundred men. But what cared his Highness for display? Was not he the actual ruler of the "Empire of the Gods"? Were not the barracks of his *yashiki* bristling with warriors? Did not twenty thousand trusty retainers await his commands at Hikoné Castle, on the distant shores of Biwa Lake? And did not eighty thousand armed Hattomotos, enrolled under the Shogun's banners, await the beck and call of Nawosŭké, Lord of Hikoné, Prince Regent of the realm? Why, then, with the forces of the realm in his hand, should he waste money on useless pomp? Thus reasoned the active and energetic mind of the Gotairo. Through the Sakurada Gate, across the broad parade ground, over the innermost moat, and into the private grounds of the Shogun's palace, swept the train that escorted his Highness, until the main entrance of his master's mansion had been reached, when the order to halt was given, and the cramped figure of his Lordship crept out of the comfortless *norimon* and stood beside the massive portals of the vestibule.

"Honorable Miyoshi," said the Gotairo in a low tone addressing one of his attendants, "command the gen-

tlemen and the bearers to return here when the shadow
of the sun-dial indicates the hour of sunset. In the
meantime they can make themselves as comfortable as
possible in the barracks beside the Exalted Gateway. It
is likely that our session will be a very protracted one."
So saying, he mounted the steps that led up to the
veranda, and then, with his councillors, passed down the
long corridor that led to the private apartments of his
master, the Shogun, in order that he might present his
respects, and also might make arrangements for the interview with the Daimios. The timid and delicate young
man before whom he and his councillors prostrated
themselves in the reception chamber of the " Barbarian
Exterminating Lord," did not much resemble the enshrined majesty held up to the gaze of the outside world
by the astute Bakufu officials,—a majesty so dread that
ambassadors and Daimios must creep into his sacred
presence on hands and knees without venturing to gaze
thereon ! Thus, in all countries do courtiers and syco-
phants pull the strings that manipulate the puppets in
whose hands the destinies of empires are presumed to
be held.

" Profoundly venerated and dreadsome sir," said the
Gotairo, after the preliminary ceremonies had been concluded, " we, your silly and incapable servants are ready
to make report to the Daimios, as to what course should
be pursued in regard to these foreigners who have vexed
the minds of the people so persistently during the last
seven or eight months."

" I have no doubt that your able report will be satisfactory, and that the solution of the difficulty therein
suggested will pacify the hearts of the people, and will
comfort the imperial bosom, thus immeasurably gratifying
and quieting my greatly perplexed mind," slowly and
hesitatingly replied Iyésada. " When I was advised to
appoint the Lord of Hikoné as my prime-minister, I was
informed that no abler vassal dwelt within the domain
of Tokugawa. Since your appointment I have had no
occasion to distrust either the loyalty or the astuteness

of your honored self. Learned sir, kindly unfold your plans without reserve, and take full charge of the august assemblage of my vassals, now gathered in this palace."

"Your unworthy servants," replied the Gotairo, "would suggest that our Lord take his place behind the screen in the alcove of the audience-hall, where his presence, not being noted, can not overawe the timorous vassals there assembled. We will sit in front of the screen, and will conduct the deliberation of the Daimios. Your Majesty will then hear all about our plans, and can whisper to us through the bamboo gauzework in the screen any question that may suggest itself to your mind, and we will write out our answers thereto and clandestinely slip the notes under the screen. Such is the humble suggestion that awaits your approval."

"Your suggestion is a wise one, and I will now authorize its immediate adoption," replied Iyésada. "Do that which you deem advisable. Affairs are now entirely in your hands. Order whatever you may wish the attendants to do without consulting further with myself. I shall now proceed to the alcove, and will there await further developments."

So saying, the ruler of the Japanese empire quietly slipped out of the room, leaving the Gotairo to do whatever might seem wise in his own eyes. And his Lordship did not hesitate to seize the reins with a firm grip. Clapping his hands, to summon an attendant, he ordered that personage, when he had put in an appearance, to instruct the ushers to marshal the Daimios in the audience-hall according to rank, and then to bring him word when every thing was ready for opening the convention. Another attendant then brought in tea and tobacco for the councillors to discuss while matters were converging toward a focus. Then some ink and paper were called for, and his Lordship busied himself with writing for the space of half an hour, until the obsequious attendants announced that the assembled Daimios awaited his pleasure. He then proceeded with his suite through a labyrinth of apartments and corridors until he came to

the stately chamber where the assembly had been convened,—a fact that was heralded by the subdued humming of many voices.

At one end of the hall was a platform raised about one
foot from the floor. This place was for the presiding
officer and his suite. To the left of this platform was
the screened alcove already alluded to. Around upon
the main floor of the hall were sitting about two hundred persons, constituting the great Daimios of the realm
and their personal attendants. They had been provided
with silken cushions, on which they knelt, and then sat
upon their heels in the peculiar manner characteristic
of the country. The *shojee* beside the platform was
slid gently back, and the Gotairo with his suite glided in
and seated themselves upon the embroidered cushions
that had been arranged there on the soft *tatamis.* When
these gentlemen had taken their seats they were the recipients of profound and profuse salutations from the
assembly, which compliments they duly returned with
salutations equally profound. After the waves of
obeisances had subsided, the Gotairo made an address,
which, if it had been condensed in terse English, would
not have taken up more than five minutes of time ; but
which, when inflated with continual bowing and sucking
in of the breath between the teeth, together with endless
circumlocutory expressions, padded to death with hon-
orific verbiage, occupied twenty-five minutes of time.
His remarks, when condensed in shockingly abrupt English, were about as follows :

"I, the insignificant and utterly unworthy servant of
the Shogun (the mighty power of whose ancestors has
smitten barbarians with abject fear for many centuries,
thereby giving peace and consolation to the imperial
bosom), have been appointed (although but a creature
of lowly rank) by the mighty Lord of Dai-Nippon to
lay before the noble vassals of the realm here convened
a matter of vast importance, and also one that will require much careful and profound investigation. After
the matter has been fully laid before you, it is the wish

of my master that you freely discuss the questions involved in so momentous a subject, so that he may be benefited and soothed with whatever valuable suggestions there may be garnered in the matured minds of thoughtful and learned vassals here convened in awesome assemblage.

"You, honored sirs, well know that last year there appeared on our coasts four ships belonging to a barbarian nation beyond some distant seas. As you have already been informed, these intruding people, with boundless arrogance and defiance, even ventured to push the prows of their ships far into the waters of our own bay,—hitherto unmolested by outside barbarians,—thus openly violating the edicts of Tokugawa Iyéyas, at which the nations of the earth have trembled for over two hundred years, and by which a profound peace has been caused to settle down upon our agitated country like heavy mists upon a mountain. Being warned to leave our waters, these barbarians persisted in remaining; and, furthermore, they insisted upon making personal delivery of a letter from the ruler of their nation to the ruler of our nation. With unparalleled impudence they refused to hand over that epistle to a *yakunin*, but they insisted on our delegating a lord of the realm to be the person upon whom they would be satisfied to make what they deemed a suitable service.

"So greatly had the country become alarmed by this unexpected advent of the barbarians, and so utterly unprepared were we to repel the intrusion by force, that we deemed it advisable then in convention to humor them in their whim, and to allow them to depart in peace. But with yet greater assurance they notified us that they would return in the spring, in order to receive our answer to their letter. And they have shown themselves to be as good as their word, for last month they again put in an appearance, and clamored most persistently and menacingly for our reply. They have rendered the situation more awkward by returning with a fleet containing twice as many vessels as were in their previous fleet. You already are familiar with the contents of that letter. Upon its reception by the worshipful and mighty Iyéyoshi last summer, he laid it before you in council. At that time I was a member of the assembly,—not yet having been appointed as servant to our puissant lord. I then counselled delay in the matter and a friendly answer, which advice the great Lord of Nippon did me the overwhelming honor to accept. But, in the meantime, momentous changes have transpired. Our Lord Iyéyoshi, soon after his friendly message to the barbarians, fell grievously ill of some mysterious malady, and entered upon the shadowy way, so that his office devolved upon our present master, the gracious and supreme Lord Iyésada, who has seen fit to constitute me to be his right hand.

"And now, gentlemen of the *Gosanké*, and of the Daimiates, what shall we do with this letter? You perceive that it is directed to the 'Ruler' of the Japanese empire, and not to the supreme and Imperial Majesty that has dwelt unseen within the sacred precincts of the Gosho for over one thousand years. Although the fountain of honors has dwelt in such prolonged seclusion within the imperial moats in Kioto, yet the Shoguns have been delegated by the invisible majesty of sovereignty to perform the functions of a ruler, and to see to it that the empire was well governed. For nearly three hundred years has the house of Tokugawa acted as rulers of Dai-Nippon, having been duly delegated by the Son of Heaven to act in that capacity. As the properly constituted and the legal rulers of this empire, it therefore falls within our province to take under consideration this letter, inasmuch as all matters relating to commerce, and all matters relating to the regulation ot intercourse with barbarians were duly delegated to Iyéyas and his descendants, when he drove forth the pestiferous *Kirishitans* and received the title of 'Barbarian Exterminating Lord' from grateful *Tenshi*.

"The question, then, is this: Shall the Shogun, the duly delegated ruler of Dai-Nippon, reconsider the action of his great ancestor, and change or modify his policy as regards the total exclusion of the barbarians ? We must first act and then report our action to Kioto, for *Tenshi* has already given us authority to act as rulers in such matters. Gentlemen of resplendent ancestry ! shall we attempt to drive away these barbarians by force, or shall we accede to their demands and allow their vessels to trade freely at two of our seaports under strict regulations ? There is no middle position that we can take in this matter, for we have already exhausted their patience with the dallying policy recommended by this august assembly when convened in such haste last summer, and these people are now surly and peremptory in their demands, although wearing smiling faces and bearing amicable outward appearances. The sharp claws lie beneath the soft hair ! The iron mouths are carrying iron balls ! What do you honorable gentlemen advise my master to do in this great emergency ? I, for my part, speaking as an individual of dull parts, must candidly say that, while it is against my wishes to subvert the long-established policy of our government regarding barbarians, yet I cannot see as any great harm will result from allowing their vessels to trade at a couple of our seaports for a few years. In the meantime, we can watch the progress of events, and be in a position at some near date to again close the ports. The matter is now before you for discussion. What say you ? "

"Well and shrewdly spoken, thou astute and diplomatic knave ! " muttered the old Prince of Mito in a savage undertone as he turned toward Konishi, who attended him as adviser on matters pertaining to barbarian customs and history. "The adroit rogue has shuffled things so that I am puzzled to know what position to take in this matter. My hate is so equally divided between him and the barbarians, that I could oppose either of them with supreme joy. Well, I shall have to take sides against him anyway. Let us hear what the Lord of Kaga has to say as he has commenced to speak."

The Daimio of Kaga was the wealthiest nobleman in the realm, and, very naturally, the weight of his utterances was vastly enhanced by the weight of his money-bags. He was not celebrated for any very brilliant qualities of intellect, but it was generally noted that his conclusions were usually sound, notwithstanding his lumbering and clumsy method of expressing himself while getting at them.

" Although it may not be becoming," said his Lordship, in measured tones, as he bowed his head downward in profound salutation of the Gotairo, " for an individual of my dull parts and obtuse faculties to criticise the statements of so capable a person as the chief councillor of the awesome Shogun, yet will I venture to state that the copy of the foreign ruler's letter that is in my possession does not purport to be directed to the ' Ruler ' of Dai-Nippon, but is very clearly addressed to ' His Imperial Majesty, the Emperor of Japan.' Such being the case, it seems to me (unskilled as I truly am in matters of diplomacy and of statesmanship) that this entire matter should be referred to *Tenshi* at Kioto for discussion and approval. When some decision has been proclaimed from the Gosho, then will it be the proper time for us to act."

The murmur of applause that greeted this most unexpected speech clearly showed that many Daimios there present considered that the phlegmatic Lord of Kaga had made a decided hit, for President Fillmore's letter was indeed addressed to ."His Imperial Majesty, the Emperor of Japan."

" Sure enough ! The entire matter should be referred to Kioto," exclaimed several lordlings, who delighted to bask in the smiles of overshadowing Kaga, and the chief end of whose existence appeared to be (figuratively speaking) to sneeze whenever their ponderous neighbor took snuff. The *Gosanké*, however, were silent, evidently not being quite prepared to give so much prominence to the Gosho, to the detriment of the long-established prestige of the house of Tokugawa. Even Mito, though prepared to take sides against the Shogun in the matter of allowing foreigners to trade with Japan, was not willing to humiliate the pride and the glory of Tokugawa by rushing off to Kioto to appeal to *Tenshi* to act as supreme arbiter in such a matter as that under discussion. The wily Gotairo, however, was not to be caught napping. He had sifted the question too carefully that very morning to be unprepared with the counter-stroke to his heavy adversary's deft and unexpected stroke. Before the approving applause of the assembly could gather any headway, he sprang to the attack with that dash and ability for which he was so greatly renowned.

"It is true, O most subtle and learned Lord of Kaga!" said the Gotairo in calm and impressive tones, "that the formal and literal address of this letter is to 'His Imperial Majesty, the Emperor of Japan.' But I was not considering the form of the superscription, but the spirit and intent of the letter. It is clearly manifest that the intention of the ruler of this foreign nation is to communicate with the ruler of Dai-Nippon in regard to commercial matters. This intent can be read between the lines throughout the entire document. I will read two extracts to prove my statements. Near the end of the letter is the following paragraph: '*These are the only objects for which I have sent Commodore Perry with a powerful squadron to pay a visit to your Imperial Majesty's renowned city of Yedo: friendship, commerce, a supply of coal and provisions, and protection for our shipwrecked people.*' And near the beginning of the letter carefully note this significant paragraph: '*The Constitution and laws of the United States forbid all interference with the religious or political concerns of other nations. I have particularly charged Commodore Perry to abstain from every act which could possibly disturb the tranquillity of your Imperial Majesty's dominion.*'

"Now, illustrious gentlemen of the *Gosanké* and of the Daimiates, please note how clearly drawn is the distinction between commercial matters and matters spiritual and political. Had the barbarians desired to treat with us on matters spiritual and political, the question might well have arisen as to the policy of referring the matter to Kioto. But they utterly repudiate any such intention. There can be no shadow of doubt about that. Furthermore, they limit themselves entirely to the consideration of commercial matters and send their squadron to the commercial capital (Yedo), where such matters have been managed for centuries. What then can be clearer than my first statement that the foreign ' Ruler addresses the ' Ruler ' of Dai-Nippon upon a subject concerning which the latter personage has full powers to act ? Was not the policy of the exclusion of foreign commerce inaugurated by the house of Tokugawa ? Has not then that same house full authority to reconsider their ancient action in the matter ? Who dare to gainsay so patent a fact ? Furthermore, who would think of referring such vulgar matters as the price of coal, wood, and provisions to the illustrious descendant of the gods ? Has not the imperial family for a thousand years referred all matters relating to the vulgar bickerings of merchants and sailors to the Shogun ? Who will dare to gainsay that such matters fall within the scope of the authority of my master? Who will dare to insult the serene majesty of *Tenshi* with long-drawn memorials and grandiloquent petitions, beseeching the scion of the immortal gods to adjust the tariff on eggs and pork ? "

The outburst of applause and laughter that followed this sally of logic and wit proved beyond peradventure that the Gotairo was master of the situation and had carried an overwhelming majority of the Daimios with him. Even Mito was seen to smile. Kaga lapsed into sullen silence, wearing on his stolid features the expression of a man who had been hard sat upon. And the long-drawn breath behind the screen betokened that the " Ruler " of Dai-Nippon fully appreciated the situation.

" No, gentlemen," continued the Gotairo, striking while the iron was yet hot, " we have decided that this entire matter falls within our legitimate jurisdiction and must not be referred to Kioto, but must be fully discussed here in Yedo by this august assembly of rulers. From this decision there can be no appeal. Let us now discuss this important matter unreservedly and fully, for the barbarians are clamoring for an answer."

After this opening passage at arms, there seemed to be a disinclination on the part of the assembly to precipitate the discussion as to whether or not the foreigners should be admitted into the land of the gods. While the Gotairo awaited the pleasure of the assembly, the Daimios quietly but warmly discussed the matter in undertones among themselves. A split speedily developed itself, wherein the minority faction rallied under the leadership of Mito, who hotly laid down his views to the meagre coterie of followers that craned their necks toward him to catch his impassioned words. An hour of verbose warfare had failed to close the breach between the factions, and it became manifest that the forlorn hope had imbibed the obstinate spirit of their leader. At this juncture the Gotairo, who, by the way, had kept himself well informed of the state of affairs by means of private communications from his adherents in the body of the house, determined to force the issue by precipitating the debate without further delay. With the suavity of a man who feels himself to be already the victor, he slowly quaffed a cup of tea as he cast his searching eyes over the assembly. Then with boundless good-humor he grasped his fan and smilingly smote the low lacquered stand that stood before him and said : "Profound and learned councillors ! The afternoon is rapidly waning and we must to-day make our reply to the barbarians' letter. What shall the answer be?"

"Yea ! Thou well sayest that the afternoon wanes," muttered the Prince of Mito in a fierce undertone, "but what carest thou for that when thou already holdest the assembly in thy hands? Yet beware ! The clouds will gather over thy fair sky at some not distant day, and I shall hold the fan and smite thy cheek as thou hast smitten yonder stand." And his choleric lordship, suiting his action to his muttered threats, smote the stand before him so vigorously, that the little cups and tiny pipes thereon quaked and rattled in dismay. The Gotairo heard the sound, and, taking it as a signal to catch the presiding officer's attention, he turned toward that part of the room and said :

"Illustrious gentlemen ! Be pleased to maintain silence while the noble Lord of Mito (worthy scion of the renowned Iyéyas) shall speak and give to us the benefit of his thoughtful observations on a subject wherein he is well qualified to express an opinion ; for, as you already know, the noble lords of Mito have always been deeply versed in the science and in the literature of western nations."

Thus introduced to the house, the Prince of Mito voiced the sentiments of the minority faction and most vigorously assailed the policy of the Gotairo in the following words [1] : "I am totally opposed to the admission of any of these barbarian nations to commercial privileges with ourselves, upon the ground that they will ruin our country, as they came very near doing three hundred years ago. At first they will give us philosophical instruments, machinery, and other curiosities, will take ignorant people in, and, trade being their chief object, they will manage, bit by bit, to impoverish the country ; after which, they will treat us just as they like ; perhaps behave with the greatest rudeness and insult us, and end by swallowing up Japan. If we do not drive them away now, we shall never have another opportunity. If we now resort to a dilatory method of proceeding, we shall regret it afterwards when it will be of no use."

The battle thus boldly begun was hotly waged for three or four hours all along the line. Reasons innumerable were adduced for excluding the horrid savages of the West. But the sentiments of the Gotairo and of his councillors, expressed in the following language,[2] finally prevailed :

"If we try," said they, "to drive them away, they will immediately commence hostilities, and then we shall be

[1] F. O. Adams' "History of Japan," vol. i., p. 112.   [2] *Ibid.*

obliged to fight. If we once get into a dispute, we shall have an enemy to fight who will not be easily disposed of. He does not care how long a time he will have to spend over it, but he will come with several myriads of men-of-war and surround our shores completely ; he will capture our junks, and blockade our ports, and deprive us of all hope of protecting our coasts. However large a number of ships we might destroy, he is so accustomed to that sort of thing that he would not care in the least. Even supposing that our troops were animated by patriotic zeal in the commencement of the war, after they had been fighting for several years their patriotic zeal would naturally become relaxed, the soldiers would become fatigued, and we should have to thank ourselves for this. Soldiers who have distinguished themselves are rewarded by grants of land, or else you attack and seize the enemy's territory, and that becomes your own property ; so every man is encouraged to fight his best.

"But, in a war with foreign countries, a man may undergo hardships for years, may fight as if his life were worth nothing, and, as all the land in this country has already owners, there will be none to be given away as rewards ; so we shall have to give rewards in words or money. In time, the country would be put to an immense expense, and the people be plunged into misery. Rather than allow this, as we are not the equals of the foreigners in the mechanical arts, let us have intercourse with foreign countries, learn their drill and tactics, and when we have made the nation as united as one family, we shall be able to go abroad and give lands in foreign countries to those who have distinguished themselves in battle ; the soldiers will vie with one another in displaying intrepidity, and it will not be too late then to declare war. Now we shall have to defend ourselves against these foreign enemies, skilled in the use of mechanical appliances, with our soldiers, whose military skill has considerably diminished during a long peace of three hundred years, and we certainly could not feel sure of victory, especially in a naval war."

Thus ended the most momentous debate that had occurred under the Shogunate, since the time when the bloody decrees against the Jesuits were promulgated. Mito was routed, but he remained undismayed and defiant. "Aye!" said he to Konishi that night at his *yashiki*, "the battle has begun, and I have well unmasked the hidden springs that control the actions of that Hikoné dog. He fears and dreads the foreigners! Our spies have indeed rendered us inestimable services. There can be no doubt but what these foreigners are greater and more powerful than we are. It will be useless for us to fight them. The councillors spoke truly there. Henceforth we must not fight the foreigners, but the Shogun himself. The glory must depart from Tokugawa, and must return to *Tenshi*. We must use our secret endeavors to set the tide of power and of influence in the direction of the Gosho. This will require much time and patience. But who that knows me will say that I do not possess the capacity to wait and watch when yonder upstart is lording it over the realm as if he were born of the gods? Yea, thou Biwa ape! Thy carcass shall some day rot, as now does that of thy sneaking minion in the woods beside the shrine!"

CHAPTER XVII.

AGAIN the scene changes. We are at Hikoné Castle, on the shores of Lake Biwa. Soon after the great debate of the Daimios, described in the last chapter, the American Commodore was duly notified that the Shogun had consented to the terms of the proposed treaty; and that document, after long negotiations, was duly signed on March 31, 1854. The fleet then departed on a cruise along the coast, for the purpose of inspecting the harbors of the two treaty ports. Early in May, the Gotairo, after a careful survey of the political outlook, came to the conclusion that there were breakers ahead, and that it behooved him, during the calm that had ensued when the foreigners had departed, to put the affairs of his Daimiate in good shape, so that, when the storms that were evidently brewing around the political horizon should break upon him, he might be ready to weather the gales. He considered the fact that he might not have another opportunity to visit his Daimiate for many years, as it was manifest that his continued presence in Yedo would be required at a very early date. He therefore set out about the middle of May with a small escort, and journeyed rapidly by way of the magnificent Nakasendo through the inland mountains toward Hikoné, where he arrived safely at the end of the month, and at once set vigorously to work to arrange his affairs, so that his anticipated long absence would not be productive of injury or embarrassments in the future.

Hikoné Castle was one of the most picturesquely located of any of the feudal strongholds of Japan. Situated about midway up the eastern shore of Lake Biwa, it looked forth upon the blue waves of that placid sheet of water, and upon the lofty ranges that bounded the western shore. This beautiful mountain mirror extended from north to south for about fifty miles, and, in its widest part from east to west, it was twenty miles wide. Its lovely shores were girt with well wooded hills and majestic mountains. Beginning with the town of Otsu, at the southern end (where our Nakashima friends sipped the farewell cup when starting on their overland journey), we follow the shore up the eastern side until we reach Shioatsu, at the extreme northern end of the lake. The southern part of this side is low and hilly ; but as the vicinity of Hikoné is approached, the country becomes more rugged ; and, as the northern part is reached, the converging shores merge into a grand mountainous region. Then starting from Shioatsu, and journeying down the western shore, we find ourselves overshadowed with magnificent mountains during the entire trip. Far down this shore, near Otsu, stand the white walls of another castle, belonging to some petty Daimio. It is perched upon the brow of a low hill, while behind it— like some majestic sentinel—rises lofty Hiyeisan, with its engroved monastery and sequestered shrines. The entire circuit of the shores is beaded with villages and hamlets. And every available spot has been cultivated, so that the waters seem to be clasped with a broad band of living green. Fishing-boats fly merrily over its surface, and " oft in the stilly night " the pleasure-seekers skim the waves in excursion boats. As before remarked, the eastern and the western shores converged toward the north, until they plunged, like a huge wedge, into the mighty mountain barriers, and the lake received into its bosom the never failing streams that poured down the glens and ravines, thus carrying vast quantities of gravel and pebbles into the lake, and scouring the northern shores so well with their sands, that the broad expanse of glittering beach and pebbly shore stood out spotless in the bright sunshine. The native legends say that this exquisite sheet of water was created by an earthquake that occurred over two thousand years ago. A whole province sank out of sight, and, simultaneously, Fujisan upheaved his towering crest upon the eastern coast three hundred miles away !

Hikoné Castle was built upon some bluffs, at a point where the shore juts boldly into the lake, thus giving a superb view up and down the shores. The general plan of the fortifications resembled that of the castle in Yedo. It was constructed, however, upon a very much smaller scale, and was far more picturesque in its details. In and about its massive ramparts had camped the legions of the league, on the eve of the fateful battle of Sékagi-hara. The misty morning of that day beheld the lusty warriors streaming forth, confident of victory, and the dusky gloaming saw the depleted ranks shrink within the moats to await the victorious swoop of Iyéyas. Multi-tudes of the vanquished warriors refused to submit to the humiliation of surrender, and plunged their keen blades into their abdomens, through the portal vein and the great arteries. The fair greenswards reeked with the fuming blood of self-immolation ; and the victors, for-sooth, found many bodies, but there were but few heads to chop off and impale on the gateposts and along the battlements. Fair and lovely, however, appeared the lawns, and sweetly blushed the roses and the peonies, on that June morning when Nawosŭké sat in the charm-ing pavilion beside the lake, and dreamily gazed upon the beauties of the enchanting scene. He had arranged his affairs, and had straightened out his financial matters, so that his revenues would flow steadily into his Yedo coffers without any vexatious delay. The succession to his estates (in case of his sudden death) had been duly secured to his son, a bright, promising lad, who now was making merry with a picnic party, fishing in one of the shady coves hard by, whence the merry laughter of the boys could be heard as they frolicked in the water and on the beach. Presently he was aroused from his reverie by an attendant bringing in tea and tobacco. After the lapse of a few minutes, another attendant brought in a despatch that had just been delivered by special courier at the outer gateway of the castle.

" Ah !   From Yedo, I perceive," exclaimed his Grace, as he glanced at the box.   " I hope it contains some news about Shimidzu.   He remains remarkably silent on this trip.   I cannot imagine what put it into his head that spies from some Yedo *yashiki* were in communication with the foreign fleet.   Surely we sowed the country around the bay with enough emissaries to ensnare any suspicious person in our nets.   But he was always a very persistent fellow, and would always work after his own fashion.   And, so long as he was successful, why should I care about his methods ?

" Well ! What is this that I am reading ? I certainly did not expect to hear any such news as this ! [He reads from the letter in his hand :] ' About ten days ago, the peasants worshipping at the shrine erected in honor of *Ebisu* near a fishing hamlet somewhere in the vicinity of of Yokoska, on the southwestern shore of Yedo bay, were afflicted with a foul and grievous stench, as if putrid flesh had been thrust under their very nostrils.   Following up the direction whence the horrible odor seemed to emanate, they went into the woods, and found the body of a *samurai*, in advanced stages of putrefaction.   The man had evidently been killed in a duel, for his sword (very valuable), his money, and his clothes were carefully concealed in the underbrush near by, thus conclusively showing that robbery could not have been the motive. The terrified peasants at once reported the matter to the nearest town, and an officer speedily visited the spot. He reported that the features had become corrupted beyond recognition ; that the man had evidently been killed with a single deep cut across the bowels from right to left ; and that the assailant had apparently met him in single combat, for reasons unknown.   A careful inspection of the clothing failed to throw any light upon his identity.   But the sword has been identified in the office of the Bakufu, in Yedo, as that of Shimidzu, the wonderful spy. It is with boundless grief that we are obliged to report the death of so faithful and valuable a servant.' "

With unmoved features his Lordship read and re-read the despatch. At last he closed it pensively, and thrust it into the folds of his sleeve, and exclaimed : "Well! It's no use mourning now. It was over with the poor fellow some time ago. So the old fox finally met his match ! I wonder who his antagonist could have been ? No tyro, I 'll warrant, but a well seasoned piece of timber, as sure as I am Nawosŭké, Lord of Hikoné. And now for revenge ! Ah ! There the prospect is not very encouraging. Not a trace of the assassin ! Not a clue ! But let me see the letter again. Yes, there is a slight clue. It says that he was deeply cut from right to left. That would indicate that the cutter was a left-handed man, to be able to give so deadly a stroke on that side. Left-handed men are not so numerous, are they ? Let us hereafter keep our eyes open for them. The outlook for revenge is certainly rather meagre, for I can't very well seize a man for being left-handed ! Never mind, my unknown enemy, my memory is excellent, and my patience is as enduring as the hills. We will wait and see if I ever come across you." So saying, he slipped the letter into his sleeve, and sadly rested his head upon his hands and lapsed into a condition of profound meditation, from which he was roused at the end of about half an hour by the attendant bringing in another letter.

"What now ?" exclaimed Nawosŭké, peevishly ; "some more Yedo despatches ?"

"No, my illustrious Lord," meekly replied the bearer ; "it is a note from the Abbot of the Buddhist monastery on Hiyeisan, who awaits your pleasure at the outer gate. He submissively presents his compliments and his homage."

"Which, being construed in the light of past experience, means that he is on one of his begging excursions, soliciting contributions for his monastery," ejaculated his Lordship, snappishly. "These fellows seem to think that I am made of gold. I wish Tokugawa had never taken the Buddhists under state patronage. That rogue always manages to find out when I am here, just as a crow scents garbage. Well, it may be some time before he has a chance to see me again, and, as I am in a mood for holy conversation, I think you may order him to come here. I shall endeavor to vex his heart with some new ideas about his religion. That will entertain me."

In a few minutes the shaven priest, dressed in elegant gowns of brocaded silk, and carrying his rosary wound about his wrist, was ushered into the pavilion. He prostrated himself before the Gotairo, and delivered a series of obeisances such as he was accustomed to bestow on Buddha in Nirvana up at his monastery.

"Well, sir Abbot, what service can I render to you to-day?" said his Lordship, after the salutations had spent themselves.

"Supremely venerated sir," slowly replied the monk in reverential cadences, acquired through having intoned the ritual so many thousand times, "it is well known to your honorable self that Gongen-sama condescended to smile upon our monastery at Hiyeisan, and that his successors have continued to show us boundless favor,—although we have but slightly merited such attentions. We have endeavored to requite such friendship by continuing to chant the services for their souls. But such ceremonies entail expenditure. Therefore, it becomes necessary for us, from time to time, to solicit assistance. Be pleased, most honorable sir, to remember us in the matter."

"It is well to be mindful of the dead, and to revere their memories with becoming ceremonies," said the Gotairo. "I have been considering the matter, and I now decide that the sum of ten thousand *kokus* of rice shall be apportioned to your institution, for the purpose of defraying the expenses connected with the services mentioned by you. I will now write out an order on the warehouse keeper for the delivery of that amount."

"Profoundly venerated sir," intoned the priest in his most solemn cadences, placing his forehead on the *tatami,* "your liberality is munificent indeed, and we shall endeavor in our mystic way to requite the favor thus shown by propitiating the unseen powers of the other world."

"And now, sir Abbot," said the Gotairo, as he handed him the order that he had just written, "as I have dealt frankly and liberally with you, I hope that you will deal with me after a similar fashion in regard to a few questions that I desire to put to you."

"Your worthy and obscure beneficiary will do all that may lie within the scope of his limited intelligence to give you satisfactory answers," replied the priest.

"Generously spoken!" exclaimed his Lordship, smiling gloomily. "Now, sir Abbot, be pleased to explain to me what you mean by that which you just now said about chanting services for the souls of the dead. If the spirit of Gongen-sama has entered upon that Nirvana about which Shaka, the founder of your religion, taught us, what need has he for your prayers?"

"Truly spoken, most honorable sir," replied the priest, "but he may now be struggling through some lower forms of existence trying to regain his human form. We therefore pray that his struggles may be shortened."

"But to whom do you pray?"

"We pray to Shaka."

"But Shaka, according to your teachings, entered Nirvana over twenty-five centuries ago. You define Nirvana to be an eternity of utter and absolute unconsciousness. How can he aid you in any way? Do you not see that your definition of Nirvana has practically annihilated him?"

"But, sir, there may be unseen powers that require propitiating."

"How can that be, O Monk, when Shaka taught that there was no creator; that this universe was a mere accident of matter; and that the destiny of the human soul was annihilation? Do you not see that such doctrines rule unseen powers out of existence? Shaka never taught any thing about unseen powers. Why then do you teach such doctrines?"

"Sir, the founders of our sect taught that there were unseen powers."

"But, O learned Monk, they had no right to tamper with the fundamental principles of Shaka's religion in that manner. The fundamental principles of any religion are those principles incorporated into it by the founder thereof. This proposition is self-evident. But you priests in Thibet, Ceylon, China, and Japan have gone to work since Shaka's death and have invented a vast mass of doctrine that does not belong to the religion of Shaka. You have made a hopeless mess of every thing. As matters now stand, a man can believe any thing he likes, and can prove himself to be a good Buddhist by citing some monastery or monk as authority. You must cite Shaka as your authority, and not the monasteries. See what you Buddhists did when you came to Dai-Nippon! You found our Shintoism recognizing the existence of some power behind the phenomena of nature, and teaching that our islands were created by the gods above, and that the inhabitants of our empire had descended from some god who had come down with his wife and dwelt here. You fellows then went to work and coined the fiction that Shaka had come back from lower animal forms to human form eighty thousand times before he finally succeeded in entering Nirvana, and that on one of those occasions he became incarnated in the form of this particular god, and became the progenitor of our race. By this fraud you captured the land and pushed our native religion into the remote valleys and glens, where but little money was to be made.

"When the *Kirishitans* came here three hundred years ago, you found that you could not capture their god by the same trick, because he happened to have been born five hundred years after Shaka had entered Nirvana. As a person cannot very well be annihilated more than once, you hadn't the face to say that their god was an incarnation of Shaka. Come, now, tell me candidly what you really do believe."

"It is manifest that your Lordship is deeply versed in matters pertaining to our religion," replied the priest.

" It will, therefore, not be well for me to converse as if I were talking to a common person having but little intelligence. I will be very frank with you, and will state exactly all of my views. Of course we know almost nothing concerning what Shaka himself taught. His teachings and sayings were not recorded in writing until (as some writers put it) two hundred years after his death, or (as other writers put it) five hundred years after his death. Under such conditions, what can be depended upon ? But the fundamental principles that he incorporated into his religion were treasured up by his followers and became so welded into the creed, that we may be reasonably certain that they were Nirvana, transmigration, and mercifulness to all living creatures. Beyond this, of course, every thing is uncertain, and abundant room has been left for speculation and inventive imaginations in the monasteries everywhere. Of course he taught that there was no creator, and that matter was a mere chance concerning whose origin he cared nothing. It was sufficient to know that organized matter entailed on humanity a most miserable existence, and that the only way out of that wretched condition was to merge the soul into Nirvana, and thus forever end matters. Of course there is no immortality. The soul becomes annihilated eventually."

" Then why do you bring in the doctrine of transmigration ? "

" Because we wish to terrify humanity into striving to attain Nirvana. We teach men that if they neglect to attain it now they will be compelled to keep coming back to human form after having lived as degraded reptiles, insects, and animals, until they finally consent to attain Nirvana."

" But what right, O Monk, have you to terrify humanity ? You have no proof that such a thing as a soul exists in man. It is a pure assumption on your part. You can no more prove the existence of a soul than you can that of a creator. There is no more evidence in support of one hypothesis than there is for the other.

If there be no creator and no Supreme Being presiding over the affairs of men, then one man has no right to dictate to another one on such matters. There is nothing to base your authority upon. Following your plan, I could invent a little scheme of my own and force it upon humanity."

"Ah ! Now your Lordship has plunged deeper into the subject than I ever knew anybody to do. You compel me to say that there is no authority for our scheme. But listen. Know, then, that all men crave immortality. That religion which promises immortality to man will win the day. Men shrink from annihilation, although such will be their ultimate destiny. Therefore, to be in a condition to meet this peculiarity of our natures, we say that men, if they do not attain Nirvana, can keep on living in lower forms of existence until they have become tired of that sort of thing, and decide to attain thereto. This, you will perceive, gives them practical immortality in this world should they chance to desire that kind of immortality."

"But, sir Abbot, you have no right to say this. You have no authority on which to base your action. Your entire scheme is a pure fabrication. You have no right to say to your fellow-men that such a thing is wrong. One man is as good as another. Only some higher power—a creator, for example—can say to his created beings : ' This is wrong, that is right.' By his mere will he may create the distinction between right and wrong, and may implant within the hearts of his creatures intuitive convictions on the subject. Right and wrong do not exist in the nature of things, as some philosophers dogmatically assert. The idea of right and wrong can only spring from the relations that some Supreme Being has arbitrarily caused to exist between sentient beings created by himself,—between man and man, between man and beasts, between man and God. If there be no such Supreme Being, then nobody has authority to set himself up as an arbiter in such matters,—to dictate to his fellow-men what they shall or shall not do.

"A fine time we would have in this world if everybody were to set up his own standard of right and wrong and force it upon humanity! Who shall dare to step between me and the gratification of every desire? Did not the *Kirishitan* priests rebuke the great Hidéyoshi and the Daimios for their lustful indulgences, alleging that such practices were against the laws of God? Were they not eventually swept out of the country for such insolent presumption? Who will now venture to dictate in such matters?

"It is all very well, O Priest, for a father with a family of beautiful daughters to lift up his hands in holy horror and pronounce debauchery to be a crime, and to assert that whoever commits such an offense must do his utmost to make full and ample restitution both in this world and in the world to come,—nay, more, he may even go so far as to grandiloquently and pompously assert that ' no man can be perfectly happy, either in this world or the other, who has by his perfidy broken a loving and confiding heart,'—but all such talk is merely the individual opinion of an interested party trying to terrify humanity into his own notions of morality, and it goes in at one ear of the libertine and out at the other, for the simple reason that none but a creator has a right to dictate in such matters. If men be merely creatures of chance, then each one becomes a law unto himself, and is at liberty to do whatsoever seemeth desirable and expedient in his own eyes, just like the beasts of the fields. What have you to say to this, O Monk?"

"Ah! you plunge yet deeper into the subject, O Lord of Hikoné. Know, then, that religion is necessary to control men. Mankind will not be submissive unless you hold out either the hope of reward or the fear of punishment. Therefore, when governments first began to rule over society, it became speedily apparent that anarchy would ensue unless these two motives were appealed to. Therefore, the rulers of the nation early saw the policy of calling to its assistance the aid of religion. The history of our government has, from the remotest times, been interwoven with religion of some kind. And if I am not greatly mistaken, you will find that in all countries the various governments have been wedded to some kind of religion. Those religions that best control men are generally the most popular with governments ; while those religons that promote seditions and disturbances are quickly rooted out as pestiferous. By nature all men are more or less religious in their inclinations. When these religious impulses are degraded by profound ignorance, they become unreasoning and fanatical, and become known as superstitions. And these superstitions can best be controlled by terror of future punishments. I presume that this is why the various sects of our religion, since Shaka's time, have invented hells of torment. Very naturally, superstitious people soon become imbued with the idea that souls of friends could be bought out of these places,—or their sufferings therein greatly reduced,—if the priests would exert their mystic influence in propitiating the unseen powers of the other world (whoever or whatever they may be). So long as the pandering to these superstitious ideas tended to soothe the disquieted minds of ignorant people, and to fill the coffers of the monasteries, there seemed to be no harm in keeping up the delusions,—especially as the government was vastly benefited by having the people kept in a tractable state of mind."

"That which you have just spoken, O learned Monk, savors largely of political wisdom. I presume that you have really given the true reason why Tokugawa took your religion under the patronage of the state. It is for this reason that I do not grudge the contributions that we have poured forth upon the various monasteries throughout the empire. But there are other matters concerning which I wish to interrogate you in a frank spirit. Our minds have become bared to each other's inspection, and you need not hesitate to speak freely and fearlessly. But at present we cannot continue the discussion. It is the hour for the midday meal. Be so kind as to dine with me, and to spend the balance of the day with me, as I am desirous of continuing the discussion. It is very rarely that I feel disposed to talk on such subjects.

"But to-day I have received the news of the sudden death of a faithful vassal, and this fact has opened up a vista of queries that reach out into unknown regions of thought and speculation. I am very much like Shaka, in that I do not believe in any creator, and do not believe in any future world. I have lived this life for all that it is worth, and I shall continue to do so. But occasionally the inquiry comes unsought,—Am I right in my belief? Is there positively no hereafter? If there be no creator and no future spirit-world, is there any spirit at all? On such occasions I desire to converse with learned and candid minds like yours."

"The honor that you confer on me," responded the Abbot, "is indeed great. I will endeavor to give you the benefit of such meagre information as I may possess. Although believing substantially as you believe, yet there has arisen in my mind, on those evenings among the moon-lit pines when we, in accordance with our ancient usages, reduce to ashes the body of some deceased member of our brotherhood, the same questionings that agitate you. As the flames leap up against the pallid features and dissolve them into dust, I would feign ask : Where is the spirit that animated those features? If there be no spirit at all, what was it then that formerly shone forth from those eyes and communicated intelligible ideas to my mind? What has become of that subtle yet real influence?"

CHAPTER XVIII.

A METAPHYSICAL SIESTA.

"O Learned Monk," said the Gotairo when he resumed his *tête-à-tête* with the Abbot at the pavilion after dinner, "reveal unto me the mystery that I am about to propound unto thee. Behold! last night a subtle influence crept over my body, my eyelids drooped, my limbs were relaxed, and I merged into a condition of profound unconsciousness until the morning light dissolved the charming spell,—and I awoke to find that seven hours of time had been forever blotted out of my existence while I slumbered. No dream, no smothered thought had crept in upon my brain ; and I started up to grasp the volume that I had been reading when I surrendered myself to the sweet influence. O Monk, tell me what was that subtle influence?"

"O awesome Lord of Hikoné," replied the Abbot, 'it was merely the lapsing of your system into a period of sweet sleep. Your brain had become tired with studious application, your nerves and muscles had become wearied with many hours of unremitting toil, and your body—unable any longer to bear the strain—clamored for repose and sank into the comatose condition that you have so well described. In short, your mighty Lordship went to sleep like all mortals are wont to do."

"O Monk, as you have well said, my body was indisposed any longer to perform its functions and drifted into unconsciousness. But where was my soul during that period? Did that also sleep? Behold! this is the mystery that I would have you reveal unto me. If it sleep not, then where abideth it while the body enters upon its temporary Nirvana?"

"O philosophic Lord, your question is indeed hard to answer. I presume the soul lapses into its natural condition,—utter and absolute unconsciousness ; but it is roused into conscious existence just as soon as the body awakes from its period of repose. So long as it is linked to a mortal body, just so long must it be subjected to the horrors of being perpetually dragged back into conscious existence. Behold ! how desirable a thing it is to enter upon that eternal repose—that Nirvana—wherein no shadowy dreams, no smothered thoughts ever flit across the midnight of the soul to vex it with the miserable consciousness of its own existence."

" But wherein does this partial and periodical annihilation differ from eternal anihilation, O Priest ? "

"In the same way that this drop of water that I hold in the palm of my hand differs from the vast body of water in the lake. I now cast it over the balcony railing, and it becomes merged into that glorious sheet."

"But, O Priest, suppose an enemy had crept upon me unawares, and had smitten off my head with one dread stroke before consciousness could have been regained, would then the unconscious condition of my soul have been prolonged forever? Would it have entered Nirvana even though I had not desired nor had ever endeavored to enter therein ? "

"Our religion, sir, teaches that nobody can enter Nirvana unless he desire to enter therein and has laboriously striven to enter therein."

"But, O Priest, if the soul sleep not, but, as you say, merely lapses into its natural condition of unconsciousness until such time as the body to which it is linked may be good enough to rouse it therefrom, what shall rouse it when that body is instantly dashed out of existence with one mighty blow? Under such conditions, what shall prevent the soul's temporary Nirvana becoming eternal—just as you forced the drop of water to merge into the body of the lake ? "

"Such a doctrine, sir, would be opposed to our theories."

"O most sagacious Monk, have you ever seen the soul ?"

"O penetrating mind, I never have."

" Have any of your friends ever seen it ? "

" They never have."

" Has anybody, to your knowledge, ever seen it ? "

" No one ever has."

'· Then what evidence have you that there is any soul at all? You say that there is no creator, or Supreme Being, no immortality for the soul, why not finish up matters by saying that there is no soul? What is the· use of a soul anyway ? Why do you halt on the thresh-cold of your own existence after having wiped out the universe ? Why are not you consistent ? Why not come forth candidly and say that there is no soul ? "

" Because, sir, there is overwhelming evidence of some personal intelligence in the human body. Surely at the present moment there is something in my body ex-changing intelligible ideas with something in your body ! "

" But that evidence is no stronger than is the evidence of some personal intelligence behind the phenomena of nature. Yet, in one case, you deny a personal intel-ligence, and, in the other case, you admit the personal intelligence. And in each case the evidence is precisely the same ! Then, again, how do you know that there is but a single soul in a body ? Each varied thought, each sentiment, each emotion, may emanate from a distinct soul lurking within our mysterious mechanisms. For all you can show to the contrary, each person may have a hundred—yea, a million—souls instead of one, as you assume."

" Sir, the unity of sentiment and of action that char-acterizes each individual, argues the existence of a sin-gle soul."

" No more, O Priest, than does the unity of design and of plan in the universe argue the existence of a Supreme Being."

" Sir, I cannot answer you otherwise than I have done."

"O Monk, be candid. You have merely assumed the existence of a soul in order to account for the phenomena of this life. In other words, know that the fundamental principle, or principles, of every theory must be taken on faith,—they can never be demonstrated."

"I do not think that you are right, sir. What room for faith is there in the science of mathematics as taught in those wonderful books imported by the Hollanders? The laws of lines, angles, and triangles are so immutable that they can measure distances in space far beyond our earth, and can calculate eclipses with the utmost precision. Pray, what fundamental principle do you accept on faith in mathematics as developed in geometry, trigonometry, and astronomy?"

"O Priest, the entire science of mathematics is based upon the single fundamental principle that there are such things as straight lines. You must accept on faith this underlying fact. You can never demonstrate that any given line is straight. But, believing in the existence of such a thing as an absolutely straight line, then you can build thereon your wonderful science that measures so many millions of leagues into space. No progress can be made unless you assume that your lines are straight."

"But, sir, observe me draw this line with this pen and ruler. Can you prove that this line is not straight?"

"I can, O Priest.

"How, sir?"

"With this lens imported from Holland. It magnifies an object many thousand times. Now look at the side of your ruler with it. See how rugged it is,—just like the teeth of a saw! How could you draw a straight line with such a thing as that? Now look at your alleged straight line with it. See how jagged and wavering it is! Do you call that a straight line?"

"I see, sir, where you are crowding me. If I accept the fundamental principles of mathematics, then must I accept the fundamental principles of the universe on faith and accept the fact that there is a Supreme Being.

Therefore, I deny that there are such things as straight lines ! I demolish the entire science of mathematics. I can be just as happy without knowing any thing about the subject."

" But what progress will humanity make, O Priest ? "

" Let humanity stagnate if it so desire. I do not care for humanity. There is no Supreme Being, I insist ! There are no such things as straight lines even in theory ! "

" But, O Priest, the books of the foreigners describe parallel lines as being straight lines in the same plane which never intersect even if produced to infinite distances from either end. Surely such lines must be 'straight in theory or in the abstract ! "

" I deny the fact that there are such things as parallel lines. I can be just as happy without believing that."

" In order to be consistent you must also deny that *two and two* make four, because there may be a class of beings in this world, or somewhere in the universe, who consider that *two and two* make forty, or four hundred, or four thousand. You must start by assuming that all minds are alike, and that to all of them *two and two* appear to make four."

" But, sir, I can prove that two and two make four."

" How will you do it ? "

" I take these two oranges and add them to these other two oranges. I now have four oranges. What better proof can there be than that ? "

" O Priest, you have utterly failed to make out your case. These oranges are all of different sizes. Now if this smallest one be your unit of measure, it follows that this next larger one must be more than one orange. You should trim it down to exactly the size of your unit of measure before adding. When you took these two small oranges and added them to these two large oranges, you must have had more than four oranges, because your units of measure were all unequal. What you mean to say is that if two equal units be added to two other equal units, the result will be four units. But you must assume at the start that there are such things in the abstract as equal units, because you can never demonstrate any given set of units to be equal. Your proof, sir, has vanished into air."

" I see your point, sir. Therefore I deny that *two and two* make four invariably, inexorably, and under every conceivable'form of existence."   •

"Yet you believe in the existence of a soul without proof ! "

" Sir, for social and political reasons it is best to teach the existence of a single responsible soul. As a matter of fact, I am quite willing to confidentially intimate to you that I deny the existence of any such thing."

"O Priest, why did you just now withdraw your hand• from the sunlight ? "

" Because, sir, the heat was so intense that it was blistering my tender skin."

" If I were to tell you that the sun had stretched forth his finger across an abyss over ninety millions of miles wide and had touched your hand, I fear you would not believe me."

" Most assuredly I could not."

"Yet as a matter of science explained in the mysterious books of the Hollanders, the sun sends forth subtle vibrations of heat and of light that travel across an abyss of *ether* and reach the earth, producing light and heat. That warm finger touched your hand and you shrank from it. In this science the theory of light and heat has reached its wonderful development by its discoverers accepting the fundamental principle that such a substance as *ether* intervenes between the sun and our earth. In order for you to be consistent it will be necessary for you to demolish all such theories. But, tell me, did you believe that you felt the heat of the sun a few moments ago ? "

" Certainly I did."

" Why ? "

" Because such matters fall within the cognizance of my senses."

" Are your senses infallible ? "

"I have never known them to deceive me in such matters."

"But do you think that they never can deceive you?"

"I presume that they may at some time deceive me."

"Then, O Priest, the basis of your belief after all is faith in the correctness of your impressions. You begin by assuming that your nerves are in sound condition and are capable of transmitting correct impressions. You cannot prove that your nerves are in sound condition, nor are you in a position to prove that you have any nerves at all, because neither you nor anybody else has ever seen them. You assume that you have a nervous system like that of mankind at large ; then, having faith in the correctness of your assumption, you proceed to act thereon. According to the wonderful books of the Hollanders treating about the science of astronomy, there are stars which we mortals can see, which have ceased to exist for many thousands of years ; but so immense is the distance intervening between those stars and this earth, that their radiance does not reach us for thousands of years,—long after the fiery worlds have ceased to exist. If I were to point out to you one of those points of light in the heavens, you would at once say that it was a star. Yet no star exists there ! How then can you trust the correctness of your senses ? It is absurd to assert that they can be always trusted. The eyes of men very frequently deceive them. All that you can allege is that because the general results of the various impressions upon our senses have been found to agree in the majority of instances, therefore we assume that our nervous organizations are similar, and that they are in sound condition and transmit impressions correctly from the outward world to our brains."

"Sir, that which you say sounds very extraordinary indeed, and I am not prepared to contradict what has been stated. Nevertheless I assert that reason must always remain the supreme and final test in all matters pertaining to this life. Whatever conflicts with our reason must be rejected as false."

"But whose reason shall be accepted as the supreme and final test? Surely not your reason, nor mine, nor that of any single individual. Is the reason of each man to be presumed to be absolutely correct? Are not you, O Priest, rendering human reason infallible? Surely you cannot believe that it is not liable to error. How often have conclusions that have appeared to be entirely consonant with our reason been shown to be entirely wrong! Then if it cannot be each man's reason that is to be the supreme and final test, whose or what reason shall it be? Shall it be the reason of this race of men or of that race of men? Shall it be the reason of this age or that of some previous age? Shall it be the reason of to-day or that of to-morrow? You must bear in mind that the human reason fluctuates like the tides of the ocean; it is as evanescent as the dews upon the lilies; it is as changeable as the clouds of heaven."

"Yet, sir, human reason is the only test. It is our only light. If you extinguish that, nothing but darkness remains. To be consistent, I presume that I must be prepared to admit that there is no such thing as human reason anyhow."

"But how do you know that no other light remains? How do you know that no other faculty may lie dormant within us? Perhaps some minds may possess peculiar faculties of comprehension quite independent of reason, —some faculty not possessed by the average man. Surely you cannot say that such may not be the case. No, sir Abbot, you must allow me to score another point; you are at your old subterfuges again. You assume, first, that your reason is generally correct, and then you assume that all men's reasons resemble your own. Then, having faith in these fundamental principles, you start out and say that whatever meets the general approval of the average intellect of intelligent humanity must be correct or nearly so. That is all that you can do or say on that point. But certain great truths that are essential to our welfare and to our happiness, we take cognizance of quite independent of reason. When you suddenly withdrew your hand from the scorching heat just now, you took cognizance of the fact without stopping to reason about it. We know positively when we are hungry, or thirsty, or sleepy, without reasoning to a definite conclusion about it. Therefore, O Priest, I say that although I individually do not believe in any Supreme Being, or in immortality, or in any soul at all, yet I am not prepared to say that other races of men may not possess subtle faculties of perception whereby to take cognizance of such tremendous mysteries. Nor am I prepared to say that minds of my own countrymen may be so peculiarly constituted that the existence of such mysteries may be certainties quite above their reasoning faculties,—invisible yet real facts of the universe."

"Then, sir, what solace is there for that large portion of humanity born under hard conditions of life? Multitudes are born poor, remain poor during life, and die poor. The few have always held the wealth in this country, while the majority have always struggled for a bare existence. Nay, more, the greater portion of humanity are born with the certainty of remaining poor during their whole lives. What possible inducement do you offer to such unfortunate ones to continue the hard and thankless struggle for existence? Upon your theory life is merely a struggle to keep forty or fifty feet of alimentary canal flush with nutritive fluids. Eat! eat! eat! What for? Oh, just for the sake of keeping up the hopeless struggle. If every thing be mere chance, and we be merely freaks of chance, then the most philosophic course for a poor man to pursue would be to take things into his own hands at once and end his ill-starred existence. In common parlance, he should call for a fresh shuffle of the cards, and see if the next deal will not produce better luck. Pray, sir what is human life worth under your theory?"

"Pray, what is it worth under yours, sir Abbot?"

"It certainly is worth more than it is under yours."

"Well, perhaps it may be so. Of course it is just as well that the people do not venture into such subjects as deeply as we do. I will admit that your theory is better for the common people. Nevertheless, when men become more cultivated in their intellects, like the *samurai*, then they adopt my theory, which, after all, seems to be the most philosophic one. As you already well know, we do take matters into our own hands when hard times come upon us. Multitudes have shortened their unhappy lives with the knightly *hara-kiri*. Multitudes of the common people have drowned themselves. What course can be more philosophic? Yes, take matters into your own hand ; that 's our doctrine precisely. Get all the pleasure out of life that you can while it lasts. Then call for a fresh deal of the cards, a new throw of the dice. Heretofore I have been studious and diligent in my habits. Henceforth I shall make the funds at my command produce the utmost pleasure. What course can be more philosophic? I now hold the reins of power, and grasp the revenues of the realm. I shall never surrender either. Having once tasted of supreme authority I become as insatiable as the tiger that has once tasted human blood. When my power shall end, then shall end my life ! "

" It is well, sir, that such teachings are not communicated to the people of Dai-Nippon. Pray, what would be the end of the horrors that would ensue?"

"Oh, it of course would not be well to instruct the vulgar crowd in matters beyond their comprehension. But when that time does come, sir Abbot,—mark my words,—when the masses shall think as I think, then matters must adjust themselves as best they can. By that time I expect to be safely out of the way. And then what shall I care about matters pertaining to humanity?"

"Your doctrine, sir, is terribly—nay, inhumanly— selfish. What progress would humanity ever make under such teachings? The results following their application to practice would be too horrible to contemplate."

"What care I for that? Your religion teaches self-extinction ; why then do you complain at the logical application of your creed? Every man has the right to destroy himself whenever he ceases to crave any further existence under hardships. Who shall dare step in and dictate to me as to what constitutes right and what constitutes wrong? There being no Supreme Being, then who shall decide such matters, since one man's opinion is as correct as another one's,—so far as we can tell? Don't you perceive, O Priest, that to be consistent with your alleged beliefs and public teachings, you must admit that there is no right, no wrong, in this universe ; that every thing is reduced to a mere question of expediency and policy for those who chance to hold the power? That is right which agrees with the will of the prince, and that is wrong which conflicts with the will of the prince. That is all there is about it. I hold the supreme power in Dai-Nippon—"

"Yea! O mighty Prince," solemnly intoned the Abbot, bowing low.

"And whoever displeases me I catch and slay, provided I can lay my hands on him."

"Verily! verily!" came the response in mournful cadences.

"In other words," continued the Gotairo, "the will of him who holds the reins of power is the only arbiter of expediency and policy in Dai-Nippon. As regards me, right and wrong have no existence. It is merely a question of whether I have the power to back up my wishes. When some mightier power overshadows mine, it then becomes expedient and politic for me to back down."

"Well and truly spoken!" chimed in the Abbot.

"Yet, O Priest, on days like this I am not satisfied with my own theories and beliefs. Restless queryings disturb the repose of my being. Deeply have I meditated on this subject, and my mind is ill at ease. I am wearied with doubt and speculation. Recently a superior power has menaced the supreme will that rules Dai-Nippon, and that will now bends before a mightier influence. It was compelled to surrender the policy of two centuries, and to submit to the arrogant dictation of a superior power that hovered on our shores. A race of beings fashioned after our own similitude is to-day mightier than we.

Our strength is but as an egg-shell compared with the power of that dread nation. Long and wearily has my heart vexed itself with speculation as to the cause of such pronounced superiority.

"In the books furnished by the Hollanders I read strange things. The history, the religion, the customs of this western nation are indeed wonderful. Through my spies I have studied their personal characteristics. Nay, more, I myself in person have studied them *nébon* on various occasions. With but trifling variations these foreigners are in all particulars the same as we are. They eat, drink, sleep, laugh, see, hear, smell, taste, and touch, just as we do. On the day when the great feast was given on board of their flagship in Yedo bay, to celebrate the ratification of the treaty, I went *nébon* unknown to anybody present except my two Commissioners. What a scene it was! Awnings were stretched overhead, and tables were spread in the shade beneath. Flags, flowers, and bunting, in most gorgeous profusion, decorated every thing. And a band of musicians performed on mighty brazen and silver instruments with such power that the massive timbers of the ship quaked beneath my feet. Multitudes of officers, gorgeously dressed in gold and silver trappings, moved about the decks. Multitudes of stately soldiers, with gleaming muskets, marched and countermarched with majestic tread to the sounds of sonorous drums and throbbing music. And immense black cannon vomited forth at intervals clouds of flame and smoke with concussions that shook the heavens and smote the very hills with terror. Truly the grandest of our state dinners would be tame in comparison with such stupendous pageantry!

"And then everybody sat down like brothers to the magnificent collation. The very gods might well have hungered after the boiled ham and wondrous wine called *champagne!* My Commissioners carried away from the feast abundant samples of every article, and I examined them at leisure on shore, and they were indeed wonderful concoctions of skilful cuisine, for the ingredient sub-

stances were familiar to me in many cases. The feaſt
flowed on like a mountain stream let loose from the uplands,—rapidly becoming noisier and more tumultuous
as it gathered volume and headway. Ye gods ! At the
close of the convivialities I could not distinguish, so far
as actions went, my own countrymen from the strangers.
They might all have been members of the same family
descended from centuries of common ancestors, so far as
methods of expressing joviality and good-fellowship
went. About the only persons not hilariously inclined
were my Commissioners and a few of the ship's officers.
Such shouting, such laughter, such affectionate embracings between foreigners and sons of Dai-Nippon, I
never could have dreamed possible ! Dignity and
decorous propriety were slid under the table to keep
company with the susceptible fellows already there.

"Of course in our own feasts we have abundance of
hilarity, but we confine our potations entirely to *saké*, so
that drinks do not get mixed. But these foreigners mix
up fully a dozen kinds of wonderfully stimulating bever-
ages, so that our systems, unaccustomed to such doses,
become unduly exhilarated. Then we drink from small
cups, while they drain large goblets. And the foreign
officers, apparently possessed with a droll combination of
humor and hospitality, persisted in pouring the wine
called *champagne* down the willing throats of my countrymen, just as soon as it became manifest that that quality
of wine was their favorite potation. I can excuse their
partiality for this drink, for it is truly a most delightful
beverage. From my vantage-ground I could observe all
these things deliberately and philosophically. And I was
forced to the conclusion that these foreigners were men
just like ourselves, but having constitutions developed
more powerfully by stronger food. Even those sailors
who were as black as this lacquered box—coming from
an entirely different race, as the Hollanders say—moved
about and acted like human beings. Yet, behind this
wonderful similarity between three different races of
men, I detected about the Commodore, his officers, and

many of his men, a loftiness of bearing and an exaltation of mien that betokened their superiority over ourselves. It was an expression of countenance that betokened a loftier mind, and a more refined sentiment and spirit."

"Yet, O Lord of Hikoné, according to your doctrine so ably enunciated just now, there can be no such thing as a spirit or a soul. You merely assumed that there was a loftier mind dwelling within those foreign bodies. You cannot prove that any such elements existed there."

"Quite true, O Priest. And that is the very thing that has puzzled me ever since. Of course I can prove nothing in the matter. Yet, just as you were bound to recognize some outside force when you withdrew your hand from the sun, so was I compelled, in the presence of those foreigners, to *feel* the *power* of something in their inner natures that impressed and appealed to something in my nature. And I am convinced that that something in my nature took cognizance of some superior force in their natures. Furthermore, this process of recognition was quite distinct from reason. And I am also convinced that this intangible power is the secret of their great physical and material power as a nation. There must be some spring whence this effect flows,—some principle that inspires their natures with exalted aspirations."

"Yet, O Prince, there can be no such spring or principle, if your theories be correct."

"I know that well enough, O Priest. Yet I am in search of power, and when I see any thing tending to promote and strengthen power, I want to get hold of it. These strangers have something in their natures that we do not possess. They have a loftiness of spirit that I am compelled to recognize, and to admit to be the secret source of their greater power as a nation. And it is this intangible something that I want to get at. We can imitate their ships, cannon, and houses, but, unless we possess ourselves of this secret inspiration, our labors will be fruitless. We shall be like the mountain boor who puts on the garments of a *samurai*—his vulgar spirit *will*

crop out and make him a source of ridicule and contempt to all the world."

"Yet, O most learned Prince, this is all a delusion,
according to your learned deductions of this afternoon."

"I know it, O Priest. But I want *power*. And, by the
shades of Taiko-Sama, I am going to have it!"

"Then, after all, O Prince, it would appear as if power
were the only reality in this universe, because you are
able to feel it. In other words, the tangible is not real
because it cannot be demonstrated to exist ; but the intangible, that appeals to something in us that is above
reason, can be felt by a responsive something that we
designate the spirit. Are you aware, sir, that, if we accept any such theory, you and I will be forced to admit
all the conclusions that we have been so vigorously re-
pudiating this afternoon concerning a Supreme Being,
the soul, and immortality ? Do you mean to tell me that,
because I cannot demonstrate the fact that I am sitting
here and talking to you, therefore this lovely lake and
yonder lordly mountains do not exist? If I shut my
eyes and sweep the vision away, yet will the substance of
the landscape exist as before. These beauties will be
here, even if there be no eye to gaze on them. Surely
this present moment is real! Surely I am here talking
to you! Surely we are environed by these fields and
mountains ! These things must be true even if every
thing else in the universe be mere phantasms !"

"Nay, O Monk, you merely assume that these things
exist. If I choose to deny your assumptions, you have
no demonstrations at hand that could force conviction
upon me. Also bear in mind that, if these things be true,
then, by the same method of assumption, a multitude of
other things are equally true. Either *every thing* exists,
or *nothing* exists. You cannot assume that just a few
things that you enumerate do exist, and then forbid the
existence of the balance of the universe, that other minds
assume to exist as well as the few things that you have
seen fit to dignify with existence."

"Then, O Prince, I presume that this intangible power

in the foreigner does exist, as truly as yonder shadow that Hiyeisan is casting upon the waters of this lake. If this concession be made, I do not see where you will land me short of the accursed doctrines of the *Kirishitans.*"

"I do not care where it will land you. All I know is that, so far as I am concerned, there are certain phenomena that I consider it politic and expedient to recognize as realities, even though they be invisible realities. Did not my mind wrestle with the minds of these foreigners over the terms that should be incorporated into the treaty, and am I not positive that in matters of diplomacy and reasoning their minds are constructed on the same plan as mine? What can be more real than that fact? Let the treaty speak for itself."

"O most profound and learned Prince, you are treading upon very dangerous ground if you intend to adhere to your first declarations about the universe."

"Never mind about that, O Priest, but look to your own laurels and to those of your religion, for I am about to make some marvellous revelations unto thee. Know, then, that in my researches to discover what was the secret power of these foreigners, and whence flowed their inspiration, I came across the following historic record: It appears that nearly four centuries ago there dwelt on the shores of a far distant sea a man who not only assumed this earth to be spherical in shape, but who also asserted the same to be a fact with endless persistency. He spent many years in navigating his native seas, and also the shores of a vast ocean contiguous thereto. All the wise and learned men of those days laughed him to scorn. Yet did he persist in his assertion, and endeavor to verify his allegation, that land lay beyond those apparently boundless waters, by showing certain berry-bushes and sundry curiously carved pieces of wood that had drifted across that vast expanse of waters and had floated upon the shores of those countries that bordered the eastern shores of that ocean. Still persisting in placing absolute faith on the correctness of his assumption, he even dared to venture upon that unexplored waste of waters, and to sail westward for many months, until he actually came upon the shores of an unknown continent. Further voyages and discoveries verified his theory beyond all possible doubt. And, within fifty years from the time that he reached the shores of that new world, another navigator, sailing in an opposite direction, came upon our own shores.

"Now, the strange part of this matter is, that the inhabitants of this new continent, who, by the way, are the descendants of the race to which the discoverer belonged, are the very people who now come to our shores and demand commercial intercourse with us. Now the actions of this great discoverer reveal unto me the principle, not only of his own success, but also of the success of the race to which he belongs. He, being convinced of the correctness of his conclusions, then by faith laid hold of things unseen, and thus out of his intangible theories revealed a new world to humanity. And the race to which he belongs are given to acting on faith in many matters that are extremely practical in their nature. They appear to have imbibed this principle from their extraordinary religion, of which this great discoverer was a very devout follower. Having accustomed their minds to this peculiar method of procedure, they very naturally drift into the habit of applying this wonderful principle of human nature to things outside of their religion. In their sciences and arts they appear to have assumed certain fundamental principles to be correct, and then to have gone ahead and constructed their comprehensive theories and their marvellous mechanical productions. This principle of laying hold on the invisible and the intangible and building thereon in accordance with their enlightened reason, appears to be the secret of their superior power as a race. The people of this very race were savages a thousand years after our nation had adopted Chinese civilization! Yet, under the subtle influence of this principle, they appear during the last thousand years to have made immeasurable progress, while we have stagnated. This race of savages has developed a boldness and a keenness in metaphysical and scientific speculation, an exalted devotion in the search for truth, and a magnanimity of spirit that will eventually cause them to crowd out of existence all races not developing such characteristics."

"But hold on, O Prince! Whither will you lead me? If that which you say be true, then the meteoric stones and foreign substances that drift across the boundless ocean of space upon our shores prove the existence of other worlds beyond this mighty abyss, for the books of the Hollanders say that the elements composing these pieces of drift from unknown realms beyond us are identical with the mineral substances entering into the composition of our earth. Pray, where will your next step lead us?"

"Now zealously guard the laurels of thy creed, O Priest. Know that this foreign race has applied this same principle of faith to the intangible and invisible spirit-world, as they call it. They assume the existence of a Supreme Being and of a soul, and they believe that this Supreme Being has promised immortality to mankind. Assuming and believing these fundamental principles to be correct, they have built thereon their hopes and their energies. They also allege that this Supreme Being has revealed unto them a magnificent and perfect system of moral ethics, whereby to guide and to direct them in this life, and to prepare them for a future life after death. Upon this system of ethics they have built their social and political institutions, which appear to have developed into something quite superior to ours. Now, even if there be no Supreme Being, no soul, no immortality, yet the very principle of laying hold on the reality of such profound mysteries by faith, and acting thereon, appears to develop a nobler spirit in mankind than the rejection of these mysteries, or the remaining in a state of uncertainty concerning them, seems to develop. The application of this principle seems to produce higher types of races. Therefore I am convinced that this is the source of the foreigners' exalted aspirations and inspired sentiments, which have developed in their natures lofty and noble impulses, that stamp their existence on their very faces.

"O Priest, what chance has your weak and childish creed against such vitalized and glorious beliefs ? Look to your laurels, sir Abbot. I foresee great changes in this country. The day may soon come when this foreign religion will again challenge your creed. Three hundred years ago it swept, within forty years, over Kiushiu like wildfire, and, but for the intervention of the State, where would your sect have been ? Beware of its second advent, and make ready your weapons. Be assured that the religion which can offer a reasonable hope of immortality to man will soothe the cravings of the human heart, and will sweep your dead creed out of existence. As for myself, I shall continue to live and to believe as I have heretofore done. I cannot understand these mysteries. Therefore I reject them. But your creed is under our patronage, and it behooves us to give you timely advice and warning whenever our forecast becomes gloomy.

"It is now getting toward the close of the day, and you must hasten homeward. My swiftest boat with eight lusty scullers will bear you across the lake directly to the base of Hiyeisan. Return, then, to thy engroved monastery on yonder summit, and ponder well my warnings. Seek the shadows of the moon-lit pines, and brood yet more deeply over the profound mysteries of life, of death, and of immortality ; and when thy sombre communings shall disclose whither hath fled the spirit that erstwhile shone forth in the countenance of thy departed brother, then hasten to reveal unto me the dread truth. Farewell ! "

CHAPTER XIX.

ON the same day that the Lord of Hikoné wrestled so nonchalantly with the Abbot of Hiyeisan on matters pertaining to the dread mysteries of life and of death, there came a messenger to the gateway of Mito Yashiki, enquiring for the sons of Nakashima. He was duly escorted to the lodge, where dwelt the two gentlemen for whom he was searching. The messenger reported himself to be the bearer of letters from their father at Atago-Yama, With reverent hands the despatches were received, and quickly opened. The one addressed to Junzo contained merely a few items of family news and some expressions of general pleasure at the auspicious commencement of his vassalage to Mito.

The letter to Tomokichi, however, was far different in its import. To the Caucasian reader it would have appeared a droll specimen of literature. It ran thus :
" My son, it has been truly said that he, who leaves no children to burn incense before his shrine, well merits the commiseration of both gods and men. To have one's name pass into utter oblivion, to become extinct in root and in branch, are calamities to be guarded against with great care by judicious and thoughtful members of the community. Has not our name been handed down from generation to generation for more than one thousand years ? Should not we, therefore, see to it at this day that the proper precautions be taken to prevent the contingency of so dire a calamity as the decadence of so ancient a family ? Profoundly have I dwelt upon this subject, until my meditations have brought me to definite

conclusions and action in the matter. It is already well known to you that our worthy friend Yamada grieves deeply over his supreme misfortune in being deprived of male offspring. In accordance with the ancient and praiseworthy custom of our country, he has offered to adopt as his heir my youngest son, your brother Kunisaburo, thus perpetuating his family and transmitting his name to posterity. It is needless for me to say how supremely honored I feel at this token of confidence on the part of so discriminating a person as this gentleman of renowned lineage undoubtedly is. Another pleasing feature of this matter was developed when our illustrious friend also proposed a marriage between his younger daughter and Kunisaburo (between which frivolous creatures it appears that a weak and silly attachment has long existed). The generous offers of Mr. Yamada have been accepted by me after long and profound reflection ; and the marriage will be consummated next month. Immediately thereafter, the adoption of my son will be ratified.

"But there is another matter, allied to the one under discussion, that more directly concerns yourself, and concerning which I now notify you. I, being consumed with the very natural and laudable desire to hand down my name to posterity, have proposed a marriage between you and Mr. Yamada's elder daughter. This proposal, after due deliberation, he has condescended to accept, thus honoring us very greatly by the alliance. We have decided to have this marriage consummated a few days before the nuptials of your brother are celebrated. Therefore I have written this letter to you asking that you will obtain leave of absence for three months from Yedo, and that you will forthwith journey home in order that the bridal ceremonies be not held in abeyance after an unseemly fashion. It will not be necessary for your brother Junzo to leave his duties in Mito Yashiki. At the end of three months you may resume your duties in Yedo, and your wife can make her home with us at Atago-Yama. We are all in good health and wish you much joy and a pleasant journey."

Such was the substance of the epistle. Strange enough does it seem to our Caucasian ears. Yet, in a land where the family and the government were based upon patriarchal principles, it was deemed just and proper that the father should dictate in what manner and with whom his name should be perpetuated,—and from his decision there was practically no appeal. If a matrimonial alliance seemed proper in the eyes of the parents, orders in council were forthwith issued to the young couple, and they meekly obeyed. Making love after the manner of the Caucasians, to them would have appeared coarse and tumultuous. For a love-lorn swain to have confessed his passion to the object of his admiration, would have been regarded as vulgar and indecent. In such matters the services of a mutual friend were always employed to discuss the affair with the young lady's parents, who pondered and rendered final decision in the premises.

As a general thing, the young people were very rarely consulted as to their own wishes in the matter. From beginning to end, the entire transaction was viewed from a purely business standpoint, and every vestige of romance was duly eliminated therefrom. Of course, if there existed a very violent antipathy on the part of one toward the other, then the indulgent parents would doubtless act cautiously and wisely. But where a match was otherwise desirable, then no question of personal preference would be allowed to intervene. The only escape from the will of inexorable parents lay in suicide, —a ghastly measure occasionally resorted to by thwarted lovers, who would tie themselves together with cords and then jump into the friendly waters of some river or inlet, whence their unhappy souls drifted out upon the unknown seas above, while their hapless bodies drifted about with the uneasy tides that ceaselessly pounded the shores.

Whilst this despotic method of procedure in the highest compact known to mankind may not be desirable, yet it would be well if we Caucasians learned to conduct our campaigns in the domain of Cupid with more sober judgment and with less of gushing and tumultuous pyrotechnics, so to speak. Now, owing to this peculiar method of match-making, I fear that there will not be found to be much of wooing and winning within the pages of this book. Romantic incidents of that description will necessarily be very meagre, because the conscientious novelist will not try to picture the Oriental lover as making love after methods peculiar to Caucasians. However much of latitude may be given to the novelist in matters of detail, yet the critical reader notices with displeasure any liberty taken with matters of general principle. To weave through the web of my romance the subtle fibres of a charming tale of wooing and winning might be very tempting, but it would be violently introducing ardent foreign methods into the mild and unpoetic marital customs of the Far East.

Yet the essence of love was the same as with us. It differed only in the manner of expression. The Japanese maiden loved coyly and demurely, scorning to exhibit any outward sign of emotion as being unwomanly and silly. The young man loved deeply, and, instead of publishing that fact to the world with serenades and motiveless meanderings about the premises of his dulcinea's parents, at once retained the services of some astute and diplomatic friend to press his suit before mademoiselle's father, who was generally disposed to give kindly attention to the young swain's advance, provided his connections were respectable.

I will not waste time, however, in moralizing upon the possible advantage to be derived by us from a careful study of the practical and business-like methods of conducting Oriental matrimonial alliances. Suffice it to say that Tomokichi read, comprehended, and obeyed. As a matter of fact, I feel justified in confidentially stating that the young man was not entirely unprepared for his father's abrupt announcement and peremptory command. He had long had his eyes open to the way matters appeared to be shaping themselves (observing young man as he was) and he perceived the thorough appropriateness of the entire proceeding. In addition to this he long had admired and esteemed the stately and modest Masago. Had the customs of the country permitted him to take the initiative in the matter, he would long before have bloomed forth in the rôle of the ardent lover. But the chilling proprieties of the social atmosphere wherein he had been brought up discouraged any open advances on his part, and so he had plunged yet deeper into his studies and had patiently awaited developments.

And how about Masago herself, I hear you asking? Had she been consulted in the matter? Nay, not as we understand such things. Her father briefly notified her one morning that within two months she was to be married to the eldest son of Mr. Nakashima, and that her arrangements must be accordingly made. She bowed her head to the *tatamis* and said : "Very well, father," and forthwith set to work to make her exceedingly simple *trousseau.* But she also had kept her eyes open and had drawn shrewd conclusions as to how matters were shaping themselves. And in her little Japanese head she saw the thorough appropriateness of the whole plan. And, then, had she not always admired the grave and courtly youth? Had she not always felt happy when he visited her father's house, and had she not felt inexpressibly lonely whenever he departed? Did she not love to recall the time when he forgot his fan and she ran after him, all blushes and smiles, and returned it to him at the gateway? Could she forget his profound and gracious acknowledgments, and how he touched her hand so gently (accidentally, of course) when he reached forth and took it back? Ah, mademoiselle, your father's announcement fell upon ready ears. It was not unwelcome news, and it filled your heart with strange joy.

It did not take long for our young knight to complete his arrangements for his overland trip. His first plan was to foot it over the Nakasendo. But when the impulsive old Prince heard about it he at once gave orders for a horse and *bettô* to be furnished from his own stables for the journey. And, when our young friend went up to take leave of his Lordship, that gracious old gentleman handed him one hundred *rios* for his nuptial expenses, quite overwhelming him with confusion and astonishment. Early on the following day he rode forth on the Nakasendo and journeyed for ten days over the road traversed nearly a year before by the fleet-footed couriers of the Shogun. About midway through the mountains he met the retinue of the Gotairo returning to Yedo. At last he drew near the base of Atago-Yama, and his heart beat with proud and happy emotions as he anticipated the pleasure that his honored return would produce. Late in the afternoon he rode into the mouth of the glen and began to ascend the winding road that led up toward the hamlet.

"A gallant knight comes riding up the glen!" whispered the children with bated breath as they rushed home to report the news to their parents in the hamlet.

"Sure enough! Who can it be?" exclaimed the startled villagers as they gathered about their gateways and gazed curiously down the road, for it was indeed an unusual occurrence to have a horseman enter the secluded hamlet, and the timid people had learned to shrink from the lawless blades that occasionally roamed abroad to test their cruel swords on any luckless subject that chanced to fall in their way. The terrible tales of reckless *ronins* had served to subdue the insubordination of many a peevish youngster in the peaceful hamlets of the realm.

Presently a little fellow, somewhat bolder than his companions, crept cautiously through the thickets that bordered the hillside and peeped down directly upon the approaching horseman as he toiled up the steep ascent. The little fellow was not long in recognizing the stranger, and dashed back shouting at the top of his voice: "It is Tomokichi, the son of Nakashima!" The last trace of fear fled at the sound of these magic words, for the young man was loved and respected by everybody who had ever known him. Fathers leading their little ones, mothers with babies tied on their backs, maidens with hastily plucked flowers in their hands, all flocked about the gateway of the Nakashima cottage to bid welcome to the returning wanderer, whom they greeted with profoundly respectful obeisances as he came up to the entrance. Great was the joy and the pride of the simple people to see one of their neighbors thus enter the gateway of his home.

Dismounting at the veranda and handing the reins to the *bettô*, Tomokichi was received by his family with that affectionate and decorous ceremony so admirable in the Japanese people. And then the neighbors poured in with warm congratulations. In the meantime the meek *bettô* held the horse beside the gateway, the centre of an admiring group. At last the animal became restive under the close inspection, and lashed out with his hoofs at an old gentleman who had ventured too near so as to obtain a good view of the handsome saddle. This manifestation of equine rudeness precipitated upon the nag's devoted head a torrent of harsh rebuke from the *bettô*, together with a volley of sarcastic admonition from the same source, to the effect that his Yedo manners had better not be laid aside, unless he was hungering "to taste a bit of stick." This cutting observation appeared to overwhelm the nag with confusion, for he forthwith subsided into demure contemplation of the scenery, and the people filled up the measure of their curiosity even to overflowing.

After the levée had lasted for about an hour, Tomokichi suddenly became mindful of the companions of his journey and came out to order that the horse be stabled. But *presto !* there was not a stable in the hamlet. The people themselves had always been the carriers of burdens, so that the interesting disclosure was made that from the remotest generations nobody had ever owned a horse. The next question was "What was to be done?" Surely, it would never do to send the noble animal down into the stables in the city. At this perplexing juncture a good neighbor came forward and offered the use of a shed, where in the winter season he was accustomed to store bags of charcoal. And he *bettô* himself was billeted to chum with the old man-servant in the Nakashima kitchen.

Having thus settled down, Tomokichi plunged into a description of his adventures and experiences that held the household entranced far into the night. In fact, the next two days were given up very largely to smoking and to conversation, and O-Hana allowed her household work to run sadly behind in order that she might hear about the thrilling wonders that were transpiring beyond the mountains that environed her home. To the Caucasian reader it may appear strange that the young man did not cut a swell on his steed and dash down to Yamada's at once to see his dulcinea. But such exhibitions of vulgar show and inordinate haste were not according to refined Japanese taste. Such matters were conducted with simplicity and decorum.

Therefore three days were allowed to pass before he called on Mr. Yamada. On the morning of that day the entire family went to Kioto, and spent a couple of days. The Misses Yamada were, to all outward appearances, the same courteous young ladies of last summer entertaining their friends. They acted their parts to perfection. And it required a keen observer to see and to appreciate the many delicate attentions of which the two young men were the recipients from their respective *fiancées.* Why was it that whenever Masago dipped out the rice the elder brother was always first helped, while, when Seisho dipped it out, the same fate befell the younger brother? Why was it that the side-dishes of the two young men always contained delicate morsels of some dainty not seen on the other less fortunate side-dishes? Why was it that the sisters always happened to be on hand when the gentlemen went out calling, so as to be ready to hand from the rack the swords of their respective lovers, while the old gentlemen had to help themselves to theirs. You do not know what Tomo-kichi's favorite flower is, yet Masago always wears it in

her hair. And Seisho always wears the silken girdle presented to her by Kunisaburo on her last birthday.   Do
you, my Caucasian friend, call these but tame manifestations of love?   Do you shrug your shoulders and remark
that such servile attentions do but disgust your more
rugged nature?

Well, well, my carnivorous countryman, it may seem
tame to your beef-fed constitution, and it may appear
servile to your modern democratic perceptions, but you
must bear in mind that the feudal theory upon which society was founded in that country rendered such attentions
eminently becoming and proper.   The structure of their
society was based upon the idea of lord and vassal.   As
every man was the vassal of some lord to whom he bowed
down in homage, so every woman was the vassal of some
man (whether father, brother, or husband) to whom she
owed allegiance and rendered homage.   Man was the
bulwark that girded the prince about with a living wall,
standing betwixt him and every danger, and he was also
the lion that stood at the threshold of the home to rend
asunder the spoiler and the ravisher.   What then could
have been more appropriate and dignified than for hands
unfitted for mortal combat to gently gird on the keen
blade and to minister to the wants of the warrior, the
guardian of the home?

We will not detain you with such scenes, but will
hasten with the story of the simple wedding that took
place within a fortnight after the return of our gallant
knight from Yedo.   It was indeed very simple.   There
were no wedding bells, no organ marches, no church
processions, no temple ceremonies.   It was viewed
almost entirely as a business transaction.   Yet to the
maidenly hearts of the sisters the occasion was one of
supreme importance and happiness.   On the morning of
the eventful day the Nakashimas went in *norimons* to the
mansion of Mr. Yamada.   A few friends had been invited to the sumptuous feast prepared by the host.   It
was spread out on the floor of the upper story, which had
been ornamented with silken hangings and flowers until

it resembled a lovely bower. A bevy of servants from some renowned caterer flitted about noiselessly arranging the dishes and the cushions on the *tatamis*.

The Nakashimas were quietly ushered into the lower rooms, where they chatted with their host and with the assembled guests, while the bearers were sent to the quarters of the gate-keeper, where a feast had been prepared for them and for the household servants. At about midday the guests were ushered upstairs, where they were duly arranged around on the floor,—and the feast began. It was one of those interminable Oriental repasts that beggars description. It comprised forty courses, served up in little messes of fish, flesh, and fowl. Of course none of the courses were very heavy. Some of them might well have been characterized as merely a nibble and a bite. Little bowls of soup, tiny morsels of some choice vegetable or fruit, and rare selections of roots and confectionery comprised the bulk of the courses. The entire afternoon was given up to eating, drinking, and smoking between times. The utmost good-humor and hilarity characterized every thing. Choice brands of *saké* flowed freely, and the band of musicians downstairs at intervals wrestled with sundry stringed instruments and flutes after a fashion that would have impressed a Caucasian with the idea that the tune was rapidly getting the better of the performers.

The bride sat with her parents on one side of the room, while the groomsman dined with his family at the other end of the room, where he was the recipient of considerable good-natured chaffing and badgering. As the feast merged into its closing courses there gradually settled down upon the convivial gathering a hush of expectancy, as if the supreme moment of the entertainment were approaching. At last an attendant brought in a beautiful tray whereon were placed a tiny cup and an exquisite little porcelain jar containing the choicest of *saké*. He ceremoniously deposited his burden before two vacant cushions beside the balcony. Then, amid the plaudits and the congratulations of their friends, the bride and the groom slowly rose, and, advancing to the cushions, seated themselves thereon. Then Masago, with nervous hands, filled the cup with *saké*, and handed it to Tomokichi to quaff; and he, in turn, refilled it and handed it back to her to quaff.

And this pretty ceremony—emblematical of the fact that from thenceforth they were to imbibe pleasures and sorrows at the same bowl—constituted the happy couple Mr. and Mrs. Nakashima. And from that time until the close of the feast they ate and drank together as husband and wife, receiving from and giving back to the company much witty and pleasant badinage. There was no kissing of the bride, no handshaking, no dancing; but verbal congratulations poured forth freely from all parts of the room. And quite bride-like did Masago appear with her blushing cheeks and lavender-colored robe. On this interesting occasion Kunisaburo and Seisho sat side by side, and graciously helped each other to choice morsels of edibles. Late in the evening the jovial revellers disbanded. The newly married couple departed in their *norimons* for the glen that very night, but the rest of the family did not return until late the following day.

About ten days after the events chronicled above, Kunisaburo's wedding came off. It was a great day in the hamlet. The guests assembled in the upper story of the cottage, and feasted far into the night. Good old neighbor Yenzo called for a fiddle, and essayed an ambitious flight in the realms of harmony, but his efforts merely served to increase the volume of the prevailing hilarity. At the supreme moment the attendant again brought in the cup and the jar, and pretty Seisho daintily dealt forth the beverage to her new lord. The congratulations of the kind-hearted neighbors then poured forth in a steady stream. Good old Yenzo, undismayed at his previous shortcomings in the realms of harmony, now launched forth into an improvised rhapsody in the dread realms of Chinese poetry to the unbounded amusement of the company. The little children of the hamlet were furnished with a juvenile entertainment downstairs, and feasted to their hearts' content on cake, fruit, and candy. Late in the evening the party broke up, and, a few days thereafter the bride and the groom returned to the house of her father, where her husband's formal adoption as the heir to the estates of Mr. Yamada was duly ratified.

CHAPTER XX.

FOUR years have elapsed since the events chronicled in the previous chapter transpired. The course of public affairs has flowed on steadily, but there have been abundant indications of ill-disguised and deep-seated resentment on the part of the conservative element in the country against the liberal concessions made to the foreign treaty powers by the Shogun's government. Unwonted earthquakes, storms, and pestilence have sorely vexed the country until the people—naturally superstitious—cry out that the gods are angry at the actions of the government in subverting the ancient anti-foreign policy of the nation. The year 1854 was one of great seismic agitation throughout the empire, and the native chroniclers assert that during that entire twelve-month the islands of Dai-Nippon never ceased to quake and to tremble in some portion or other with continuous vibrations. The Vries islands, situated to the eastward of the mouth of Yedo bay, were in a state of violent and continued eruption, so it is not unlikely that the native accounts are true.

In the month of November, just after Tomokichi had returned from Atago-Yama, these seismic disturbances seemed to culminate in intensity around Yedo as a centre, and produced one of the most terrific disasters on record. In the vivid language of the native historians, Yedo was reduced to a rubbish heap. The massively built *yashikis* and temples were not thrown down ; but all of the common structures were demolished. The shocks commenced early in November, and continued for many days almost uninterruptedly, and spasmodically stirred the country even up to the close of December. Tomokichi was in his room at the lodge manfully wrestling with the mysteries of a Dutch grammar, when the deep-toned booms, like suppressed thunder, caused him to start up and listen to what seemed to be a distant cannonade. Presently the leaves of the trees began to rustle as if blown by some unseen tempest, and the shock struck Mito Yashiki with a rush and a roar that threw him off his feet.

Then ensued scenes of appalling horror. Shrieks and yells could be heard arising from all parts of the city. With one impulse the inmates of Mito Yashiki rushed forth from the buildings and sought the groves that filled their spacious grounds, so that in case the earth should split open, then would the interlacing roots of the trees keep them from falling into the yawning fissures. The shocks were so violent and rapid that before Tomokichi could regain his feet he was most unceremoniously rolled about the room and out upon the veranda, whence he was tumbled out upon the ground, along with the débris of numerous flower-pots and porcelain vases. He picked himself up and staggered out under a tree and tried to stand up beside it, but the swaying motion rendered him so deathly sick that he felt constrained to lie down on the grass and allow himself to be rolled about at the mercy of the successive waves that beat against the hill. It seemed as if the lodge would surely be set on end. Large patches of tiles slid off until the rafters were laid entirely bare. It swayed from side to side like a ship in a gale. The *shojees* were twisted out of their grooves and thrown down, while the timbers creaked and groaned most dismally. The long lines of barracks were thumped and twisted until their roofs slid off with horrid din. They writhed and squirmed like vast serpents when the seismic waves rolled beneath their foundations. The stately palace, with its massive roof, sustained but little damage, although it swayed and rattled with deafening turmoil. During the intervals between the shocks, our young friend hastily removed the *tatamis* from the lodge, and spread them out under the trees, so that his companions and himself might spend the night there if necessary. He then started out to find his brother. Whenever the vibrations commenced he threw himself flat on the grass and waited until they had subsided. Everywhere the wildest confusion and consternation prevailed. Twenty thousand men had simultaneously rushed forth and sought the open air, and were now scattered all about the lawns and groves, excitedly discussing the catastrophe. During the intermissions, *tatamis* and bedding were brought forth, and they prepared to camp out all night. Finding his brother at last, he returned with him to the trees beside the lodge, and there awaited further developments. The shocks continued at intervals all through the night, and the crash of falling houses, together with the glare of conflagrations caused by overturned *hebachis*, made it a scene of indescribable horror. And from that time onward to the close of December they camped out most of the time in the open air. According to estimates, twenty thousand houses and sixteen hundred fire-proof *godowns* were destroyed during the continuation of these shocks. Over one hundred thousand people were reported killed. The great cities along the southern coast were nearly destroyed. . Osaca and Hiogo were well-nigh demolished, and Kioto was very badly shaken up. The little hamlet in the glen of Atago-Yama was off the great vein of seismic vibration, and escaped with a slight shaking up.

Toward the close of November the disturbances seemed to break up the fountains of the great deep, for the ocean rose up and dashed itself in mighty billows against the coast, and created incalculable havoc to harbors and seaside villages. The Russian frigate *Diana* lay at anchor in Shimoda, one of the two ports just thrown open to foreign commerce, and the water rushed out of the harbor, leaving her bumping on the rocks, while the thoughtless people on shore, following their first impulse, rushed down the beach to catch the fishes floundering in the mud. Then back came the wave from the ocean in a billow thirty feet high and rushed over the town and broke in surges against the base of the bluffs beyond, while the *Diana*, on beams' end, was swirled around her anchor with sickening rapidity. Then back went the wave, and crash went the frigate against. the bottom of the harbor. Five successive times did the mighty billows advance shoreward, and then recede oceanward, until the town had been washed away, and all the mud had been swept off the floor of the harbor, thus utterly destroying it for commercial purposes ; and the noble frigate was so badly wrecked that it sank shortly afterward. Then the water resumed its normal level, and so peacefully lapped the beach of Shimoda that a stranger would not have known any such disaster had befallen the place, until he beheld the fields covered with the mud and slime deposited there by the ocean waves. It truly seemed to the native mind as if the gods had stepped in and had destroyed the harbor that had been desecrated by foreign anchors,—for the place had to be abandoned as a seaport.

By the commencement of 1855, however, nature settled herself down, and matters resumed their accustomed course. During the three years that succeeded the great earthquake, Tomokichi and Junzo pursued their perilous vocation with great success, and without exciting any suspicion as to the real nature of their presence at Mito Yashiki. And Mr. Yamada, at Kioto, pursued so peaceful and exemplary a life that he regained favor in the eyes of the Shiro people, and his name was accordingly crossed from their lists. About a year after the wedding of his brothers, Junzo was duly lassoed with the paternal halter, and was meekly led up to the marital altar—so to speak,—where he was tied to a very delightful morsel of humanity, known as Miss Akashi. She was the only daughter—in fact the only child—of a warm friend of Mr. Yamada. She was pretty, blithesome, and highly educated according to Japanese ideas. Her father was the retainer of a *kugé*, and, unlike most gentlemen of that description, he was quite wealthy, and owned a very choice tea plantation not far from Kioto. The marriage was celebrated with great zest, for the old Prince of Mito had generously put down another hundred *rios* wherewith to celebrate the nuptials. This showed to the Kioto people that the Lord of Mito was highly pleased with his new vassals from Atago-Yama, for some reason unknown to the public. As old Mr. Akashi had no heir, he very naturally adopted this surplus son of Mr. Nakashima as the heir to his estates.

With matters thus arranged, these two brothers had most excellent pretext for alternately visiting their homes in Yamashiro every six months or so, and staying a few weeks with their wives and children, for at the date of the opening of this chapter, Masago rejoiced in two robust sons, while young Mrs. Akashi smiled upon a lovely daughter. Nor was Seisho to be outdone by her sisters, for she boasted of a sturdy son and a merry little daughter, the very image of herself. It would be needless to say that on the occasion of these visits our young spies fully posted Mr. Yamada on all that was going on in Yedo. With young Konishi in the office of the Bakufu in daily communication with the ministers of state, it is not surprising that they were able to keep marvellously well informed about affairs in general, without any apparent exertion on their part. No wonder the Gotairo frequently found himself headed off in many of his pet schemes, and felt obliged to sharply admonish the commandant of the Shiro in Kioto to increase his vigilance over suspected characters in that city. Yet, in spite of every thing, matters at Kioto shaped themselves after a fashion that plainly showed that secret information was being regularly transmitted from Yedo. It became manifest that there was a leak somewhere. In vain did the Gotairo storm at his subordinates. The foxy Yamada only laughed the more in his sleeve while his crafty lieutenants demurely and unobtrusively plied their vocation without exciting the least suspicion. Could the sands of the Kamogawa shoals have voiced the many conversations that took place in their picnic booths during these years, the Gotairo would soon have stopped the leak in his office.

During the years 1855 and 1856, it became manifest to the Gotairo that a knowledge of the English language would be indispensable in the office of the Bakufu, inasmuch as that language appeared to be the commercial vernacular of the outside world. Accordingly, orders were given to discourage the study of Dutch and to take up that of English. As Mito ranked as the most scholarly of all of the clans, he very naturally looked in that direction for material wherewith to organize a corps of English linguists. Through young Konishi, he had already heard of Tomokichi's scholarly attainments, and accordingly gave orders that he and Konishi should go down to Shimoda and connect themselves with the custom-house at that port, in order to learn as much as possible from the American and English merchants trading there. With diligent application, they not only acquired a fair mastery of the English language during their sojourn there, but they also gained an insight into foreign commercial usages that was of great service to them. They also reaped a rich harvest of information as to the peculiar methods of the Bakufu in conducting a custom-house.

In all countries a prejudice of corruption has always existed against those who "sit at the receipt of customs." It will not be too much to say that under the Shoguns' administration this service was probably as corrupt as any thing that ever existed in the political history of this world. The officers of the government well understood the unfriendly spirit of their master toward foreign commerce, and were aware that they were at full liberty to make trade as uncomfortable as possible, both for the native merchant and for the outside trader. They hovered like a flock of harpies over every transaction. Every sale had to be conducted under their directions. They craftily compelled their own countrymen to tuck on the prices, and then pounced down upon the luckless dealers and plucked them of their inflated profits.

As produce and merchandise began to be drained from the country, scarcity and corresponding high prices began to prevail everywhere. The people groaned, the merchants tamely allowed themselves to be plundered of their profits, and the Bakufu grew enormously rich with ill-gotten spoil. This, in connection with storms, pestilence, and earthquakes, which seemed to be rampant during these four years, created deep-seated and widespread murmurings throughout the empire. But what cared the Gotairo for that? With the purse in his hands, he could afford to smile at the situation and continue on his course. At no time had his power been so great. And it seemed to grow stronger every day. With this vast source of foreign income he was rendered independent of the Daimios. He defied the conservative element in the land, and, metaphorically speaking, snapped his fingers in the face of the Emperor himself. In the estimation of his own party the Gotairo was the ablest and most upright individual in the empire. But in the estimation of his adversaries he was a cesspool, wherein stagnated the slimy ooze of villainous corruptions and fiendish cruelties. Thus, even in that remote corner of the globe, did political nomenclature enshrine public characters in a manner to indicate very strongly the common origin of the human race.

And thus opened the year 1858. Shimoda had been abandoned as a treaty port, and Kanagawa, just eighteen miles below Yedo, was opened as a new port in lieu thereof. In addition to this, Osaca and Hiogo on the Inland Sea—or rather at the entrance thereof—were to be thrown open in the following year, thus bringing the hated foreign traffic within a day's march of the sacred precincts of the Gosho. Loud and bitter were the imprecations of the conservatives against this unhallowed action on the part of the Gotairo, but he laughed them to scorn. So threatening, however, became the attitude of the hostile clans, that his Lordship deemed it prudent to persuade the foreigners to settle in Yokohama, a little fishing village a short distance below Kanagawa, thus getting them off the line of the Tokaido, where hostile clans were perpetually streaming along with thousands of fierce retainers. Thus he still held the reins with a firm grasp and seemed assured of an indefinite lease of power, when an event occurred that seriously disturbed his calculations and threatened dire disaster to his cause.

CHAPTER XXI.

"IYÉSADA the Shogun is dead!" exclaimed a breath-less messenger from the citadel one morning in August, when he had been ushered into the presence of the Go-tairo at his *yashiki*. This abrupt communication fell like a thunder-clap upon his Lordship. Doubtless the reader but dimly comprehends the full significance of this dread message. It meant that the Gotairo was down. His authority to govern the realm had lapsed. A new Shogun must now be chosen by the grand council of Daimios—for there was no heir,—and he well knew that their choice would be Keiki, the seventh son of the old Prince of Mito, a brilliant young man who had been adopted by the house of Hitotsubashi. With the scion of the hostile house of Mito in power, then Nawosŭké becomes merely Lord of Hikoné, a common Daimio of the realm. Then, being thus stripped of his power, would his enemies jump on him for his alleged misdeeds while in office, and badger and humiliate him until his life would cease to be desirable. Nay, they might even bring against him charges of treason toward the Emperor, and send him to the blood pit.

This was the direful situation in which his Lordship was placed by the death of Iyésada, his liege lord. It all flashed upon him in one moment. Yet did he not lose his balance. Even his enemies credited him with prompt energy and daring boldness in action, although they took pains to modify this complimentary admission with the allegation that he was thoroughly unscrupulous as to his methods of securing an end. Admirably did his great qualities shine forth in the present emergency, and his spirit rose to the momentous struggle with wonderful promptness. When the messenger was so hastily ushered into his presence, he was in his office looking over some papers relating to the new treaty recently negotiated with the Shogun by the American Minister, Mr. Townsend Harris. This fresh batch of concessions had created boundless fury among the conservative Daimios, and had given rise to dark threatenings against Iyésada and himself. Although he was overwhelmed with astonishment and regret at the message, yet did he not for one moment show by any outward sign how deeply he was affected by the sudden announcement. He coolly invited the messenger to sit down, and then ordered in some tea and tobacco. With the utmost deliberation he then proceeded to sip, to whiff, and to interrogate. .

"Your master's illness appears to have culminated very suddenly," said his Lordship. "I was aware that he was ailing last night, but I did not understand from the physician that any thing serious was to be apprehended. He seemed to be troubled with slight spasms in his stomach. I understood that the symptoms merely indicated a slight attack of indigestion."

"Quite so," replied the messenger, "but soon after the spasms commenced they increased very rapidly in frequency and in violence. In a very few hours they culminated in the most frightful convulsions, and he died in great agony."

"Why did nobody send me word?"

"Every thing was in such utter confusion," replied the messenger, "that it never occurred to anybody. Besides that, none of us for one moment anticipated death. Our master was too ill to give orders, and there was nobody to assume authority. The attendants were running about in every direction bringing warm water, plasters, and hot drinks. The members of the household were so overwhelmed with the suddenness and the terrible violence of the spasms that they were dazed. The truth is, that we all thought that by morning the illness would yield to treatment. Alas ! sir, but that was not to be."

"This matter must be kept profoundly secret until a successor has been chosen," replied his Lordship. "Speak to nobody concerning it, and carefully caution every one at the citadel to keep the matter quiet until notice from me. I will now accompany you to the saddened home of our unfortunate master and arrange matters." So saying, he clapped his hands and ordered the responding attendant to notify his retinue to be in readiness within half an hour.

At the appointed time, he was borne down the hill, through the Sakurada Gate, and up to the main entrance of the citadel. Every thing was quiet. There was nothing to indicate that so momentous an event as the death of the ruler of the land had taken place. To the outside world Iyésada was still the Shogun. And he continued to be such for many days thereafter. Leaving his retinue at the entrance, his Lordship went with two of his officers to the palace, where he met the weeping ladies of Iyésada's household. They were overcome with grief and horror. He was then ushered into the darkened chamber where lay the body. So sudden had been the catastrophe, and so unnerved had all the members of the royal household become, that the lifeless form of the unfortunate prince had been left just as it was when the spirit fled, lying in the middle of the room on a heap of silken quilts. His Lordship carefully examined the body and satisfied himself that life was extinct.

He then gave orders that the body should be prepared for private burial until such time as a public funeral became feasible. Then, convening the entire household in the audience-hall, he enjoined on everybody the strictest secrecy until such time as a successor might be chosen. He then went to the death chamber and called in each inmate of the palace and instituted searching inquiries as to the cause of the illness,—(for the preceding Shogun had died under very suspicious circumstances at the time of the granting of the first treaty in 1853, and it was doubly suspicious that his successor should suddenly die just after signing the second treaty). In fact, his Lordship felt morally certain that there had been foul play. A searching examination revealed nothing of importance. Everybody told the same story. The master had been taken ill with slight spasms in the stomach on the previous day ; the illness rapidly increased in intensity toward night, but was still supposed to be nothing serious ; but in the night the spasms merged into horrible convulsions, causing an agonizing death before morning. It was so terrible for one so young and so amiable to be thus stricken down !

But his Lordship was not yet satisfied. He submitted the personal attendants to a further series of questions as to what their master had been eating and drinking just before his illness. It did not appear from their replies that the diet of the deceased had varied from the usual routine. It is true that he had eaten some watermelon and had taken a glass of foreign wine ; but these articles appeared to have come from proper hands, so that no suspicion of poisonous substances injected therein could arise. Had the science of chemical analysis been understood in those days, the body of the deceased would surely have been subjected to a post-mortem examination ; but, nothing of the sort being known, the secret locked up in the tissues of the stomach remained untold. His Lordship then subjected the entire premises to a close scrutiny for some clue that would indicate the presence of intruders, but every thing appeared in good order. He then placed guards in all parts of the palace with strict instructions not to allow any one to go forth or to come in until further orders.

He then returned to his *yashiki* and sent for his councillors. These elderly gentlemen were the head men of the Hikoné clan, and had been his advisers from youth upward. On all important matters they were invariably consulted.

" Revered Councillors," said he when they had assembled in his private office, " it is my sad duty to notify you that our noble and generous master, the Shogun Iyésada, has entered upon the shadowy way. We are now without a head. It therefore becomes of paramount importance for us to take counsel and to devise measures to prevent popular panic and public disturbance until matters have become again settled. For this purpose have I caused you to be here assembled in consultation."

"Most worthy Lord," replied the senior member of the council, a gray-haired gentlemen whose wisdom and loyalty had rendered him highly esteemed by the entire clan, "this news is sudden and terrible indeed, but not altogether unexpected in view of the threats breathed forth lately by those who opposed the second treaty. Of course our mighty Lord perished by violence?"

"There I am at a loss to answer you," replied his Lordship, smiling at the clever declarative interrogation of the senior councillor, "because there is no appearance of any violence on his person. Of course I am morally certain that there has been foul play somewhere. Matters would be somewhat simplified if I could establish death by violence."

"What are the facts in the case?" enquired the senior councillor.

"It appears," replied his Lordship, "that he was in good health until taken ill yesterday. The case seemed to be merely an attack of indigestion, or some such slight stomach ailment. But he grew rapidly worse toward night, and, before morning, died in terrible convulsions."

"Then, sir," said the councillor, "in view of the political situation, it seems to me that the presumption is conclusive that there has been foul play. This is the second time within five years that this thing has happened under precisely similar circumstances. I have no doubt but what some attendant is in collusion with our enemies. He has been bribed to mix some deadly foreign poison with the wine. Either this or some attendant has allowed an outsider to scale the ramparts at night and to clandestinely mix the poison in the wine.

I do not doubt for a moment but what this thing has been done in some such way. In this corrupt age, what will money not accomplish? Dangle before the eyes of the average *samurai* the prospect of a grand carouse in the Yoshiwara and what can you not induce him to do? Under such circumstances, honor and loyalty become shadows that vanish in the glare of the brothels. Sir, we should trim our sails to the breeze that whispers 'foul play,' and act accordingly. This is my humble advice."

"You have spoken wisely, most revered councillor," replied his Lordship. "Your theory as to the cause of the death of our most unfortunate Lord, agrees with mine. I shall therefore adopt it as correct in view of the circumstances of the case. I have long since come to the conclusion that there is a powerful coalition of conspirators somewhere in Yedo working against us. And recently I have, through my spies, come across some clues that indicate Mito Yashiki as the head-quarters of this gang of traitors. I need but one or two more connecting links to complete my chain of evidence. And then beware, you sneaking curs over there! The operations of these fellows are conducted with consummate skill. They never leave behind them any footprints. This work of last night is a fair specimen of their way of conducting their campaigns of iniquity. Not a clue! Not a shred of evidence! Yet, beyond doubt, traitors have murdered their liege lord. O my fine fellows, don't laugh in your sleeves too much. I shall yet run you down."

"The manner of death rather indicates the use of some powerful foreign poison," suggested one of the councillors.

"Quite true," replied his Lordship.

"And who can more easily secure foreign poison than these same Mito men, who are continually communicating with the foreigners?" suggested another one.

"Equally true," replied his Lordship.

"And who but Mito will reap the benefit of this deed?" suggested yet another one.

" Who, indeed ? " queried his Lordship.

" It would appear," said the senior councillor, " as if we had a very strong case against Mito, and I fail to see how this case can be shaken. We are all familiar with their ancient grievance against the Shoguns ; and we also are well aware of their present hostility against the Bakufu. We all know that they expect to reap vast benefits from the death of Iyésada, inasmuch as young Hitotsubashi will surely be the choice of the Daimios. And we are fully informed of their recent threats, and well know the readiness with which they can procure subtle and deadly substances from foreigners wherewith to poison their adversaries. Thus, having the means and the disposition to perpetrate this foul deed, they traded on the weakness of human nature somewhere and gained access to the royal premises. With the aid of a friendly rope let down from above, a person could easily scale the ramparts in the rear of the garden at night and slip into some closet in the palace, where he could mix up his accursed drug in a glass of wine, and have it slyly administered by his coadjutor when the victim (perhaps) is in a condition not to be cognizant of any peculiar taste about any thing he may chance to put into his mouth. Promises of promotion under a Mito Shogun would be a powerful inducement just now, when so many are dissatisfied with the present administration of affairs. Sir, after all, the fault in this disaster will be found to rest very largely with us, for we did not carefully weed out from the members of our master's household all persons suspected of having conservative ideas. In case we secure control of the next Shogun, we must carefully select his household and know exactly what people serve him. Even his concubines should be thoroughly scrutinized. Women frequently make very dangerous conspirators."

" Well and truly spoken," exclaimed his Lordship. " Our plan, then, shall be to accuse Mito of causing the death of the Shogun by violence. This, of course, they will deny. But the effect of this public announcement will be to create a prejudice against their candidate for the office. I do not anticipate that this will defeat his election by the grand council of Daimios, but it will serve as a cover under which to introduce my candidate and force him on them. Desperate cases require desperate remedies. We are not going out of office in the natural order of things, but are being forced out by our adversaries resorting to foul and treasonable methods. This patent fact will justify us in using extraordinary methods to circumvent our enemies. We are compelled to meet violence with violence. The sympathies of a large part of the people are with us in our foreign policy ; and when it shall be proclaimed that Iyésada was the victim of the enemies of this popular policy, then will our violent course be deemed praiseworthy. The people will say that Mito had been justly punished for such unscrupulous and treasonable conduct. Then, in addition to this, our enemies are scattered, while we are concentrated here in Yedo,—thanks to the wise policy of Tokugawa Iyéyas. Their forces cannot successfully cope with our army here. I hold the power, and shall not resign it without good cause. The murder of our gentle master I shall certainly feel called upon to punish."

" But, sir, have you selected your candidate ? " enquired the councillors.

" I have been thinking over that matter very carefully," was the reply, " and I have decided upon the young prince of Kii-shiu."

" But, sir, he is only twelve years old ! "

" So much the better for me, inasmuch as I myself cannot be a candidate for the office."

This witty reply provoked loud laughter among the councillors, who shook their sides immoderately over the shrewd scheme of their lord.

" Besides that fact," continued he, " this plan has the merit of placing the minds of you councillors at ease concerning female conspirators within the citadel, for we shall not be called on to select his wife and concubines for a long time to come. In the meantime we can have the most absolute control of his household matters, and shall see to it that nobody enters his service until we have passed upon him. How does all this impress you, my worthy councillors?"

This sly hit was received with unbounded good-humor by all present. The details of the plan were then fully discussed, and the minutest points were carefully analyzed with that exhaustiveness which rendered his Lordship so difficult a person to catch unprepared. It was midnight before the council adjourned, and by that time a scheme had been perfected to keep the power in the hands of his lordship for an indefinite period.

CHAPTER XXII

IYÉMOCHI.

" Long live Iyémochi the Shogun ! " Such would have been the greeting of a Caucasian mob to their new ruler. But no such welcome awaited the new Shogun. In fact, the populace knew nothing about the death of the prior incumbent until the successor had been duly installed in office. The Lord of Hikoné had again carried the day, and the little Prince of Kii-shiu was now the " Ruler of the Four Coasts " and the " Barbarian-Exterminating Lord." His Lordship continued on as the Gotairo, and could afford to smile upon his enemies, who sneered at him as the " swaggering Prime-Minister." Truly he had carried matters with a high hand, and had done most unprecedented things that had filled the hearts of the conservative Daimios with rage and fear.

On the day following the death of his liege lord, as set forth in the preceding chapter, the Gotairo succeeded in extracting from the attendants at the palace evidence that criminated the old Prince of Mito. Popular rumor alleged the use of torture, and it is not unlikely that such measures were resorted to by this bold and desperate man. At all events, depositions were procured by some means or other to the effect that the luckless Iyésada had come to his death by poison administered at the instigation of the old Prince. Without delay the Gotairo sent notice to Mito Yashiki, ordering that old gentleman to retire at once into banishment at Mito,—for reasons best known to himself,—and to remain there in close confinement in his palace until permission to come out had been decreed by the Bakufu. This peremptory mandate was accompanied with a suggestive intimation that, if he instantly obeyed, matters would be allowed to rest, but that, if he did not at once obey, then he would be compelled to perform *seppuku* (hara-kiri), and his estates would be confiscated. This ominous notice it was deemed best to obey, and the old Prince forthwith departed from Yedo, vowing eternal vengeance against the wily author of his woes, as well as against "that nest of robbers," the Bakufu. When the choleric old gentleman arrived at his place of exile, he allowed his wrath to explode in terms of unmeasured denunciation at the outrageous indignity imposed upon him, and, in the highly expressive political colloquialism of the nineteenth century, "he painted the town red." The reverberations of his wrath reached Yedo, and he received speedy notice to subside, else extreme measures would be taken against him. Pressed against the Pacific Ocean, surrounded by powerful Tokugawa clans, with fiery Aidzu on the northwest ready to swoop down on him like a mighty avalanche, his position was indeed isolated and defenceless. He sulkily subsided. But his deep mutterings reached Kioto through underground channels, and found the imperial ear ready to listen to his complaints.

But the Gotairo did not stop here. He preferred charges against the most powerful of the conservative Daimios (even Satsuma and Tosa), and commanded that they should consider themselves under arrest and imprisonment within the seclusion of their respective *yashikis* until further notice, under penalty of incurring the dire displeasure of the Bakufu. Loud, angry, and ominous were the threatenings of the enraged clans at this extraordinary action. A less intrepid man than he would have quailed before the storm of indignation that arose from within the walls of almost every *yashiki* in Yedo. But, unterrified, he steadily pursued his course and heeded not the mutterings of the tempest that he had created.

With these preliminary steps thus energetically taken, he proceeded to convene the Daimios with a fair chance of winning the election. His manœuvrings would have done credit to the methods of a modern ward caucus. How admirably convenient to be able thus to bottle up your opponents until after the campaign ! Nevertheless, even with this handicapping, the election was a most hotly contested one, for young Hitotsubashi was not only exceedingly popular, but was also eminently fitted for the office both by maturity and ability. Most stubbornly did his adherents wage battle for him in the convention, and most eloquently did they urge that the national crisis demanded a man and not a boy at the head of the state. Vain ! When the tide seemed setting in their favor, and when victory seemed almost within their grasp, the Gotairo played his trump card and won the game. He asserted that Iyésada had verbally designated to him the young Prince of Kii-shiu as his heir and successor. True, no formal adoption had ever been consummated, but the wish and the intention to adopt had been so strongly and so frequently intimated, that the behest must be looked upon as a binding will. Such being the facts in the case, he felt called upon to see that the wishes of his late master were scrupulously complied with, and that his estates and his succession should revert to that one whom he had manifestly chosen to inherit them, and who, but for an unexpected contingency, would have inherited them.

This statement overwhelmed the Daimios with amazement and confusion. The wishes of the dead are respected in all lands. And when, as in this case, those wishes are urged for adoption by a man who clearly intimates that, unless they are adopted peaceably, then he must endeavor to enforce them with all the power at his command, the chances stand decidedly in favor of their adoption. In the present case they were adopted. The shrewd schemer precipitated the balloting just as soon as he had played his trump card and before his adversaries could put their heads together for consultation ; and, as a very natural consequence, the young Prince of Kii-shiu was declared elected. The little fellow was brought from chasing butterflies and flying kites in the vast enclosures of his father's *yashiki*, and was duly installed in the stately halls of the palace amid all the pomp and circumstance of royal power, and was bowed down to and reverenced by every one who entered his presence as Iyémochi the Shogun. And the crestfallen Daimios were dismissed to their respective *yashikis*, to chew at leisure the cud of bitter reflection over this brilliant illustration of how the realm was indeed ruled by one master-mind, and how helpless they all were to frustrate the ambitious schemes of this bold man.

The Gotairo then announced the death of Iyésada to the public and allowed the people to manifest whatever emotions they pleased. The English and the American Ministers, who had recently come to Yedo to reside, were duly notified of the event and were allowed to send in their somewhat tardy condolences. Lord Elgin, the Plenipotentiary from Great Britain, whose fleet had been riding at anchor before the city, found that he had been negotiating with a Shogun dead, for nobody knew how long a time. But he did not allow this Oriental idiosyncrasy to disturb his diplomatic relations, and, with the *sang-froid* of an experienced hand, he proceeded "to sign, to seal, and to deliver" as if nothing had happened.

Then did the councillors of the Gotairo arrange the household matters of the new Shogun after a fashion to suit themselves. There was a thorough overhauling of the domestic economy of the entire establishment. In the first place, all the attendants of their late master suddenly found themselves out of employment, being summarily dismissed under the vague charge of implied negligence in the matter of the sudden death of Iyésada. Then their places were slowly filled with persons whose loyalty could not be in any way doubted. The guards about the citadel were doubled. And the gardens surrounding the palace were placed under the surveillance of the keenest spies. So thoroughly did the councillors perform their work, that the new treaties of that year, granting greater concessions to foreigners than had ever yet been conceded, were not followed by the usual death of the Shogun.

Having thus rendered his position almost impregnable, the Gotairo turned his attention to punishing his political adversaries in Yedo and Kioto, and he entered upon one of the bloodiest and most cruel campaigns of vengence on record in Japanese history. He arrested his enemies on every side and consigned them to the blood-pit and to disembowelment. He sent orders to the commandant of the Shiro at Kioto to arrest and send to Yedo, under close guard, all persons known to be plotting against the Shogun. Thanks to his vigilant spies, he knew exactly where to lay his hands. Scores of avowed imperialists were arrested and forwarded to Yedo, where some were beheaded and others were granted the privilege of performing *seppuku*, in order to save their estates from confiscation and their families and kindred from blood-attainder, consequent on their overt acts of treason. The old Prince of Mito was ordered to remain in perpetual banishment. He was also compelled to hand over all authority to his son. Having thus finished off his more formidable enemies, his Lordship exultingly turned to crush the ring of spies that had so long been pestering him at Mito Yashiki. With the tiger's thirst for blood, and with deep rancor long goaded beyond endurance by the gadflies that had so long buzzed about his ears, he set out upon a campaign of inhuman atrocity, in order not only to gratify his thirst for revenge, but also to strike terror into the fearless spirits that had tampered with his secret plans.

CHAPTER XXIII.

IN the spring of 1859, the Gotairo one morning was deeply involved in consultation with his councillors, when a messenger handed to him a note from a gentleman waiting at the gateway of the *yashiki*. After reading the note, he hastily dismissed his cabinet and ordered the attendant to usher the visitor into his private office.

"Well, sir Fox," said he, good-humoredly, when the spy (for such was the gentleman) had been brought into his presence, "have you succeeded in kidnapping your man ?"

"I have, most honored sir," modestly replied the spy.

"Well done !" exclaimed the Gotairo. "Now we shall have some fine sport I can assure you. Pray how did you manage the matter ?"

"I heard last week that the fellow was going back to Mito with some horses for the stables of the old Prince, so I lay in wait for him among the groves beyond the tombs of the Shoguns, north of the suburbs, and arrested him just as he came out on the *Mito-kaido*."

"Was he alone ?"

"Entirely so."

"What, then, became of the horses ?"

"I turned them loose to take care of themselves," said he. "They will wander back to Mito Yashiki, and the powers there can puzzle their heads over the spiriting away of their *bettô* at their leisure."

"Ha ! ha !" chuckled the Gotairo, as he gleefully rubbed his hand, "now we shall soon see whether we have caught the right man. Does Yamagata still frequent the Yoshiwara ?"

" He does, sir ; and whenever he becomes exhilarated over his cups he invariably launches forth into that same old tale that he has been rehearsing down there for the last four or five years, about his wonderful cleverness in bleeding a couple of high officials travelling *nébon* one dark night whilst shadowing the fleet of Commodore Perry. He keeps adding to the amount levied on those gentlemen until his hearers will some of these days gather the impression that he struck a gold mine that night."

" Nevertheless," said the Gotairo, " the bloated fool has given me the clue whereby to follow up the assassin of Shimidzu the spy."

" I am well aware, sir, that you have always regarded that tale as a clue of some sort, but I must confess that I have never been able in any way to connect it with the murder."

" Do you remember the testimony of the fishermen near Yokoska ? "

" Certainly, sir. They said that two Bakufu officials stayed there several weeks about the time of Perry's visit, and appeared to take great interest in the fleet, visiting it in their boat at all hours of the day and night. They also said that the young men were in the habit of climbing the neighboring hills and spending hours in watching the vessels. But how does that connect them with the murder of Shimidzu ? Surely *samurai* travelling *nébon* would not ruthlessly slay an inoffensive gentleman sight-seeing like themselves."

" Very true," said the Gotairo, " but the testimony of the villagers further stated that one afternoon, when one of those young men came back from a solitary tour among the hills, he reported himself so badly injured from a fall that it would be necessary at once to leave for home, in order to consult a physician, and that forthwith they all hurried off that very night. About two weeks after their departure, Shimidzu's body was discovered on a neighboring hill-top, having evidently been slain in single combat with somebody. It always seemed extraordinary to me that he should have fought on that lonely hill, so I visited the place and clearly saw that he must have walked inadvertently into a trap, and was compelled to fight for his life."

"But, sir, at that time many of our Yedo people went down the bay *nébon.*"

"Very true, but the two men shadowing the fleet wore the Tokugawa crest, according to this Yamagata. Therefore they belonged to the *Gosanké*, for I know that none of the Bakufu officials were down there. This limits the investigation to the three clans of Kii, Owari, and Mito. I am on good terms with Kii, and know that none of their men were down there. The issue, then, is narrowed down between Owari and Mito. I am reasonably certain that no Owari men were down there. Therefore during nearly five years I have confined my investigations to Mito. My theory is that the old Prince sent these men down the bay to spy out the foreign fleet, and that Shimidzu, in some unknown manner, got wind of the matter and started down to catch them, and that he inadvertently came upon one of them on that lonely hill-top, and, being recognized, was obliged to fight to the death. At any rate, the animus of Mito makes my theory seem very plausible.

"Now, the people at Mito Yashiki are so exceedingly close-mouthed that I have not been able during these years to obtain a single clue. Every batch of the rollicking blades that has visited the Yoshiwara has been shadowed by my most expert spies, and not a single compromising word has ever passed over their cups. This convinced me that they knew nothing about the matter, and that it was a close secret limited to a few persons within the *yashiki*, and that those individuals were evidently not in the habit of visiting the Yoshiwara. This limited me to a very small circle indeed, as you may well imagine. I have long known that the two sons of Nakashima from Yamashiro were studious young men, not given to corrupt practices, and that they have always been exceedingly interested in the affairs of foreigners.

Furthermore, they are exceedingly expert swordsmen. The slayer of Shimidzu must indeed have been expert ! But just at this point I am non-plussed. It seems manifest that the antagonist of Shimidzu must have been a left-handed person. But both of these young men are right-handed men ! But for this fact I should have laid hands on them long ago. But I think that we shall catch them this time. If they be so close-mouthed in Yedo, perhaps they are a little more communicative when they visit their homes in Yamashiro. It occurred to me some time ago that the human propensity to brag and to swagger might manifest itself in the bosom of one's family when it did not show itself away from home. And now we shall see what this clever *bettô* has heard during his frequent visits to Yamashiro. Where have you put him ?"

" He is at the guard-house beside your gateway, in the care of my two assistants."

" Bring him in at once."

Within ten minutes the pale and trembling *bettô*, filled with a nameless fear at the uncertainty that clouded the reasons for his arrest, came slowly into the dread presence of the Gotairo, where he prostrated himself in the grovelling fashion that characterized the salutation of the plebeian in those days of despotic oligarchy.

" Bid the fellow sit up," commanded the Gotairo. An attendant forthwith punched the prostrate form in the back with a stick, saying : " You are bidden to arise ! " Then the attendants took their positions,—one on each side of him and one behind him,—and tapped his bare pate with sticks whenever his answers came slowly and his ideas seemed to need enlivening. When the unhappy fellow sat up, he found himself looking into the keen eyes of the Gotairo, who cast upon him a fierce look that smote him with terror. Those snapping gray eyes seemed to pierce his very soul.

" Fellow ! " said his Lordship, in severe tones, " in affairs of this kind the safety of the culprit always depends upon the truthfulness of his replies. Let that one tremble who dares to conceal facts, or to prevaricate when I question him."

" Tremble, indeed ! " groaned the attendants, in harrowing tones as they mildly punched the culprit in the back, and gently tapped his head to emphasize his Lordship's awful statement.

" Know, then," continued the Gotairo, " that satisfactory answers must be given to all of the interrogatories that will now be put to you, and that false and careless replies will entail nameless miseries and profound anguish."

" Lay this well to heart, fellow ! " moaned the assistants in doleful accents, as they proceeded to emphasize as before.

The luckless culprit murmured his willingness to answer all questions, and replied falteringly to a long series of inquiries as to his name, birth-place, age, kindred, occupation, and so forth. A brief summary of his replies divulged that he was Kochiki Bandu, of the city of Mito, aged thirty years, a *bettô* by birth and by choice. Thus far his answers had been entirely satisfactory to the dread tribunal, and no enlivening of ideas had been necessary. But as his remorseless interlocutors plunged deeper into matters concerning which he, in his confidential relations to the Nakashimas, had become conversant, the interview became much less cheerful. By a long series of questions the Gotairo had elicited from him the fact that, in the beginning of 1854, he had accompanied the two young men on a trip to Mito, and that after several weeks he had returned with them. But he was unable to give any information as to where his young masters had gone during the interim,—except that he supposed that they had amused themselves at the seashore villa, where he left them while he tarried in the town of Mito.

The unfeigned exultation with which the Gotairo received this information revealed to the *bettô* that his terrible inquisitor was upon the track of his young masters and not upon his own track. His little black eyes saw far deeper than anybody credited them with seeing ; and, behind the mask of his stolid features, he was taking in the situation and maturing his course of action. Now, beneath the boorish exterior of this man, there dwelt a kind and a brave heart. He was bound to the Mito clan by sentiments of loyalty and affection. His ancestors for many generations had served the house of Mito in the capacity of *bettôs*, and had received kind and considerate treatment. An unwritten law of honor bound him to the masters of whose salt he had partaken. In addition to this, the kind and generous treatment that he had received from the entire Naka-shima family had kindled within his simple mind feelings of gratitude and sincere affection. And now, when he clearly saw from the trend of the questions that his replies were manifestly getting his young masters into trouble, he determined to suppress and to equivocate. He well knew that he had overheard at Atago-Yama suf-ficient confidential matter to condemn the young men to a cruel death, if divulged before this heartless tribunal. At first he denied having accompanied the young men on their trips home. But his Lordship coolly informed him that he himself had seen him on the first trip about half-way down the *Nakasendo*, and that his subsequent visits could be proved by a witness on hand. Addressing an attendant he ordered him to usher in Mr. Honda. Very soon a tall, well-dressed *samurai* responded to the sum-mons, and came in and sat down where all could clearly see him.

" Do you recognize this gentleman ? " said the Gotairo, softly, as he exultingly beamed upon the astonished *bettô*.

" I do, most revered sir," faltered that luckless indi-vidual.

" Who is he, then ? "

" It is he who formerly kept a stand for fruit and confectionery beside the road that entered the glen of Atago-Yama," replied the crestfallen culprit.

" Precisely so, fellow ! " thundered the Gotairo ; " and

he has seen you on every occasion that you went there in company with your young masters. He is my pet spy. It is manifest that you are not giving heed to my admonition about veracity. Be admonished now to adhere henceforth to rigid and exact statements. Failing in this, you shall feel my power in unpleasant ways!"

"Take heed and tremble!" shrieked the chorus of assistants, as they proceeded to admonish him with a series of sharp taps and vicious punches.

But the poor fellow had more pluck than they credited him with possessing. His regard for his masters was so great, and his sense of gratitude and loyalty was so strong, that he determined to adopt the perilous course of keeping his mouth shut about every thing pertaining to his visits to Atago-Yama. The same spirit that is shown by the North American Indian while under torture is frequently found in the Japanese nature. That admirable vein of fortitude and endurance crops out among all classes at the most unexpected times. Bandu, the *bettô*, belonged to this type. In vain did the whacks rain down upon his defenceless head. In vain did blows and punches descend upon his poor shoulders and back. He remained as mute as an oyster whenever the questions related to the visits of his young masters to their home. His Lordship wheedled, badgered, and bullied to no purpose. Smiles, cajoleries, and threats were all thrown away. In a moment of extreme wrath his Lordship so far forgot his dignity as to draw forth his fan from his belt and smite the sulky culprit a stinging blow on the cheek. All in vain! The man was obdurate.

"It is manifest," said his Lordship, finally, in savage tones, "that we shall be compelled to put our questions under less comfortable surroundings. Adjourn to the warehouse!"

This warehouse was a large fire-proof *godown*, built into a distant wing of the palace in order to store valuables in case of fire. Its immensely thick walls and massive flanged doors fitted it admirably for a dungeon and a torture-chamber. Cries and groans would not

reach far beyond its solid masonry. Of late it had witnessed the agonies of many political offenders. In about
half an hour the tribunal reassembled within the dark
chamber of the *godown*,—the judge and his associates
having refreshed themselves betimes with some hot,
spiced *saké*, wherewith to restore their shaken equipoise.
They seated themselves on a little platform at the farther
end of the gloomy vault, and ordered the culprit to
be brought in for further questionings. The dim candles
flickered in a ghostly fashion as the poor fellow was led
into the sepulchral place by two fierce-looking tormentors, whose naturally savage features had been painted
and blackened in a hideous manner, in order to strike
terror into the heart of the timid peasant. The Gotairo
did not condescend to put the questions in person, but
handed a written list of interrogatories to the inquisitors,
who savagely shouted them forth at the culprit, and
menacingly demanded answers thereto. There was no
response. Then, with fierce imprecations, they rushed
upon their trembling victim and roughly removed the ·
cords that bound his arms and hands. Then they rudely
stripped him, and laid him face downward on the ground.
Calling a couple of assistants, they directed one of them
to hold his head down, and ordered the other one to
press his toes close together on the ground, while holding
the heels as far apart as possible,—a position in itself
painful. Then the tormentors, with rods in their hands,
stood, one on each side of the victim, and thundered
forth the final question :
"Base-born fellow ! Do you still refuse to answer the
questions put to you ?"
There was no reply. Then the luckless fellow was
most unmercifully flogged from neck to heels. His pluck
was indeed admirable. Nothing but a few groans indicated his anguish. Whenever he writhed in his agony
the cruel assistants crowded his face into the ground and
violently wrenched his heels from side to side, thus adding sprained joints to the torture of the mangled back.
Fully two hundred blows had poured down before a stop

was called. He still refused to answer. It was manifest that the man would permit himself to be beaten to death before any answer could be elicited. This was not what the Gotairo desired. "That will do for to-day," said he. "To-morrow you may apply the copper *moxa* to the raw spots on his body. Perhaps that course of treatment will loosen his tongue a bit." Accordingly, the court adjourned.

On the morrow the court again convened in the *godown*. The miserable *bettô* was carried in, for he was too stiff and lame to walk. Again the tormentors shouted at him the interrogatories of the previous day. Again did he refuse to answer. And again was he stripped and thrown flat on his face. A glowing *hebachi* holding an iron pot brimful of molten copper was then brought in. While the assistants held the wretched fellow down, the tormenting fiends dipped forth small quantities of the horrible fluid and poured it upon the raw spots on his poor back. But the only response that they could elicit was a heartrending groan. With devilish deliberation they applied *moxa* after *moxa*, but with the same unsatisfactory results. It soon became manifest that the fellow would allow himself to be burnt to death before he would reveal any information damaging to his masters.

"That will do for the *moxa*," finally exclaimed the Gotairo, "now apply the stomach test, and let him die under that if he chooses so to do."

This stomach test was a horrible form of torture invented during the days of persecution against the Jesuits. The victim was thrown on his back and held down. A funnel was then thrust down his throat and water was forced into his stomach until it was full. Then a board was laid across his body just over the distended member, and a man would jump upon it with all his might, thus causing water and blood to gush from the victim's nose, mouth, and ears, causing the most excruciating agony. This operation would be repeated again and again, until the unhappy wretch either recanted or died. Now, this *bettô* would probably have stood any amount of external torture, and have died under it, rather than to have revealed any thing detrimental to his young masters ; but he was filled with a peasant's superstitious horror at having his internal organs tampered with. When the funnel was thrust down his throat and he perceived the devilish atrocity of the torment about to be inflicted on him, then arose in his mind a feeling of undefined terror at having the mysterious organs of his existence wrenched, ruptured, and mangled in this horrible manner. In his ignorance he conjured up agonies not only more painful than what he had already endured, but also anguish of an unknown description, concerning which he could form no conception in his mind. He had defied that which was known, but he surrendered to that which was unknown. He therefore made a sign, and the funnel was withdrawn.

" What do you wish to say ? " inquired the torturers.

" I will answer the questions," was the feeble reply.

" The culprit consents to answer your Lordship's questions," reported the tormentors.

" Then remove him at once to my private office, and let us note his replies," was the brief response.

In a few minutes the conclave reassembled, and the unhappy culprit was laid on his face before the inquisitors. The Gotairo took up the list of interrogatories, and proceeded to catechise.

" Have you ever heard the two elder sons of Nakashima, during their visits to Atago-Yama, tell about any extraordinary experience or exploit in or about Yedo ? " was the first question.

" I have," was the reply.

" Clearly state what you heard."

" On the night of Tomokichi's wedding I heard him state to his father that Junzo had killed in terrific combat a Bakufu spy."

" Well, what else ? "

" When Junzo went down on the occasion of his wedding I heard the family inquiring about the particulars of the affair. He told them that he and his brother had been sent by the old Prince of Mito to shadow the American fleet in Yedo bay, and that while so engaged he one day met the famous spy Shimidzu, on a hill-top near some woods, and that he killed him after a long fight, in order to shut his mouth. On one or two occasions I have heard the family discussing the matter."

"Is Junzo a left-handed man?"

"No, but he is equally skilful with either hand. I have heard him say that in that combat he held his left-handed stroke in reserve, and then suddenly delivered it at an unexpected moment, and gashed Shimidzu across the bowels from right to left. He is celebrated at Mito Yashiki for this peculiar stroke."

"I understand every thing now," graciously responded his Lordship. "Remove the culprit to the dungeon, and keep him there under close guard until I send for him."

Like a bloodhound that has caught the scent, so sped the Gotairo on the track of his victims. He at once sent a messenger to Mito Yashiki, requesting young Konishi and the two sons of Mr. Nakashima to call on him at his *yashiki* in reference to some business of importance. He had rightly conjectured that their suspicions had not yet been aroused, and that it would not occur to them that the notice was any thing more than to do some translating for the Bakufu. His surmises were sound. The messenger delivered his message at the gateway of the *yashiki,* where it did not excite any thing more than a passing comment. The note was then duly forwarded to the Konishi lodge, where it found Tomokichi and young Konishi playing chess. Junzo was down on the parade ground and had to be sent for. Within an hour they all met at the main gateway, where the messenger awaited them. Interchanging a few bantering remarks with their friends as to the probability of their notice being the harbinger of promotion to some fat office, they started down the hill, crossed the moat, and walked straight into the trap.

CHAPTER XXIV.

THE CAT PLAYS WITH THE MOUSE.

As soon as our young friends stepped within the gateway of Hikoné Yashiki, the heavy portals were closed behind them, and they were requested to step into the guard-room. Somewhat surprised at such unusual proceedings, they nevertheless did as they were directed to do. Presently ten *samurai* came into the room, and ranged themselves around its sides, so as to completely surround the visitors, who were demurely sitting in the middle of the floor warming their hands over a *hebachi*. Nothing was said, and no salutations were interchanged. In about five minutes three gentlemen of forbidding aspect came in bearing huge bundles of stout hempen cord in their hands. Bowing low, they demanded of the three young men the surrender of their swords, which were reluctantly handed over without comment. After having complied with this order they were directed to stand up and permit themselves to be bound. At this juncture the strangeness of the proceedings caused Konishi to exclaim that they were being made prisoners for some unknown reason. "Oh, no, indeed," replied the gentlemen in waiting; "you are merely to be the honored guests of the Lord of Hikoné for a brief period."

"You will kindly excuse our rudeness," said the three jailers (for such they were) as they unrolled the cord, "but we are acting under the orders of our master. Our noble lord sometimes honors his guests after an extraordinary fashion. Be pleased to hold forth your wrists in order that we may tie your hands together, most honorable sirs."

"We fail to comprehend the meaning of such actions," said Konishi, with affected surprise and nonchalance.

"His Lordship will soon explain matters to you," was the reply. "Who knows but what this is merely a prelude to some delightful promotion?"

"Sure enough! Who knows?" exclaimed all the *samurai*, as they bowed low in mocking salutation.

It took fully half an hour to perform the very intricate operation of binding the prisoners. First the wrists were tied so tightly together as to nearly stop the circulation of the blood. Then the elbows were drawn as far back as possible and tied together behind the back as closely as possible. Then a complicated system of knots and loops was woven all over the upper part of their bodies, so that it appeared as if a net had been cast about their trunks. These knots and loops were drawn so tight that respiration became difficult, and the arms and shoulders became almost immovable. The position was not only uncomfortable, but was positively painful. When prisoners· have been left bound for many days there have been instances where the flesh on the hands and arms has mortified. When the binding had been completed, each jailer tied a rope about the neck of his charge and prepared to lead him out of the guard-house into the presence of the Gotairo. In the meantime the news had spread like wildfire throughout the Yashiki to the effect that his Lordship having, after years of patient burrowing, finally unearthed a nest of dangerous Kioto spies in Mito Yashiki, was going to amuse himself by perpetrating one of his grim jokes on them by receiving them as if they were imperial ambassadors worthy of distinguished notice.

When the prisoners reached the courtyard they found an elaborate guard of honor waiting to escort them to the Gotairo's palace. A trumpeter sounded the signal, and the procession took up its line of march. Throngs of retainers crowded the roadside, and showered profuse salutations with mocking humility upon the unfortunate ones. Everybody caught the spirit of the huge jest with that marvellous readiness of impersonation so prominent in the Japanese character, and profound bowings and scrapings were showered upon the party as if they indeed were ambassadors, and not culprits, whose appearance presented a laughable contrast to the elaborate ceremony of their mocking reception. With due decorum the young men were slowly led by their jailers through the maze of courtiers up to the main entrance of the palace. Here they were reverently received by the entire staff of councillors, all dressed in regalia costume. It took them fully five minutes to sufficiently humble themselves in the presence of such renowned personages as their visitors presumably were. The contrast presented by the crestfallen and forlorn appearance of the prisoners caused the immensity of the joke to dawn with such power upon the crowds of retainers flocking about the entrance that they could no longer suppress their merriment, but exploded in fits of jeering laughter, which swelled into roars of derision as it was communicated to the outside mob.

The prisoners were then escorted through long corridors and lofty suites of chambers, where the household attendants carried out the colossal jest of receiving imperial ambassadors from Kioto by prostrating themselves on the floor as the solemn procession stalked majestically along. After endless marchings and countermarchings for the sport of the palace, the jailers finally led their prisoners into the private office of the Gotairo, who arose to meet them with the most elaborate exhibition of the profoundest respect. Bidding them to be seated upon some elegant cushions, he ordered an attendant to set tea and tobacco before them. The drollery of this bit of humor was too good to keep within the palace, and was speedily communicated to the barracks, where shouts of immoderate laughter greeted the announcement of how his Lordship had set refreshments before fellows who could not even brush away the flies that tickled their noses ; and he was the recipient that evening from the flunkies of the palace of many compliments on the extreme brilliancy of his most amusing paradox.

And how did our young friends take all this bitter mockery? They were mortified beyond expression. It was bad enough to be ridiculed by strangers, but to see the faces of their numerous acquaintances distorted with derision and contempt was unendurable. When the farce commenced at the guard-room they had not time to make up their minds as to the meaning of the strange proceedings, but, as the play progressed, they overheard remarks among the retainers that left no doubt that they were under arrest on the charge of being secret spies in the service of the Kioto faction. Gradually the grave seriousness of their position dawned upon them. They had no opportunity to converse with one another, but they all came to the same conclusion as to the nature of the proceedings. The deep blushes of intense humiliation and overwhelming mortification that had at first tinged their cheeks slowly faded into the blanched pallor of suppressed fear and stern resolve. The equipoise that had been so sadly disturbed in the guard-room was speedily regained in the court-room. From behind screens and shades his Lordship had watched with intense gratification the shame of his victims, and, when he perceived that the gibes and the scoffs of his retainers were beginning to lose their force, he cut short further teasing, and ordered the prisoners into his private office, where he hoped to continue the sport for a while longer. He well knew that he could not have chosen a more distressing method of revenge than to badger the proud and sensitive spirits in his power by such refined mockery as that to which he was subjecting them, and he purposed keeping up the game just as long as it produced the desired effects.

"Most honorable gentlemen from Kioto," said he, in the blandest tones, as he bowed before them, "permit me to congratulate you on your safe arrival after your long and circuitous journey. Allow me to express the hope that your health may continue good in this insignificant city, and that you may successfully prosecute your mission in behalf of your august master within the Gosho."

" We do not understand you, most honorable sir," replied Konishi, putting a bold face on the matter in order
to compel his Lordship to fall back on his proofs to meet
this plea of *Not Guilty.*

" Oh ! indeed, do you not ? " exclaimed his Lordship,
with leering eyes and sneering lips.

"Indeed we do not," was the reply.   " We are the
vassals of Tokugawa, and now you intimate that *Tenshi*
is our master.   Pray, sir, what is the meaning of this
unexpected treatment to which we are now being subjected ? "

" Oh ! indeed, do you not understand that ? " slowly
drawled his Lordship, as he daintily filled his pipe and
quizzically ogled his prisoners with half-closed eyes.

" Will you kindly explain this matter to us ? " said
Tomokichi.

" Oh ! you have found your tongue, have you ? " said
his Lordship, as he turned a severe look on him.

" Sir," exclaimed Junzo, "there must be a mistake
somewhere in this matter.   Will you kindly explain your
action, in order that we may justify ourselves ? "

" And so you thought it about time for you to commence your little speech, did you ? " replied his Lordship, as his eyes lit up with a dangerous glare.   " You
also are hungering after an explanation, are you ?   You
must be very obtuse, young man, not to be able to read
the signs of the times.   Don't you see that I am tender-
ing you folks a reception as the accredited envoys of his
Imperial Majesty, the Mikado ? "

" How can that be, sir, since we are in the employ of
the Shogun, and have been so employed for many years
past ? " exclaimed Konishi, with a well-feigned air of
bland astonishment.

" Oh ! you gentlemen speak by turns, do you ?   And
it has swung around again for you to open your mouth,
has it ? " was the insulting reply.

Thus did the Gotairo chaff and dally with his prisoners for fully an hour, to the unbounded amusement of
his retainers.   Scores of listening ears, pressed close to

the *shojees*, caught each choice repartee and reported it to the courtiers outside, who duly published the brilliant saying in the barracks for the edification of their comrades. Sometimes he was humorous ; sometimes severe. Sometimes he would appear on the point of making some explanation, when the spirit would suddenly move him to branch off on to a line of cutting sarcasm and biting irony intended to crush the recipients thereof into abject silence. Sometimes he insulted them. Sometimes he spoke in elaborate riddles or lengthy parables. Sometimes he indulged in familiar jests. Sometimes he gave expression to harsh and gloomy threats of mysterious torments. But the young men adhered to their policy of demanding an opportunity to justify themselves, and would neither be cowed nor silenced, so that the sport finally lost all savor of interest. In addition to this, his Lordship's supply of wit was becoming rapidly exhausted. At last he smote the rim of the *hebachi* a sounding blow with his pipe and exclaimed :

" So it is an explanation that you fellows want, is it ? Well, you shall have it. Dost thou, Junzo, son of Nakashima, recognize this sword that I now place upon the stand before thee ? "

" I fail to recognize it," replied Junzo, after looking at it carefully. It is needless to remark that the sword was the one with which Shimidzu the spy fought his famous duel. As a matter of fact, Junzo did at once recognize it, but there was nothing in his creed of moral ethics to prevent his prevaricating under the somewhat foreboding circumstances that environed him.

" If you fail to recognize the sword," leered his Lordship, " perhaps you will remember the circumstances under which you murdered its possessor."

" I do not understand you, sir. I have never murdered anybody. My life has been peacefully spent in Yamashiro, and in attending to my duties at Mito Yashiki."

" Nevertheless, you went down the bay spying out the American fleet five years ago," replied his Lordship, fastening his piercing eyes upon the young man with a searching gaze. This unexpected announcement might have thrown a less ready antagonist into confusion. But Junzo betrayed not the slightest trace of surprise, and he returned the gaze with a look of bland innocence and said :

" You are mistaken, sir. I never went on any such expedition."

" Nevertheless, you did do so. And, furthermore, when caught on the hill-top by my spy you foully slew him and concealed his body and sword in the adjacent woods."

" I deny this most respectfully."

" Nevertheless, you did do so. And, furthermore, you boasted.of the act in the presence of witnesses."

" Never having done the act, it would have been impossible for me to have boasted of it."

" Perhaps this little document will refresh your memory," said his Lordship, as he spread out before his eyes the confession of the luckless *bettô*.

Junzo read it with a terrible sensation of fear at his heart. But, after a careful perusal, failing to see any name attached thereto, he concluded that it would be best to put in a bold denial of its truthfulness.

" I do not know what this paper means. It is quite true that I have been to Kioto on visits during the last three or four years. It is also true that I described the exciting incidents of my Yedo life to my friends. But no such story as that contained here ever passed my lips. This thing is a pure fabrication."

" Perhaps this distinguished gentleman here is also a pure fabrication," sweetly replied his Lordship, as he drew aside a screen and showed the unhappy *bettô* held up by two stout *samurai*.

It would be very difficult to describe the exact feelings of our young friends, when they recognized in the pale and pitiful countenance before them the features of their *bettô*. In a brief period of time their minds had travelled over much ground, and speedily arrived at the same conclusions as to what course of action to pursue. To all outward appearances they were cool and self-possessed, yet at heart they were faint and sick as the utter hopelessness of their position dawned upon them. The Duke of Wellington defined a brave man as one who clearly perceives his danger, yet faces it. In the light of this definition our young friends were indeed brave, for during five years they had faced the perils of their situation, and now when entrapped by their crafty enemy they intrepidly faced torture and death. For years past they had again and again discussed their line of action in case of detection. They well knew that the detection of any one of them would involve the conviction of all of them, and so they had planned that in case any one of them should be caught, that then the others should at once become *ronins* and fly to the mountains of the interior, and organize bands of *ronins* to prey on the Bakufu at all points, and to annoy them as much as possible. By becoming *ronins* they formally severed their allegiance with the Prince of Mito, and thus absolved him from all responsibility for their acts. In case all of them should be caught at the same time, they had decided to stand and fall together without implicating any one else.

That time had now arrived. During the past year Konishi had noticed a growing coldness on the part of the Gotairo toward himself, and had felt that the eyes of suspicion were upon him. He was shrewd enough to perceive that criminating evidence had been wrung from the hapless *bettô*, and that a network of evidence had been woven about himself and his friends quite sufficient to crush them. The same conviction forced itself upon the minds of the brothers. In advance they had discussed this precise situation so frequently that they were prepared for it, and were ready without consultation to act harmoniously. The *samurai* was taught to despise death, so that when he was brought face to face with it he defied it. When he had abandoned all hope of life he hurled defiance at his enemies, and courted their utmost fury with the reckless coolness of the North American Indian. Our young friends, with fainting hearts, read the handwriting on the wall, and then sorrowfully but unflinchingly faced their destiny. With unruffled demeanor they met gibe with suavity, and parried insolence with urbanity.

"Well, young gentlemen," said his Lordship, after a long pause, "are you prepared to pronounce this individual a pure fabrication?"

"Oh! he is genuine enough," replied Junzo. "I perceive that he appears quite ill. Probably he is under your charge for medical treatment."

"None of your impudence, you beast!" thundered his Lordship; "answer me and tell me if you recognize him."

"He is one of the *bettôs* belonging to Mito Yashiki. But I do not see what he has to do with our case."

"Don't you? Well, he is the author of that document. And by that document your heads fall into the blood-pit at noon to-morrow. Do you see any connection now?"

"I see that you have kidnapped him, and have tried in vain to get some voluntary testimony out of him, and, failing in that, you wrung out of his mangled body some sort of crazy confession like what you have there in writing. Under torture a peasant like that will confess any thing after a while. If you deem it proper to convict *samurai* on such testimony as that you are at liberty to do so. But we assert our innocence, and continue to demand some proof of the charges made against us. Of course you have us in your power, and can do what you like with us, but we are true *samurai* and shall fear nothing."

This bold reply awakened a feeling of admiration in the hearts of those who stood by, but it was like the flaunting of a red flag in the face of an enraged bull so far as the Gotairo was concerned. His passion had been steadily rising for some time, and now it burst forth in ungovernable fury and broke upon the unprotected heads of the prisoners.

"Yea! you speak truly. Most assuredly are you in
my power, and most assuredly shall I do with you as I
deem best. Know, then, ye miserable whelps," roared
he, as he drew forth his fan and smote each one of them
a stinging blow on the cheek, "that I have this year
condemned fellows like you on evidence far less satisfactory."

The look of hatred and defiance that gleamed forth
from their eyes in response to this shameful insult but
stimulated his Lordship's wrath, and he proceeded to
beat upon the shaven tops of their heads a series of re-
sounding tattoos, remarking meanwhile that their skulls
made most excellent drums. This vigorous exercise
served to cool him down somewhat, and he called for
his papers and proceeded to read off his sentence against
them.

"Know, then, ye miserable abortions of monkeys,
that have so long disturbed my peace," said he, in savage
tones, "that according to the ancient customs of Dai-
Nippon nobody is executed until after he has made due
confession of his guilt. Although your iniquity has
been established beyond peradventure or doubt, yet
you persist in stubbornly denying it. But we have
means of loosening tongues. Beware! beware! therefore to-morrow morning you shall feast to your heart's
content on stick, copper, and water, and if you choose
to die under that course of treatment,—well and good.
It is a matter of utter indifference to me how you die.
But by putting your signatures at any time to this confession that I hold in my hand you can be ushered out
of this life at once and with but a single stroke."

"Take heed! take heed! Beware! beware! beware!"
groaned in harrowing accents a chorus of doleful voices
in an adjoining room.

"Furthermore," continued his Lordship, when the
impressive admonition had subsided, "know that the
punishment will not end with your death. By ancient
custom, whosoever perpetrates treason against the Shogun, thereby entails blood-attainder on his family and

kindred, and they become extirpated root and branch. Therefore, O Konishi, I condemn your father and his entire family to death, and his entire estate to confiscation. As regards you, O sons of Nakashima, I condemn your father and his entire family, together with his remotest kindred and your own families, and all of their estates shall escheat to the Shogun. And your respective fathers, as heads of the family, being responsible for the acts of all members thereof, shall die by crucifixion. All the others shall die by ·decapitation and impalement. But in your case, O Konishi, I am pleased to be lenient in view of the services rendered by you to the Bakufu. I therefore commute the sentence passed on your family to perpetual banishment in the island of Yesso, and your father shall be allowed to wipe out the blood-attainder for treason by being permitted to perform *seppuku*. But thou shalt die like a dog to-morrow at high noon! And thy head shall grin from the gate-posts of Mito Yashiki before sundown! As for you, ye sneaking curs from Yamashiro, I decline to remit one jot or one tittle of your sentence. Die like dogs! And may the soil of Dai-Nippon be forever purged from such an accursed litter of traitorous whelps! Ye and your polluted breed shall perish root and branch so that coming generations shall point to the dunghills and say : ' There lie the remains of the malignant and treacherous Nakashima family ! ' This, then, shall be your doom. To-night I shall send my orders to Kioto, and within twenty days the heads of your corrupted kindred shall be impaled on spears, and shall garnish the shoals of the Kamogawa as a warning to the traitorous dogs hovering about the Gosho when they cross and re-cross the bridge on their sneaking tours. As they gaze down upon the long row of picketed heads that roll their sightless eye-balls upward toward the moon and open their gaping mouths as if to speak, then shall those who pass by know what it is to arouse the lion of Lake Biwa. Ye have had your sport for full five years. Behold the accounting ! "

A deep silence followed the uttering of this horrible sentence, that had been raked up from the fearful annals of the Ashikaga period, when proscription perched as invariably on the banners of the victor as buzzards flock around carrion. Five centuries had failed to expunge from the unwritten law of the land the horrible customs of a most cruel age, thus leaving it in the power of the infuriated "swaggering prime-minister" to resurrect a sanguinary law that had, during the dark times of the thirteenth and sixteenth century, swept hundreds of families out of existence amid scenes of the most hellish cruelty. The prisoners had not anticipated such a terrible sentence. They were chilled to the heart with horror, and their countenances became as stone. Many of the attendants had sympathetic hearts and could not endure the pitiful sight of the mute agony of the prisoners. One by one they slipped away and whispered with bated breath to those outside the details of the awful decree. Terrible indeed was the wrath of Nawosŭké, Lord of Hikoné!

But his Lordship glared on his victims with an expression of the most devilish hate, and cruelly taunted them in their silent misery with gibes and jests so heartless and brutal that his own councillors would fain have interposed to check the torrent of his fury. His vituperation poured forth in raging floods until his courtiers trembled and wondered whether or not their master was beside himself. Finally his foul denunciation subsided, and he mopped the dripping perspiration from his brow and wiped the frenzied foam from his mouth, glaring meanwhile with the most unutterable hate at his victims, and spasmodically clutching at his sword-hilt as if he could hardly restrain himself from drawing the keen blade and hewing them to pieces on the spot. As the swollen veins in his forehead relaxed their tension he became more composed, and gazed with manifest satisfaction upon the compressed lips and blanched faces before him. Our young friends had defied all that his Lordship might have been able to heap upon themselves individually; but they had affectionate hearts, and they loved their families and kindred, and were appalled at the frightful catastrophe overshadowing them. Too haughty to make any plea for themselves, yet did they relax their pride to beg mercy for their families. They bowed low and said as follows in humble and eloquent tones :

" Do as you please with us. But spare the old men, the women, and the little children, for they are helpless and in no way to blame for our actions. We alone are guilty. We have plotted against the Shogun entirely unbeknown to our kindred and families. Punish us but spare them."

" Ha ! ha ! " roared the Gotairo, " then you confess every thing charged against you ? "

" We do, most humbly," was the low response.

" Then sign this written confession," said he.

" We will sign it if you will remit that part of the sentence relating to our family and kindred and will limit your punishment to ourselves," was the noble answer.

" Dogs ! " yelled his Lordship in uncontrollable fury, " Dare you dictate terms to me ? I swear by the gods of Dai-Nippon, not only that you shall sign it, but also that your accursed breed shall be exterminated before the new moon ! Were it not for the lateness of the hour I would commence operations on you to-day."

" We shall not sign it until the sentence be remitted," replied the young men, as their meek expressions changed into glances of deadly hate and unconquerable determination.

" Then to the dungeon with them ! " yelled the Gotairo to the jailers.

" What shall we do with the *bettô ?* " inquired those gloomy and forbidding gentlemen.

" He is of no further use. Finish him off to-night in reward for his obstinacy, and send his head up to Mito Yashiki with my compliments when you go up after the old Konishi. Who knows but what that may bring down some weak-kneed *bettô* up at the stables ? "

And so the meeting adjourned.

CHAPTER XXV.

AND THE MOUSE ESCAPES.

THE prisoners were conducted from the dread presence of the Gotairo into a long corridor that led out toward the distant wing where was located the so-called dungeon, or, more properly speaking, the *godown* that had been extemporized as a dungeon. It had already become dusk when they reached the gloomy chamber, so that candles were needed to illumine the place. The heavy doors were swung back and the funereal procession entered the sombre vault whose massive walls had so often stifled the moans of agonized victims. The dim flicker of the lights revealed a room comparatively bare. In the corners and along the sides were stored sundry articles of *vertu* and value. There were no windows, and the black walls rose up on four sides like lofty shadows and were merged in the deep gloom above. The jailers brought in three *tatamis* and laid them in the middle of the room and seated their prisoners thereon. Then they brought in some rice and fish and invited their unwilling guests to partake thereof after their arms had been sufficiently loosened for them to feed themselves. But the poor fellows made but a sorry meal, for their hearts were heavy and they were parched and feverish. The merest nibble seemed to appease their hunger. Then the food was removed and they were tightly bound hand and foot. Some pillows and quilts were then brought in and they were requested to lie down on the mats and allow themselves to be covered up for the night.

Then the guards bid them good-night and withdrew to the outside of the doorway, where they made preparations for making themselves as comfortable as possible for the death-watch during the long hours of the night. They divided the time into three equal parts, arranging that while two of them kept awake smoking and sipping *saké* the third one should sleep in a room adjoining the one into which the *godown* doors swung open. A light was left inside the dark vault so that they could observe every movement of the prisoners through the open door-way. Then they ensconced themselves on the *tatamis* just beyond the threshold and chatted away late in the evening. At about nine o'clock one of them retired to rest according to the plan already agreed upon. The other two talked and smoked for another hour and then began to yawn very vigorously over their pipes. Occasionally they would turn their eyes in the direction of their prisoners and then would nod and doze over their tea and *saké*. They felt that their prisoners were absolutely secure. In the first place, no human being could possibly break loose from that complicated network of knots. In the second place, they were within the walls of Hikoné Yashiki, surrounded by thousands of valorous warriors within easy beck and call. In the third place, their master, the Gotairo, was the lord of the realm with the armies of the nation at his back. Who then could have the rashness to beard the lion in his den? What possible contingency could arise wherein the prisoners could escape? The poor fellows indeed seemed doomed.

In the meantime, how fared the prisoners? When the jailers withdrew they had their first opportunity to exchange ideas since the time when the gates had closed behind them that afternoon. Their swollen hands and aching arms were giving them great pain, and their feverish blood was beating and throbbing violently against their burning temples. Their parched throats and mouths could hardly articulate the trembling words to which they gave utterance when the guards had retired beyond earshot.

"Well," said Konishi, "I fail to see how we are to extricate ourselves from this scrape. And yet I do not see how we could have avoided it."

" Nor I either," replied Junzo. " The *bettô* could hardly have been blamed in any way. I did not credit him with the great pluck that he has manifestly shown in this matter. Poor fellow ! Whatever shortcomings he may have been guilty of he has ere now most dearly atoned therefor. I consider myself to be the chief one to blame in this whole matter, because of my ill-starred loquacity at Atago-Yama."

" I do not see as anybody is to blame," said Tomo-kichi." The simple fact is that the Gotairo has thoroughly outwitted us, and we are fairly caught in his net. When I consider what a sly old fox he is, I am amazed at our success in evading him for so long a time. I have the mournful consolation of knowing that Yamada has derived much valuable information through us which he could not otherwise have obtained. I can at least die feeling that our great cause has perceptibly advanced during the last five years, and that though we may not live to see the fruit of our efforts, yet have we been the means of that fruit ripening. So far as I am concerned, I have but little to regret. But the dire calamity that I have brought upon our families is breaking my heart. It is cruel ! It is awful ! I swear by all the foul fiends that infest the Buddhist hells that if there be a soul in this body of mine it shall roam heaven and earth in its endeavors to wreak revenge on the savage beast that has crushed us ! Unseen hands shall stretch forth from those shadowy regions and shall terrify and torment him with their subtle influences ! Flaming tongues and hideous faces shall haunt his life until his misery shall become unbearable ! I shall lead the pestilential miasms from swamps and cess-pools into his palace, and shall rot him with their fetid breath ! I shall discover the springs of corrupting disease and shall fill his bowl to overflowing with the deadly mildew of corroding leprosy and the blasting virus of dropsy and marasmus, until his fevered limbs shall split open and crumble to pieces in the fierce viewless flames that warp and twist his tortured nerves ceaselessly both day and night ! And when his foul spirit shall be withdrawn from the putrid tissues that enchain it, I shall be there to seize it and to drag it through the torments of the deepest hells, where it shall steep in the seething dregs of substances that will dissipate his molten copper into vapor—so intense will be their heat ! "

" Well spoken ! Well spoken ! " exclaimed his two companions in fierce and exulting whispers. " We swear by the same powers that we shall be there to aid thee in thy praiseworthy work. This miserable fiend shall find that there are kindred spirits somewhere in the vast universe that also delight to feed on anguish and despair."

Thus they conversed in low and sullen whispers for nearly two hours. They had arranged all the details for the horrors that they anticipated on the following day. Each one agreed to watch for a favorable opportunity when their cords were removed, preparatory for torture, to snatch one of the short swords from the belts of the jailers and, after disabling or killing those gentlemen, to slay themselves, thus escaping the agonies about to be inflicted on them. There was a very good prospect of this scheme being successfully carried out, for those gentlemen seemed to repose absolute confidence in the power of their master, and were careless and exceedingly deliberate in all of their actions, thus rendering themselves fit subjects for some such sudden onslaught. In vain did our young friends try to sleep. Slumber deserted their eyelids. They turned restlessly from side to side until midnight. At this hour they heard one of the guards go and rouse the sleeping man in the adjoining room. They could plainly hear him calling to the man that his turn to watch had come, and they heard the drowsy fellow shuffle out and take his place beside the doorway. In a few minutes his loud snoring proclaimed the fact that he had again succumbed to the sweet influence of his interrupted slumbers. Presently the responsive snorings of the other two men proclaimed the fact that the entire guard was asleep.

But still the poor fellows vainly courted the shadowy

influence. They rolled from side to side in feverish uneasiness. Finally Tomokichi dropped into a troubled slumber and dreamed that he was riding his horse over the mountain passes of the Nakasendo in frantic efforts to escape from some enemy. Onward he rushed at break-neck speed, for the pursuers were close upon his heels. He wound the reins tightly about his wrists and arms. This gave him great pain, but there was no time to con-sider that, for it was of the utmost importance that he should reach Atago-Yama before his enemies, so as to warn his family to fly to the mountains.

Twice did the sun rise and set on his mad gallop. His head spun with aching pain, his wrists writhed within the agonizing grip of the reins, his blood boiled with fever, but he could not stop. The life of his entire family depended on his efforts! Though fainting and sore and almost ready to drop from his horse, yet he chased the western sun until he drew near to his native glen. One more supreme effort and all would be well! He had gained on his pursuers, and there was yet time to save his loved ones. Onward he dashed into the glen just as the lengthening shadows were commencing to coquet with the mists that rose from the brook. Over the bridge, past the shrines, and up the steep road he rushed with reckless speed until the gateway of his cottage home had been reached. He was just making ready to dash through, when somebody from behind seized his arm and held him back. Without turning to see who had thus rudely grasped his arm, he shouted to his loved ones to fly. But they did not seem to hear, for nobody paid him the slightest attention.

His father was calmly smoking his pipe on the balcony and was gazing vacantly down at the very spot where the frantic horseman was struggling to enter. Masago sat demurely on the veranda sewing on some children's garments. O-Hana was under the cherry-trees romping with her little nephews in noisy glee. Loudly did he call to her, but she heeded him not. Drat that girl! Would she not cease her frolic even on the threshold of death?

What could all this mean ? Nobody paid him the slight-est attention—and he there shouting forth tidings of life and death ! Perhaps he was not calling loud enough. He must make a greater effort. Then somebody from be-hind clapped a hand tightly over his mouth and bent his head backward. As his eyes rolled upward he saw Mr. Yamada standing on the balcony serenely looking at him. Surely he would hear him and help him ! With a supreme effort he shook the hand from his mouth and shouted out at the top of his voice : "O Mr. Yamada ! Bid my people fly at once to the distant mountains ! An enemy is at the gate ready to destroy them ! Oh ! Save my wife and children from cruel death !"—But Mr. Yamada heeded him not. With provoking indifference he stared blankly down at the gateway as if buried in profound thought. Oh ! The horror of the situation ! Again was the hand clasped over his mouth, and he was dragged from his horse and shaken most violently. And he awoke dripping with perspiration and sobbing bit-terly, to find that there was indeed somebody's hand pressed tightly over his mouth, while another hand was holding him tightly by the arm and shaking him most violently.

"Be still, Tomokichi ! In the name of Jimmu-Tenno, don't ruin us with your uproar ! Wake up, sir ! Wake up, I say ! There, that is better. Now keep quiet. I came just as you reached the climax of your nightmare, and if I had n't taken hold of you with a strong hand, every thing would have been lost."

Tomokichi lifted his head from somebody's shoulder and stared about him in the dim light with a bewildered gaze. Junzo and Konishi were sitting up looking at some apparition behind him, with eyes that seemed to be starting from their sockets in unutterable amazement. The voice had sounded strangely familiar, and he turned around in joyous haste that was almost delirious in its excess, and found himself face to face with the smiling countenance of——

"Mr. Yamada !" exclaimed Tomokichi, in wild aston-ishment.

"It is indeed Mr. Yamada!" whispered Junzo, in a low tone to Konishi. "How under the wide heavens he ever got here, I can't imagine. I thought I heard an unusual gurgling and shuffling sound outside the door a few moments ago ; and after that I heard somebody creeping toward us. But I did not pay any attention to the sounds, as I attributed them to the guards. I could not be more surprised if a thunderbolt had dropped from the skies. Surely this man is the veriest devil for adroitness and boldness ! "

"Honorable sirs, I salute you," said Mr. Yamada, in a low voice, as he bowed down to the ground. "You seem surprised at my visit. Nevertheless, I am here at your disposal."

"How came you here at so opportune a moment?" inquired Junzo.

"That would take a long time to explain,—in fact, rather more time than I have to spare. Nevertheless, while I am cutting loose your bonds, I can give you the general details of this my latest trip. I heard mutterings of coming trouble over three weeks ago in Kioto. Ha! ha! The old fox does not forget its cubs. If that Bakufu dog can burrow, he will find that I can also burrow. If he can have his spies under the "phenix-car" in Kioto, I can have mine beneath his latticed windows in Yedo. Through underground channels I have long known that this vicious cur was scowling on you, and, as soon as I heard that some blow was about to be directed at you, I at once announced that my regular attack of spring fever was at hand, and forthwith disappeared. I left my family most assiduously nursing an old dummy carefully tucked beneath the quilts, with instructions to report slow convalescence of the invalid. Vanishing from Kioto, I went to Osaca and engaged a stout and swift boat for a coast trip. When we had left the city far behind we put to sea, and with favorable winds, together with steady sculling, we reached a secluded village on the shores of Yedo bay, within ten days. I ordered the boat to be pulled up on the beach in line with some other boats, and left it in care of the headman of the village.

"Then I hired a much smaller boat to take me up near to Yedo and land me. I left my own crew down the bay, with instructions to go out fishing every day in our large boat and await my return. During the last week I have been in the Yoshiwara taking notes. If that Bakufu cur can make men drunk and extract information from them, he will find that to be a little game at which two can play. This afternoon I found out all about your arrest, and I heard about the abusive treatment heaped upon you through hordes of Hikoné retainers that flocked down to the brothels for their regular carouse. I kept my eyes open, and laid my plans accordingly. I first secured a stout rope and a small saw, which I hid away under my clothes. I then retired to my room and drew forth my plan of Hikoné Yashiki, which you gentlemen kindly sent me a couple of years ago. I found by the specifications there laid down that in a certain part of the walls there was a window that was but a short distance from the ground. I then hunted up a jovial Hikoné *samurai* and invited him to partake of a repast that I had prepared, and, in the course of a long conversation, elicited from him the very interesting fact that that portion of the barracks was at present used for a kind of store-room for armor and spears. As it was getting very late, and as he was pretty far gone in his cups, I accompanied him home, under the pretext of seeing that he came to no grief. This brought me up to the gates of his *yashiki*, where I parted company with him, he going inside, while I prowled about the dark walls until near midnight, when everybody appeared to be asleep.

"I then cautiously crept to the designated window and listened carefully. All was silent. To one end of my rope I fastened an iron hook that I had secured for this purpose. With a stick I managed to hook it around one of the wooden bars in the window. Then I pulled myself up, and looked in to inspect the room. There was nobody there. Then I went to work and quietly sawed out two of the bars and let myself into the room. I had found out from the tipsy braggarts in the Yoshiwara precisely where you were confined, and so had no difficulty in marking out my course. Slipping out of the room, I picked my way through the shrubbery and crept about under verandas, until I came to the wing where this dungeon is located. I crept up on the veranda and wet the *shojee* with my tongue and pushed my finger through it. Through this aperture I could see the two guards asleep beside the *hebachi*. I then slipped the *shojee* back and crept in upon them. The nearer one was lying flat on his back, so that I had a splendid chance at his throat, and was able to cut it so deeply that no outcry or noise was made, the windpipe having been entirely severed. But the other fellow turned partly over as I crept upon him, and turned his drowsy eyes upon me, so that I was obliged to clutch him tightly by the throat to prevent an outcry, and then stab him through the heart. This created a slight disturbance. When every thing had settled down, I crept in to inspect the inside of the dungeon, and found this young man wrestling with a nightmare, and came just in time to prevent an outcry."

Thus this extraordinary man kept up in low tones a running conversation while he cut the cords that bound the prisoners and brought in the swords of the guards and armed them therewith. It was found that there was need of another set of swords for Konishi.

"Was there not another jailer?" inquired Mr. Yamada.

"There was, sir," replied Junzo.

"Where is he, then?"

"He is asleep in that room to the right."

"Well then, please wait here a moment, and I will bring another pair of swords. Our dangers are but beginning, and we must be well armed. We must be prepared to die like *samurai*, and not like dogs."

So saying, Mr. Yamada crept cautiously across to the room where slept the third jailer. A dim light was burning within the chamber. Slyly making a hole in the paper, he carefully inspected the premises. The man appeared to be soundly asleep. Noiselessly sliding back the *shojee*, he stealthily crept upon his victim. The sleeper had buried his head beneath his quilt, and heard nothing. Mr. Yamada slowly folded back the heavy coverlid, and unintentionally disturbed the sleeper, who, supposing that his time to relieve guard had come, sat up in bed and began rubbing his eyes, thus exposing the back of his neck to a fair blow. Mr. Yamada rose with cat-like rapidity, and with one swift stroke severed the head from the body. It fell forward noiselessly upon the well-padded quilts, while the body sank back on the floor with a sighing sound, where its flounderings were quickly smothered beneath the heavy coverlids at once drawn over it. In a moment every thing had quieted down. Mr. Yamada then took possession of the coveted swords, and hastily returned to the young men, who had been watching him from the doorway of the dungeon.

"That was no mean stroke," remarked Junzo in an undertone.

"I have not been practising fencing with Kunisaburo during the last two years for nothing," was the laconic reply. "Now, gentlemen," continued he, "we have but little time to spare. Here are some straw sandals for you to put on while I am washing my sword in this bucket of water here. Make great haste, for we have no time to lose. Our perils now begin."

In about five minutes all were ready to start. Leaving the lights burning, Mr. Yamada directed the young men to form in a line behind him, and take hold of each other's skirts in order not to become separated in the darkness. Then sliding back the *shojee* they slipped out into the yard, where they were soon obscured by the gloom. The lynx-eyed leader, however, seemed to be familiar with every nook and corner of the *yashiki*, for he picked his way along with the most unerring certainty. Every thing was hushed in the profoundest repose. Finally they reached the room where the entrance had been forced. It was undisturbed. Going to the window, Mr. Yamada directed the young men to slide down the rope. Then he slid down after them. Again they formed line, and with stealthy step stole down the edge of the moat to the Sakurada gateway. Here they turned abruptly to the right and directed their course toward the Tora gateway that led beyond the outermost moat of the castle.

Mr. Yamada had entered this same gateway but a short time before with the rollicking Hikoné *samurai,* and had carefully remembered the password hiccoughed forth by that very jovial gentleman. In addition to this he was dressed in one of the garments of Tomokichi bearing the Tokugawa crest, which he had been far-sighted enough to borrow from that young man on one of his visits to Kioto over a year before. These crests on their dresses at once stamped them as men intimately connected with the Tokugawa interests. So that when Mr. Yamada boldly stepped up to the drowsy guard and gave the countersign he was at once allowed to pass through the wicket-gate with his companions. Once outside the castle and their course was much simplified. They turned abruptly to.the left, and followed the moat for a long distance towards the bay. At intervals they met revellers returning from some rollicking cruise. But no one interfered with them in any way. Finally they reached the waters of the bay, and followed its shores southward a short distance to where it made junction with a deep and broad canal.

Here they paused while their leader peered into the darkness as if looking for some person with whom he had pre-arranged a meeting. Finally he spied a boat moored close to the bank. He crept up to the top of the embankment, and uttered a word, to which the countersign at once came back from somebody in the boat. After a short conversation with the invisible person, he returned to the young men and said that every thing was ready for immediate embarkation, as this was the boat he had engaged by secret messenger that very afternoon. It was now about three o'clock in the morning, and daylight was drawing on apace. Quickly they cast loose from their moorings, and slipped out into the bay. They sculled far out beyond the Shinagawa shoals, and then spread their sails, and went scudding down the bay before a brisk breeze. About midday they reached the hamlet, where Mr. Yamada had beached his large boat. Sending the smaller boat back to Yedo, they launched their sea-going boat without delay, and by nighttime were far out to sea, scudding southward on the swift wings of the northeast monsoon.

CHAPTER XXVI.

AGAIN at dawn a swift-footed courier is standing beside the western gateway of Yedo castle patiently waiting for the delivery of the despatches that he has been ordered to call for and forward to the next station. Long does he wait, but the despatches come not. The guards have swung back the massive portals, but still he lingers there on the threshold while the glorious sun rides high into mid-heaven. After long hours of monotonous delay a messenger rushed up with a despatch-box for the commandant of the Kioto *shiro*. The courier overheard sundry remarks about the delay being caused by the intense excitement prevailing in Hikoné Yashiki over the miraculous escape during the night of three dangerous spies under sentence of death, who were immured in the *godown* under a strong guard that had been found by the attendants early that morning butchered in cold blood. Great was the anger of the Gotairo! Everybody in the *yashiki* trembled lest the rigid examinations that had been instituted might bring some friend or companion under the suspicions of that dreaded man. It was manifest that there must have been a coadjutor, for how could human beings have escaped unaided from the meshes of the net woven so strongly about their bodies? But all clues ceased abruptly at the window whence flight had been effected. Beyond that point nothing was known,—not a trace of the prisoners could be found anywhere to tell in what direction they had fled. Couriers had been hurried off to all the mountain passes to caution the guards to exert the utmost vigi-

316

lance in examining all suspicious characters. But of what consequence was all that, since the prisoners had escaped torture and execution anyhow?

Such were a few of the hurried and excited remarks caught by the ear of the courier as he gave his receipt for the box and made his preparations for starting. Then away went the box like a hunted deer from station to station, until it reached the distant mountains. As it was borne deeper into those mighty ranges its progress became much slower, for it found the streams swollen by the melting snows of the highlands. Although the skies were bright and clear overhead, yet angry floods filled the ravines, and the little rivulets were raging torrents. Frequent delays were experienced, and many vexatious *détours* became necessary.

In one place a rivulet deep down in a valley had received an unexpected accession of water, so that the stepping-stones had disappeared far beneath the yellow waves. The stream was not deep, and could easily have been forded under ordinary circumstances, but the swiftness of the current was such that no person could have kept his footing on the slippery stones. There was no bridge at this point, for the stream had always been forded, even during freshets. So the courier had to sit on the banks and wait for the floods to subside. Not until late on the following day was he able to resume his interrupted journey. Then the box flew from summit to summit until it came to a place where the torrents had swept away a bridge. A long and vexatious *détour* here became necessary. Far up the rugged valley the courier slowly picked his way through paths overgrown with underbrush and reeking with mud, until he came to a place that could be safely forded ; and when he came back on the other side and resumed the road, he found that he had lost nearly an entire day. But onward sped the box.

At one or two other points on its way through the mountains it was delayed in its course for a few hours, so that the despatch was fully three days behind time when its bearer finally leaped forth from the frowning gorges of Shinano and sped across the plains of Mino toward the hill country encompassing the southern shores of Lake Biwa. Toward evening a fresh courier seized the box, and plunged into a ravine among the hills. With bated breath and bowed head he rushed along as if he were some express train behind-time. His glistening body gleamed through the trees as he sped by copse and thicket. Now he has reached the base of the range, and is slowly climbing the steep road that winds up through the woods. He has reached the summit, and is starting off on another spurt of speed when he suddenly utters a wild screech of pain and terror, and tumbles down in a heap in the middle of the road,—hamstrung in both legs. The next instant, his head rolls into the dust ; and the body, that but a moment before had been bounding along with the grace and the buoyancy of a gazelle, now lies twitching and floundering convulsively on the ground.

This bloody deed was perpetrated by a band of *ronins*, who had sprung from a thicket with the swiftness and the fury of a man-eating tiger. As they washed their swords in a spring that bubbled along the roadside, they glanced hurriedly up and down the road to make sure that nobody was in sight. Then they dragged the body far into the thickets, and sprinkled sand over the bloody traces along the road. Then they seized the despatch-box and bounded into the woods. They picked their way for a mile or so along a wild and rugged foot-path until they came to a deserted hut, near a little stream that flowed down the rugged sides of a deeply wooded ravine. Here they took up their quarters, and eagerly broke open the box and proceeded in the dim light to peruse the contents thereof. But, O quick-witted reader, you have already guessed who these *ronins* are. Therefore an introduction will be needless.

Our friends had scudded day and night before the favoring monsoon all the way down the coast until they had outstripped the tardy couriers. On the third day after their departure from Yedo, they entered Owari bay and beached their boat at a fishing village in the friendly Daimiate of Isé. Then they had cut across country by forced marches, and had intercepted the fatal despatches. Within an hour after leaving Yedo bay, Mr. Yamada had fully posted himself about the details of the Gotairo's horrible sentence. When he realized that Kunisaburo, Seisho, and the children were included within the text of this exterminating decree, he became moody and silent for several hours. There did not appear to be any earthly chance of saving these innocent and unfortunate victims of the Gotairo's savage fury. Allowing four days (the usual time) for the despatch to reach Kioto, then that would mean the arrest of the proscribed individuals on the morning of the fifth day after the escape of the prisoners from Hikoné Yashiki. And how could he himself possibly reach Kioto in less than ten days? Impossible! All seemed lost.

Far into the night he sat on the deck buried in deep thought. The young men respected his grief, and sought the cabin, where they quietly discussed the thrilling incidents of the last twenty-four hours. They were indeed *ronins*, and could now do just what they pleased, without any danger of involving their Mito friends, for it appeared that the far-sighted Yamada had sent, on the afternoon of the previous day, a letter with their (forged) signatures to the Daimio of Mito, announcing their intention of immediately withdrawing from his service for political reasons, and of forthwith becoming *ronins*,— thus absolving him and his clan from all responsibility for their acts. Henceforth they were to be lawless desperadoes! Long and anxiously did they discuss their future prospects, until overpowering drowsiness, superinduced by the protracted vigils of the previous night, settled down upon them and buried them in the profoundest slumbers.

But Yamada slept not that night. His bold and busy brain was exerting all of its extraordinary powers to extricate his friends from their horrible dilemma. How

could it be done ?   Ah ! there lay the supreme difficulty.
In vain did he struggle in the meshes of the perplexing
net.   Toward midnight he rose with a sigh and went below.   He soon found it utterly impossible to sleep, and
so returned to his former position on deck.   Whether or
not the motion had quickened his circulation, and had
thus brightened his ideas, I cannot say.   But his eyes
now lit up, as if inspired with a hopeful thought.   He
called the captain of the boat, and inquired whether there
were any more sails that could be set to his craft.

"There are two other sails that can be set, most honored sir," was the humble reply.

"Then spread them at once," was the laconic order.

"With such a strong wind, most honored sir, it would
be dangerous, for our boat is already struggling under as
much sail as she can safely carry."

"Do as I tell you, Mr. Captain, and spread every sail
you can.   I will be responsible for the risk," was the
prompt command.

"Very well, sir," replied the startled captain, as he
proceeded to set the sails.   It was indeed a risky thing
to do in that stiff gale, for the boat careened as if about
to capsize, and the masts bent as if about to snap off.

But Mr. Yamada had well balanced the chances and
had come to the conclusion that nothing but this course
of action could save his friends.   He knew that the
monsoon blew steadily from the northeast for many days
at a time during this time of the year.   Instead of stopping at night he purposed to keep right on through the
entire period of darkness.   With such a breeze he calculated that they were averaging fully six miles per
hour.   If the wind kept up they would make during
twenty-four hours fully one hundred and forty-four
miles.   The distance from Yedo to Osaca would be fully
four hundred miles by sea.   But he well knew that he
could not make this distance under eight days, even
under the most phenomenal circumstances, because the
course would have to be changed into the teeth of the
wind after rounding the Kii promontory.   By that route

he could not possibly reach Kioto under ten days. And that would be too late ! But the Daimiate of Isé lay on this side of the promontory, and was only about three hundred miles from Yedo, and it could be reached on one tack with the present winds. This, then, would land him at Isé within three days after leaving Yedo. So far, so good.

But the courier with his fatal despatch would by that time be nearing the southern end of Lake Biwa, fully two days' journey to the northward. Too late to intercept him ! But then he bethought himself of the fact that the freshets in Shinano were always very bad in the spring, owing to the floods of water let loose by the melting snows that had draped the mighty crests during the winter. The despatches might be delayed ;—they frequently were at this season. But how long would they be delayed ? Two days' delay would suffice to carry out his daring scheme. Should he take the risk ? Certainly ! It was his only hope. Accordingly they had scud along under full sail for nearly three days. The boat was an unusually swift one, and the breeze favored them all the way down the coast, so that on the third day they were enabled to land at their destination safe and sound. At once they pressed northward across the hills and mountains.

When they reached the Tokaido, the southern highway between Yedo and Kioto, the thought occurred to Mr. Yamada that possibly the Gotairo might have sent his despatch by this route instead of the midland one, thus avoiding delays from freshets. But he well knew that important despatches were far safer on the secluded Nakasendo, away from the frisky antics and kittenish humors of the swarming retainers of the hostile southern Daimios, who invariably travelled by the southern road along the coast. The bare bodies of the couriers presented too tempting a bait for the endless groups of rollicking *samurai* from Satsuma, Tosa, and Choshiu, to render it advisable to trust them to the fickle moods of those dangerous gentlemen. A fleeting courier bound-

ing around a sharp bend into a company of these irascible characters would probably never have been heard
from again. And for a courier to surrender the right of
way invariably demanded by these punctilious gentlemen, would have entailed endless delays. Better take
the Nakasendo with its freshets, than the Tokaido with
its swaggering blades. So thought the Bakufu. Nevertheless, Mr. Yamada made diligent inquiry at this point,
as to whether any couriers had come through lately from
Yedo, and was informed that there had been none except a few local ones from cities along the road.

Accordingly he pressed swiftly northward toward
where the Nakasendo made junction with the ranges
skirting the eastern shores of Lake Biwa, and had arrived at the lonely spot on the highway but a few hours
before the arrival of the ill-fated courier. That half a
day of delay in Yedo had rendered this possible. But
they still did not know whether they were attacking the
right man. They took their risks on that. They knew
that a courier came through from Yedo every four or five
days or so, but they could not tell whether this one was
carrying the fatal orders presumed to have been sent on
the morning following their escape. With nervous hands
Mr. Yamada tore off the coverings and unrolled the
despatch and read it through with features absolutely
unruffled in their cool placidity. The young men
watched him anxiously but could draw no inference
from his countenance. Schooled in the art of self-con-
trol, the *samurai* wore an air of nonchalance where a
Caucasian would have thrown his cap into the air and
have shouted himself hoarse. At last Mr. Yamada
cleared his throat and quietly remarked :

" It is all right. This is the despatch that we are after.
Read for yourselves."

The young men eagerly conned the contents of the
letter. It ordered the commandant of the Shiro to place
the entire Nakashima family under arrest, because of the
blood-attainder that had been decreed against them for
treason toward the Shogun. Directions, however, were

given that the prisoners should not be removed from
their houses, but should be allowed to remain there
under the surveillance of strong guards secreted about
the premises, in order that when the condemned sons of
Nakashima, who had recently escaped, should be de-
coyed thither, they might be pounced upon and captured ; but, if after the lapse of thirty days they did not
put in an appearance, then the prisoners were to be executed in accordance with specifications to be forwarded
from Yedo within a few days.

"The miserable scoundrel has laid his plans with his
usual foresight and cunning," remarked Konishi, after
the perusal.

"He has indeed," replied Mr. Yamada, thoughtfully.

"I see that while Kunisaburo and his family are speci-
fied within the terms of this sentence," said Junzo, "yet
you and your wife do not come within its terms. It is
manifest that suspicions have not yet been excited against
yourself. It is only the unlucky Nakashima family that
is to be exterminated."

"That seems to be the case," was the mournful reply,
"but what will life be to me without my children and
grandchildren ? My house will be as desolate as a
sepulchre ! That Bakufu whelp might just as well have
made a clean job of it while he was about it, and have
swept me also out of existence. However, things are
very much simplified by the fact that I am free from
suspicion as yet. But we have not any time to lose if we
wish to save our friends. It is evident from the terms of
this letter that another courier will be on the heels of this
one in a few days. Until then we can walk the streets of
Kioto with impunity. Do you feel equal to the exertions
of a night march ? "

"I am ready for any thing," replied Konishi.

"And so are we," exclaimed the brothers in one breath.

"Then let us be off now," said their leader. "There
will be a bright moon to-night, and we can reach the
city by daylight, for we can resume the road and press
on with greater speed than we made while cutting across
the country through by-paths."

CHAPTER XXVII.

THE FLIGHT.

WHEN the moonbeams had faded away from the lofty crest of Hiyeisan, and the blue peak of that lordly mountain stood forth clear and sharp against the hues of dawning day, our band of *ronins* had just crossed the granite range of high hills that serve as a water-shed between Lake Biwa and Yamashiro. Yonder lay Kioto, embosomed in the shadows of the vale. The mists that had risen up from the rice-fields and from the Kamogawa shoals during the night had become chilled by the cool breath of the morning, and had shrunk down near the earth, until their white billows vied with the myriad clouds of cherry blossoms that embowered the foothills around the city. The throbbing, deep-toned bells of the engroved temples and monasteries were calling in mournful tones the many thousands of priests to chant the orisons before numberless altars. The stupendous voice of the Chionin bell boomed forth accents of despairing melody that trembled through the vale at regular intervals.

But what cared the *ronins* for all this? Rapidly did they descend through the woods on the reverse slope of the hills, and hasten along the highway toward the city. As they neared Mr. Yamada's house, that crafty gentleman left them at the gateway, while he stole around behind and entered the premises through a wicket in the boxwood hedge. The members of his household had become accustomed to his abrupt methods of appearing before them, and consequently were not alarmed when he crept up-stairs and blandly inquired after the health

324

of the invalid. He found all well. Going to the gateway he directed Tomokichi to hasten at once to Atago-Yama and warn his people to prepare for flight that
very night. Junzo was ordered off on a similar errand
in the direction of Mr. Akashi's plantation. Konishi was
to come into the house and rest for the day. And as soon
as darkness came on they were all to journey by circuitous routes to a given point on the rugged borders of
the friendly Daimiate of Iga, thirty miles southeast of
Kioto. After resting for a day or so at that point he
would lay out their future line of march. So saying, he
dismissed them with the admonition to keep their hoods
well drawn over their faces, so as to disguise their
features.

Tomokichi hastened home as fast as he could, and
arrived there just as the folks were sitting down to
breakfast. Nobody recognized the cowled figure as it
came up to the veranda. Mr. Nakashima approached
with a stately bow, and inquired what might be the object of the stranger's early call. A low voice from the
depths of the hood replied that there was business of the
utmost importance that must be communicated privately.
Accordingly Mr. Nakashima led his strange visitor upstairs and ushered him into one of the back rooms. His
surprise was unbounded when the disguise was removed.
For several minutes he stared at his son in blank
amazement before he could find words to express his astonishment.

" There seems to be no doubt but what my son Tomokichi is now before me ; but what is the meaning of this
unprecedented freak ? " exclaimed Mr. Nakashima when
he had recovered from his dumbfounded wonder.

"It means, my father, that we have been detected as
spies in Yedo, and have escaped to warn our families to
flee to the mountains," replied Tomokichi.

"Oh ! Is that all ? " was the quiet response of his
father. " Well, I am free to admit that this event was
not entirely unexpected. I did not think that you boys
would be able to play your game as long as you have

already done.　During your first year at Mito Yashiki I lived in constant dread of exposure.　Since that time, however, I have become calloused and indifferent, just like people who live at the base of a volcano.　I might almost say that I feel somewhat relieved to know that it is all over with.　But why should I and my family fly as you suggest ?　It seems to me that you and Junzo are the ones to fly.　Let us be up and planning without delay.　There are lots of monasteries about here where you can easily secrete yourselves."

"O father !　You little know that our entire family now trembles on the very brink of a raging volcano.　It is concerning this that I have hastened to warn you."

"My son, what do you mean ?　I perceive from the serious aspect of your countenance that you are profoundly agitated,—otherwise I would deem you to be jesting."

"Know then, O father, that the Gotairo, in his blind rage, was not satisfied with sentencing Konishi, Junzo, and myself to a painful death, but, in his savage fury, he leaped beyond all bounds of moderation, and decreed blood-attainder for treason against all of our families, thus exterminating them root and branch.　As an act of special favor he allowed Konishi's father to perform *seppuku*, thus wiping out the blood-attainder as to his family.　But the unfortunate Nakashima family he has doomed to utter extermination, root and branch.　It is cruel !　It is horrible !　Little did we dream that our plottings would terminate so terribly !　The thought that my deeds should bring such misery upon so many innocent people has filled my heart with unutterable horror and anguish, causing me boundless humiliation and grief."

"Compose yourself, my son," gently replied Mr. Nakashima, "and do not fret yourself needlessly.　We must now act like men, and not like children.　So that fiend has decreed blood-attainder, has he ?　Well, I presume he has precedent in his favor.　What a great misfortune it is that our nation has no written laws, such as exist in foreign countries! Here is this unscrupulous savage raking up an ancient and obsolete custom to glut his frightful vengeance, and there is no help for it, simply because this humane age has not had sense enough to close the gates of the barbaric past with a few statutes of definite purport! Well, well, there is no help for it. Our enemy holds the hilt, and it behooves us to get out of the way of the blade. Have you any plans for escape?"

"Every thing is already arranged. Make your preparations for flight to-night. Leave the house in charge of our faithful servants. Then we will journey around to the borders of Iga, and meet the others. From that point we will journey in accordance with further instructions from Mr. Yamada. I must sleep as much as possible to-day, for I have had but little rest for several nights."

"I will order the breakfast to be served up here," said Mr. Nakashima, "and we will break the news as gently as possible to the women. The time has now come when they must be made conversant with every thing."

The old gentleman then called to his wife, and requested her to bring the breakfast up-stairs. In a few moments the three ladies came up,—Madame Nakashima carrying the dishes on a tray, Masago carrying the tub of rice, and O-Hana carrying the little side-dishes. As they modestly entered the room, with downcast eyes, they did not at first recognize Tomokichi, but, when they had set their burdens on the floor, they looked up and saw him. The old lady stared in mute astonishment. O-Hana gasped forth "Tomokichi!" in tones of mingled joy and surprise. And Masago, utterly oblivious of all proprieties, and acting on her first impulse, rushed forward, clasped her soft, plump arms about his neck, and kissed him lovingly,—for all the world like a demonstrative Caucasian! The little boys, who had brought up the rear of the procession, stood looking in at the door upon the strange actions of their mother, and seemed undecided whether to advance or retreat.

When Masago had recovered her equilibrium, and had sat down beside her husband, with hands demurely folded in her lap and a countenance wreathed with beaming smiles, the little fellows then had a chance to see their father's face, and they toddled forward and bowed their heads to the floor in reverential salutation,—well-bred sons of a well-bred mother as they were. Then followed the tardy salutations of the mother and daughter, together with a flood of congratulations and questions. By degrees the sombre nature of the catastrophe that had befallen the Nakashima family was revealed to the poor creatures. It took them long to understand the matter fully,—for the reader must bear in mind that they had never been informed as to the real nature of the young men's mission at Mito Yashiki, but had always supposed that they were gentlemen-in-waiting on the Daimio of Mito. When the full extent of the disaster had dawned upon them, the reaction was most painful to witness. The old mother seized the hands of her son and bowed her head down to the floor, overwhelmed with grief. O-Hana buried her face in the wide folds of her sleeves, and wept convulsively. Masago clung to her husband and hid her face in his bosom. The little boys, seeing such universal grief prevailing on all sides of them, began to cry. Old Nakashima alone remained unmoved. But his blanched face told plainly of the bitter sorrow at his heart. He reached forth his hands and drew the little ones toward him, and patted their heads, while his bright eyes shone with moisture.

It took a long time for this distressing exhibition of grief to subside. Finally those qualities of fortitude and devotion, that have rendered the frail and gentle counsellors of men so admirable in the estimation of mankind, gained the mastery of their emotions, and they settled down to a joyless breakfast and a quiet deliberation of their perils. Toward the close of the meal the happy volatility of the native temperament had gained the complete ascendancy, so that a stranger glancing at the group would never have imagined that they were sitting under the shadow of death.

"It is one consolation," sighed the mother, "to know that if we must perish, we can all die together."

"Yea, verily!" exclaimed Masago, with an emphasis suggestive of a fierce exultation, "and also to know that I shall not die by the hand of a stranger, and that my face shall not mirror itself in the waters of the Kamogawa. Oh, my husband, remember that you have pledged me this upon your knightly word."

"But why talk of death at all?" chimed in the blithesome sister, unable longer to endure the gloomy tone of the conversation. "Surely we all have many days of life yet to live, and who knows but what we may escape entirely? We, too, are *ronins*, and shall join this desperate band of wayward desperadoes in their wild rambles over the country. How gay! How gay!"—and the merry young lady actually clapped her hands in glee at the thought.

"Daughter, be still!" said her father in rebuking tones. "This is no time for merriment. Our condition is far too serious to be discussed otherwise than in the most solemn manner."

"Sir," said Tomokichi, "I do not know but what she is adopting the wisest course. Let us all act cheerfully even if we feel gloomy, and let us try to live the balance of our lives as happily as possible."

"Perhaps you are right, my son," sadly replied his father, "perhaps it would be better to get all the enjoyment we can out of what remains to us of this life. But we must now be making our preparations for flight. You women keep up your spirits and act just as if nothing had happened. You, my son, go to sleep and take no further care about things until we wake you up to start. And I will go out and engage some *kagos*."

And so the sad company dispersed. Tomokichi slept peacefully until sundown. The ladies packed up a few small bundles and were ready for the journey,—so simple a thing was it in that land to go travelling! The stranger glancing in at the gateway would never have imagined that the quiet and cheerful household were beneath a sword that hung by a thread. The evening meal was served an hour later than usual, and the sleeper was duly roused to partake of it. When it was over the house was closed and placed in charge of the faithful servant who had served the family so long. Instructions were left to answer all inquiries by saying that the family had gone to Osaca on a visit. Then the ladies and the children were carefully put into the *kagos*, the bundles were tied on the top, and the party was ready to depart.

" O, dear me ! " exclaimed that maiden O-Hana, " I surely must not forget my battledoor aud shuttlecock. And there is my precious kitten also ! It would never do to leave her behind. That would indeed precipitate bad luck." And out she jumped from her *kago* and rushed into the house to secure her treasures.

" Silly child, come back ! " exclaimed her father in severe tones. " This is not the time for such folly. When will you ever learn to act otherwise than as a foolish child ? "

" Never mind her whims, father," interposed Tomo-kichi ; " let her have them. It will be good policy to put on an air of pleasure as we are starting, in order to give our neighbors the impression that we are pleasure-seekers. It will not do for our departure to have either the appearance of a flight or of a funeral procession. The more jolly and cheerful we seem the better will it be for us."

" Very well, my son," replied the old gentleman, as the scowl faded from his brow while watching the young man help to chase the frisky kitten about the yard. When it had finally been caught and placed in the *kago* in the lap of its mistress, he slowly shook his fan at his wayward daughter and exclaimed : " Take warning, young woman ! I am going to marry you to the very next eligible young man that makes application for you. Too long have I put this matter off in deference to your childish protests. Before I know it I shall have an old woman on my hands. Now remember that hereafter no excuses will avail. You are entirely too lively. We shall see if there be any way of sobering you down a bit at a very early date."

" Oh, my father ! Do not overwhelm me with confusion before these strangers," protested that lively young lady, as she fanned the kitten vigorously with her battle-door. "Indeed I am very obedient, and will marry the very next young fellow that you may choose for me !"

"Remember your promise, young miss," said her father, as he gave the signal for starting.

They went down the glen as far as the Kioto road, and then turned southward toward Osaca, and journeyed many miles until they came to a village where they changed bearers. Then they changed their course and went eastward, passing across the flat region of country that lay south of Kioto. All night did they travel. Every few miles they changed their bearers. Toward morning they entered the delightful hill country border-ing the Daimiates of Iga and Yamato. For mile after mile did they press onward through this beautiful region, gradually approaching the mighty mountains of those two Daimiates. Late in the day they reached the designated village on the frowning borders of Iga. Here they met the tearful families of Junzo and Kunisaburo. These sorrowful people had been through scenes much resem-bling those already described in this chapter. Mr. Ya-mada and Konishi were to arrive on the next day. Until their arrival everybody was to make time pass as pleas-antly as possible. Four rooms were engaged in a hotel picturesquely situated near a stream that rushed down the glade. The ladies at once got together in an upper room and had a good cry ; after which they appeared as fresh and bright as a June day after a shower.

CHAPTER XXVIII.

THE territory that stretches for one hundred and fifty miles due south of Kioto, and which terminates in the magnificent promontory of Kii, comprises one of the grandest mountain regions of the Japanese empire. Jutting boldly far out into the deep waters of the Pacific Ocean, where the mighty whales sport amid the waves that wash its stupendous foundations, the rugged shores of this rock-bound promontory bend back and trend toward the northwest and toward the northeast, thus forming a gigantic wedge, cleaving the ocean's bed. The northwest bend terminates in the peaceful waters of the Inland Sea, while the northeastern one terminates in Owari bay. In the widest part—about midway up the coasts—this Alpine region is about one hundred and fifty miles wide. The important Daimiates of Senshiu, Kawachi, Kii, Yamato, Isé, and Iga were situated within this large district.

The Daimiate of Kii, or Kii-shiu as it was generally designated, was the southernmost one, and, conforming as it did to the coast lines, it was triangular in shape. It was grandly and superbly rugged throughout its entire length and breadth, especially so along its eastern face. With its southern exposure, and with the tepid floods of the Black Stream laving its shores, it had a mild and delightful climate. The mighty ranges behind it screened it from the north winds, thus making it the choicest orange district in the empire. Forty different varieties of this delicious fruit were cultivated upon the slopes of the hills fringing the shores. To descend into the sweet

332

valley of the Arida during the heavenly winter months, when the hills, as far as the eye could reach, were covered with the golden fruit, was one of the sights of earth. Kii-shiu was truly one of the choicest Daimiates in the realm. Watered with innumerable streams that dashed across it in speedy course from the highlands to the sea, bathed in perpetual sunshine, and fanned with the warm southern zephyrs,—what wonder that this should have been the home of the camphor tree and of the citrus ? Here the camellia shrub grew to the full stature of a tree, and the magnolia and the cape jessamine assumed gigantic proportions. Verily, the place might well have been the home of the gods, for temples innumerable were scattered all over the province,—from the magnificent monastery of Koya-san, that lifted its deeply shaded crest nearly five thousand feet above the sea, down to the little shrines beside the deep inlets where the devout fisherman needs must ring the bell to rouse the drowsy gods from their dreamy siestas.

Then came the classic province of Yamato, which was yet grander in its mountain scenery. This Daimiate split its way deep into the back of Kii-shiu like a gigantic plough, until its southernmost point came within twenty miles of the Pacific Ocean. Its scenery was surpassingly sublime and beautiful, the superb mountains being packed together in awful grandeur, and rolling away in adamantine billows as far as the eye could reach. The lofty peaks towered to an altitude of over six thousand feet. Here dwelt the bear, the wild boar, the goat-faced deer, the monkey, and the panther. The oak, the beech, the chestnut, the cryptomeria, and the camphor tree draped the landscape with sylvan beauty. Hamlets, shrines, temples, and monasteries were scattered in all available spots. In the heart of this province, near the town of Tosamachi, was located the tomb of Jimmu Tenno, who founded the dynasty of the Mikados over twenty-five centuries ago.

To the northeast of Yamato lay Iga, which was almost equally mountainous. The Daimiate of Isé skirted the shores of Owari bay, and was quite flat in its northern part, but became very rugged and grand in its southern portions.

Thus, it will be perceived, our refugees had succeeded in escaping into a region where it would be very difficult to catch them. They could most effectually secrete themselves among the vast solitudes of this promontory. It would take a large force to hunt them down in those secluded regions, where they could easily fly from valley to valley without leaving any tracks behind them. When driven from human habitations they could fly to the vast and pathless forests upon the remotest slopes, and defy pursuit. Even if driven from these forest solitudes they still could slip down to the shore and escape to the broad ocean in a boat. And if supreme misfortune should overtake them, they could with their own hands free their spirits from further pursuit and vex their enemies with the empty cages. But it was not at all likely that the Gotairo would have either the time or the inclination to send an army chasing over the mountains after the fugitives. His plan would be to wait until his spies made report as to the Daimiate into which they had fled, and then to demand of the Daimio their immediate surrender, and holding him responsible for their capture and delivery. But with Daimios hostile to him, as were those of Iga and Yamato, this would not be a very easy task, for these magnates would probably refuse to take official cognizance of the presence of strangers within their borders, and thus deny the allegation of the Gotairo that any such individuals were there. If, upon proof, the presence of strangers should be forced upon their attention, then they would probably be so dilatory in their movements that the fugitives would be thereby enabled to escape over the border into somebody else's jurisdiction. Secret warnings could always be communicated in advance, so that capture would be impossible. In those days they managed such things very well in Japan.

Therefore, the Nakashima family was comparatively safe for a time at least. But Mr. Yamada did not intend to let them remain where they were ; he intended to send them southward, far into the mountain fastnesses of Yamato. He selected a lofty plateau nearly five thousand feet above sea-level, known as the Odaigahara, and situated in the wildest and most broken section of the promontory, at a point where the three provinces of Isé, Kii, and Yamato join corners, about twenty miles from the ocean. They would thus be in a position to step from province to province with the utmost ease, and finally to take to water in case the land became too hot to hold them. With such admirable foresight did that cunning man lay his plans !

After resting a day, the journey was resumed along the rapidly ascending road that led up into the mountain barriers that looked down upon the rice flats of Isé and the blue waters of Owari bay. Here Mr. Yamada took leave of the party and returned to Kioto, bent on further schemes of daring espionage. He placed Mr. Nakashima in command of the expedition, and left in his hands a full description of the country through which he was to pass ; for this far-sighted man had during the five previous years of leisure made extensive and minute geographical surveys of this entire promontory in anticipation of some such emergency. While the young men were on duty at Mito Yashiki he had improved the time in making pilgrimages to all the shrines and temples south of Kioto. As the entire promontory was full of holy places, this devout man tramped over every section of Kii-shiu, Iga, Isé, and Yamato, thus becoming perfectly familiar with the entire country and able to follow every by-path. Every village was known to him, for he had maps showing every thing. He had taken particular precaution each summer, as he started out on his pilgrimages, to let everybody know the object of his journey, so that his reputation for sanctified devotion permeated even the moats and walls of the Shiro where the commandant took special delight in twitting Captain Murata about his early suspicions concerning this holy man of pilgrimages and prayers.

By degrees he had footed it over every road in the promontory without exciting the slightest suspicion, for, during the summer months, multitudes flocked through that region visiting the innumerable shrines and temples scattered by sea-shore and mountain stream. Nor had he confined his exertions to this region, but had diligently visited the shrines to the east, north, and west of Kioto also. It was thus that he was able with such swiftnesss to cut across the country from Isé to Lake Biwa and intercept the despatches. He was thoroughly familiar with every by-road and mountain path. While he had found much wild and rugged mountain country to the north of Kioto, yet did he prefer the confused medley of ranges in the promontory to the south, partly because of the friendly character of the Daimios of Iga and Yamato, partly because of the proximity of the ocean, and partly because of the extreme difficulty involved in finding anybody once lost in those vast forests and broken valleys.

And so he left them with cheerful words of parting and journeyed back to Kioto to await further developments. He had calculated that the despatches from Yedo would be due within four or five days after his return. In the meantime he could be industriously circulating the report that the Nakashima family had gone on a pilgrimage to some shrines among the mountains north of Kioto. With the system of espionage that he had so carefully developed during the last few years in and about the city he could keep posted on all the movements of his enemies without being detected. Although as yet free from suspicion, nevertheless he very well knew that this state of affairs could not very long continue. He weighed the chances carefully, however, and had come to the conclusion that he could do more good at home for the present, and that he would stay there until his spies signalled the approach of somebody from the Shiro, when he would leave his wife and servants in charge of the premises and would retire from the scene until the purport of the visit should be disclosed. The risk was certainly very great, but the man was eminently daring and crafty.

After taking leave of Mr. Yamada, the party journeyed by easy stages for many days far into the mountains toward the point of destination. Sometimes they would spend nearly an entire day in slowly climbing the precipitous sides of some lofty range where human habitations were very few and very far between ; where, for hours, at a time, they heard nothing but the voices of the cascades and torrents echoing the breezes that whispered through the immense forests of oak, cryptomeria, and chestnut ; where, from some overhanging crag, the goat-faced deer peered at them curiously as they climbed upward ; and where the spotted gazelles fled deeper into the sylvan solitudes as the unaccustomed sounds of shouting and of laughter disturbed the silence of those rocky heights. They would spend the night at some hamlet perched far up among the crags at the summit, where they would find the startled inhabitants ready to fly at the sight of such an unusual incursion of strangers. But their fears would soon be put to flight by the friendly appearance of the party, and then they would hasten to place at the disposal of their guests the best accommodations in the hamlet. Brook trout from the neighboring streams would be daintily broiled over the *hebachi.* Delicious sweet potatoes, that had been cultivated in stockaded clearings to save them from the depredations of wild-boars and porcupines that dearly loved to revel over them, were nicely boiled in earthen pots and made ready for the evening meal. The good people then brought forth their treasures of *soy*, pickled plums, and salted shrimps, to tempt the appetites of the travellers.

When the rice was thoroughly cooked the meal would be served in that room whence the most picturesque outlook could be obtained. As far as the eye could reach, the blue mountains rolled away to the horizon in endless waves and were bathed in the shadows and mists that heralded the speedy approach of night. Joyous and hearty would be the repast. After it had terminated the little ones would be carried off by their mothers to be duly put to bed, where they would soon be found asleep beneath the heavy quilts, for in those altitudes the night air was very chilly even in mid-summer. Then the company of ladies and gentlemen would gather on the veranda overlooking the vast and motionless panorama stretched before them, and would view the serene majesty of the scene as they talked over the events of the day and ventured timid surmises as to the future. Long after the moon had cast its spectral mantle over the billowy landscape did they tarry and sip their tea. At length they dispersed and were soon buried in slumbers known only to those who have journeyed over lofty mountains and have quaffed with their lungs the crisp atmosphere of great altitudes. But the moon shone on, and cast his beams into the dark ravines where dwelt the panther, the wolf, and the fox, to guide them as they scoured the remote fastnesses for their prey.

Bright and early in the morning our friends would descend the reverse slope of the range. Down, down, down through the endless forests of beech, maple, *kayaki*, *hinoki*, and camphor trees, would they slowly sink like a balloon settling in clouds. The monkeys gibbered at them from the boughs. The ibex glanced askance at the uncanny sight and leaped into the bamboo copses to ruminate over the matter at leisure. An occasional wildboar, returning from his depredations in some barley field or potato patch, halted as he crossed their path and then fled in terror lest these might be the avenging Nemesis of his night's devastations. Down, down, down, yet lower into the land of terraced rice fields and millet patches, down where the trout sported in the brooks and where the complaining wheel of some rustic mill filled the valley with its dreary music,—went the straggling procession. The peasant shades his eyes and gazes in blank amazement at the sworded knights and fair ladies, and wonders whether these people have fallen from the clouds upon his native village. A few kind words,

however, dispel all fears ; and the gracious manners of
the ladies quite win the hearts of the simple rustics, who
forthwith bestir themselves to prepare the midday meal
for their unexpected guests. Then the journey is resumed
up the other side of the deep valley, and evening overtakes
the travellers at a romantic little hamlet about half-way
to the summit where they pass the night and resume
their journey in the morning.

And thus they journeyed for ten days, doing little else
but to commence climbing one mountain just as soon as
they had descended one. Sometimes, however, the road led
among the hamlets at the base of the valley. Sometimes
it followed the mountain side for many miles. But such
variations were not common. The road soon became
tired of the monotonous level and sought the air of the
bracing altitudes. On the morning of the tenth day
they began to climb up to the lofty plateau of Odaigahara, where they were to rest until further orders. The
grandeur and the magnificence of this promontory
seemed to culminate about this black mass of mountains.
Up, up, up through vast forests of *hinoki*, cryptomeria,
beech, yew, oak, chestnut, and maple, crept the *kagos*
until they had attained an elevation of nearly five thousand feet above sea-level. Here, as they emerged from
the woods, they came out upon a grassy district, containing fully thirty square miles of meadow and forest,
around which towered summits to yet loftier heights,—
that of Odaigahara-yama, attaining an altitude of nearly
six thousand feet. From its top there was a superb outlook.- On one side you gazed down upon Iga, Isé, and
Yamato, while on the other side your eye took in the
coast of Kii-shiu, the deep-blue billows of the Pacific,
and (on a clear day) even the crests of Fujisan, fully two
hundred miles up the coasts. Beautiful groves of maple,
oak, and chestnut were scattered about in this vast
mountain basin, and many wild animals similar to those
found in the regions already traversed by our party
abounded in the vicinity, while the streams were filled
with trout.

Mr. Nakashima decided to halt here for the midday meal. Accordingly, head-quarters were established beneath an immense maple tree that overshadowed a brook. While the children tumbled about on the grass the *kago* bearers industriously built an oven with stones from the stream and proceeded to boil the rice in a large iron pot that had been brought along in anticipation of such " camping out." And the young men, after securing some bait, went a little distance up stream and tried their luck at fishing. In a short time they had captured a dozen fine specimens of trout and brought them back to be broiled for lunch. It was a very jolly pic-nic party that gathered about the steaming rice and demolished innumerable bowls full of that snowy substance. While they ate their meal, the bearers respectfully withdrew to a deep pool some distance down stream and bathed and shouted to their hearts' content. After that they came back with most formidable appetites and utterly annihilated the allowance of rice and fish that had been set aside for them. Mr. Nakashima, in token of his appreciation of their faithful and arduous services, warmed up some *saké* and dealt it out liberally to them until the happy fellows were ready to pledge themselves to carry him to the uttermost limits of the empire.

Everybody was in the most jovial spirits when the journey was resumed, and they set out on the last stretch that intervened between them and their destination. Journeying slowly through this beautiful region of verdure and streams, they finally reached its southern boundary, where they took a road that led out to the edge of the mountain barrier overlooking the ocean, that lay but a few miles beneath. At that point there was a little monastery romantically perched among the crags. Mr. Yamada, on one of his excursions, had noted the delightful spot, and, on his return to Kioto, had used his influence to have one of his friends appointed as the abbot of the institution. To this individual Mr. Nakashima was now carrying letters of introduction. Late in the afternoon our party rounded a bold spur of the mountains and saw before them, through the trees, the blue waves of the ocean rolling against the rock ribbed shores far beneath them. A few more steps brought them to the sequestered retreat of the monks.

The massive bell was booming forth in melancholy tones the vesper summons, and the yellow-robed priests were marching in solemn procession from their dormitories toward the main temple to chant Sanskrit rhythms before the gloomy altars. The priest at the main entrance directed our friends up the steep mountain side to the house of the abbot. They climbed up quite a distance through the forest and finally came to a terrace having its front walled up to a height of about twenty feet with rough stones. Hereon was perched the very comfortable abode of the abbot, which was approached by a long flight of moss-grown steps leading up through the cryptomeria groves on the right-hand side. But that reverend gentleman was at that moment conducting the services in the temple. An attendant hastily went down and handed to him Mr. Yamada's letters of introduction. Quickly summoning his assistant, the abbot directed him to continue the services and then hurried up to the house, glancing over the letters as he went. He at once comprehended the situation. With great cordiality he invited his guests into the house, after having soundly berated the servants for having left them standing at the gateway. The *kagos* were then carefully stowed away in a shed, and the bearers were paid and dismissed with a few presents, which the grateful fellows dropped flat down on the ground to acknowledge.

Orders were then given for the hot bath to be prepared for the stiff and weary travellers, and for the larder to be taxed to its uttermost capacity in preparing the evening meal. Cushions were spread on the *tatamis* in the front room, *hebachis* filled with glowing charcoal were brought, —for the evenings were as yet quite chilly,—and the choicest tea and tobacco were served. After a little rest the ladies were allotted the corner room that opened out on the veranda, and which adjoined the reception-room, where they were then sitting ; and the gentlemen were allotted the other corner room on the opposite side. Then the bath was announced to be ready. When everybody had boiled themselves therein to their full satisfaction, the rice was declared ready. An assault thereon was at once delivered, which speedily developed into a systematic and well sustained attack that lasted until the host feared that with such appetites on his hands there would soon be a famine in those regions.

After dinner the gentlemen gathered in the reception-room and fully discussed the situation. The letters had only furnished information of a general nature, so that Mr. Nakashima was obliged to explain matters more fully. When the abbot had thoroughly grasped the situation he most cordially extended the hospitality of his roof to the fugitives for an indefinite length of time, —for he detested the Bakufu most heartily and rejoiced in being able to aid in sheltering its enemies.   *   *   *

Four months have passed away. The fugitives are still at the monastery. A few days after their arrival Konishi and Junzo were absorbed in a game of chess upon the front veranda, when they were disturbed by a small pebble falling on the ground near them. Looking up they perceived the head and shoulders of a strange man peering over the boxwood hedge at them. This beautiful barrier of evergreen surrounded the premises on all sides, and, at the point where the stranger was standing, it separated the yard from the forest. When he saw that their attention had been attracted he cautiously beckoned for them to approach. Puzzled at this curious proceeding, Konishi and Junzo went toward the man, and, after noting that he was quite alone and apparently unarmed, they came close up to the hedge and inquired what he wanted.

"I am the bearer of private despatches from Mr. Yamada to Mr. Konishi," was the low response, "and I must deliver them in person and take his receipt. Can either of you gentlemen tell me where he is ?"

"I am Konishi," replied that young gentleman.

"Then if you will kindly come into the woods here I will deliver the despatches," said the stranger, "and I have a receipt already drawn up and ready for your signature, so that you need not take more than a moment of time. I do not wish to be seen by anybody, for in my line of business it is the safest policy to be seen by as few persons as possible. By the way, here is the countersign which you can compare with the code placed in your hands by Mr. Yamada, and thus identify me to your entire satisfaction. I will now hasten to the large rock beside the spring back there in the woods, and will meet you there."

The young men hurried back to the house, and found that the countersign tallied with the code. Then they slipped out by a wicket gate in the hedge, and were soon lost in the forest. After a brisk walk they reached the spring, and found the stranger sitting on the rock, with writing materials spread out ready for immediate use. He drew forth from beneath his garment a small package, which he respectfully handed to Konishi, at the same time politely requesting him to sign the receipt without delay, as he must start on his return at once. Konishi did as the man requested.

"Honorable sirs, I bid you adieu," said that mysterious gentleman, as he took the receipt and vanished into the forests.

Konishi then sat down upon the rock and unrolled the paper wrappings from the parcel, and found a short sword and a letter in Mr. Yamada's handwriting addressed to himself. Konishi at once recognized the sword as his father's, and, drawing it from its scabbard and perceiving the blood-stains along its keen edge, he at once read the ghastly tale that it told. An extract from Mr. Yamada's letter will make the matter clear to the reader : " Soon after my return to Kioto private despatches were received from Mito Yashiki, stating that your father had been compelled to perform *seppuku* by the enraged Hikoné beast. It was his dying request that the weapon with which he made the fatal stab should be carefully preserved and forwarded to you, with the request that you should bide your time and some day plunge it into the body of this mortal enemy of the house of Konishi. I, having received this weapon from secret messengers, do now with reverent hands send it to the son and heir of him who has been so greatly wronged, and do most devoutly hope that the day may be near at hand when this blade shall drink the blood of the foul aggressor."

Konishi held the bare sword in his hands in a dazed sort of fashion, and gazed upon it with moistened eyes. Junzo fully comprehended the situation, and stood by with silent lips and pitying face. Not a word was spoken for several minutes. At length Konishi dreamily slipped the sword back into its scabbard, and handed the letter to Junzo without comment. He read it through, and then handed it back in silence.

" This means," said Konishi, in determined tones, " that either the Lord of Hikoné or I must perish by this blade."

" Verily ! verily ! " responded Junzo, with decision, " and at no very distant day either. We must, while we now have leisure, lay our plans for ridding the country of this ferocious beast."

Returning to the house the young men told the sad news to their friends, and Konishi at once became the recipient of sincere and sympathetic condolences. The tender-hearted ladies wept over the letter, and shuddered at the sword. In deep and angry voices the men proclaimed a vendetta of eternal duration between the houses of Konishi and Nakashima and that of Hikoné. And the abbot, not to be behindhand in maledictions, launched upon the Gotairo's head bitter curses in pure Sanskrit, the very translations of which would doubtless have frozen the hearers with horror ; and he decreed that daily during the hundred days of mourning that were to be observed by the son the monks should chant at the vespers the mass for the dead.

One day, after the period for mourning had terminated and Konishi had allowed the razor to touch his head, the young men were returning from a fishing excursion in the Odaigahara when they were stopped in a lonely part of the road by the same mysterious messenger, and were politely requested to sign a receipt for another despatch from Mr. Yamada. This time the letter contained no disagreeable news. It stated that a clandestine message had come through from the Prince of Mito to the effect that if the son and heir of the Konishi estates could be found it would be well for him to secretly return to the city of Mito and attend to his property, inasmuch as matters were becoming confused owing to the long absence of a responsible head. The letter went on to state that the son, although under sentence of death, could easily evade capture, as he would be in the midst of friends who would conceal his presence. In conclusion, Mr. Yamada stated that his position in Kioto was becoming so dangerous that he might be compelled to fly at any time. The Shiro people had now commenced to follow him with suspicious and angry looks, and were evidently on some strong scent. The announcement that the Nakashima family were off on pilgrimages had long since been branded by Captain Murata as a most outrageous "cock-and-bull" story, and that shrewd officer fairly fumed to lay hands on the "old fox." But the commandant of the Shiro hesitated to take this step without positive evidence of guilt. That observing gentleman had noted how the tide of power had begun to set toward the Gosho. The authority and the ancient prestige of the Mikado were commencing to revive and to assume formidable proportions,—such as they had not borne for many centuries. The powerful southern Daimios were already transferring their allegiance from the Shogun to the Emperor (Mikado). Their fierce warriors were gradually gathering about Kioto for some bold *coup-d'état.* Five years ago it would have been quite safe to have carried matters with a high hand ; but as affairs were now shaping themselves it behooved the emissaries of the Shogun in Kioto to conduct themselves circumspectly if they did not wish to precipitate a revolution.

On the day following the receipt of this second despatch (and after a very exhaustive discussion thereof), the ladies took the children and went down to a rustic arbor on a jutting crag, whence a most glorious view could be obtained of the ocean and sunny coasts. There they spent the morning in sewing and chatting over the Kioto news. Mr. Nakashima and his two sons borrowed an old musket from a hunter in the vicinity and went off into the forests to shoot deer and wild-boar. Konishi complained of a headache and remained at home. The day was very warm. So he placed a mat upon the grass beneath one of the magnificent cryptomeria that so deeply shaded the terrace, and lay there meditatively smoking his pipe and gazing down through the trees on the blue waves beneath. Finally, he appeared to have been smitten with a brilliant idea, for he eagerly called to the abbot, who was lounging on the veranda, to come out and keep him company. That jovial gentleman was always ready to converse with his intelligent guest, and at once hastened to spread his mat also beneath the shade trees. After having exhausted quite a number of topics of conversation, Konishi suddenly turned to his companion and said in a grave voice :

"I have something of great importance to communicate to you. It is a matter wherein I shall need your friendly assistance. Can I rely on having it ?"

"Surely, surely !" replied the abbot, somewhat taken aback. "I very willingly place my humble services at your disposal. Whether or not I can aid you much, remains to be seen."

"Be quite easy on that point," replied Konishi, "for I have carefully considered the matter and feel assured that your services will be of the utmost benefit to me."

"What will be the nature of the services ?" languidly inquired the abbot after a pause which he had improved by taking several brisk whisks from his pipe.

"I wish you to act as a go-between to negotiate a marriage for me," replied Konishi with charming bluntness and a mischievous smile.

The startled priest looked incredulous at this announcement. He, a priest sworn to celibacy, negotiate a marriage contract! Shades of Kobu-Daishi! What could this mean? Was protracted loneliness making the young man crazy? Konishi laughed at his friend's confusion and then tapped him on the shoulder and exclaimed :—"Don't be frightened, austere and holy priest, for I shall not ask you to speak to the lady herself. Her father is living, therefore your communications will be addressed to him. This will remove all awkwardness from the situation."

"Ah! Very well. That is as it should be," replied the abbot, greatly relieved : "In that case I will very willingly assist you. Speak freely that which you have on your mind."

"Know then, O man of prayers, that I have decided to return to my home in Mito within a few days."

"So I heard you say last night. I congratulate you on being so soon re-united to your friends."

"That is all very well, O priest, but I do not wish to return alone."

"Ha! ha! I now see where the lady comes in," chuckled the priest as he patted Konishi on the shoulder : "I have not been blind, my young friend, during these months of your sojourn here. Your choice is a good one, and I will gladly assist you. Of course it would be too much to expect that a susceptible young layman like you should be travelling around with a bright and pretty girl and not be smitten with her charms. Love-making is, by the rules of our order, prohibited on our premises. But I can afford to shut my eyes on this occasion and help the thing along."

"O priest, your guesses do credit to your powers of observation. Know then that I have long loved the daughter of Mr. Nakashima, and do now desire to make her my wife and carry her back to Mito. Now will you kindly favor me by interviewing the old gentleman and obtaining his consent to the match? I imagine the young lady will not be shocked at the proposal, for she has manifested increasing kindness toward myself during many weeks past, so that I am inclined to think that she and I are in the same predicament and that we both need go-betweens. What say you ? "

" I will arrange matters this very afternoon," was the hearty response.

And he was as good as his word. For the midday repast had no sooner been concluded than he beckoned to Mr. Nakashima to follow him into his room. Having closed the *shojees,* he proceeded to open the negotiations with a lengthy and verbose exordium wherein he contritely begged his guest's pardon for intruding in family affairs, but humbly justified his action by pleading friendship for the scion of the house of Konishi. After patiently listening for quite a while to this oratorical effusion, it finally dawned upon Mr. Nakashima's mind that the abbot was acting as a go-between to secure the hand of his daughter for Konishi. It is hardly necessary to add that he was not at all averse to this state of affairs. In fact, he also was not blind and had been watching the course of events with great inward satisfaction. Consequently he was not quite unprepared for the present demonstration. So the negotiations dragged their slow length along most amiably and satisfactorily. After the lapse of an hour, the abbot was duly commissioned to inform Konishi that his suit had been favorably considered and that the wedding would be celebrated in time for him to return with his bride to Mito and with whatever ceremonies the peculiar environments would permit. Then Mr. Nakashima called O-Hana into the room and stated the case to her with abundance of flowery verbiage. That young lady became very sober and very pale. She sat with downcast eyes and with hands demurely folded in her lap, listening respectfully. When her father had concluded by expressing it as his wish that she should now accept the suitor, thus pressing his claims, she bowed her head to the floor and signified her willingness to obey his wishes in the matter. She then retired into her room where her mother and her three sisters-in-law crowded around her to know what the matter was.

"My father has commanded me to marry Mr. Konishi," said O-Hana in response to their inquiries.

"Indeed!" exclaimed Seisho; "well, you do not look as if that were going to be a very hard command to obey."

"I presume that it will be my duty to obey my father," said O-Hana, with an air of resignation.

The ladies all laughed at her when she had given utterance to this martyr-like sentiment, and commenced to tease and to banter her most unmercifully; for they revelled in this delicious opportunity to turn the tables on this lively young lady who had teased them all, individually and collectively, on so many occasions.

"She is indeed to be pitied!" exclaimed Masago, in tones of mocking condolence, as she offered her some sugar on a tray.

The clever innuendo that lurked beneath this act made them all laugh again. Then Masago got hold of one of her hands, and Seisho got hold of the other one, and they all sat down and discussed matters at length. Before the afternoon was half spent she was as gay as ever, and laughed at her sombre first impressions of matrimony. It was arranged that the wedding was to take place within a week, and that she was to depart with her husband immediately thereafter.

The appointed day came around and the feast was spread in the reception-room. It did great credit to the ingenuity of the cook. The limited nature of the market rendered it impossible to have over a dozen courses, but the *saké* was most excellent, and the good-fellowship was unbounded. None were present save the members of the family and the abbot. It may seem incredible, yet the presence of the strangers was hardly noticed by the monks. In those days it was a common thing for fugitives escaping from the vengeance of political adversaries to fly to the monasteries for protection. So that when our party of fugitives had settled themselves in the house of the abbot, the only comment provoked by this event was that they were merely political refugees. That explained every thing to the satisfaction of everybody, and no further questions were asked and no acquaintanceship was sought. Consequently our friends were as much strangers as they were on the day of their arrival. The feast progressed, nevertheless, with great *éclat.* The bride and groom drank from the same cup, and duly were declared husband and wife amid the usual banterings. Late in the afternoon the entertainment came to an end.

Then the happy couple prepared to depart. The *kago* was ready at the gate, and the boat was ready on the shore. After a season of protracted farewells the ladies finally surrendered the bride to her husband to be carried off. The children were greatly grieved at her departure, for she had indeed made herself one of them, with her sprightly ways and joyous temperament. After she had been tenderly packed in her *kago* the gentlemen escorted her down to the shore. The road was exceedingly steep and rugged. It wound down through most magnificent scenery. Although the distance traversed was not over twenty miles, yet it was late in the evening before they reached the deep inlet where the boat had been moored. It was a bright moonlight night, however, so that they were enabled to embark without difficulty. The scullers then made for the open sea, where the sails were quickly spread, and the wings of the southwest monsoon bore them rapidly up the coast toward the bridegroom's home, where they arrived, in leisurely course of sailing, in about three weeks, and settled down in the Konishi homestead, where they were warmly received by innumerable friends.· * * *

It is now autumn, and still the fugitives linger at the monastery. Mr. Yamada continues to tarry in Kioto, as if bent on challenging fate itself. News has just been received of the safe arrival of Mr. and Mrs. Konishi at their home in Mito, and the ladies have been made exceedingly happy thereby. On the day following the receipt of this information the three brothers started out for a day's fishing among the streams of the Odaigahara. They were returning well ladened with spoil, late in the afternoon, when they were met in a lonely part of the road by a monk coming in breathless haste toward them.

Upon nearer approach they were much surprised to recognize the abbot.

" O worthy monk, what brings you to this spot in such haste at this unseasonable hour?" inquired Junzo, as the priest stood panting before them.

"Alas! There is reason enough, my luckless young friends," replied the abbot, ruefully. " Dire disaster has most unexpectedly befallen your family, and I come to warn you not to return to the monastery, but to fly to parts unknown."

" Your words are freighted with fearful significance ; yet I am unable to catch your meaning," said Kunisaburo, anxiously.

" Then I might as well frankly tell you the worst at once, as you are men, and can stand the shock," replied the abbot. " Know, then, that a short time after you left the house this morning, as I was going down to the gateway, I was much surprised to find several strange *samurai* standing guard there. I asked them who they were and what they wanted. They replied that they were the retainers of the Daimio of Kii-shiu and had come to arrest, in the name of the Shogun, the members of the proscribed Nakashima family abiding in my house. I at once told them that we were not within the jurisdiction of their Daimio and that consequently they had no authority to come across our borders and seize people by violence. To this they respectfully replied that it had long been in dispute as to which Daimiate had jurisdiction over my monastery, as boundary lines and landmarks had long been in a very confused state in that vicinity. They said that the Daimio of Kii-shiu had always laid claim to the jurisdiction,—although they were quite willing to admit that the Daimios of Isé and Yamato had contested that claim as being one that conflicted with their own claims.

" But it seems that the foxy Gotairo had found out through his spies that the Nakashima family had sought refuge in my monastery and were being harbored in my house. That man appears to be able to ferret out any thing! As soon as he had satisfied himself that his information was correct, he laid his plans accordingly. He induced the Kii-shiu people to trump up this ancient claim as to jurisdiction and to quietly submit the matter to him for arbitration. Of course he decided in their favor. And this decision cannot be reversed except by the Shogun or the Emperor. The Shogun, being of the house of Kii, will not reverse it, and the Emperor has no power to do so at present. In other words, your crafty enemy has stolen a march on you. He quietly sent word to Kii-shiu to have a strong force of armed men steal up to the mountains and surround the monastery, and, after capturing the Nakashima family, to hold them there under arrest subject to his further order. The entire place is now surrounded. The very woods are alive with soldiers. During the conversation with the *samurai* at the gateway, I looked about me and beheld guards stationed at every wicket and at every angle of the hedge about the premises. Escape was impossible. They were all very respectful, however, and were not inclined to use violence. In fact, it was merely a nominal arrest. Their orders were to keep the prisoners confined within the house and yard, and not to touch their persons unless they ventured to escape. These Kii-shiu gentlemen seemed to be somewhat ashamed of the whole business, and were disposed to grant every privilege consistent with their orders. Their captain then accompanied me back to the house and made a list of all the prisoners and notified them of their arrest.

"When your father comprehended the unfortunate situation it was as much as I could do to prevent his slaying the entire family and himself. Your wives were almost beside themselves with hysterical frenzy, and begged him to at once end their unhappy existence and thus save them from falling alive into the hands of their cruel enemies. I finally succeeded in quieting them all down by explaining that the arrest was nominal for the present, and that there would be abundant time thereafter to resort to violent measures. I told them that I would slip away to give you warning at the time when I was supposed to be conducting the vesper service, and that I would tell you to hasten to Kioto and lay the matter before Mr. Yamada, who might perhaps prevail on the Emperor to exert some of his ancient authority in this matter and thus save them from the Gotairo's fury. By forced marches you can reach Kioto long before the news will reach Yedo. Therefore fly with all speed. I will take good care of your families in the meantime. A month or two anyhow will elapse before definite orders will be received from the Gotairo. Hasten ! Fly at once ! "

" All except me," said Kunisaburo, firmly.

" Are you crazy ! " exclaimed the abbot.

" No ; but you will bear in mind that I am not under sentence of death like my brothers. I merely come under the blood-attainder for treason. Two can attend to the business in Kioto just as well as three. I shall be needed at the house. If my brothers succeed in having the blood-attainder set aside, I shall be free. If they do not succeed, my position will be no worse, and I can then be of service to my father in cheating the fox of his prey. I will therefore return with you to the house and deliver myself up to nominal arrest."

" Well spoken ! Well spoken, indeed ! " exclaimed the abbot in admiring tones.

And so they parted. The two elder brothers started off with heavy hearts, but with an unconquerable determination. They journeyed far into the night and tarried a few hours for rest at a little hamlet beyond the plateau. Then they pressed onward by forced marches for five days, until they drew near to Kioto. At night they stole through the deserted streets, and came to the gateway of Mr. Yamada's house. The gate-keeper recognized them and ushered them into the house, where an attendant desired them to sit down while he summoned his master. On this occasion it will be necessary to record that Mr. Yamada was surprised. He cautiously glided into the room as if in doubt as to whether these gentlemen might not be enemies in disguise. Then, subduing all manifestations of surprise, he ordered the attendant to bring in tea and tobacco, while he suavely inquired after the health of their respective families. His manner was so cool and matter-of-fact that you or I would never have dreamed that his heart was thumping in the utmost agitation, as his keen eyes read in the faces before him a tale of serious import. It was not long, however, before he was fully posted on the exact state of affairs, and then his countenance became exceedingly grave, and for full half an hour he smoked in silence, while he gazed upon the floor in an absent-minded fashion. At last he drew his pipe from his mouth and vigorously smote the rim of the *hebachi*, as if inspired with an idea.

"This is truly a sad predicament," he ejaculated. "That Hikoné beast has indeed stolen a march on us! He could outwit a fox,—so devilish is his cunning! But never mind. We shall see if we cannot head him off in his little game. Have you that pen-holder containing the imperial signet and the cake of yellow ink? You will remember that I gave it to you six years ago when you were commissioned by our imperial master to act as spies in Mito Yashiki."

"I have it here in my sleeve," replied Tomokichi. "You instructed me always to carry it about my person, and I have not failed to do so these many years. Here it is."

"That is well," said Mr. Yamada. "I see that you obey orders most faithfully. I hope that you may now reap your reward. You will remember that I told you that this paper, ink, and signet were only to be used in some great emergency, when it became necessary for you to go over my head and address the Emperor in person. That time has now come. You gentlemen will now go up-stairs and sleep on the bedding that has been spread out for me. While you slumber I will draw up a memorial stating all the facts in your case, and respectfully petitioning the Emperor, in view of your faithful services in his cause, to exercise his authority over the Shogun and secure the repeal of your cruel and unjust sentences. You see, Yamato was the ancient heritage of the Mikados, and the Gotairo has trespassed on this ancient domain. I think that he feels rather weak himself in this matter, else he would have acted with his usual vigor and have used extreme measures at once. This transgression we shall magnify and make political capital out of. I shall have this petition all neatly copied before daylight. Then I shall rouse you up to sign it and to seal it with this signet. Then you must at once return to the little hamlet on this side of the Odaigahara and there await my coming. To-morrow I shall have this memorial presented to the Emperor. A grand council of *kugés* will probably be convened to consider this, in connection with some other matter that I have to submit, and immense pressure will be brought to bear on the Gotairo— both directly and indirectly—to compel him to reconsider his action and rescind his barbarous decrees. Our party has grown so much in power during the last year that I have great hopes of your petition being successful. As soon as something definite has been accomplished I will hasten to join you at the designated hamlet."

So saying, that able and crafty man bid his guests good-night and labored over the important memorial far into the small hours of the morning. Then the servant, in accordance with his previous instructions, brought in the breakfast and went up-stairs to rouse the young men. After the meal the important document was duly signed and sealed. Then the young men stole forth like mountain wolves into the darkness and were far beyond city limits before sunrise. By nightfall they had again reached the hill country and were again comparatively safe. They rested abundantly and journeyed leisurely for seven days, at the end of which time they reached the designated hamlet at the base of the Odaigahara, where they took up their quarters in a comfortable cottage belonging to the headman of the place, who received them with that mixture of fear and veneration that so peculiarly characterized the peasantry of old Japan in their intercourse with the *samurai.*

They waited there nearly a month without hearing any

thing from the outside world. As day after day rolled away they began to feel very uneasy. Yet, as they were under orders, they patiently waited for further developments. At last Mr. Yamada arrived one evening in a drenching rain. Laying aside his dripping garments to be dried beside the kitchen *hebachi*, he plunged into the hot bath, and then emerged to don some dry garments, kindly lent by the gracious host. Then he proceeded to discuss over the evening meal the results of his efforts in their behalf. It appeared that a grand council of *kugés* had been summoned early in the year to consider the outrageous actions of the Gotairo in arresting and executing so many of the prominent imperialists in Kioto, as well as for his arbitrary imprisonment of so many great Daimios in Yedo. It was thought that the occasion was a proper one, either for imperial interference or for some manifestation of disapprobation on the part of the Emperor. After a protracted and exciting session it was decided that the edge of the wedge could best be inserted by notifying the old Prince of Mito that his protests had been duly considered and that the Emperor had commissioned him to look after the imperial interests in Yedo.

Accordingly, the following letter was drawn up and clandestinely forwarded to that irascible old gentleman while in banishment, who went into ecstasies of delight over its receipt : " The Bakufu has shown great disregard of public opinion in concluding treaties without waiting for the opinion of the court, and in disgracing princes so closely allied by blood to the Shogun. The Mikado's rest is disturbed by the spectacle of such misgovernment when the fierce barbarian is at our very door. Do you, therefore, assist the Bakufu with your advice, expel the barbarians, content the mind of the people, and restore tranquillity to his Majesty's bosom." [1]

Accordingly, many of the Mito *samurai* at once became *ronins* and began prowling around the treaty ports

[1] Kinsé Shiriaku.

to slay some of these fierce barbarians, in order to create
diplomatic complications between the Bakufu and foreign
governments. During the past few months several French
and Russian sailors from the men-of-war in port had been
hacked to pieces in the streets of Yokohama. No clue as
to the assassins could be obtained by the government.
These atrocities had caused the Bakufu great annoyance
and uneasiness, inasmuch as if they were to be continued
there would surely be trouble with the foreign powers.
Consequently it became manifest to the officers of the
government that it would be good policy to conciliate
the hostile clans and to curry favor with the Mikado, and
thus to check these outrages on foreigners. Accordingly,
when it became known that the court had championed
the cause of the proscribed Nakashima family, tremendous pressure·was at once brought to bear on the Gotairo
to prevail on him to repeal his cruel and barbarous sentence. That vindictive and savage man, however, was
for a long time deaf to all appeals.

Then the councillors of the Hikoné clan were induced
to use their powerful influence to secure the repeal of
the sentence. Those able and astute gentlemen had
many interviews with their lord, and finally led him to
see that the times had changed, so that it would not be
advisable for him to do now what he might have done a
few years before. The old Prince of Mito, with the imperial commission in his hands, loomed up as a possible
rival in the near future, when the tide of power had set
more strongly toward Kioto. In short, so skilfully did
the councillors analyze the political situation, that they
finally induced their .obstinate lord to reconsider his
action. After a long and stubborn contest he was finally
prevailed on to allow that portion of his sentence, which
had decreed confiscation and blood-attainder against the
Nakashima family, to be wiped out by allowing the head
of the family to perform *seppuku.* But no inducement
could make him rescind the sentence of death passed on
Konishi, Tomokichi, and Junzo. According to Japanese
ideas this adjustment of the matter was a just and merci-

ful one. As the Gotairo was obdurate, the imperial party was obliged to be contented with this compromise. Two Bakufu officers were then sent overland to Kioto, bearing the decree of *seppuku* against old Mr. Nakashima. They were instructed to be present at the ceremony which was to take place in the monastery among the mountains. These officers had arrived in Kioto about ten days before, and were now journeying toward the monastery by a longer but easier route along the coast.

Such was the sad situation as described by Mr. Yamada during the course of the meal. The brothers heard the recital with mingled feelings of grief and anger. Yet, according to the customs of that country, the penalty was a very mild one. *Seppuku*, or *hara-kiri* (belly-cut) as Europeans term it, was a merciful institution that originated during the terrible civil wars of the Ashikaga period in the twelfth century of our era. By immemorial usage the victorious party in war had the right to proscribe its adversaries and to exterminate them root and branch. The scenes of carnage that invariably ensued when a victorious party came into power were more frightful than the proscriptions that soaked Rome with the blood of her best citizens during the memorable contests between Marius and Sylla. First one faction and then the other would be victorious, and the land was filled with the slaughtering of multitudes of innocent and helpless people, until it was found that the flower of the land was being ruthlessly swept out of existence. The wild horror of the scenes beggared description. The kind nature of the natives shrank back from the spectacle, and set about devising some scheme whereby needless bloodshed might be spared and innocent lives might be saved.

They finally hit upon the horrible yet beautiful ceremony of *seppuku*—horrible when considered in its ghastly details, and beautiful when considered in the light of its humane and beneficent effects. By this ceremony the leaders of the vanquished party were allowed to take their short swords and cut through their bowels into the portal vein, and thus terminate their lives. By this sanguinary act they washed away blood-attainder from their families and kindred (thus saving them from proscription) and also cleansed their own honor from all stains. Their political shortcomings, whatever they might have been, were thus fully atoned for. After a battle, thousands of warriors, instead of flying from the victors, would calmly kneel down and perform this ghastly rite upon the bloody field, thereby limiting the consequences of their political acts to their own persons.

As the nation settled down to its long repose under the Tokugawas, it became customary to extend this ceremony so as to include the families and kindred of offenders guilty of treason against the Shogun. But in such cases it was discretionary with the Shogun to grant or withhold the privilege of *seppuku*. It was necessary that the Bakufu should make a judicial decree or sentence permitting the offender to perform the ceremony, otherwise his bloody act lost its efficacy so far as confiscation and blood-attainder were concerned. It was essential that the government should grant him permission to disembowel himself in the presence of two duly appointed officers. Without this formal permission a man might slay himself and yet not redeem his property from confiscation and his kindred from extermination. Viewed in the light of a redemption of innocent people from the fearful effects of blood-attainder, the ceremony of *seppuku* was indeed grand and beautiful. It was a great boon to the families of political offenders. In the case of the Nakashima family the Gotairo had intended to withhold this favor and to extirpate them in a spirit of bitter revenge. But, as already stated, the pressure brought to bear on him had compelled him most reluctantly to forego his fierce resolve.

On the following morning Mr. Yamada started out to climb over the Odaigahara. As the two brothers were yet under sentence of death, he directed them to remain at the hamlet until he returned with the fugitives. They gloomily obeyed. That energetic man was soon far up the deeply wooded slopes of the mighty range, and toward evening he drew near the monastery.

As shadows of the parting day hasten in their course, so must our closing scenes be brief and quickly told. It was dusk when Mr. Yamada halted before the gateway of the abbot's house in response to the challenge of the guard stationed there. Upon due explanation of the nature of his mission he was permitted to enter the yard. Every thing was quiet and orderly. The guards had never intruded themselves within the barriers, so that the prisoners had remained undisturbed in their possession of the premises. Crossing over to the veranda, he surprised his friends at their evening meal. Great was their joy at his unexpected appearance. But no questions were asked as to the nature of his visit until after supper. Then, when the little ones had been put to bed, they all crowded around him and anxiously inquired for news. The entire evening was given up to discussing what had transpired since the abbot had met the brothers in the woods more than a month before. That portion of the narrative which related to the freeing of their property from confiscation and the redemption of the family from blood-attainder was received with unbounded delight by the ladies. But, when the woful recital of *seppuku* was rehearsed, a dark cloud rested upon the household. Mr. Nakashima was perfectly composed, but wore a solemn countenance that told full well how he realized the gravity of the situation.

"After all," said he, during a lull in the conversation, "I do not know but what the termination of this affair is about as satisfactory as I could desire. I have well-nigh lived the full span of my life, and I now have an honorable opportunity of terminating it in a highly distinguished and creditable manner. By the way, I will now nominate Kunisaburo as my second in this matter. And I desire, O most worthy abbot, that my body shall be incinerated under your friendly supervision, and that the ashes shall be carefully placed in an urn and taken back to Atago-Yama and deposited in the cemetery behind the upland temple, where repose the bones of my ancestors. I appoint you, Mr. Yamada, my trusted and honored friend, as my executor, to see that my wishes be properly carried out. As a matter of course, my estate will descend to my eldest son and his heirs. And this short sword, with which I shall terminate my life, I bequeath to my sons, to be used as an avenging blade upon the accursed carcass of the miserable villain who has hounded me to death. It is my wish that from henceforth you shall all be cheerful and thus render the balance of my life as pleasant as possible. On such occasions tears are useless and merely serve to cast a gloom over the departing spirit. Let us now all retire to rest, inasmuch as you, my kind friend, must be very weary after your long and toilsome journey."

Several days elapsed before the Bakufu officers put in an appearance at the monastery. When they arrived it did not take very long to complete the simple preparations for the awesome ceremony. Mr. Nakashima was imbued with the classical ideas about *seppuku* and disdained all modern degenerations of this ancient rite. Under his directions the ancient régime was most scrupulously adhered to. Four lofty cryptomeria that grew in the backyard, very nearly on the corners of an imaginary quadrangle, were selected as the spot where the ceremony should be performed out under the open heavens. The abbot then suspended several temple curtains between these trees, thus enclosing a large rectangular space. Then he took a *tatami* from the house and laid it at one end of the enclosure, and placed two camp-stools at the other end, in order that the judges might sit above the culprit. This completed the arrangements for the performance of the bloody rite.

In order to conform to his punctilious notions, Mr. Nakashima delayed the ceremony until night in order that it might take place under the starry heavens amid the baleful flickerings of torches and paper lanterns. At the appointed hour he left the house and entered the enclosure, where he knelt down upon the *tatami* awaiting the coming of the officers. Presently those elegantly dressed personages came in and seated themselves on the camp-stools. Mr. Yamada and Kunisaburo then seated themselves on the grass behind the principal. After profound salutations had been interchanged, one of the officers drew forth from his bosom a long scroll which he slowly unrolled and proceeded to read in solemn tones. It was the sentence of death pronounced by the Bakufu on the responsible head of the Nakashima family for allowing members of said family to disturb the Shogun's peace of mind by hatching conspiracies in Yedo and elsewhere. Could the Generalissimo of the Four Coasts allow such things to transpire with impunity under the very shadow of his citadel? After the reading of this solemn document, Mr. Nakashima bowed low to signify his submission to the decree, and then returned to the house to make ready for the ordeal.

On these supreme occasions the true *samurai* never manifested the slightest emotion, and treated death with the utmost contempt. Nor was it considered proper for his family to give way to grief. Every thing was conducted with such cool and hideous precision that the blood of the foreign spectator would have been well-nigh frozen at the sight. Bidding adieu to his heart-broken wife and children and friends, the stately old gentleman reëntered the screened enclosure dressed in garments of pure white. After he had seated himself again, Mr. Yamada brought in upon a white tray the short sword with which the deadly cut was to be made. This he placed within easy reach in front of the principal. A bucket of water and a bamboo dipper were then brought in and placed near the tray.

While this was going on within the curtains, the trembling women and the terrified children huddled themselves together on the back veranda, where they could be present at the ceremony, and yet not actually witness its ghastly details. Down in the temple the abbot and the priests were intoning a solemn mass, while the booming drum responded in measured tones to the mellow notes of the mournful bell. And yet farther down, the eternal ocean rumbled amid the caverns along the shore. Truly it was a weird and dreary scene !

After a brief silence Mr. Nakashima reached forward and grasped the sword with one hand while with the other one he threw open his robe and laid bare his abdomen. According to modern usage it was not necessary to do more than inflict a slight wound and then bend the head forward for the stroke from behind. But the old warrior scorned such effeminate proceedings, and plunged the cruel blade deep into his bowels in the most approved ancient style, and then drew it entirely across his abdomen, making a sickening gash nearly a foot long. By this time an expression of intense pain had settled upon his rigid features, and he bent his head forward for the stroke that should terminate his existence. Kunisaburo, who from behind had been watching every gesture with the utmost vigilance, now swept his sword from its scabbard, and, with one swift and sure blow, severed the head from the body with such force that it bounded against the enclosing curtain. Mr. Yamada hastily threw a cloth over it until the facial contortions had subsided. Then he lifted it tenderly and washed off the blood and the sand. After which he held it up by the top-knot, and exhibited it to the two officers. After due inspection, those gentlemen retired. And within a few minutes they and the guards had disappeared and thus left the fugitives free to go and come as they chose.

On the following day preparations were at once made for incinerating the body. In the grove beside the main temple there was a large open space where the bodies of the brotherhood had been consumed for many centuries. Here was speedily collected a huge pile of underbrush and resinous fagots. The body was then placed on top of the heap, and the severed head was placed upon the breast. The torch was quickly applied, and in a short time nothing was left of Nakashima Yotori except a few handfuls of ashes. These were sorrowfully collected by the widow, and were tenderly placed in a small bronze urn presented to her by the abbot. After which, the lid was tightly soldered down by one of the monks who had grown very expert in that occupation. The bereaved wife carried the receptacle up to her room and carefully wrapped it in a piece of yellow brocaded silk, which the thoughtful abbot had provided for this purpose. Then she placed it on a shelf preparatory to departure for Atago-Yama.

As there was now nothing to detain the fugitives at the monastery, they made preparations for an immediate return homeward. Two days after the tragic death of the head of the family, the *kagos* were brought up to the side of the veranda, and the ladies and children were duly seated therein, while the grunting coolies speedily bore them out through the gateway into the road that led to the Odaigahara. The abbot escorted them far into the woods and finally bade them a reluctant farewell as he turned his steps back to the solemn groves of his sequestered retreat, there to intone for one hundred days a Sanskrit requiem for the dead. Late in the day, as Tomokichi and Junzo were strolling along the road that led up from their hamlet into the mountain, they perceived a procession of *kagos* coming down the mountain side, and at once surmised that their families were returning from the monastery.

Hastening forward they first met their mother, who, as she recognized her sons, immediately removed the silk from the urn that she was holding in her lap, and held it up for them to view. The procession at once came to a dead halt, for all understood the significance of the gesture. Not a word was spoken by anybody. And the young men, at once comprehending the mournful meaning of these proceedings, prostrated themselves in the dust before the ashes of their father. Long did they thus kneel and rub dust by the handful into their hair in token of boundless grief. At length they slowly arose and saluted their mother. Then Tomokichi, as the present head of the family, reverently took the urn and led the way back to the hamlet. The reunion was sad, yet joyful. The incidents of the mournful scenes at the monastery were rehearsed with a fierce exultation, and the tarnished blade was received as a sacred trust. Then and there the brothers vowed that it should taste the Gotairo's blood at no distant date. Ah ! Nawosŭké, Lord of Hikoné, beware ! beware ! The avenger is abroad !

CHAPTER XXIX.

SEVERAL months have elapsed since the closing scenes of the last chapter. We are again at the sea-shore villa, whence our young spies started down the coast in a boat on their famous shadowing expedition six years ago. It is the first day of March, and the blustering gales are sending the frothing billows rolling far up the beach in their vain attempts to smite the keen-prowed boats that the experienced fishermen have taken the precaution to draw up far beyond their insidious attacks. The square-trimmed boxwood hedge surrounding the front of the yard is coated on its seaward face with salt spray, and the garden paths of broken shells resemble strips of driven snow ; so that there is a wintry aspect to the landscape even though it be the first day of spring. The villa appears to be closed, and the rain-doors are rattling noisily as the boisterous winds dash against them as if clamoring for entrance.

That appearances are deceptive is an old adage and one that is very true in the present instance, for behind those doors is gathered in the seclusion of the inner chambers of the villa a band of eighteen *ronins* discussing in excited tones the details of some blood-curdling scheme of carnage. The bright sunlight sifts through the rifts in the doors sufficiently to reveal the faces of these fierce men. They were formerly Mito *samurai,* but they have recently absolved that clan from all responsibility for their acts and have dedicated themselves to wage eternal warfare against the Bakufu. Their faces are mostly strange to us ; yet, as our eyes become accustomed to the dim light, we recognize the countenances of the centre group near the blazing *hebachi.* Yes, the blood-avengers are in grave and earnest consultation with their friends from Mito Yashiki as to the best method of assassinating the Gotairo. Mr. Yamada has just spread out a large map of Yedo upon the floor near a lamp, and is addressing in his usual free and easy style the company crowded about him.

"Honorable sirs," said he, "this enterprise upon which we are now engaged, is one of the utmost gravity. It is not likely that any of us will come out of it alive. Do you fully comprehend this, and are you willing to undertake it ?"

A hoarse shout of assent, more resembling the deep-chested growling of a wild beast than the utterances of human beings, was the response.

"It is well spoken," exclaimed Mr. Yamada ; "Now let us proceed to business. In the first place, however, I must apologize to you, honorable gentlemen, for my tardy appearance here. A succession of mishaps has delayed me and my three friends until we began to think that the gods were not propitious to our enterprise. In returning to Kioto from the Odaigahara we were storm bound among the mountains for many days, inasmuch as we could not face the tempests while escorting women and children. Then it took much time to arrange our affairs at home, as they had become confused during our absence. Then, again, I had to wait until the spring season was reasonably near at hand before I could succumb to my regular attack of spring-fever. Even then I was compelled to seclude my person from the public gaze a month ahead of time. But as it will probably be my last attack, I do not know as it will make much difference. After leaving Kioto and rejoining my two young friends in the hamlet at the base of the Odaigahara, we journeyed through the mountains and descended upon the shore of Isé, where we had made arrangements for a boat to meet us and bear us up the coast to this place. We had a very rough time beating up in the teeth of the gales, and were so delayed that we could not reach our destination until last night. This is our humble apology for detaining you for so many days at this bleak place."

This speech was interrupted by peals of laughter that shook the house when the playful allusion was made to the spring-fever, for Konishi had been regaling his companions during the long evenings of their waiting with humorous accounts of those mysterious spells of illness, until the subject had become a standing joke at the villa. At the conclusion of the speech they all begged him to make no excuse for this delay and to take no account of their detention. They one and all expressed themselves ready for whatever he might propose, and urged him to divulge his schemes without delay.

"Well, honorable sirs," resumed Mr. Yamada in response to their request, "the plan itself is simple enough; it will be the execution of it that will tax to the utmost our ingenuity and courage."

"Say on, say on. We are ready for any thing," was the hearty response.

"Well, then," said Mr. Yamada, "we will consider the subject under three general heads. First, how shall we get to Yedo? second, what shall we do there? third, how shall we get away? Now as to the first part there will not be much trouble. You can all embark in my boat, and sail down the coast. When we enter Yedo bay a dozen of you must consent to be stowed away under the planks, so as to be kept out of sight. The rest of us will seclude ourselves in the cabin. We will arrange so as to approach Yedo after dark, and will land at this point here on the map just below the southern suburbs. We will then leave our boatmen under the command of the captain, with instructions to go down the bay and play fishermen, returning each night to this point for secret orders from us.

"After landing, we must break up in small parties, and take these various roads here to this point in the citizens' quarter, where we will meet at the house of a friend. There we can keep concealed until the morning of the appointed day. In an upper room of that house have been clandestinely collected eighteen suits of chain armor, together with an equal number of oil-paper overcoats for rainy weather. Having reached our destination, we will act as follows : Every morning the Gotairo goes, in the discharge of his official duties, from his *yashiki* to the palace of the Shogun, by way of the Sakurada gateway. We will wait for the first rainy day ; then put on our water-proof overcoats over our armor, and will lie in wait for his Excellency at the bridge that crosses the moat before the gateway. We will then slay him without delay. Should luck favor us we must take his head and escape with it to our boat, and come back to Mito.

" This, of course, is a very rough outline of the matter. I shall now go more into details, and will divide up the work, so that we may act like a single machine. On the first rainy day after reaching Yedo we must, after putting on our chain armor and overcoats, as just described, firmly tie on our feet strong straw sandals, so that we can run about nimbly on the slippery and muddy ground. Around our legs we will tie oil-paper, in accordance with the custom of travellers in rainy weather, thus completely covering up the chained mail protecting our calves and thighs, and inviting our enemies to waste many harmless blows on those parts. Thus disguised, we will leave the house in little groups, and make our way over toward the Sakurada gateway. We will loiter about there in a manner not to attract attention, and will await the approach of his Excellency's retinue. You will perceive from this map that the distance between his *yashiki* and the gateway is less than five hundred yards. Being within the first moat of the castle, he feels comparatively safe. As soon as he crosses the second moat and enters the Sakurada gateway into the second system of ramparts, he feels absolutely safe. The only place then where any danger can befall him is on this short stretch of causeway that comes down the hill from his *yashiki* to the gateway. Once over the bridge, and none but traitors can touch him.

" Now during the last five years he has gone back and forth between the *yashiki* and the palace, until he has become careless and indifferent about his body-guard. Not over two hundred persons comprise his retinue,—and these are not all *samurai.* No member of the Gosanké would move out of his *yashiki* so ill attended. None of the great Daimios would condescend to enter the castle with less than five hundred retainers in his retinue. I presume he considers himself merely moving from one part of his grounds to another when he goes from his *yashiki* to the palace. Except on very extraordinary occasions, his men are never in armor. He usually starts out with about twenty swordsmen and spearmen in his van-guard. Then he follows close on their heels in his *norimon,* with three *samurai* walking on either side. Then the rear-guard of about a dozen *samurai* follow at a short distance behind their master. And after that come the rest of the retinue, comprising led horses, coolies, relief-bearers, servants, and quite a number of *samurai,* all straggling along behind in a most careless and demoralized fashion, so that it frequently happens that when the *norimon* has reached the bridge, the tail end of the procession is only just emerging from the *yashiki,* thus leaving great gaps between the van-guard and the rear. I presume his Excellency rather enjoys thus swaggering down to the palace, just as if he were merely nonchalantly straggling in slippered feet with his personal servants from his room to the bath-tub. He seems to regard the entire castle as merely a part of his *yashiki,* and that he can lounge about from one part to the other regardless of strict etiquette and ceremony.

" Now you gentlemen can readily see that when eighteen mailed warriors hurl themselves against the *norimon,* that the inmate thereof is liable to sustain serious injuries,—the long, thin column cannot concentrate with sufficient quickness to avert such a catastrophe. So far, so good. The slaying of our enemy can thus be readily accomplished, but it will be quite another thing to get away with the head in order that we may hold it up to well-merited public scorn and contempt. But that matter must be left to me alone,—I will shower personal attentions upon it. Now, the order of attack will be as follows : My young friend, Junzo, must avail himself of his previous knowledge of your skill and prowess, and must select four of the best swordsmen, whose duty it shall be to throw themselves across the line of march of the van-guard as it approaches near to the bridge. Of course every member of his Excellency's escort will rush forward to punish the insolence of these presumed country boors. The four gentlemen selected for this purpose must be prepared to fight to the death. Then two other skilful swordsmen must rush upon the rear of these *samurai* of the van-guard and body-guard, and thus not only serve to confuse them, but also to prevent their turning back to the *norimon.* Then seven other men must throw themselves into the gap behind the *norimon,* and rush upon the approaching rear-guard with the utmost fury.

"These assaults, if properly delivered, will so confuse and demoralize the enemy that the *norimon* will be left entirely exposed for at least a minute. This time will be faithfully and vigorously utilized by Konishi, the three sons of Nakashima, and myself, to pay our personal compliments to his Excellency. Then I will secrete his head under my water-proof cloak, and will run down this road here on the map to the gateway that crosses the first moat ; and escape through the suburbs to our boat. At the moment I fly from the *norimon,* one of you must cut off the head of one of the bearers whom we shall have cut down, and run down this long stretch of road beside the moat in plain view of everybody, toward the other gateway. He who does this must be prepared to fight to the death, for he will surely be overtaken and slain. It will not be possible for me at this moment to designate who shall perform this heroic feat. In the *mêlée,* let him, who can, at once avail himself of the opportunity.

"You will please to note very carefully this part of the map. Here near the centre is the Sakurada gateway.

This bridge crosses to it from south to north. The road from the Hikoné Yashiki comes down the hill from the northwest, and, when it reaches the southern end of the bridge, continues on past it due east for a long distance beside the southern side of the moat toward the gateway through which the man with the decoy head must dash when he has led the pursuit down in that direction. This road that trends nearly due south from the bridge is the one down which I will run with his Excellency's head. It is built up with *yashikis* on both sides, so that my movements will be well screened until I escape beyond the first moat into the streets of the city. Just as soon as you observe me run from the *norimon*, all of you who are able to do so must form a line across the road down which I have escaped and must fight to the death. While the hue-and-cry goes off on the wrong trail, your desperate struggles across the true line of retreat will so retard pursuit that I shall be enabled to effect my escape to the boat. From the time when the signal for attack is given by the four men flinging themselves across his Excellency's line of march until I run off with the head, *ten seconds must not elapse.* So you must now improve your time in practising the details of a sham attack and by studying this map with the greatest minuteness."

Such in substance was the running talk of Mr. Yamada, that lasted for the entire morning, being frequently interrupted with eager questions from the excited listeners. The afternoon was given up to the arrangement of details and to practising rapid manœuvres. The building shook beneath the rush of many feet and the struggles of an imaginary conflict. By nightfall the situation had been thoroughly mastered. On the following day the entire company embarked and went scudding down the coast under tempestuous gales, very much to the discomfort of everybody aboard. In due course of sailing they reached Yedo and concentrated their forces at the designated rendezvous in the citizens' quarter.

CHAPTER XXX.

ON the 23d day of March, 1860, there prevailed in in the city of Yedo a violent storm. The equinoctial torrents, hastening up from the south, had come in violent collision with freezing blasts from the north, and came down in blinding sheets of sleet and snow. The conspirators had been impatiently waiting for a rainy day, and were up bright and early on this tempestuous morning, making their arrangements for the momentous work of the day. Breakfast was speedily washed down with abundance of *saké*, and the *ronins* quickly donned their armor and rain cloaks and slipped out of the house in groups of twos and threes. Mr. Yamada and his young assistants were the last to leave, as it was necessary that they should remain behind to superintend matters, and to aid the others in dressing.

At length the last greave was strapped on and the last sandal thong was knotted. Then Mr. Yamada, the three brothers, and Konishi slipped down-stairs and made ready to depart. As they stood there on the veranda, equipped with large straw rain-hats, and cumbersome oil-paper cloaks, they looked like a company of harmless travellers,—for they carried their swords close to their bodies, beneath their water-proofs, and their legs were well wrapped in oil-paper. The lull before a naval battle, when the decks are being sprinkled with sand, has been pronounced to be the most depressing part of an engagement. The quaffing of several cups of warm *saké* by our friends at this point, rather indicated that this was their *mauvaise quatr' heure*. When they went forth

373

into the streets they found the weather all that they could have desired. The fitful gusts that always accompany these changes of the monsoon,—blowing from all points of the compass within an hour,—render travelling very disagreeable. Nobody, who can avoid doing so, will venture out on such occasions. The streets are abandoned to the sweeping deluge, the rain-doors are partly closed, and the people huddle within doors over blazing *hebachis.* Nothing but urgent business will take a native out-doors on such days.

Our friends, therefore, found the streets entirely deserted. Even the patrols found the inside of their guard-houses unusually comfortable. In addition to all this, the sleet and snow alternated so as to greatly aid the conspirators in their enterprise. When the snow came down heavily it became impossible to see very far ahead, and, when the stinging sleet hurled itself into the face, the head had to be bent downward so that the broad-brimmed hats might protect the eyes, thus greatly obscuring the vision. Altogether it was an ideal day for a dark deed. After strolling about for nearly an hour they crossed the first moat and leisurely picked their way through the mud toward the Sakurada gateway.

Nobody appeared to be abroad. Reaching the causeway that ran alongside the southern border of the second moat, they turned their steps towards the bridge described at the villa. With their heads bent well forward against the wind that came rushing down the wide stretch of moat and causeway, our *ronins* looked innocent enough. As they drew near the gateway they saw three or four groups of travellers dressed just like themselves, straggling along at irregular distances down the road. These turned out to be their coadjutors. The time was now not far distant from the hour when the massive portals of Hikoné Yashiki on the hill-top were usually flung back to let pass the retinue of the Gotairo. It was, therefore, full time for Mr. Yamada to dispose of his forces. Approaching the four young men, who had been delegated to commence the attack by flinging themselves across his Lordship's line of march, he directed them to stroll leisurely up and down the causeway bordering the moat until they perceived him signal to them that the *norimon* was approaching, at which juncture they were to go toward the bridge so as to arrive there when the van-guard was but a few feet distant from it. Then he distributed the rest of the band in such a manner as not to attract attention, at irregular distances along the street that ran southward from the bridge. Then he and his assistants loitered up the road that led to Hikoné Yashiki. The snow and sleet served greatly to screen their movements.

Just then occurred two unexpected events that nearly dashed his well-planned schemes to the ground. As he was strolling back to the beginning of his beat at the bridge, he chanced to look down the street, and saw approaching the large retinue of the Daimio of Kii-shiu, brother of the Shogun. At the same moment he dimly espied the head of the retinue of the Daimio of Owari coming up the causeway beside the moat. They were both headed for the bridge, and would cross it not many moments apart. It seems that this day had been previously selected as the one whereon the great Daimios were to make congratulatory visits to the Shogun's palace. If the Gotairo were now to approach he would be surrounded by a multitude of allies, for the retainers of these powerful members of the Gosanké numbered fully three thousand men.

At first it seemed to Mr. Yamada as if the execution of the scheme must be postponed to some future day. Then he remembered that, after all, the objective point was the Gotairo's death, and that that could probably be accomplished even in the midst of such an array of friends,—for the attack would be so sudden and unexpected that the opposing *samurai* would not have time to disengage themselves from their cumbersome rain-cloaks and clumsy lacquered hats before they would be cut down while their swords remained sheathed. Of course, there would be no prospect of getting away with the head. But, however gratifying that exploit might be, the brave man bore in mind that the main object must not be sacrificed to a secondary consideration. He therefore resolved to slay the Gotairo, and then die selling his life as dearly as possible.

He accordingly signalled to his companions to hold themselves in readiness for speedy attack. Feudal etiquette prescribed that travellers should stand aside when a princely procession came along the road. Accordingly the *ronins* respectfully gave up the right of way, and stood to one side. Just as the head of the retinue of Kii-shiu stepped upon the creaking planks of the bridge the portals of Hikoné Yashiki were flung back and the lacquered *norimon* of the Gotairo was borne forth and was escorted slowly down the hill. Here, then, were three processions converging toward the same point, and likely to meet at nearly the same moment! The situation was indeed a most critical one. A weaker head or a fainter heart would have succumbed to the dilemma.

But Mr. Yamada never for one moment lost his head, although his cool courage was taxed to its uttermost capacity. He took his position at the corner of the street a few feet westward of the bridge. All the groups were in position ready for the attack just as soon as the retainers of Kii-shiu had crossed over the bridge, and just before the head of Owari's column—now slowly approaching in the teeth of the wind, that was hurling the sleet hissing into the murky waters of the moat—could debouch thereon. Therefore they could with good excuse, and without exciting either comment or suspicion, stand around until the Daimios had passed them.

The Kii-shiu men, having sighted the approach of the Gotairo's *norimon*, hastened their steps so that their last man had disappeared through the gateway just as his Lordship's van-guard came abreast of Mr. Yamada. With a stately tread the two spearmen, who held aloft on their long shafts the tufts of black feathers that always indicated the presence of a nobleman of the realm, slowly led the way to the bridge. Ah! Nawosŭké, Lord of Hikoné, Prince Regent of the realm, hast thou made thy peace with God? The avenger is at hand! Beware!

When the van-guard had almost reached the bridge, and when the *norimon* had come abreast of Mr. Yamada, that gentleman of iron nerves gave the first signal, and instantly four mud-bespattered travellers trotted across the line of march. As had been anticipated by the conspirators, everybody around the *norimon* rushed forward to punish the vile peasants for their infamous conduct. Instantly the second signal was given, every rain-coat fell simultaneously to the ground, and eighteen mail-clad demons, with drawn swords, rose from the earth and hurled themselves upon the dumbfounded warriors with a yell so fierce and wild that the startled teal among the sedges of the moat arose in a cloud and fled to less noisy regions. It will take my slow pen a long time to describe what transpired within the next few seconds. The Hikoné men lost their wits, while the Owari men stared in helpless bewilderment. Many of the van-guard were cut down before they could draw their swords; some of them fled over the bridge to call back the Kii-shiu men to their aid; some, in their efforts to secure a firm foothold on the muddy ground, slipped and fell never again to rise; others were dashed over the embankment into the waters of the moat, and a few were able to draw their swords and wage a desperate but unequal combat.

In an incredibly short space of time the entire van-guard had been swept away. At the very instant that this assault had been delivered on the van-guard, seven *ronins* hurled themselves with the utmost fury against the rear-guard. The astonished Hikoné men, unable to quickly draw their swords, as they were encumbered with their rain-cloaks, were cut down in great numbers. The head of the column was swept away, and the long line was rolled back up the hill in the wildest confusion. A few *samurai* made a desperate, but unavailing, struggle to resist the onslaught. They were either cut down, or were tumbled over into the moat. The majority of those behind at once took to their heels, and, after casting aside their rain-gear and drawing their swords, returned valorously to the attack.

Simultaneously with these two assaults, Mr. Yamada and his four assistants rushed furiously upon the *norimon* and instantly cut down the bearers, together with a solitary *samurai* lingering behind. The *norimon* fell to the ground. The door was slid back, and Mr. Yamada grasped his Lordship by the hair, and dragged him out upon his hands and knees. Instantly the avenging blades of Konishi and Tomokichi stabbed their way deep into his back, while the long sword of Kunisaburo went whistling and crashing through his neck. Quick as a flash Mr. Yamada placed the head beneath his arm, caught up a rain-cloak to throw over his shoulders, and started to run down the street. Three or four *samurai,*— perhaps from the ranks of Owari—rushed forward to intercept him, but they were instantly tackled by the young assistants, and were cut down after a brief but ferocious struggle.

By this time the routed *samurai* of the rear-guard had rallied, and were pouring down the hill, and bearing back their assailants, several of whom had been slain ; and the men of Kii-shiu were now swarming back over the bridge like angry bees from a hive. Quick as a flash Junzo sprang forward and cut off the head of the *samurai* lying beside the body of the Gotairo, and, grasping it by the top-knot, brushed past the pursuers down the long causeway beside the moat. The hue-and-cry went after him in full halloo. By this time five of the *ronins* had been killed. The remaining ones now threw themselves across the true line of escape, and prepared to die inflicting as much loss as possible upon their adversaries.

Tomokichi, Kunisaburo, and Konishi were ordered by the *samurai* who had assumed command upon the departure of Mr. Yamada, to run down the street and escape with that gentleman, as he would undoubtedly require their further assistance. Catching up their water-proofs, they dashed off, and soon disappeared in the falling snow. This entire series of transactions had transpired within one minute! The remaining eight *ronins* now formed a line across the street, and dearly sold their lives in a furious combat with the on-coming Hikoné men, in which several of the leading men of that clan were slain. Before the last *ronin* had been cut down the young men had overtaken Mr. Yamada far down in the southern suburbs.

But what had become of Junzo? He had led the chase far down the causeway past the entire length of the Owari column, whose petrified warriors gaped in stupid wonder at the wild proceeding. By degrees they realized the nature of the catastrophe that had happened at the head of the column, and some of them joined in the pursuit. It was a long and a hard one. Down the long stretch of causeway, through the gateway, over the bridge, and beside the edge of the outermost moat, did the swift *ronin* lead the hounds. Panting for breath and sadly hampered with his armor, he steadily lost ground. At a short distance from the bridge he was overtaken by two *samurai*. Throwing the head into the waters of the moat, he turned suddenly on them, and cut them both down before they could check their speed. Then he turned to resume his flight, but found that the delay had enabled several other *samurai* to head him off.

Escape was now impossible. The pursuers were closing in on all sides. Like a lion at bay he fought, with his back to the moat for quite a while with the grim fury of despair, and cut down so many of his adversaries that they grew cautious, and sent for some spears in the guard-house at the gateway. Then they formed a semicircle of bristling steel, and advanced to impale him. But our hero did not relish this kind of a death. So he slid down the sloping side of the moat and waded out waist-deep into the water, where he defied his adversaries to come on. But they had no desire to expose their unarmored bodies to the strokes of a mail-clad madman, who fought with the fury and the skill of an incarnate devil. So they proceeded to lay siege to him. Several spears were hurled down at him, but he deftly parried them with his sword. Presently an arrow from behind whizzed past his ear and went hissing into the reeds in front of him. Turning around, he beheld the ramparts lined with archers and spearmen. He was now merely a target for arrows and spears. Escape was absolutely impossible. With sullen visage he glared up at his enemies and signalled his intention to avail himself of the privilege of a *samurai*. The warriors at once sheathed their swords, the spearmen held their shafts at rest, and the archers unbent their bows and slipped the arrows back into their quivers. Everybody waited in respectful silence for the sanguinary act that was to end the tragedy. Junzo first thrust his long sword deep down into the mire. Then he slowly drew forth his short sword and cut the leathern thongs that bound the armor to his body. Then, throwing open his tunic, he plunged the blade deep into his abdomen and severed the great veins and arteries of that region with one swift and skilful stroke. With his expiring strength he withdrew the dripping blade and thrust it through his throat, amid the admiring murmurs of his adversaries. His arm then fell powerless to his side and he sank slowly down beneath the crimson waves.

When the last bubble had come to the surface, two men waded out and drew the body to the shore and laid it upon the greensward beside the road. Thus perished Junzo, the second son of Nakashima Yotori,—as brave a youth as any whose deeds have been chronicled in classic song. When the head had been fished up from the depths of the moat and had been pronounced to be merely a decoy, then the old warriors, gazing upon the refined and youthful features that lay there on the grass before them, knew full well the heroic nature of the deed that had been accomplished by the devoted *ronin*.

When the fight was over, the warriors of the Hikoné clan crowded around the *norimon* to see whether their lord had sustained any injury. Nothing but the headless trunk remained. According to the traditions of feudalism, any Daimio who allowed himself to be caught napping and to be ignominiously slain beyond the walls of his *yashiki* might have his estates confiscated by the Shogun. Therefore the body was hastily put back in the *norimon*, and the Hikoné men, by a legal fiction, carried him back grievously wounded to his *yashiki*, where his subsequent death was duly and formally reported. When the foreign ministers residing in Yedo made inquiries after his Lordship's health, they were graciously informed that he was "no worse." Within two hours of the assassination, every ward gate in Yedo was closed, so that nobody could leave the city without the knowledge of the Bakufu.

CHAPTER XXXI.

THE FATE OF THE HEAD.

MR. YAMADA and his young companions settled down to a long swinging trot when they reached the suburbs, and they kept it up all the way to the point on the bay where they had ordered their boat to meet them. They met but few people, and these did not pay them the slightest notice, as they were also hurrying along to get out of the storm as soon as possible. Even the patrols at the ward gates gazed unsuspiciously after them as they trotted past,—evidently considering it quite natural for travellers to make all haste to shelter themselves from such weather. Within half an hour from the time when the attack was made on the Gotairo, our *ronins* had passed the last ward gate, and within an hour they were at the point of embarkation. Here they paused a moment to take breath.

"Where is Junzo?" inquired Mr. Yamada, with anxious surprise, as he for the first time noticed the absence of that young gentleman.

"It was he who ran off with the decoy head," replied Konishi, ruefully.

"Ah, well, then he has ere this died the soldier's death!" exclaimed Mr. Yamada.

"It was a brave and gallant deed," said Konishi; "he put us all to shame in the matter, for, after your departure, we were like people without heads, and were stupidly gazing around, not knowing what next to do. He alone kept his wits about him and remembered your directions about the decoy head. The Kii-shiu men took after him like hunters after a wild boar, and left only a few Hikoné men to settle accounts with us."

" How, then, did you manage to escape so as to rejoin me ? "

" Mr. Tanaka assumed command after your departure, and ordered us off to aid you in escaping with the head," replied Konishi.

" He indeed acted wisely and honorably," said Mr. Yamada, thoughtfully.

" We have paid a dear price for our revenge," remarked Tomokichi, sadly.

" Well, we have the beast's head anyhow ! " exclaimed Mr. Yamada, as he drew forth the gory trophy from beneath his water-proof and held it out at arm's length, shaking it savagely by the ear. His companions crowded around it and contemptuously spat in its face.

" Now, gentlemen, jump into the boat without further delay," said Mr. Yamada, as he replaced the luckless head beneath his arm.

In a minute they were under full sail, and were soon far down the bay, rushing before the gale at a terrific pace. All day long the billows broke over them, and the frightened boatmen begged repeatedly to be allowed to shorten sail and to seek shelter under some headland. But the stern command was to proceed at all hazards. After dark they put into a secluded cove and waited for daylight.

" Bring those two casks of *saké* that I ordered to be placed under the planks when we left the villa," said Mr. Yamada, addressing one of the boatmen.

The casks were accordingly brought and placed in the little after-cabin. On the downward voyage the contents of one of them had become well-nigh exhausted. The top of this one was removed, and the Gotairo's head was placed therein. Then the top was replaced and the hoops were driven tightly down. After that the bung was removed, and the *saké* from the other cask was poured in until it was full. When the bung was replaced there appeared to be nothing but a very innocent cask of *saké*, and no one would ever have imagined that it contained the head of the ruler of the Japanese empire.   On the following morning the gale had subsided sufficiently to render it safe to put to sea, although the billows were exceedingly tempestuous outside.   The voyage up the coast was a long and stormy one.   They finally reached their destination in safety, however, and ran their boat on the beach in front of the villa, where they tarried until a pack-horse could be engaged.   Then they tied the *saké* cask on his back and started off inland to pay their respects to the old Prince of Mito at his capital.   They had so timed their departure from the villa that they entered the city under cover of darkness.   Mito is built upon and around a high hill that rises abruptly from a wide plain.   The lower town is built about the southern and eastern base of the hill, and the upper town is built upon the high ground westward of the summit.   The crown of the hill is occupied by the castle,—one of the most picturesque and beautiful in the whole empire.   The precipitous sides of the hill have been used to form mighty grassy ramparts for the eastern and southern sides of the massive fortifications,—while immense cuttings separate the other sides from the parks and gardens of the upper town.

Our party wended their way unobserved through the long street that led around by the southern ramparts to the upper town.   Reaching the summit they followed a clean broad street out toward the outskirts of the town, where was located the estate of Konishi.   At about ten o'clock they reached the gateway and roused up the gatekeeper, who thrust forth his head from a window to inquire what was wanted.   Hearing his master's voice, he at once threw back the heavy doors and admitted the party into the courtyard.

"Where is the honorable mistress ?" inquired Konishi.

"She has long since retired to rest," replied the gateman.

"Well, do not disturb her until morning," said Konishi, "but at once unload this *saké* tub from the horse, and place it in your room for the night.   We will sleep in one of the chambers of the western wing of the house. Order the servants to prepare the bath in the morning. Serve breakfast at the usual hour. Let the horse occupy our stables for the night, and in the morning pay off the man and let him depart. Deliver this letter to the chief councillor of the Prince early in the morning."

So saying, Konishi led the way quietly across the yard and around by the gardens until he came to the entrance of the western wing. Here he gently roused the attendant and gained admittance into the apartments, where a comfortable night was made of it. O-Hana was an early riser, and was speedily informed by her maids on the following morning of the arrival of her husband during the night. Rushing over to that part of the house, she bounded into the room while the gentlemen were yet vigorously snoring. In an incredibly short space of time their slumbers were terminated, and their gay and amiable hostess was nearly beside herself with delight at the unexpected presence of her brothers. She poured forth a perfect torrent of orders to the servants, and deluged her guests with a multitude of questions,—the answers to many of which had to be diplomatically doctored in order to suppress information not intended for anybody but the Prince and his councillors.

"I am so glad that you were so thoughtful as to visit me in my new home!" exclaimed that vivacious young lady, as she dipped forth the rice at breakfast. "But why did not you bring Junzo along with you? Surely he has not lost his interest in what concerns me, has he?"

"He could not very well get away from his duties this time," replied Mr. Yamada, with a forced smile;—"but you will surely hear from him very soon."

After breakfast the attendant announced the presence of a visitor at the gateway. Konishi hurried out, and, in a few minutes, word came back for the other gentlemen to join him at the gatekeeper's lodge. When they arrived there they were introduced to a very distinguished-looking gentleman, who turned out to be the chief councillor of the Prince. After profuse congratulations upon the brilliancy of their daring exploit, he requested them to meet him with their trophy at midday beside the western gateway of the castle. Accordingly, when that hour drew near, they secretly removed the Gotairo's head from the cask, and, slipping it into a blue silken bag, hastened toward the designated spot. The councillor received them most graciously, and escorted them over the bridge into the exquisite gardens of the Prince. Tarrying at a beautiful pavilion long enough to place the head upon an elegantly lacquered tray, they covered it with a piece of red brocaded silk, and handed it to an attendant to carry.

Then the councillor led them through the winding paths of the lovely garden-like park to another pavilion where the old Prince was busily engaged in reading some Chinese classic. Prostrating themselves in his presence, they remained in that position until the old gentleman bade them rise and state the nature of their mission. As they rose up he recognized Tomokichi and addressed him in kind and courteous phrases, inquiring after his health and that of his family. It appeared that no news had been received from Yedo for many days, as the Bakufu had established so strict a surveillance over the city that even the matter of the assassination had been suppressed. When the facts in that thrilling episode had been laid before him his excitement and exultation were boundless. His eyes gleamed with alternate flashes of anger and triumph, while his face fairly beamed with jubilant emotions. He apostrophized the heroic deed in the extemporized measures of a Chinese sonnet that he evolved on the spur of the moment from his inner consciousness, and praised in exalted strains the magnificent achievement. He ordered an attendant to place refreshments before his honored guests. Again and again did he go over the details of the tragic affair until it seemed as if he would never get through with his interrogations.

After two hours of the most animated conversation imaginable, Mr. Yamada bowed down low, and modestly begged leave to present a small gift. The old gentleman graciously consented, and the covered tray was accordingly brought forward by Tomokichi and placed upon a low marble table that stood before the Prince. The cloth was then removed, and the ghastly eyes of the Gotairo leered up into the countenance of his deadliest enemy. At first the old gentleman was somewhat taken aback,—for all information about the head had been suppressed. Not expecting such a surprise, he failed to recognize at once the blackened visage before him as that of the Gotairo. When he finally did recognize the features, however, he became wild with rage and hate. He poured forth a torrent of bitterest malediction upon the defenceless head, and repeatedly spat in its face. Then he drew forth his fan and smote its cheeks repeatedly, in order to give emphasis to the flood of abuse that he was showering upon it. When his fury had spent itself, he gave orders that the head should be stuck on a pole, and be exhibited in the streets of Mito. He took a pen and wrote a vile and scurrilous placard, to be exhibited along with it. Shortly after this the interview terminated, and the *ronins* went back to Konishi's house, while the councillor busied himself with carrying out his master's instructions. On the following day, after the luckless head had been exposed to the insulting jeers and taunts of the populace, it was returned to Mr. Yamada, with the compliments of the Prince.

It was again placed in the *saké* tub, and carried back to the sea-shore villa for another voyage. Here Konishi bade farewell to his fellow-*ronins*, and returned to his home in Mito, inasmuch as his services were no longer requisite. The others embarked, and, after a quick passage down the coast, landed on the shores of Isé and journeyed through Iga and Yamato in the guise of *saké* merchants, transporting a cargo of that beverage on pack-horses. They slipped into Kioto under cover of night, and, after ascertaining that every thing was peaceful at Mr. Yamada's house, entered therein and stored the fateful cask in an upstair closet.   Then they dismissed their horsemen and went to bed.   On the following morning word was sent to the Emperor that the head awaited his pleasure.   In a few hours orders came back that it should be exposed for two hours upon the public execution ground with the following placard posted over it :   " This is the head of a traitor who has violated the most sacred laws of Japan,—those which forbid the admission of foreigners into the country." [1]

It was quite safe to make this exposure, because the features had become unrecognizable, so that the Shiro people could not suspect that the head of their late master was being thus ignominiously treated.   At dusk it was taken down, and clandestinely conveyed back to Mr. Yamada's house.   That indefatigable gentleman then repacked it, and, after leaving Kunisaburo in charge of his house, and directing Tomokichi to secretly abide with his own family at Atago-Yama until his return, he set out alone for the coast of Isé, where he arrived with his load of *saké* in due course of pack-horse travel.   Embarking again in a boat, he set out for Yedo, where he arrived after the excitement connected with the assassination had entirely subsided.   Storing his merchandise in a remote part of the city, he sought the brothels of the Yoshiwara, and soon had posted himself on all the news of the day, and particularly about what was going on at Hikoné Yashiki.

Two or three nights after his arrival, he escorted one of the rollicking blades of that ardent clan through the Tora gateway up the road toward his home.   The tipsy fellow hiccoughed forth innumerable barbaric odes all the way up the hillside, and on one or two occasions, when he lurched unexpectedly and violently to starboard, came very near overturning his obliging companion into the moat.   After endless trouble Mr. Yamada finally brought him up to the gateway of his *yashiki*, where he handed him over to the care of his friends, who thanked

[1] Alcock's " Capital of the Tycoon."

the courteous *samurai* most cordially for his kindness in the matter. Tarrying in the shadow of the walls until the gates had been closed, Mr. Yamada then opened a silken bag and drew forth the ill-fated head that but a short time before had proudly emerged from those same portals, and, waiting until all was quiet within the *yashiki*, he threw it over the walls and glided away in the darkness. Passing the Tora gateway on the strength of the countersign, adroitly filched from his late boon companion, he made his way back to his quarters. On the following day he started back overland for Kioto, journeying by secluded mountain paths well known to himself, and arrived there safely in about three weeks to find every thing serene.

CHAPTER XXXII.

A BRIEF HISTORIC RÉSUMÉ.

EIGHT years have slipped away since the closing scenes of the last chapter transpired. During this time momentous changes have taken place in the empire of Japan. The Shogunate has been swept away, and the Mikado is now in Yedo (rechristened Tokio), ruling the land as Emperor in fact as well as in name. The current of political events during these years has ebbed and flowed with the swift impetuosity of the tides that sweep through the straits of Shimonoséki. The star of Tokugawa slowly faded as the imperial splendor rose above the political horizon and cast its rays over the entire land. In order that we may fully understand the present situation, let us review briefly the principal events of this epoch of mighty changes.

The death of the Gotairo proved to be an irreparable loss to the Bakufu. With the fall of that able, daring, and unscrupulous man, the speedy decadence of feudalism became inevitable. Without his strong and crafty hand to direct the course of events, bewilderment, confusion, and gloom settled upon the councils of the government. Its enemies (and they were legion!) plagued it unceasingly. Since the incoming of foreigners the price of rice had steadily risen, until it had trebled in value, so that the people were in great distress, and the Daimios were no longer able to support such swarms of retainers, and were compelled to disband multitudes of *samurai*, who, being thus cast adrift, became desperate *ronins*, roaming over the country, carrying terror whithersoever they went on their expeditions of lawless depredations. These dangerous gentlemen foraged on the country at will. Scattered through the mountains of the inland provinces, they descended like birds of prey upon the highways, and plundered travellers and caravans in order to supply their necessities. Many of them crept like tigers into the treaty ports, and mercilessly slew those foreigners upon whom they could steal unawares. In Yokohama alone there were twenty-three persons cut down.

On the night of July 5, 1861, a band of about twenty Mito *ronins*, under cover of darkness, broke into the large temple, in Yedo, where the British Legation had its head-quarters, and came very near slaying Sir Rutherford Alcock and his entire suite. But for the darkness and the skilful use of firearms nobody would have escaped, for the attack was a complete surprise and was skilfully conducted until the assailants seemed to lose their way in the maze of rooms and corridors, from which they were forced to make a hasty retreat, leaving many of their comrades dead in the yard when the Bakufu guards attacked them.

As a matter of course, the odium of all these deeds fell heavily upon the government. Between the showers of complaints poured upon them by the country people and the angry protests and threats of the foreign ministers, the lot of the Bakufu officials was far from being a happy one. To add to their confusion, there happened a most extraordinary event about this time that fairly took away their breath. The Emperor served a notice on the Shogun to come to Kioto and explain the charges of misgovernment that were pouring in from all sides ! What was coming to pass ? Where would things end ? No Shogun had visited Kioto since the year 1634, and here was the proud descendant of Tokugawa Iyéyas summoned to the imperial court to give an account of himself like an ordinary vassal ! Truly, a mighty change had come over the spirit of the times when the imperial puppet should dream of so unprecedented an exercise of authority. A copy of this historic document, as translated by Mr. Adams in his diplomatic history of Japan, will be here inserted, as its quaint and picturesque phraseology gives a pathetic epitome of the state of affairs that prevailed at that period, and also illustrates most grotesquely and touchingly the utterly inadequate idea of foreign power that prevailed among the higher classes in Kioto and elsewhere throughout the interior :

" Since the barbarian vessels commenced to visit this country, the barbarians have conducted themselves in an insolent manner, without any interference on the part of the Bakufu officials. The consequence has been that the peace of the empire has been disturbed and the people have been plunged into misery. The Emperor was profoundly distressed at these things, and the Bakufu on that occasion replied that discord had arisen among the people, and it was therefore impossible to raise an army for the expulsion of the barbarians, but that if his Majesty would graciously give his sister in marriage to the Shogun that then the court and camp would be reconciled, the people would exert themselves, and the barbarians would be swept away. Thereupon his Majesty good-naturedly granted the request and permitted the Princess Kazu to go down to Kuantô (Yedo). Contrary to all expectations, however, traitorous officials became more and more intimate with the barbarians and treated the imperial family as if they were nobody ; in order to steal a day of tranquillity they forgot the long years of trouble to follow, and were close upon the point of asking the barbarians to take them under their jurisdiction. The nation has become more and more turbulent. Of late, therefore, the *ronins* of the western provinces have assembled in a body to urge the Mikado to ride to Hakoné, and, after punishing the traitorous officials, to drive out the barbarians. The two clans of Satsuma and Choshiu have pacified these men and are willing to lend their assistance to the court and camp in order to drive out the barbarians. The Shogun must proceed to Kioto to take counsel with the nobles of the court, and must put forth all his strength, must despatch orders to the clans of the home provinces and the seven circuits, and, speedily performing the exploit of expelling the barbarians, restore tranquillity to the empire. On the one hand, he must appease the sacred wrath of the Mikado's divine ancestors, and, on the other, inaugurate the return of faithful servants to their allegiance, and of peace and prosperity to the people, thus giving to the empire the immovable security of Taisan (Mountain in China). Or, secondly, in accordance with the law laid down by Taiko-Sama, five of the maritime Daimios should take part in the government with the title of the five *tairos*, defend the country against the barbarians, and keep up the defences properly, and should then perform the exploit of driving out the foreigners. Or, thirdly, Hitotsubashi Giobukio should be directed to assist the Shogun, and the Daimio of Echizen should be appointed *tairo* to assist the Bakufu in its conduct on domestic and foreign affairs. One of these three proposals must be accepted in order to prevent the disgrace of having to fold the left lappet over the right."

The Shogun promised to obey the commands set forth in this extraordinary letter. In July, 1862, he duly appointed as Gotairo the Daimio of Echizen, a man thoroughly in sympathy with the Kioto faction. He also promised to visit Kioto in the following spring. Furthermore, he made Keiké (Hitotsubashi Giobukio) his guardian, thus giving great prominence to the Mito clan by placing a son of its old Daimio in authority over himself. In April, 1863, the Shogun went in great state to Kioto to render homage to his lord-emperor, the Mikado, and to escort him to the Shinto shrines "to appease the sacred wrath of his divine ancestors." The camp having thus bowed down to the court and having promised to obey its commands, the Shogun begged leave to return to Yedo, where important business demanded his attention. Upon his return he issued his famous order (through the Lord of Echizen) releasing all the Daimios from their compulsory residence in Yedo. This was an overwhelming concession and admitted more plainly than words how terribly shaken was the dreaded power of the once supreme house of Tokugawa. Accordingly, within one week, more than half a million warriors marched forth from the Yedo *yashikis* and dispersed to their native provinces all over the empire "like wild birds let loose from a cage"; and thus the romantic *yashiki* life of that city, that had existed nearly three hundred years, disappeared forever. A few retainers were left in charge of the palatial residences of the feudal dukes, and the glory of Tokugawa faded away never to bloom again.

At this point I cannot forbear quoting the graphic words of the native historian as found in Adams' history: "In consequence, all the Daimios and the Hatta-motos, who owned land, sent their wives and children to their country residences, and, in the twinkling of an eye, the flourishing city of Yedo became like a desert; so that the Daimios allied to the Tokugawa family, and the vassals of the Shogunate of all ranks, and the townspeople, too, grieved and lamented. They would have liked to see the military glory of Kuantô shine again; but as the great and small Daimios who were not the vassals of Tokugawa had cut at the root of this forced residence in Yedo, and few of them obeyed any longer the commands of the Bakufu, they also began to distrust it, and gradually the hearts of the people fell away. And so the prestige of the Tokugawa family, which had endured for three hundred years; which had been really more brilliant than Kamakura in the age of Yoritomo on a moonlight night when the stars are shining; which for more than two hundred and seventy years had forced the Daimios to come breathlessly to take their turn of duty in Yedo; and which had, day and night, eighty thousand vassals at its beck and call, fell to ruin in the space of one morning."

On August 11, 1863, a powerful British fleet, in revenge for the slaughter of several of her subjects by

Satsuma *samurai*, bombarded Kagoshima, the capital city of that warlike clan. The place was laid in ruins. This event seemed to put fresh life into the expiring Shogunate. Up to this date the political tide had borne the Bakufu along with irresistible force. But now, with a mighty effort, the current was turned back for a couple of years. During 1862 and 1863 anarchy had prevailed in Kioto. Multitudes of *ronins* swarmed in from all parts of the country, and made their headquarters there. Many of the adherents of Tokugawa were cut down in the streets, and their heads were pilloried on the Kamogawa shoals. Matters came to such a pass that nobody could safely venture into the streets after dark. The brutal *ronins*, running short of available material whereon to try their lawless blades, began to cut each other down in a spirit of pure wantonness. Many a man while walking the streets in broad daylight would receive a mortal cut from behind, delivered by some frolicsome fellow who had crept upon him unawares from some alley. Frequently tipsy fellows rushed forth from the brothels and slashed away at any thing animated with the breath of life. Dogs became obsequiously retiring in their habits, and beggars girded up their loins and fled to safer regions. Desperate street-fights between rival *ronins* were of daily occurrence. Such a carnival of riot and bloodshed had not been witnessed in Kioto for many centuries. At the same time the city was a scene of bustle and splendor unknown since the thirteenth century. Daimios flocked hither with their trains to tender homage and service to the Emperor, and the place rivalled Yedo in its pageantry.

Soon after the bombardment of Kagoshima the Shogun began collecting a powerful army around Kioto. Suddenly his forces concentrated around the Gosho, and expelled Choshiu from the city upon the ground that the scheming members of that clan had formed a conspiracy to capture the Emperor, and to compel him to issue a decree abolishing the Shogunate. Without delay the staunch Tokugawa clans gathered around the imperial palace, and placed powerful guards of Aidzu men in charge of its nine gateways. A formidable body of troops camped in the imperial flower-gardens in anticipation of some sudden assault on the part of crafty Choshiu, and due preparations were made for repelling a violent attack. Proceedings were instituted against a large number of persons supposed to be implicated in the plot. Seven *kugés* and a large number of ringleaders were convicted (according to Bakufu methods) of complicity in this affair. The reader will not be surprised to know that Mr. Yamada found it very convenient to permanently leave Kioto at this time. All the convicted persons were compelled to fly to the distant Daimiate of Choshiu, so as to escape the wrath of the Shogun.

Shortly after this some Choshiu troops marched upon the Gosho, and delivered a series of fierce assaults that lasted for two days, and during which the greater part of the city was reduced to ashes. In the history already quoted it is stated that 811 streets, 18 palaces, 44 large *yashikis*, 630 small *yashikis*, 112 Buddhist temples, and 27,000 houses were destroyed. Twelve hundred fireproof *godowns* were knocked to pieces by the cannonading, in order to prevent their serving as shelter for the enemy. Multitudes of people fled into the mountains to escape the bullets and the shells. In the picturesque diction of the native historian : " The city, surrounded by a ninefold circle of flowers, entirely disappeared in one morning in the smoke of the flames of a war fire. The Blossom Capital became a scorched desert." Finally Choshiu was routed and driven forth with great slaughter, and quiet was restored. In the following year, when the allied fleets destroyed the Choshiu forts at Shimonoséki, the humiliation of that warlike clan seemed to be complete.

Having thus gotten rid of his persistent enemies for the time being, the Shogun, in 1865, prevailed on the Emperor to ratify the treaties that had been made with the foreign powers. For many years the Bakufu had vainly tried to secure the imperial sanction to these unpopular documents, but had always been balked by the machinations of the Kioto faction, headed by Satsuma and Choshiu. Now they were triumphant, as they had gained their great diplomatic victory. Flushed with success, they secured an imperial decree, commissioning the Shogun to raise an army and march against Choshiu and punish them as traitors. Here the tide turned against them most unexpectedly. During 1866 disaster after disaster fell upon the Bakufu armies that undertook to handle this political hornet. The Choshiu men had clandestinely adopted foreign methods of warfare, and were able to completely rout the clumsy mediæval legions of Tokugawa that marched against them. Rifles, ammunition, and foreign instructors had been brought across the sea from Shanghai, and landed on the coast. Before the close of the summer the Shogun's forces had been driven back upon Kioto in great confusion. So mortified and worried was Iyémochi by these disasters that he fell into a fever, and died on September 19, 1866. On January 30, 1867, the Emperor Komei Tenno died of small-pox. His son, the present Mikado of Japan, succeeded him. The new Emperor at once appointed Keiké (Hitotsubashi Giobukio) as the new Shogun. Thus was the house of Mito honored at last. But the old Prince was not there to enjoy the triumph, for he had died in the autumn of 1861.

Hitotsubashi was either a very weak leader, or he was at heart an imperialist, and inclined to let the office of Shogun become extinct. There is every indication that the politicians of that period were disposed to let the Shogunate down easy. The new Shogun repeatedly resigned his office, and tendered his power to the Mikado. But his Majesty refused to accept the resignation, and urged him to continue in office. Then did the enemies of the Bakufu pluck up courage and plot to seize the imperial person, and establish a new order of things. The warriors of Satsuma, Choshiu, and Tosa concentrated their armies about the imperial city. Desperate battles ensued between these fiery spirits and the forces of Tokugawa. The Bakufu men were finally driven out of Kioto with great slaughter, and the Emperor passed under the control of the southern Daimios. Hitotsubashi, impelled by fiery Aidzu, rallied the routed forces at Osaca, and returned with numerous reinforcements to the attack. Before he quite reached Kioto, however, he was met by the imperial army under the command of the immortal Saigo, and was driven back upon Osaca in hopeless confusion. The discipline and the weapons of the nineteenth century again triumphed over the clumsy paraphernalia of feudal warfare. Hitotsubashi resigned his office, and went into retirement at the castle of Shidzuoka, about one hundred miles southwest of Yedo, where he is yet living in seclusion. The victorious imperialists then marched upon Yedo, and abolished the Bakufu, and the Emperor went up there and occupied the citadel of the Tokugawas, whence had issued the mandates at which his ancestors had trembled for so many generations.

CHAPTER XXXIII.

THE DAWN OF A NEW ERA.

ONE bright sunshiny day in the autumn of 1868 the Pacific Mail Steamship Company's steamer *China* lay at anchor in the harbor of Yokohama. Huge paddle-wheel vessels like this one h&d been plying regularly for two years between San Francisco and Hong Kong by way of Japan. Every month one of these black leviathans of modern commerce awoke with its hoarse bellowings the echoes that slumbered among the green hills around the bay, as it sought the shelter of the peaceful waters after its long battling with the turbulent waves of the broad ocean. The strong arm of the nineteenth century had indeed stretched itself forth, and snatched the empire of the rising sun from the category of hermit nations. On the afternoon of the day above alluded to a sharp-prowed native boat put off from the shore, bearing three *samurai* toward the massive hulk that loomed up in the bay.

When these gentlemen reached the foot of the long gangway that led up the side of the vessel they hesitated a moment, as if in doubt whether to ascend or not, but the elderly gentleman in the group speedily settled the question by quickly mounting to the deck, with the other two close at his heels. There they made inquiries for the captain, and were directed to go up the main stairway to the hurricane deck, where his cabin was located. Following these directions, they came out on the upper deck, and then, instead of turning toward the bow of the ship, they went aft toward a group of passengers who were lounging about in steamer chairs enjoying themselves with comparing notes on their day's excursion ashore. Here they again made inquiries for the captain,

399

and were escorted by one of the obliging travellers to the cabin of that august individual.

"Who are those gentlemen?" inquired the companions of the accommodating passenger when he had returned to the group.

"I believe they are custom-house officers, who desire to see the wonderful foreign steamer," was the reply. "They seem to be a fine set of fellows."

"How exceedingly gracious were the manners of that tall young man who spoke English so well," exclaimed a young lady.

"They are not ordinary Japs, I'll bet," put in a young Californian, as he blew a ring of smoke from between his lips and watched it float up against the awning overhead.

"I rather took a fancy to the intelligent features of the elderly gentleman," observed another passenger.

"And I am free to confess," replied the young lady, "that I did n't like him at all. I did not like the cunning and cruel expression of his eyes when he half closed them and took me in from head to foot. I felt afraid of him. I instinctively knew that the eyes of a bold and crafty creature were searching me through and through. I presume, however, that I am the first white woman he has ever seen. Therefore, I will condone his staring me out of countenance."

"Now I must say that I rather liked his face," exclaimed the Californian; "there was a dashing and daredevil expression about it that I really admired. I'll bet he would make things mighty hot if he ever got to swinging those knives that he carries in his belt. Great Jupiter! what an orbit he could sweep with that long blade of his. We would have to hustle around mighty lively to get beyond his reach. I would most dreadfully hate to have him get the drop on me."

"Oh, well, you men always admire a countenance that has lurking about it a suggestion of blood and thunder," retorted the young lady; "but I don't, and I never shall. Now, I must say that I really admired the faces of the young men. They were so refined and intelligent."

"They were fine-looking fellows, that's a fact," replied the Californian; "I wonder who they are anyhow? There they go with the quartermaster on a tour of inspection. Well, when they have gone I will pump his royal highness as to their pedigree."

Accordingly when, after a thorough examination of the ship, the quartermaster had bidden adieu to his guests at the top of the gangway, the young Californian approached him and inquired: "Who are those chaps?"

"I 'll be blowed if I know who they be," exclaimed the quartermaster. "They do beat any thing I ever tackled in all my days for downright, undiluted, up-and-down, double-twisted curiosity. They poked their noses into every nook and cranny of this ship. That old codger,—well! he do beat any monkey I ever seen. He fingered every part of the machinery until his hands were as greasy as the piston-rod! When I offered him some soap and water he did n't seem to understand their use until I explained the matter to the young man who spoke English. I do believe that old Jap would have had his head inside the steam-chest if I had left him alone for a single minute. By gosh! I breathe freely now that they are gone. No, sir, you can't prove by me who they be."

This unique and graphic description of the doings of the three *samurai* was duly reported to the group on the quarter-deck, who listened to its recital with great merriment. As the vessel lay there on the bosom of the peaceful waters they discussed late into the evening the strange sights and sounds that surrounded them, and ventured numberless conjectures as to what was transpiring beyond the distant mountains that rose up so sublimely against the dark horizon.

But who were these inquisitive *samurai?* The reader has probably already surmised that they are our old friends, Mr. Yamada, Tomokichi, and Kunisaburo. How came they there? Let us take a brief retrospect and inform ourselves on that point. Mr. Yamada, as before stated, after having thrown the luckless head of

the Lord of Hikoné over the walls of his *yashiki*, returned
overland to Kioto. He lived there quietly with his
family until the *kugé* whom he served was compelled to
fly to Choshiu. As there existed no doubt in the minds
of the *Shiro* people as to Mr. Yamada's complicity in his
master's plottings, and as they felt strong enough to take
him vigorously in hand, this crafty gentleman deemed it
best to take his long anticipated departure from Kioto.
He retreated in his usual masterly manner, with his entire family, to the glen of Atago-Yama, where Tomokichi
had been quietly living with his family ever since his
return from the tragedy of the Sakurada gateway.
Nobody had molested him because the exciting events
in Kioto had so absorbed the attention of the Bakufu
people that no time could be given to hunting down the
victims of the former Gotairo's wrath. When, therefore, late one night Mr. Yamada and his family entered
the gateway and announced that the time for flight had
at length arrived, there was considerable commotion in
the Nakashima family.

Without delay Tomokichi prepared to join him in his
flight. His mother was dead, so that there would only
be his wife, himself, and the four children to pack off.
The old lady had died within one year after the mournful death of her husband at the monastery. She never
recovered from the shock, and pined away like a crushed
flower until the mysterious messenger summoned her to
the shadowy realms whither had fled the stern spirit of
her departed lord. Leaving the house in charge of his
faithful servant, he set out before daybreak of the following day in company with the Yamadas, and climbed over
the lofty mountains north of the glen, and descended to
the shores of the Japan Sea by secret paths well known
to Mr. Yamada. Here they embarked on board of a
junk, and sailed down the coast until they reached Choshiu, where they remained for three years.

During the bombardment of Shimonoséki by the allied
fleets, Mr. Yamada, Tomokichi, and Kunisaburo watched
the fighting from a neighboring hill-top. Like nearly all

of their countrymen of that period these gentlemen had supposed that in warfare the only difference between foreigners and the Japanese lay in the fact that the weapons of the former were superior, and that just as soon as the Japanese had adopted these weapons then they would be able to fight the foreigner on equal terms. It was therefore with great surprise that they witnessed the ease with which the foreign vessels destroyed the native forts and batteries that had been fortified with imported rifled cannons. Their surprise was even greater when they saw the foreign soldiers land and attack the Choshiu warriors in their own strongholds. With their keen military instincts they beheld with unbounded admiration the scientific formation of the troops in order of battle. As the gleaming line of bayonets advanced up the slopes, it was violently attacked by bands of furious *samurai* with swords. With amazement Mr. Yamada saw his countrymen swept away like chaff before an advancing tempest by that invincible line of steel. Whatever might have been the individual bravery of the assailants they had no chance against the organized troops upon whom they so madly hurled themselves. Down they went like grass before the scythe, doing but little damage to their enemies.

As Mr. Yamada beheld the complete discomfiture of the Choshiu warriors, "a change came over the spirit of his dreams." Hitherto he had fondly imagined that his countrymen by introducing foreign weapons might be able to drive the intruders out of the country and thus restore the peace of the realm. With profound astonishment he now perceived that superior weapons formed but a single element in the problem. He realized now that behind the rifle and the bayonet there lay a moral power that made those weapons irresistible in the hands of those possessing that subtle force. This peculiar fact has made itself very conspicuous during the many wars waged by the troops of Great Britain and France against the warriors of India and China during the last hundred years. A mere handful of European troops conquered Hindostan. In the last war between England and China, twenty thousand British and French soldiers marched from the Taku forts up to Pekin, driving before them in complete rout an army of Chinese warriors estimated as high as half a million men. And they captured the city without firing a single gun !

When the sepoys of India went into revolt in 1857 they were armed with muskets and bayonets and had been drilled for so many years in their use that they could handle them quite as well as European troops. Yet a few shiploads of British soldiers subdued the great mutiny ! Fifty thousand of the flower of the East Indian sepoy army garrisoned the fortified city of Delhi, whose massive ramparts had been constructed by skilled European engineers so as to be as formidable as the vaunted ramparts of Strasburg, planned by the renowned Vauban. Yet a little army of Englishmen (I had almost said company), comprising barely six thousand soldiers, unhesitatingly laid siege to the place, and, after effecting a barely practicable breach near the Cashmere gate, unflinchingly breasted the storm of shot and shell that poured down upon them from the machicolated battlements, and carried the city by storm, driving forth ten times their own numbers ! The sepoys on that occasion fought desperately and skilfully, yet were unable—although using the same weapons as their adversaries—to stand before them, and were swept out of the city like dust before a tempest. Such has been the result whenever the Christianized warriors of Europe have come in collision with the pagan hosts of Asia.

"Wherein lies the power of these foreigners?" exclaimed Mr. Yamada, as he admiringly watched their operations ; "whence is the source of their superiority? Surely it cannot lie entirely in their weapons, for our soldiers have armed themselves with the same weapons. Nor can it be merely a matter of courage, for our soldiers are equally brave, as is clearly shown by the way they threw away their lives just now in rushing on the bayonets."

"Nor can it lie entirely in their knowledge of the science of war," remarked Tomokichi, "because these Choshiu *samurai* have been for many years studying the science of war from Dutch and French treatises, and have had foreign officers to drill and instruct them."

"I do not think," said Kunisaburo, as he watched the troops with a powerful field-glass that one of his Choshiu friends had lent him for the occasion, "that their superiority can lie entirely in their bodily strength, because our men are very nearly as strong when you take them man for man."

"Yet this organized aggregation of foreign soldiers," exclaimed Mr. Yamada, "has crushed the troops of Choshiu as if such work were mere child's play! If reports be correct, there are in the foreign ranks many men contemptible in their character and not over-brave in their natures, yet some unseen power seems to seize them and hold them in line of battle as parts of some vast machine. Some inspired purpose animates the entire body of men with unity of motion and action. Some invisible but mighty force sways them as one body and hurls them with overwhelming momentum upon our unorganized bands of brave fellows."

"The single mind that controls those forces," said Tomokichi, "you will probably find in the brain of the commanding officer who is now standing on the deck of the flagship watching the operations with his glass."

"Yes," replied Kunisaburo, "but his mind has been instructed by the military books in his cabin. Therefore you may say that the principles of those military treatises constitute the controlling force moving those troops."

"Yes," rejoined Tomokichi, "but those military principles have been evolved by other minds out of many bitter experiences in war, and have been collected and printed by some mind having but little practical knowledge of war,—by some theoretical student perhaps. Now tell me whose mind is controlling those soldiers. Is it the mind of the author writing the book? Or is it the mind of the general (or generals) from whose experiences

the military principles have been evolved ? Or is it the
mind of the officer there on the flagship who is now applying those principles ? "

" Those are all factors in the problem," said Mr.
Yamada. " The mind of the officer is undoubtedly the
most prominent one. But, in addition to all this, it is
manifest that the moral qualities of the troops must be
the secret of the success of those organized movements.
You might drill our low-bred peasants in the same school
of science along with those foreigners, and yet I apprehend they would make but a poor showing against them
in battle. Intelligence, exalted devotion to their purpose, manly courage, and self-sacrifice are the most powerful factors in this matter. Now, the question in my
mind is as to the process by which these foreigners have
developed such moral qualities in their troops. The
rank and file of their armies are composed of common
people. Yet these sons of vulgar plebs when brought in
contact with our brave and intelligent *samurai* are able
to vanquish them with the utmost ease ! Truly, we are
no nearer the solution of this mystery than when we
started. I must investigate this matter, and endeavor to
ascertain the cause of the foreigners' superiority in battle. Until that has been done we can never hope to
cope successfully with them."

Thus reasoned those keen and observing pagan intellects. They went back to the little temple where they
were living, and discussed the matter at great length.
The results of this battle profoundly moved the thoughtful minds of the Japanese empire. It effectually opened
the eyes of the people to the fact that imitation of the
manners and customs of foreigners would be of little use
to the country unless they also assimilated the principles
on which those manners and customs were based. From
that time the outcry against the "barbarian" subsided,
and the treaties were forthwith ratified. Progressive
Japan then set out to thoroughly investigate the institutions of foreign nations, and to ascertain the reasons for
their superiority. From that time our exiles in Choshiu

spent their leisure hours in diligently studying foreign treatises on political science and the arts of peace, and their interest in fighting the " barbarians " entirely subsided. Their thirst for knowledge became insatiable. They soon found that they needed more favorable surroundings under which to prosecute their studies and investigations. They felt greatly the need of a foreign instructor to explain many things that were obscure.

When the tide of war turned against the armies of the Shogun, our friends joined the forces that marched toward Kioto, and fought valiantly in the fierce struggles around the imperial city. When the Shogun's forces had been driven back upon Yedo, they followed on their track, and took part in the severe battles at the Uyéno Park on the bluffs north of the city. When peace had been restored they embarked on one of the Pacific Mail steamers that plied on the branch line to Shanghai *via* the ports of the Inland Sea, and reached Shimonoséki in four days, instead of forty days as of yore. Bringing back their families to Kioto they found every thing desolated by fire. Not a vestige of the Yamada mansion remained. The flames of war had done their work only too well. Everybody that could do so was moving away to the treaty ports in order to start in the new commercial life that seemed to be opening up to the country.

Our friends decided to follow the tide. Accordingly, Tomokichi sold out all his property at Atago-Yama, and Mr. Yamada sold out all of his interests in Kioto, and the entire party embarked on the steamer at Kobé, and reached Yokohama within thirty-six hours. Shortly after their arrival they received lucrative custom-house appointments at this port, in grateful recognition for their many services in behalf of the Emperor's cause. At the same time Konishi was summoned from Mito, and appointed to fill a prominent position in the Foreign Office, a position for which his experience and great linguistic abilities well fitted him. Our Yokohama party forthwith purchased a fine piece of property on one of the picturesque hills near the bay, and at the time of the opening of this chapter had well established themselves in housekeeping to the great satisfaction of the ladies, who had become thoroughly disgusted with journeying from one end of the empire to the other. And Mr. Yamada and the young men spent all their leisure hours in visiting the ships in the harbor and in watching the members of the foreign settlement as they engaged in their business and sports. They made their observations timidly and shyly at first, but gradually became bolder as they perceived that the strange foreigners rather enjoyed having crowds of natives at their horse-races and athletic exhibitions.

CHAPTER XXXIV.

LIGHT BREAKS THROUGH THE CLOUDS.

MR. YAMADA was sitting on the veranda of his house one morning, and was gazing in an absent-minded fashion out upon the azaleas and chrysanthemums blooming in his back-yard. At intervals he filled his pipe and listlessly sucked the smoke into his mouth, whence he slowly and meditatively puffed it forth as he ever and anon sipped the hot tea that his good wife occasionally brought in upon a tray. The old lady had become so thoroughly acquainted with her husband's moody spells that she knew just how to manage him during their continuance, and therefore she judiciously let him entirely alone,—taking the precaution, however, as already intimated, to soothe his nerves with periodical quaffs of the national beverage.

Thus did he sit and meditate during the greater part of the forenoon. The elder children had gone off to school, and the younger ones had accompanied their mothers to a distant wing of the house, where their noise would not disturb their grandfather. And what was that old gentleman so profoundly meditating about? He was absorbed in wrestling with the mighty problem as to what constituted the foreigner's superiority over the Japanese people. He had studied and observed all phases of the characteristics of these aggressive Caucasians without solving the mystery, or even coming nearer to a conclusion than when he started out on his investigations. He had studied these energetic creatures in all parts of the settlement, and had availed himself of every opportunity to visit the ships in the harbor. But he had found himself puzzled and confused with his inability to see through the clouds. He had carefully watched them at their business, and at their pleasures ; he had seen them walking, riding, boating, running, and swimming ; he had seen them eating, drinking, smoking, and lounging ; he had noted their many virtues and their grossly sensual dissipations ; he had observed their bodily prowess as exhibited in athletic sports ; he had greatly admired their exuberant energy in all their enterprises ; he had keenly scrutinized their public behavior, and had carefully posted himself on their domestic affairs ;—he had indeed subjected them to a most searching analysis. And what was the result of all his investigations ? Had his keen intellect torn aside the veil that seemed to obscure the cause of the foreigner's superiority ? From the great mass of facts so carefully collected had his bright perceptions evolved any principle that could explain why one set of human beings should be so much in advance of another set of human beings constituted after a precisely similar fashion ? He is soliloquizing. Let us listen to his musings.

"My perplexity in this matter seems to increase in proportion as I plunge deeper into the subject," mutters he, as he dreamily poises his pipe between his fingers, and gazes upon an orange shrub that is blooming in a porcelain jar beside him. "I cannot make out what it is that appears to inspire the lives of these foreigners with such boundless animation, so that their existence seems to be buoyant with joyousness, and not depressed with hopeless and despairing indifference. They do not possess a single bodily organ that we Japanese do not also possess. They have hands, arms, legs, heads, and cuticle almost exactly like ours. They eat, taste, drink, hear, and smell just as we do. They walk, swim, run, jump, and ride just as we do. Even their internal organs are similar to our own in all respects. The blood in their veins is of the same color and temperature, and circulates in exactly the same way.

"It is true that their food differs somewhat from ours,

but that alone cannot explain this difference of temperament, because the constituent elements entering into
their diet will not be found to differ very much from the
elements entering into our diet. They eat more meat
and consume greater quantities of cereals and vegetables,
but that fact will not account for the exalted and hopeful conceptions of human existence which my eye detects
in their actions, lives, and customs. Although these foreigners be not cowards, yet they seem to regard human
life as something strangely precious and exalted in its
nature. In this respect how greatly do they differ from
ourselves! Although we inhabitants of Dai-Nippon have
a natural shrinking from death, and an instinctive clinging to life, yet we treat dissolution with fearless contempt,
and meet it with defiance. Upon very slight provocation
we do not hesitate to slay ourselves. But these foreigners, though brave as lions in battle, deem it a crime to
take matters into their own hands by terminating their
existence, even under the most adverse circumstances,
choosing rather to face the bitterest vicissitudes of misfortune to avoiding them by their own hands. How very
strange this is! Why should they consider human life
of so much value? Does it not become worthless when
supreme misfortune overtakes us? How can it be otherwise? Yet these strange foreigners, from the highest to
the lowest, seem to be imbued with a queer idea about
its sanctity and desirability! Truly in this respect they
differ vastly from us people of Dai-Nippon.

"And pray what can be the cause of this exalted conception of the sacredness of human life? It surely cannot be the outcome of any mental difference, for our
brains are precisely similar; neither do they possess any
faculty of mind with which we are not also endowed.
Whence, then, this peculiarity of ideas? Does there
dwell within the human body some faculty of mind,—
some subtle and invisible spiritual essence,—with which
they have become familiar, and with the secret of whose
development they have become informed? Surely there
is a mystery about this matter that appears to defy analy-

sis! On this subject my mind is enswathed in the mists of ignorance, just as the clouds envelop the distant cone of Mount Fuji."

Thus pensively mused that pagan philosopher. As high noon drew on he roused himself from his reveries and called for some writing materials. After writing a letter he joined his family in the midday meal. In the afternoon he went down to his office at the custom-house to see how things were getting along.

"How is the health of the American officer on the man-of-war who was reported so dangerously ill yesterday?" he inquired of Tomokichi soon after entering his office.

"He died during the night," was the reply.

"It is much to be regretted that one so young should die before half the span of his life has been crossed," observed Mr. Yamada; "I understand that he was a great favorite among his companions."

"Even so," replied Tomokichi, "and there is universal lamentation over his untimely end."

"While I regret his death," said Mr. Yamada, "yet I must confess that I am rejoiced to have an opportunity to observe the funeral rites of these foreigners. At what hour and at what place will the services take place?"

"The body will leave the ship at about four o'clock this afternoon, and will be escorted to the chapel in the settlement, where the ceremonies will be conducted by a foreign priest."

"How can we gain access to the chapel?"

"That can be easily arranged," replied Tomokichi; "I go there every Sunday to practise my ear by listening to the English preaching. In this way I have become acquainted with the Japanese sexton who has charge of the place. He will without doubt allow us to enter if we take the precaution to get there about twenty minutes ahead of the funeral cortége. We can then seat ourselves in an obscure corner and watch the proceedings without interruption. These foreigners are remarkably liberal and good-natured about allowing strangers to observe their religious services."

" Very well," said Mr. Yamada, " you and I will attend the services, while Kunisaburo remains in charge of the office.   Let me know when the boats leave the ship."

Accordingly, at the appointed hour our two friends left the custom-house and strolled toward the chapel.   They were graciously received by the sexton, who ushered them into a pew beside a pillar, where they could sit in the shadow and note all proceedings, without themselves attracting attention.   Never before had Mr. Yamada been inside a Christian edifice, and it must be confessed that the altar with its flaming red cross and the stained glass windows with their array of Apostles and scriptural texts made a weird impression upon his mind.   Although the place was deserted and silent, yet they conversed in whispered tones as to the meaning of the strange emblems and words on tablet and window.   Long did they wait there in the chilly room.   The short December day had begun to fade away before the long roll of the muffled drum and the mournful notes of the Dead March announced the arrival of the funeral procession at the entrance to the churchyard.   Before the echoes had died away in the vaulted roof overhead, a side door near the altar suddenly opened, and a tall, white-robed figure entered the chancel and walked slowly down the long middle aisle of the chapel toward the main door.   Ghostlike and spectral enough did it look as it rustled past them in the dim light.

" Who is that ?" inquired Mr. Yamada, addressing his companion.

" That is the officiating priest in his ceremonial robes," was the murmured response.

The clergyman—for such it was—reached the doorway just as the heavy wooden portals swung back and the coffin draped with the stars and stripes was borne in on the shoulders of eight stalwart men in full naval uniform. There was a momentary halt.   The clergyman placed himself in front of the procession and opened his book as if to read therefrom.   Then in deep and solemn tones that broke the sepulchral stillness of the room and re-echoed in the vestibule outside the door, he uttered in measured cadence the grandest and most thrilling words in human speech, while he slowly led the way down the shadowy aisle toward the altar :—"*I am the resurrection and the life, saith the Lord : he that believeth in me, though he were dead, yet shall he live : and whoso-ever liveth and believeth in me shall never die. I know that my Redeemer liveth, and that he shall stand at the latter day upon the earth. And though after my skin worms destroy this body, yet in my flesh shall I see God : whom I shall see for myself, and mine eyes shall behold, and not another. We brought nothing into this world, and it is certain we can carry nothing out. The Lord gave, and the Lord hath taken away ; blessed be the name of the Lord.*" Thus spake the minister as he walked down the aisle and took his position within the chancel railing, facing the audience. The coffin was placed before him, and the people noiselessly glided into the pews on either hand and awaited in silence his further utterances. The shadows in the room were deepening, and the purple light that came through the stained windows cast tremu-lous and gauzy colors upon his white robes as he stood there and solemnly uttered the immortal words of the Psalmist, whose wailing accents, though venerable with age, have never ceased to inspire the human heart with exalted hope and strange joy : "*Lord, let me know my end, and the number of my days ; that I may be certified how long I have to live. Behold thou hast made my days as it were a span long, and my age is even as nothing in respect of thee ; and verily every man living is altogether vanity. For man walketh in a vain shadow, and disquieteth himself in vain ; he heapeth up riches, and cannot tell who shall gather them. And now, Lord, what is my hope ? Truly my hope is even in thee. Deliver me from all mine offences ; and make me not a rebuke unto the foolish. O spare me a little that I may recover my strength, before I go hence, and be no more seen. Lord, thou hast been our refuge from one generation to another. Before the mountains were brought forth, or even the earth and the world were made, thou art God from ever-*

lasting, and world without end. For a thousand years in thy sight are but as yesterday : seeing that is passed as a watch in the night. As soon as thou scatterest them they are even as a sleep ; and fade away suddenly like the grass. In the morning it is green, and groweth up ; but in the evening it is cut down, dried up and withered. The days of our age are threescore years and ten ; and though men be so strong that they come to fourscore years, yet is their strength then but labor and sorrow ; so soon passeth it away, and we are gone. So teach us to number our days that we may apply our hearts unto wisdom."

Then followed the exultant words of the apostle Paul, that were penned a thousand years later within the damp vaults of some Roman dungeon : "*Now is Christ risen from the dead and become the first-fruits of them that slept. For since by man came death, by man came also the resurrection of the dead. For as in Adam all die, even so in Christ shall all be made alive. If after the manner of men I have fought with beasts at Ephesus, what advantageth it me, if the dead rise not ? Let us eat and drink, for to-morrow we die. Be not deceived : evil communications corrupt good manners. Awake to righteousness, and sin not. But some man will say, How are the dead raised up ? Thou fool ! That which thou sowest is not quickened except it die. And that which thou sowest, thou sowest not that body that shall be, but bare grain, it may chance of wheat, or of some other grain. But God giveth it a body as it hath pleased him, and to every seed its own body. All flesh is not the same flesh; but there is one kind of flesh of men, another flesh of beasts, another of fishes, and another of birds. There are also celestial bodies, and bodies terrestrial ; but the glory of the celestial is one, and the glory of the terrestrial is another. There is one glory of the sun, and another glory of the moon, and another glory of the stars ; for one star differeth from another star in glory. So also is the resurrection of the dead. It is sown in corruption ; it is raised in incorruption : it is sown in dishonor ; it is raised in glory : it is sown in weakness ; it is raised in power : it is sown a natural body ; it is raised a spiritual body. Now this I say, brethren, that flesh and blood cannot inherit the Kingdom of God ; neither doth corruption inherit incorruption. Behold, I show you a mystery: we shall not all sleep, but we shall all be changed, in a moment, in the twinkling of an eye, at the last trump : for the trumpet shall sound, and the dead shall be raised incorruptible, and we shall be changed. For this corruptible must put on incorruption, and this mortal must put on immortality ; then shall be brought to pass the saying that is written, Death is swallowed up in victory. O death, where is thy sting ? O grave, where is thy victory ? The sting of death is sin ; and the strength of sin is the law. But thanks be to God, which giveth us the victory through our Lord Jesus Christ. Therefore, my beloved brethren, be ye steadfast, immovable, always abounding in the work of the Lord, forasmuch as ye know that your labor is not in vain in the Lord."*

"What was the meaning of those impressive utterances to which the people gave such close attention ?" inquired Mr. Yamada of Tomokichi, as they strolled homeward after the burial.

"They were quotations of profound import culled from the sacred writings of the sect called *Kirishitan*" (Christian), was the reply.

"Did you fully grasp the meaning? or is your knowledge of the English language not yet sufficient to comprehend sacred phraseology ?"

"Had the words of the service been entirely new to me, I presume that I should have been much puzzled to understand their meaning. But fortunately the entire matter was very familiar to me."

"How does that happen ?"　　　　　·

Tomokichi hesitated a moment as if greatly embarrassed how to reply to this abrupt question of his companion, whose keen scrutiny seemed to confuse him the more.

"There seems to be some mystery about this matter, sir," said Mr. Yamada, as his young friend still hesitated in his reply.

"There is, sir," replied Tomokichi ; " but I do not

know as there is any reason now why you should not
know all about it. This is a matter, sir, that I have kept
secret for many years. As the Bakufu no longer exists,
however, no harm can result from making the matter
public. The fact is that nearly twenty years ago I was
one day rummaging in an old book-store in one of the
obscure streets of Kioto. I have always been an ardent
student of foreign literature, and in those days my thirst
for information led me into all sorts of out-of-the-way
places. Not finding any thing in the regular stock to
suit my tastes, I was about to depart, when the proprietor
of the shop laid before me a box filled with ancient and
curious manuscripts that had come into his possession
from various sources at different times. I spent nearly
half a day in examining this heap of literary rubbish, and
finally came across a strange manuscript that impressed
me as being something entirely out of the usual line of
literature, and which bore on its face the most unmis-
takable evidence of being of foreign origin.

" Purchasing it at a merely nominal price, I hurried
home with it, and subjected it to a close and careful
study. This mysterious document turned out to be a
voluminous treatise on the religion of the dreaded sect of
Kirishitans. As you well know, that sect was at that
time branded by the Bakufu as accursed, and those
daring to study its proscribed teachings were visited with
the severest punishments. Although our family was
dreadfully frightened at the discovery of the exact nature
of the document in my possession, yet, after long discussion, it was deemed best to keep the matter as a profound
family secret, and to allow me to retain my troublesome
prize, on condition that I used the utmost precaution in
preventing anybody outside of the family becoming
aware of its existence. At first, the greater part of the
language in the manuscript was quite unintelligible to
me. It appeared to be composed of abundant quotations
from the sacred writings of the *Kirishitans*, together with
the notes and comments thereon of some teacher of that
religion. Those portions of it which I could understand

impressed me as being profoundly mysterious and wonderfully sublime in their nature. When I went to Mito Yashiki, I found in the archives of that clan several books descriptive of this sect of *Kirishitans.* I also found a full account of the rigid examinations to which the Jesuit priests had been subjected more than a hundred and fifty years ago, during their imprisonment on *Kirishitan-zaka,* just behind Mito Yashiki. I also found several ancient pamphlets, explaining in detail the mysteries of these strange doctrines. I was amazed to find that these things threw a flood of light upon my Kioto manuscript, making clear much that had been obscure to me.

" All my leisure hours at Mito Yashiki were spent in studying this matter, until I found out that the principles of this foreign religion were something infinitely superior to any thing that we could boast of in all of our religions combined. I also found much that was profoundly mysterious and incomprehensible. When the foreign priest to-day began to read from his book, I was startled at the strangely familiar sound of the words. I at once recognized them as the words contained in my manuscript. My careful study of the *Kirishitan* literature at Mito Yashiki enabled me to understand the language of the funeral service from beginning to end. This was not only a most extraordinary circumstance, but it was also a most fortunate one, as it thus enables me to explain the meaning of what he read."

" That which you say is indeed wonderful," exclaimed Mr. Yamada. " Pray, what was the import, then, of those solemn utterances,—for I judge them to have been such, inasmuch as the countenances of the listeners seemed moved with the deepest emotions. The nonsensical mummeries of our priests never create such feelings in our breasts. Why should the utterances of a foreign priest, then, be so very solemn ?"

" Sir, he was reading the utterances of their sacred writers, as found in their sacred book. The theme of the discourse related to the profound mysteries of life, of death, and of immortality. The service commenced with the mysterious words of the founder of the Christian sect, who claimed to be the son of the Supreme Being that created the universe. He promises immortality to mankind upon condition of belief on him as the son of the Supreme Being. By so doing, even those who are spiritually dead will be quickened into eternal life. He sets himself up as the Redeemer of the human race from the destructive effects of sin. He promises to mortal beings an immortal existence of endless duration and development, in case they will but adopt his teachings and practise his precepts. Truly the utterances of this being have awakened in my mind supremely lofty and magnificent conceptions of the nobler faculties of my spirit, and have suggested bewildering ideas of the possibilities of a future life that overwhelm me with thrilling hopes and morbid conjectures !

"After the weird language of this mysterious Christ came the words of an extraordinary man of the same nation who lived many centuries before his advent. The words in which he pours forth his sublime communings are grand and thrilling. In prophetic vision he seems to catch glimpses of his Redeemer, and to clearly see the blissful existence beyond the grave, where his soul shall take cognizance of the Supreme Being. After this superb rhapsody came the poetic inspirations of a monarch who was the earthly ancestor of this Christ. In sublime reveries the uncertainty and the frailty of human life seem to float before him like mists hovering over the cascades on a moonlit night, and he earnestly implores the Supreme Being in strains of magnificent eloquence to teach him to be mindful of his fleeting years, and to prepare himself for the nobler and the happier life after death,—a life concerning whose existence these sacred writers all seem as positive as if, forsooth, they had soared into those unseen realms, or had skimmed the waves of that boundless and invisible ocean.

" The closing words of the service are taken from the writings of a man who was a cotemporary of this Christ,

—a person who, although never having seen Christ, yet implicitly believed in him and in his teachings. He shows that unless the facts connected with the life and death of Christ be true, then his teachings as to a future life must fall to the ground. He also shows that a future existence would be in analogy with the facts of nature. The life of the plant depends upon the death of the seed. The life of the butterfly depends upon the death of the worm. The life of the bird depends upon the destruction of the egg from which it is hatched. So must the life of the soul hinge upon the death of the body. This learned and profound writer claims that Christ taught men how to control their bodies, so that after death the spiritual essence might enter upon an immortal existence of boundless happiness. If the seed be decayed, then no plant can sprout therefrom,—or, at best, but a weak and sickly one. If the body be corrupted by evil and unhallowed practices, then there can be no blooming of immortal happiness. Such, sir, is a feeble statement of the wonderful language to which we have been listening."

It was long after dusk before our friends reached the door of their house ; for the foregoing paragraph, though quickly read, contains in condensed form the substance of many lengthy replies made by Tomokichi in response to the eager and searching inquiries of his companion during their homeward walk.

"I can now understand much that was obscure to me," exclaimed Mr. Yamada as they entered the gateway of their yard ; "that which you have just told me fully explains a matter over which I have long puzzled my brain in vain. Up to the present moment my profoundest investigations have not availed to clear away the mystery that surrounded the foreigner's exalted conception of so trivial a matter as human life. I have been able to trace much of the foreigner's superiority to this exalted conception of the great value of human life ; but, hitherto, I have been utterly baffled in my attempts to analyze the principles and the reasons that underlay that conception. It is all as clear now to me as daylight. Of course if there be a Supreme Being, and if we human beings be the creatures of his creative powers, then our relations with the universe become grand and important. If we have been endowed with immortal spirits by this Creator of the universe and have been placed on this earth to develop the subtle and mysterious powers of our souls, then this life becomes supremely valuable. If there be a God, if there be a soul, if there be immortality for that soul after death, then this life becomes worth the living even under the most adverse circumstances. No condition of human existence, no matter how wretched and contemptible it may be, should be despised. Like sentinels on the fields of war we are to stand on guard until relieved from duty by our commanding officer. It thus becomes wrong for us to take matters into our own hands and to end our own existence by violent methods when adversity overtakes us.

" I now understand why the Christian warriors of Kiushiu, captured by Tokugawa Iyéyas at the battle of Sékigahara, refused to perform *seppuku* when overwhelmed by defeat but allowed themselves to be ignominiously executed and to have their heads pilloried on the Kamogawa shoals as targets for the insulting jests of the victors. This theory of immortality is truly grand and elevating ! Even if it be merely based upon the vagaries of the brilliant imaginations of highly poetic minds, and should appear on closer investigation to have absolutely no foundation in fact, yet the very belief in such a theory would ennoble and beautify human existence as nothing else possibly can do. Herein lies the secret power that has elevated the Caucasian race ! Buoyed up by the hope of a sublime existence beyond the grave, and believing that they have been created by a merciful and fatherly God, whose will they are obeying by living this life in accordance with his directions, they very naturally count the vicissitudes of this world as nothing when compared with the immortal glories for which they are preparing the soul. Light now shines through the rifts in the clouds ! I see ! I understand ! "

CHAPTER XXXV.

THE LIGHT OF THE WORLD.

Verily, verily, I say unto thee, except a man be born of water and the Spirit, he cannot enter into the kingdom of God.—St. John iii., 5. But an angel of the Lord spake unto Philip, saying, Arise, and go toward the south unto the way that goeth down from Jerusalem unto Gaza : the same is desert. And he arose and went : and behold a man of Ethiopia, a eunuch of great authority under Candace, queen of the Ethiopians, who was over all her treasure, who had come to Jerusalem for to worship ; and he was returning and sitting in his chariot, and was reading the prophet Isaiah. And the Spirit said unto Philip, Go near and join thyself to this chariot. And Philip ran to him, and heard him reading Isaiah the prophet, and said, Understandest thou what thou readest? And he said, How can I, except some one shall guide me? And he besought Philip to come up and sit with him. Now the place of the scripture which he was reading was this :

"He was led as a sheep to the slaughter;
And as a lamb before his shearers is dumb,
So he openeth not his mouth :
In his humiliation his judgment was taken away :
His generation who shall declare?
For his life is taken from the earth."

And the eunuch answered Philip, and said, I pray thee, of whom speaketh the prophet this? of himself, or of some other? And Philip opened his mouth, and beginning from this scripture, preached unto him Jesus. And as they went on the way, they came unto a certain water ; and the eunuch saith, Behold, here is water ; what doth hinder me to be baptized? And he commanded the chariot to stand still : and they both went down into the water, both Philip and the eunuch ; and he baptized him. And when they came up out of the water, the spirit of the Lord caught away Philip ; and the eunuch saw him no more, for he went on his way rejoicing.—Acts viii., 26–39.

THE above picturesque and simple language, recorded nearly two thousand years ago, is descriptive of the process by which the stupendous spiritual phenomena of the last eighteen centuries have been brought about. The zealous missionaries of the Cross, armed with the immortal words of the Redeemer, first above quoted, have preached Jesus to every kindred and to every tribe in Europe, until they have changed the face of that continent in a most astonishing manner. From century to century the hearts of devout men and women have been fired with apostolic zeal, and they have gone forth into strange lands as missionaries bearing the Gospel tidings of joy and peace to mankind. The leaven of the kingdom of heaven and the sword of the Spirit have been carried into communities where barbaric stagnation prevailed and have stirred up and awakened the hearts and the brains of the people in a manner unknown in the history of nations. Spiritual quickening has produced intellectual commotion, that has moved human society to its profoundest depths and has resulted in the evolution of the great nations of the present century. The process by which such tremendous results have been achieved is truly a most simple one. By merely preaching " Christ crucified,—to the Greeks foolishness, and to the Jews a stumbling-block,"—there has been instituted in this world of ours a moral reformation that has blessed and elevated all the social and political institutions of the nineteenth century and has developed the grandest civilization of all time.

Yea, simple and foolish enough does the process appear to the reason of humanity. Yet such was the process ordained by the Redeemer, and, judging from its wonderful efficacy, there seems to be no good reason for modifying it even if the philosophers and the skeptics of modern times do sneer at its workings and endeavor to belittle its results. The language of that immortal missionary of Tarsus is as true to-day as it was eighteen hundred years ago : " God hath chosen the foolish things of the world to confound the wise ; and God hath chosen the weak things of the world to confound the things that are mighty ; and base things of the world, and things which are despised, hath God chosen, *yea*, and things which are not, to bring to nought things that are."

The cultured philosopher and the snarling cynic of the present day do not appear to differ much from the Greek and the Jew of the time of Paul. With sneering comments the modern critic ridicules the great missionary endeavors of our times. With note-book in hand he swings round the circuit of the globe and loudly clamors for figures and statistics wherein to express the results of apostolic labors in pagan lands. Silly fellow! What would there have been to jot down in thy book on that day when gloom settled down on Calvary? A mangled corpse, twelve scattered and apostate disciples, a howling mob of bitterly disappointed Jews! Was ever failure more complete? Yet the seed had been planted; the principles of a system of divine moral ethics, illustrated by the life of the Son of God, had been enunciated and promulgated among men; the leaven had been placed in the measure of meal; and the sword of the Spirit had gone forth to subdue the nations of the world. Was that failure? Of course not, you may perhaps say. Yet, pray tell me, how could you have expressed in figures the subtle spiritual influence that had then already gone forth among men to elevate and to bless them? Can you take the measure of the sword of the Spirit as you would that of a piece of merchandise? Can you circumscribe with metes and bounds that resistless power that has transformed the savages of Britain, Gaul, and Germany into civilized human beings? Who shall duly estimate by mathematical equations the force of those principles that have ground up and are yet grinding up the institutions of paganism and evolving therefrom higher and nobler forms of human society?

Vain task! Worry not thyself about the harvest. Do thou but plant the seed. Such is God's command. Such is God's method,—and such has it been in all ages. Simple, do you say? Yea, verily,—but profoundly efficacious and scientific nevertheless. And until God shall reveal unto mankind some other method of carrying on his work in this world, it is more than probable that Christ's kingdom will continue to be built up by this "foolishness of preaching,"—this sending of missionaries to preach " Christ crucified " among the heathen everywhere. Among all the wonderful scientific discoveries and inventions made by the Christianized intellects of the nineteenth century there has been no solution to the problem as to how a man shall be redeemed from his sins. To institute reformation of desire in human nature, and to rouse the sluggish spiritual faculties into a life of progressive and endless development, is a task that either lies beyond the powers of human mind or that lies far beneath the notice of selfish human indifference. The reformation of desire, the quickening of the soul into active life through this sincere desire being operated upon by the Holy Spirit,— this is the only method known to humanity whereby men may be redeemed from their sins. Except a man be born of water and the spirit, he cannot enter into the kingdom of God.

This principle is as true to-day as it was eighteen centuries ago. And its faithful promulgation among the nations of the earth has brought the world to the dawn of an era whose spiritual possibilities defy human computation. The soul of man gazes down a vista of development that broadens out into fields of such glorious and never-ending progress that the imagination becomes dazzled at the sight. And this stupendous result has been accomplished by the " foolishness of preaching." Stuff and nonsense do you call it? You do not speak scientifically, my friend. It is spiritual evolution. As the beauteous forms of organized matter have sprung (according to modern belief) from protoplasmic germs and have been developed by the influences of the supreme will operating thereon, so has the higher spiritual nature of mankind been evolved from the germ of repentance operated upon by the Holy Spirit. In all ages man has been the divinely constituted agent for conveying to his fellow-men the tidings of the necessity for repentance and moral reformation. When the soul has been awakened to a consciousness of sin then it is in a condition to be operated on by that subtle and mysterious power which we designate in human speech as the Spirit of God.

It was in accordance with the command of the Master that the Christian churches of America sent missionaries to the empire of Japan very soon after the conclusion of Commodore Perry's treaty. In those early days the journey to Japan was not the pleasure trip that it has since become by means of railway and steamship travel. It required at least four months to make the voyage from New York to Yokohama. Five months were frequently required for the passage. Adverse winds and calms could easily protract the voyage from six to eight months. In those days it required much self-sacrifice to become a missionary. Not many offered themselves for the service, and there were but few calls for volunteers made by the home churches because of the restricted nature of the field of operations in that distant realm.

During the first decade after the advent of Perry there were barely a dozen missionaries in Japan. Among that number was a young man whom I shall call Mr. Plympton. This young man, soon after completing his collegiate and theological studies at home, had felt called of the spirit to preach the Gospel of Christ to the heathen. Offering himself to the board of missions connected with his church, he was delegated by them to carry the tidings of salvation to the far-distant shores of the empire of the rising sun. With tearful partings with sorrowing friends he embarked with his young wife on one of the stately clipper ships that plied between New York and China around the Cape of Good Hope. A favorable voyage of one hundred and twenty days brought them to the port of Hong Kong, where they embarked on a smaller vessel that was loading for Yokohama, where they safely arrived after a fortnight's sailing.

His first efforts were directed toward securing a comfortable home for his family. Then he plunged into the mysteries of an unknown language with the utmost energy. His progress was necessarily slow and laborious in the absence of dictionaries and grammars. When, after a long struggle, he had obtained a fair mastery of the language, he found nobody disposed to listen to what he had to say concerning Christianity. The minds of the people were engrossed with the intense political excitement that was then running high. Besides that, the lower classes stood in abject terror of the very name of Christ as being that of the founder of a creed that had been proscribed for more than two centuries.

Very naturally Mr. Plympton's evangelical labors were of a most limited nature and were confined entirely to the servants of his household and to their friends. Nevertheless he prosecuted his work with the utmost zeal, so that by the end of the imperial revolution of 1868 he had acquired a correct and elegant use of the vernacular, and had formed a Bible class of young *samurai*, who were anxious to obtain a knowledge of the strange religion that the new government appeared to look upon with more favor than the Bakufu did. During the great conflagration of 1866 the residence of Mr. Plympton was swept away, along with nearly the entire European settlement. Instead of rebuilding his house on the low land around the bay, he secured an elegible site upon the garden-like bluffs half a mile back from the water, and built a neat American cottage, where his wife and children could have more sunshine and fresh air than were available in their cramped quarters in the settlement. He had just settled down in his new home when our Kioto friends received their appointments at the Yokohama custom-house.

Several weeks after the events set forth in the last chapter two Japanese gentlemen were standing before the gateway of Mr. Plympton's house on the bluffs. After some hesitation they entered the yard and inquired of the obsequious gatekeeper if his master was at home. Receiving an affirmative reply, they went down the broad gravelly path that led to the house, and mounted the short flight of steps to the front veranda, where they

announced their presence by tapping a little bronze bell
that hung there beside the door. In response to this
signal a servant soon appeared and inquired the object
of their call.

"We have come to pay our respects to the foreign
priest living here, and also to make a few inquiries of
him," replied Tomokichi, for he it was in company with
Mr. Yamada.

"I will at once report to him your honorable presence," bowed the obsequious servant.

In a few minutes he returned saying : "My honorable
master will be pleased to see the honorable gentlemen in
his study in a very few minutes. If you will follow me
I will guide you there."

Leaving their wooden clogs at the door, the visitors
walked noiselessly across a neat and spacious hall into a
large room to the left-hand side of the doorway. Here
they were duly seated in a couple of chairs, and were
requested to wait until the master of the house should
come down-stairs to see them. This study was a model
of neatness and comfort. Broad windows opened out
upon the sunny veranda, where two little children were
romping with a half-grown Newfoundland dog that had
been presented to the younger members of Mr. Plympton's household by a friendly captain commanding one
of the superb clipper ships plying between America and
Japan. The floor was covered with matting, while
tables, chairs, and bamboo settees were set around the
room in convenient places. Beside one of the windows
stood a commodious desk covered with writing material
and manuscript that abundantly betokened the studious
nature of the occupant of the room. Against the white
walls stood wide book-cases containing a library of theological, historical, and philological literature. Pictures and
maps filled in all the bare spaces on the walls, so that the
general appearance of the room was such as would have
at once stimulated the literary appetite of the scholarly
visitor. Our friends took all this in with a few quick

glances while they awaited the coming of their host. That gentleman did not keep them long in abeyance. As he entered the study the visitors prostrated themselves on the floor in profound obeisance after the custom of the country.

"Arise, most honorable sirs, and be seated," said Mr. Plympton, addressing his guests in their own language.

"Most honorable sir," said Mr. Yamada, after the usual preliminary greetings had been interchanged, "we have heard many things concerning your great learning and scholarly attainments, and we have long been desirous of calling on you and making inquiries concerning certain matters of profound interest to us, but we have hesitated, being doubtful as to whether such insignificant persons as ourselves would be deemed worthy of admission into your honorable presence. Yesterday, however, we attended the services conducted by your honored self in the chapel down in the native town, and heard you kindly invite inquirers after the truth to call at your house and seek for information. We have therefore availed ourselves of this invitation, and have come with much hesitation and trepidation to ask certain questions that have long puzzled us."

"Honorable sirs," replied Mr. Plympton, "it is the delight of my heart to converse with those who sincerely seek information concerning the pure and noble religion that I preach to your people. You are most welcome visitors. Be perfectly at home and ask whatever question may occur to you. I cannot promise, however, to answer all of your questions, because mystery environs reality on all sides, the most commonplace tangibilities baffle analysis, and we are daily compelled to admit the existence of many things concerning whose cause we remain in profound ignorance. I will endeavor, nevertheless, to answer all of your questions to the best of my ability, and can only hope that the good Father of the Universe will throw light upon my feeble remarks and may enlighten your minds."

" O most honorable sir," exclaimed Mr. Yamada, " we offer up a myriad of thanks for your most generous hospitality, and we shall make inquiries concerning matters that have long troubled us. When you just now spoke concerning the good Father of the Universe, you struck the keynote of our inquiries. This is indeed the mystery of mysteries, concerning whose existence you foreigners appear to have but little doubt. Sir, we have carefully studied your sacred book, and are prepared to admit the sublime morality therein expounded by parable, allegory, historic narrative, and direct precept. We find throughout the pages of this extraordinary book three stupendous statements set forth with endless and unvarying persistency and positiveness,—statements that loom up above all other matter therein contained, as Fuji-san towers above the bosom of Dai-Nippon, and which, if they be true, dwarf into insignificance the teeming records of wonderful achievements and miraculous events.

" The first statement is to the effect that there exists a Supreme Being, the creator and ruler of the universe. The second statement is to the effect that the only son of this Creator became incarnated in human form about eighteen centuries ago, and was known as Jesus Christ. The third statement is to the effect that men possess souls that live after the death of the body. Sir, my questions are briefly stated : Is there a Supreme Being ? Was Jesus Christ his son ? Is there immortality after death ? Answer these three questions, and I will admit all the rest claimed in your sacred book.

" Of course, if there be a Supreme Being that created the universe, then it follows that he can do what he likes with that which he has created. The Creator can do as he pleases with the creature. With such a Being in the universe, of course miracles can happen. He can do as it pleaseth him with his own. That which appears impossible to us becomes possible with him. It goes for the saying that if there be such a Creator, then miracles may happen ; they become, in the legal parlance of your country, merely part of the *res gestæ*, or subordinate matter in dispute, whose existence depends upon the settlement of the main point in dispute, as to whether or not there be any Creator at all. I shall have no difficulty, sir, in believing in the existence of miracles as stated in your sacred book, if you will only show me with reasonable certainty that a Creator does really exist. Then when you shall have shown to my satisfaction that Christ was the son of that Creator, I shall be prepared to accept all of his wonderful teachings concerning morality and immortality."

"You surprise me by your candor," exclaimed Mr. Plympton, gazing steadily into the half-closed eyes of his visitor, as if endeavoring to fathom the depth of his sincerity ; "your concessions are reasonable enough, but they are very unusual ones to be made by a person presumably hostile to the Christian religion. Do you then have no difficulty in understanding the doctrine of the Atonement? This tenet of our faith has been the one most ridiculed by infidels. They loudly assert that 'no power can step between acts and consequences ; that there is no forgiveness, no atonement.' They jeeringly ask : 'How can a criminal be washed clean and pure in the blood of another?' They make merry over the fact that the 'wrong fellow' gets punished. And they boldly proclaim that 'every human being must bear the consequences of his own acts.' Before entering upon our regular discussion, kindly let me hear your views concerning this much ridiculed article of faith."

"Sir," replied Mr. Yamada, slowly, "I have thought over the matter carefully, and am in a position to say that I have no difficulty in believing your doctrine of the atonement. Granted that there be a Creator and that Christ was his son, then there would be nothing at all impossible in that son offering himself as a substitute for humanity to receive punishment for the violation of some inexorable law of the universe that had been broken by the erring children of the earth. It is, perhaps, easy for us Japanese to understand such a doctrine, because we have a political custom that somewhat resembles it.

Know, then, O most learned sir, that in ancient times the family of a political offender was exterminated for his offences, whether those luckless individuals were innocent or guilty of complicity in the deeds of their kinsman. I am informed that this same doctrine of blood-attainder prevailed in the countries of Europe for many centuries, and that it was so repugnant to the humane feelings of the framers of the American Constitution that they expressly declared, in that famous charter of human rights, that blood-attainder should never attach for any offence whatsoever.

" Now, in our country the gentler feelings of our race also revolted against this cruel custom, and it was decreed several centuries ago that blood-attainder should be wiped out by the act of *seppuku,* wherein the offender was permitted to take his own life, and thus save his family and kindred from cruel extirpation. Therefore, when I hear of the innocent and guileless son of the God of the universe offering himself as an atonement for the sins of humanity, in order to propitiate some supreme sense of violated justice, I am carried away with admiration for the magnificent sacrifice. To my mind there is nothing improbable about there being some violation on the part of our progenitors of some great universal law or principle of creation whereby countless miseries would have accrued to the human race, leading to extermination perhaps, were it not for the ' blood-attainder ' having been washed away by the noble sacrifice of a single individual. Why not ? What do we mortals know about the principles involved in the creation of the universe ?

" But, sir, all such considerations are purely secondary. It will be useless to spend time in speculating thereon until we have come to some agreement as to whether or not there be any Supreme Being at all. And just at this point there arises in my mind a question that seems impossible of an answer. I lay it down, sir, as a universal and unalterable proposition, that every thing that exists must have had a cause. We trace back on this line of cause and effect until we come to the question as to who made the universe, and you reply that .God made it. Now I ask you who made this God of yours ? Surely he must be the effect of some prior cause, because it is a universal law that every thing must have had a cause."

" Honorable sir," slowly replied Mr. Plympton, as his guest concluded his lengthy remarks, " it is manifest that your questions come from a full heart and a keen brain. You have propounded a question that has been agitating the human race from the remotest times. It will not sur-' prise you, therefore, if I should make but a lame attempt at answering so profound a query as that which you have just propounded. I will, however, do my best to throw some light on the subject, so that it may appear to you as it does to me. In the first place, I positively deny your proposition as to the universality of the law of cause and effect. You appear surprised and incredulous at this assertion. Yet I boldly say that the law of cause and effect is not of universal application. Now if I can show but a single exception to this law, I shall shatter your proposition. I positively assert that the space enclosed by this room has always existed and has never had a cause. The limitless realms of space that stretch beyond the uttermost confines of the universe have eternally existed and have had no cause. I insist that space *never* had a cause. Yet space is a reality and has always existed.

" Therefore, I say that your proposition is *not* of universal application. I can show another exception to it. Time, or duration as some metaphysicians designate it, has always existed and has never had a cause. Back through the cycles of eternity there never was a time when prior time did not exist. Time *never* had a cause. Yet it is a profound reality. And it exists just as truly as you or I exist. Therefore, I have shown two exceptions to your sweeping proposition. And who knows how many more may exist ? Consequently, when we Christians say that God was never created, we do not assert an impossibility. You are not in a position to say that it is impossible, owing to its conflicting with a universal and unalterable law of cause and effect, because I have already shown you that your proposition is not of universal application."

"Sir," exclaimed Mr. Yamada, "your reasoning is shrewd and just. But how do you answer this question : If God made all things, who then created time and space ?"

"Your question is a reasonable one," replied Mr. Plympton, "and I will answer it thus : God has no beginning nor end ; time and space have no beginning nor end ; therefore I believe that time and space are but attributes of God. If you ask me to explain how or why, I candidly reply that I cannot. My intellect was evidently made for use in this world only, and it cannot grasp subjects of such vast scope. I can merely state my belief. And I think that you will admit that my belief is not an unreasonable one. Surely it is more reasonable to assume this position than to take the other horn of the dilemma, and assert that no God exists. Humanity has attained to more exalted spheres of development by taking my attitude, than by taking the degrading and cowardly attitude of the infidel."

"You have well spoken !" exclaimed Mr. Yamada.

"Having thus shown to you," continued Mr. Plympton, "that there is nothing inherently impossible about there being a Supreme Being existing from all eternity and never having had any cause, I will now endeavor to state my reasons for believing that such a Being does really exist in this universe. Do you think it more probable that the material universe was the result of chance, or that it was brought about by some intelligent cause ?"

"It would be impossible, sir, for us to arrive at so ridiculous and improbable a conclusion as that it came about by chance," replied Mr. Yamada, after a brief pause ; "the Buddhists teach such a doctrine, but they are notoriously credulous in all things. Should we assume any such position as that, we could not blame you if you were at once to shut off all debate and to pronounce us to be too silly to converse with. It appears more reasonable and probable to me that the material universe was brought about by some intelligent cause,— although I am free to confess my inability to comprehend how or why. As there does not appear to be any third hypothesis in this matter, I feel compelled to choose what appears to my mind to be the more reasonable of two very mysterious propositions. Should I deny the existence of a creative cause in the universe, you would be in a position to force me to deny my own existence, to say nothing of compelling me to deny the existence of all material objects. I can no more prove the existence of the material universe than I can prove the existence of a creative cause. Yet my mind is so constructed that I am compelled to believe in the former, and to attribute its existence to the latter."

"I thank you for your candor," replied Mr. Plympton earnestly, "it will make a difficult task easier. I will now give you my reasons for believing that a Supreme Being does exist in the universe. But before plunging into this difficult subject, I must say a few words about the kind of evidence needed for my purpose. You must bear in mind that each department of human learning has processes of proof peculiar to itself. You must not expect me to prove a historic fact otherwise than by historic methods of proof. As a matter of fact, no fact can be demonstrated. All that you can do is to adduce sufficient evidence to satisfy reasonable belief that such and such a fact did actually happen at some time or other, whether recent or remote. In mathematics you demonstrate your propositions by means of lines, angles, and figures, after assuming said lines, angles, and figures to be correct. In chemistry you demonstrate the correctness of your theories by experimental tests with various chemical substances, after assuming that any given set of substances are really what they purport to be.

"As an eminent scientific gentleman of modern times has expressed it,—'the bases of both science and religion are grounded on faith.' That is to say, you are compelled to take the fundamental principles of all sciences on faith, just as you are compelled to take the fundamental principles of the Christain religion on faith. In the domain of history and of law you prove your propositions by means of certain well-established principles of testimony. To demand that a mathematical proposition should be proved by the methods used for proving chemical or legal matters, would be absurd. Equally absurd would it be to refuse to believe an historic fact because it is not susceptible of mathematical demonstration.

"Now you gentlemen must bear in mind that all proof at best—no matter in what department of human learning it may chance to be—is but approximate: Nothing can be proved absolutely, beyond peradventure or doubt. There is no such thing as infallible demonstration. You must always exercise your faith and assume certain fundamental principles to be correct, before you can proceed with proof of any description whatsoever. All that human law requires in adjusting the most momentous affairs is that the evidence brought forward to prove any given proposition shall be sufficient to satisfy reasonable belief. When the reason of the average community has been satisfied upon any given point, it will generally appear that the evidence adduced to sustain that point was sufficient. Now the existence of God and of Christ can only be proved (so to speak) by testimony, and this testimony I hope will be sufficient to satisfy your reasonable belief, as it has been sufficient to satisfy the reasonable belief of the Caucasian race for many centuries."

"Sir," exclaimed Mr. Yamada, "your remarks are indeed to the point. It is only with the testimony that has satisfied you and your race that I wish to deal. The entire field of argument deducing the existence of a Creator from analogy and design I have carefully gone over with my intelligent young companion here, who has studied the subject from your books during many years. I am prepared to concede the arguments of your learned writers. There is certainly sufficient evidence of design in this world of ours to suggest an intelligent Creator. The tables, books, and chairs in this room here denote an intelligent cause so clearly that nobody but a blockhead would question the fact. Your watch and clothes also indicate an intelligent cause. Houses, ships, roads, castles, steam-engines, and a myriad of other things about us indicate, beyond peradventure or doubt, intelligent causes. Therefore I am prepared to admit at once that the material universe about us gives such abundant evidence of design that by analogy we are compelled to attribute some intelligent cause to the existence of all the wonderful things that we see about us. Thus having the existence of a Creator so powerfully suggested to us on every side, and also having in our hearts a well-defined intuition that such a Creator does really exist somewhere in the universe, it remains for us to search for testimony asserting his existence as a positive fact."

"Do you see that orange-tree growing in the yard?" said Mr. Plympton, abruptly, as he turned toward the window.

"I do," replied Mr. Yamada.

"What was its origin?" was the next question.

"It grew from an orange seed, sir," was the prompt reply.

"Excuse the simplicity of my question," continued Mr. Plympton, "but pray tell me whence came that orange seed?"

"It came, sir, from an orange that had been produced by some other orange-tree."

"Precisely so," exclaimed Mr. Plympton, "and it is thus that you trace back from tree to seed for many centuries, till you come to the original seed (brought from China perhaps), whence have sprung the myriads of orange-trees that to-day adorn the islands of Dai-Nippon. Yet none of us ever set eyes on that original seed. The millions of seeds and trees that have sprung into existence during the past centuries have long since become dust. Nobody to-day living has ever seen them. Even the seed from which yonder tree sprouted has long since disappeared. Yet there is no reasonable doubt but what the present orange-trees of Japan have descended from the orange-trees of the middle ages, and that in turn those trees were the descendants of some primeval seed that first took root in the soil of Dai-Nippon many ages before. These facts are established by human testimony handed down from generation to generation. This testimony is the only evidence obtainable in the premises. You may call it weak and unsatisfactory, yet it is sufficient to satisfy humanity of the reasonableness of the proposition, that orange-trees grow from orange seeds and have always done so even to remotest ages."

"Sir," exclaimed Mr. Yamada, "your proposition is certainly well proven. Should anybody be silly enough to reject it upon the ground of insufficiency of evidence, I would decree that he be forbidden to taste the fruit of the trees until such time as his perceptions had become clearer."

"Do you see this Japanese book that I am holding in my hand?" continued Mr. Plympton, taking up a volume from the table.

"I do," was the reply.

"What is it?"

"It is a native history of the great warrior Taiko-sama who lived three hundred years ago."

"How do you know such to be the case?"

"Because I recognize the volume as being similar to one in my possession. The two books manifestly belong to the same edition of the historian's work."

"Precisely so," replied Mr. Plympton; "and upon the testimony of this book you believe that such a character as Taiko-sama existed three centuries ago and did really perform the deeds credited to him. You believe all this even though you never saw him nor have ever seen anybody who has spoken to him. All the witnesses of his deeds have long since passed away, and many generations intervene between you and the historian who chronicled his achievements. The original manuscripts of the author have long since crumbled to dust. Successive editions of his works have disappeared from the face of the earth. Yet I take up this modern edition of his work and say that, like the orange-tree, it has sprung from the seed of previous editions back to the original manuscript of the author, and that his statements as embodied in that original manuscript and based upon the testimony of his cotemporaries who were familiar with the doings of Taiko-sama I believe to be substantially correct. By the methods of historic proof the life and deeds of that great warrior are thus sufficiently proved to satisfy reasonable belief. But what book is this that I now hold before you?"

"Sir," replied Tomokichi to whom Mr. Yamada had passed the book as being in an unknown language, "it is an English translation of the "Commentaries of Julius Cæsar"—a great Roman warrior who lived two thousand years ago."

"Precisely so," observed Mr. Plympton, "and it establishes with reasonable certainty the doings of that wonderful man, even though his original manuscripts have long since crumbled to dust, even though all the first copies of his seed-germ have disappeared from the face of the earth, even though not a single copy of the innumerable editions of his work issued during nearly seventeen centuries are to-day extant, and even though nearly two thousand years have elapsed since the time when he was on earth. And I have no hesitation in saying that I believe this English translation that you now hold is a substantially correct copy of the statements contained in the original manuscript that came from the hand of Julius Cæsar. The historic proof is sufficient to satisfy reasonable belief, and as such it is accepted as satisfactory by humanity. The people of the present age take judicial cognizance of the fact that great historic characters have existed whenever a satisfactory chain of evidence certified by successive generations of human testimony reaches back through the centuries to their deeds.

"And whoever refuses to be convinced by this method of human testimony generally has some special reason for so doing. Pride of intellect has led some scholars to question the existence of the great Greek poet, Homer, even after the very foundations of ancient Troy—the subject of his most famous poem—were discovered. Even the authorship of the poems of the illustrious English poet Shakespeare, who lived about the time Taiko-sama did, has been denied by modern critics, who seem to think it presumptuous for a common plebeian schoolmaster and despised playwright to produce such sublime thoughts, and consequently attribute their authorship to a nobleman of the realm. In short, honored sirs, I wish to lay down this simple proposition, that to the candid mind of average humanity the existence and the deeds of all historic characters can be sufficiently well established to satisfy reasonable belief, and that to the bitterly prejudiced mind nothing whatever can be proved. Now let me ask you, my young friend, to tell us what is the nature of the book that I now hand to you."

"It is the sacred book of the Christians," replied Tomokichi.

"Precisely so," said Mr. Plympton, "and in it you will find the record of the birth, the life, and the death of the founder of the Christian faith. The original records were made by four eye-witnesses of the facts, who all substantially agree in their statements. The truthfulness of the records of these four historians was not questioned by the generation in which they lived. Their assertions related to matters of common knowledge. It did not occur to anybody in that age to doubt them. During the past eighteen centuries innumerable editions of these four histories have been issued and scattered over the face of the earth. Successive generations of men have testified to and verified the authenticity of the various editions. Copies of several of the ancient editions are to-day extant,—same issued five hundred years ago, some issued over one thousand years ago, and one issued fifteen hundred years ago. Critical and scholarly comparisons show that these editions all substantially agree in their statements. This powerful and overwhelming cumulative evidence does not exist in the matter of Cæsar's Commentaries.

"Therefore, while I do not hesitate to allege that the English translation just shown to you is a substantially correct copy of Cæsar's original manuscript, with how much greater assurance am I able to assert that these four Gospels are correct copies of the original manuscripts of the four disciples of Christ. Had these histories been false, their veracity would have been impeached by the cotemporaries of the Apostles. But their truthfulness has been so well established by eighteen centuries of successful defence that the rules of testimony will not permit them, nor any portion of them, to be ruled out of evidence by the pompously dogmatic and fanatically prejudiced infidels of the nineteenth century. I therefore lay down this proposition, which I think all candid minds will accept as a reasonable one—namely, that about eighteen centuries ago there lived in the vicinity of Jerusalem a person named Jesus Christ, and that he lived, taught, and died substantially as alleged in the book that you are now holding in your hand."

"Sir," exclaimed Mr. Yamada, "what candid mind could dispute such a proposition? Your sacred book is better authenticated than any ancient work in existence. When grains of wheat were discovered in the ancient tombs of the Egyptians, the scientific men of Europe felt justified in asserting that wheat grew in the valley of the Nile several thousand years ago. No reasonable mind will question this assertion. When a copy of your Gospels, fifteen hundred years old, was found at a monastery among the mountains just south of Palestine, the scientific theologians of Europe were justified in alleging that at that early date your sacred book was in circulation among the people. Your chain of evidence connecting the statements contained in this book with the birth, life, teaching, and death of Jesus Christ is too strong to be broken. I must admit that the allegations of these Gospels actually transpired as herein asserted.

But what has all this to do with proving the existence of a Supreme Being?"

"I will now proceed to show you the relevancy of this chain of evidence, my friend. Having shown that such a person as Jesus Christ did actually exist as stated in this volume that has received the judicial cognizance of humanity, and that he was a just and good man, as herein alleged, I therefore produce him as my first witness as to the existence of a Supreme Being. His testimony, made in anticipation of immediate death, while he was in the full possession of all his faculties and in the presence of a court of justice, is in its nature a most solemn legal deposition,—than which nothing more trustworthy is known in the realm of human jurisprudence. Dying declarations have ever ranked as the best evidence in courts of law.

" Now what did this person testify? Let us see. It will appear upon examining the records that he not only asserted that there was a Supreme Being, seen and known by him, but also that he was the son of that Supreme Being, incarnated in human form. He asserted that this Supreme Being was the creator of the universe and of the human race, that he had existed from all eternity and would continue to exist for ever, and that he had sent his only begotten Son into the world to redeem men from their sins, and to prepare their souls for the immortal existence that lay beyond the grave. He persisted in making these stupendous statements from boyhood up to mature years.

" The Jewish nation had already admitted the existence of the Supreme Being upon the testimony of their great lawgiver Moses, who, according to the well-authenticated volumes of the Pentateuch, had seen and talked with him on various occasions, fifteen hundred years prior to Christ's birth. During those fifteen hundred years a long line of patriarchs, prophets, and kings testified repeatedly from personal knowledge that there existed behind the phenomena of nature an intelligent creative power or Supreme Being. Their testimony was reduced to writing and was handed down in volumes as well authenticated as the 'Commentaries of Julius Cæsar.' From Adam downward, testimony of this description had repeatedly been made both orally and by manuscript, until there existed no doubt in the minds of the Jewish people that such a Supreme Being did actually exist. They worshipped him with the profoundest veneration, and adopted the moral and political code that he gave to Moses. So solemn was the veneration for this Being, that they had decreed that any Jew guilty of claiming to be his equal should be put to death as being a blasphemer.

"According to this law, when Christ made his stupendous claims he incurred the death penalty unless he could make good his assertions. During the days of his youth, but little attention appears to have been given to his claims by the Jewish authorities. But when he had attained to years of discretion and still persisted in his claims, there arose angry protests and ominous threatenings. And when he began to preach his astounding doctrines and to verify his allegations with miracles, then multitudes believed on him and accepted him as the Son of God. Three years of such work produced the profoundest agitation in Judea. The authorities were reduced to the necessity of either proclaiming him to be a blasphemer worthy of death or of admitting his claims and surrendering their own power. In their own minds they rejected his claims, but they dared not arrest him in public because of his numerous following.

"At length they succeeded in capturing him one night, through the treachery of one of his disciples. Without delay they carried him before the highest tribunal of the Jewish nation,—the renowned Sanhedrim. The issue presented at the trial was a very simple one : 'This man claims to be the Son of God. Is he, or is he not?' In the most solemn manner the presiding judge of the court put the question to the prisoner : 'I adjure thee by the living God that thou tell us whether thou be the Christ, the Son of God!' Jesus answered, 'I am.'

"Then the judge pronounced him to be a blasphemer, and the court condemned him as being worthy of death. On the following morning the Sanhedrim with great difficulty secured a permit for the execution of their prisoner from the Roman pro-consul of Judea, who would not grant it until he had made public protest as to the injustice of sentencing an innocent man to death. The Romans, being pagans, did not consider blasphemy to be sufficient ground for passing sentence of death on a man. Christ was accordingly condemned to a lingering death on the cross in order to pacify the tumultuous mob of Jews that followed the Sanhedrim. Even in his death agonies he persisted in his claims. He promised to open the gates of Paradise to the soul of the dying thief beside him, and when his own sad hour had come he exclaimed in a loud voice, ' Father, into thy hands I commend my spirit,'—and died amid seismic and atmospheric manifestations of so supernatural a character that the pagan soldiers of the Roman guard stationed at the foot of the cross exclaimed: ' Truly this was the Son of God.'

"Therefore, my inquiring friends, I introduce in evidence upon the issue whether or not there be a Supreme Being the duly recorded living and dying declarations of Jesus Christ, who was crucified for claiming to be the Son of that Supreme Being, and who died testifying to humanity the existence of an immortal life after death. In the second place, I introduce in evidence the documentary testimony of Moses and of the Hebrew prophets and kings cited in the Old Testament, — the correctness of whose records has been vouched for by the Jewish people for over two thousand years, and whose pages unequivocally predicted the coming of Christ, and also taught the doctrine of immortality. In the third place, I introduce in evidence, to offset the verdict of the Sanhedrim pronouncing Christ to be a blasphemous man, the testimony of eighteen centuries of intelligent worshippers of all nations under heaven, declaring themselves to be satisfied with his claims and believing that he was indeed the Son of God.

Multitudes of these witnesses have perished in the arena and at the stake declaring the reality of the invisible communion between their redeemed souls and God, thus bearing testimony to the consolation which had been promised by Christ to his followers in all ages and lands,—that Comforter which he would send upon his departure from this earth. And finally, I introduce in evidence the steady growth of this belief since the time of Christ's crucifixion, until to-day it is almost universally adopted by the Caucasian race.

" This universality of belief is powerful evidence, notwithstanding the infidel allegation that ' in the world of thought majorities count for nothing and that truth has always dwelt with the few.' Did not the idea of one God dwell with a few at first ? Did it not first spring from one family, then from one tribe, then from one nation, until it became largely spread over the world ? Has it not been slowly accepted by reasoning mankind as the most reasonable hypothesis ? Did not the religion of Christ spring from a single thoughtful individual, then from a few families, and then merge into the thoughtful portions of a few nations in the teeth of the bitterest opposition that the world has ever seen ? Has not this truth dwelt with a thoughtful few ? Whilst the pagan world went wild with the mad carnival of war, rapine, and lust, whilst the Roman epicureans pronounced all of the countless gods enshrined within their Pantheon to be merely myths and phantoms born of the imagination, and whilst the Greek philosophers declared intelligence, the expanding of the human intellect, the practice of virtue, the discoveries of science, the inventions of genius, and the cultivation of the imagination through art and music to be sufficient to redeem the human race—to be the saviors of mankind !—did not a few thoughtful Christian communities become in those ages of shameless debauch and nameless cruelties the conservators of virtue and call the world to order ? "

" O most learned sir," exclaimed Mr. Yamada, deeply impressed with the long and eloquent address of the missionary, "that which you say has great power of conviction. So far as the laws of human testimony and of historic evidence are concerned your position appears to be impregnable. A reasonable mind should be satisfied that Christ was crucified for claiming to be the Son of God, that the thoughtful portions of the Caucasian race for eighteen centuries have allowed his claim to be a well-founded one, and that the most intelligent, the most powerful, the most scientific, the most inventive, and the most cultured and virtuous nations of the nineteenth century are at least nominally Christian.

"But I am troubled with two questions that I will now propound to you, sincerely hoping that you may be able to answer them as satisfactorily as you have answered those already put to you. The first question has been culled from infidel literature by my young friend here, and is as follows : ' The sentence *there is a God* could have been imprinted on every blade of grass, on every leaf, on every star ; an infinite God has no excuse for leaving his children in doubt and darkness ! ' Of course it would be grotesque to think of God as scribbling his name all over the universe, and from that standpoint the demand is stupid and unreasonable. But it seems to me that on so important a matter as the existence of a Supreme Being there might have been some evidence beside mere design and historic evidence corroborating our intuitions on the subject. It seems to me that there should be some evidence so convincing that nobody could dispute it. My second question is as follows : Why could not God—aside from the question of the atonement—have devised some other method of redeeming men from their sins without having his Son pass through such a frightful ordeal of suffering. This second question is more speculative than the first one, and I do not know as it can be answered. In fact, both questions are childish and petulant, but I ask them in order to obtain your views on the subject."

"Your questions, sir," replied Mr. Plympton, "are very natural, and have puzzled the speculative minds of

Christendom for many centuries. Of course I can only give speculative answers, as God in his wisdom does not appear to have deemed it essential to man's salvation to explain such matters to him. Your first question, I think, has been indirectly answered by Christ in the famous parable of Dives and Lazarus.

"You will remember that Dives, after having lived the life of an Oriental voluptuary, finally died in his sins and was consigned to a place of torment as punishment for his numerous transgressions. Lazarus, on the other hand, was found at death to be pure in heart, and was admitted to the abodes of the blessed. In this cele-brated allegory Dives is represented as calling to Abra-ham across the impassable abyss that intervened be-tween paradise and hell, and begged him to send Lazarus to earth in order to warn his (Dives') kindred and friends to flee from the wrath to come by leading purer lives than he himself had led while on earth surrounded by luxury and refinement. The answer that went back across that fathomless gulf touches a very peculiar chord in human nature: ' *They have Moses and the prophets ; let them hear them. If they hear not Moses and the prophets, neither will they be persuaded though one rose from the dead.'* In the matter of choosing between right and wrong man has always shown himself to be a very obsti-nate and perverse free agent. In all matters left open to him to form opinions and beliefs about he has gen-erally shown himself to be erratic and stubborn in his views. In such matters it is useless to drive him. Your only course is to reason with him and to persuade him. Failing in this, you had better let him alone. Such is the matured verdict of humanity. If you cannot convince a man after having laid before him a reason-able amount of evidence—such an amount as would satisfy the average reasoning intellect of mankind,— then no amount of cumulative evidence that you may choose to heap up will be likely to convince him. This is a peculiarity of human nature that appears to be uni-versal.

"Therefore, when men refuse to believe in the existence of God, after having the testimony of Moses, the prophets, and of Christ endorsed by the sanction of eighteen centuries of devout disciples, and powerfully corroborated by the analogies of nature and the intuitions of the human heart, it is not likely that any accumulation of testimony would avail—not even if 'one rose from the dead,' or if God were to 'scribble his name all over the universe.' I lay it down as a proposition verified by the experience of mankind, that when a reasonable amount of proof fails to convince a man then any amount of superabundant testimony rarely suffices to convince him.

" This has been found to be so even in matters of profoundest importance. People have been warned not to live in certain malarious districts, yet they have done so in spite of friendly advice and have perished in untold thousands. People have been warned not to live at the base of volcanic mountains, yet they have persisted in doing so and have perished miserably. People have lived in narrow valleys with vast bodies of water insecurely dammed up in the highlands, whence, if once set free, the descending torrents would surely scour out the valley. Yet people have persisted in living in such dangerous places even after repeated warnings so strong in their nature that nothing could have been more convincing. I knew of one case where such a dam had been known to be unsafe for many years ; where, during a rainy season, the people had been warned weeks beforehand that it was daily weakening ; where, on the very morning of the disastrous day, skilled engineers had warned the people to flee to the mountains to escape the flood ; where, but an hour or so before the catastrophe occurred, urgent messengers had sped down the valley and begged the people to escape to places of safety ; and where, in the very face of death the people laughed to scorn all warnings and were swept to destruction by the down-pouring torrents. In this case reasonable proof of danger failed to convince the general community. Then cumulative and overwhelming proofs were produced with the same results. Though one were to have risen from the dead, though God were to have scribbled danger-signals all over the universe, I doubt whether the people living in that valley could have been convinced after the failure of reasonable proof.

"What can be more momentous than matters of life and death? Yet men have repeatedly ignored reasonable warnings of physical danger. So is it in matters pertaining to the welfare of the soul. Men persist in ignoring reasonable proofs and warnings, and perish in their sins. Men have received sufficient notice of the existence of a Supreme Being and of a future life. Those who will not be convinced now, I feel assured, will not be convinced though one were to rise from the dead. Nothing can be proved to those unwilling to believe. Thus I answer your question."

"It is ingeniously and well answered," exclaimed Mr. Yamada.

"As regards your second question," continued Mr. Plympton, "I shall answer it somewhat after this fashion : According to the Gospel records Christ proclaimed his visit to our world to have a twofold object. In the first place, he came to atone for the sins of humanity. This mysterious doctrine I accept on faith. I am free to confess that I do not comprehend it. It is a matter that lay between God and his Son. I take Christ's word for it, and assume that his sacrifice was essential to the redemption of mankind. In the second place, he proclaimed himself to mankind as the founder and the exemplar of a new divine system of moral ethics that he desired the human race to practise even as he practised it.

"This second object of Christ's coming is of vast importance. The great trouble with all human systems of morality has been that the expounders thereof failed to practise what they themselves urged other men to practise. Even in those exceedingly rare cases where the founders of systems of morality actually practised their own doctrines, yet men in general would not practise those precepts because they denied the authority of fellow-mortals to set up such standards and force them on humanity. The result has been that while moral teachers have said to men, 'you ought to do this and you ought not to do that,' nobody obeyed beyond their own inclinations in the matter, and each one did as he pleased. Under such conditions no lofty system of morality requiring self-denial and the crushing of base animal instincts could ever prevail among men, because neither inducement nor authority were at hand to urge men to lead lives of rigid and austere virtue. When men came to the point where some pet appetite had to be curbed or some passion had to be subdued, they graciously said: 'Excuse me, if you please,' and passed over to the other side of the way, upon the principle that in moral matters men were born free and equal, and that nobody had the right to dictate to his fellow-creatures what he should do and what he should not do.

"But Christ came teaching the most sublime system of moral ethics that the world has ever seen,—a system most difficult to practise in many of its details, and directly opposed to the strongest appetites and passions of the human race. He not only taught this system of morality, but he practised it literally and rigidly in all the details of his own life, and required all of his disciples to do the same. As an inducement for thus running counter to the currents of their inclinations, he taught that the objective point of man's existence was immortal life with him in paradise. He proclaimed that he was the Son of God, and that all power in heaven and on earth had been given to him, and that men must obey and practise his precepts. Thus was his system of moral ethics based upon authority from which there could be no appeal, as it was the highest in the universe. He taught and practised his teachings even to the bitter end, and allowed himself to be slain by mankind, thus forever shutting the door by which men had been perpetually escaping from the rigid practice of austere virtue.

"The disciples of Christ cannot excuse themselves from practising Christian morality because it is difficult and runs against the fierce currents of their appetites and passions—against the downward tendency of all their animal instincts. The Son of God allowed himself to be crucified for proclaiming and practising a divine system of moral ethics, and his followers must practise in the same way, even if called upon to suffer martyrdom (as vast multitudes have actually done). Based upon such authority this noble religion has overcome all obstacles, and has shown itself to be a priceless gift to humanity. It is fulfilling the prophecy of its founder, and is spreading to the uttermost parts of the earth with joy and healing in its wings. Do you wonder that we Christians glory in the cross of Christ? Are not the results worth the sacrifice? The cross has become to the devout followers of the crucified Redeemer the sign of their divine authority to preach to perishing humanity. Armed with this emblem of the bitterest anguish that the world has ever witnessed, we shall conquer the world for Christ. All the powers of evil—the very gates of hell—shall not prevail against us. This is the only answer, honorable sirs, that I can give to your question."

"O most learned instructor," exclaimed Mr. Yamada, "that which you have just spoken makes clear much that was obscure in my mind. It is manifest that you Caucasians are a matter-of-fact race of people, who take a common-sense business view of every thing. Recognizing the fact that men are religious by nature and possess ineradicable intuitions concerning the existence of some supreme and intelligent power behind the phenomena of nature, you then select that religion which offers proof of its divine origin, and give it to the people as being reasonable and just in its claims. As in all your commercial transactions your operations are based, more or less, on speculative estimates that appear to be reasonably certain of producing certain results, so in your religious calculations you proceed on faith and hard-headed common-sense.

"Certain facts in this world are like mules,—if you ig-
nore them and dash yourself against them you are liable
to be kicked to death. You Caucasians have found out
that popular morality cannot be developed without a
religion of some sort, that in moral matters men are free
agents and refuse to be dictated to by their fellow-men,
and that for fully ninety per cent. of humanity this life
from beginning to end is but a series of hardships and
cheerless strugglings for a bare existence. You have
found out that life for the toiling masses of humanity is
not worth the living. You have found out that men need
encouragement and sympathy to enter the bitter and piti-
less contest for existence that rages around the world.

"Therefore, when Christ proclaims the fatherhood of
God and the brotherhood of men, and enunciates a
matchless system of morality based upon divine authority and offering priceless inducements to the struggling
creatures of this world to bear up cheerfully under their
heavy burdens, then you gladly accept his teachings on
faith as he directed his followers always to do, and you
make human life a glorious and magnificent period of
probationary existence. And then, when you observe
the stupendous effects of the principles of Christianity
upon the spiritual, the mental, and the physical development of your race after eighteen centuries of practice,
you very naturally deem the prophecy of Christ as fully
verified,—you insist that the effects of his teachings on
humanity satisfactorily demonstrate all of his claims to
being the Son of One who thoroughly understood the
minutest peculiarities of human nature. Sir, your position is impregnable. It is based on the matured conclusions of the shrewdest race on the face of the earth. I
also believe in God, and in Christ his Son! But, sir,
how am I to enter on this life of Christian development?"

"Sir," exclaimed Mr. Plympton, with great feeling,
"you have already entered upon the path. Continue as
you have begun. Read the Scriptures daily. Pray at
seasonable and regular periods to the Almighty Father.
Never allow the spark of reformation of desire to be-

come extinguished in your soul. Make public profession of your new beliefs before your countrymen, by means of the beautiful ceremony of baptism. Then indeed will you be born of water and the Spirit! Then will you enter upon that glorious life of self-conquest and of spiritual development that our blessed Redeemer has promised to every soul that God has sent into the world.

"Sir, I extend to you the right hand of fellowship. It matters but little to me with what Christian denomination you may choose to identify yourself. When I first set foot upon your shores I was zealous to propagate the theological views of my own peculiar sect. But now, thanks be to God, the beauty and the grandeur of Apostolic Christianity—the teachings of Christ himself—have dawned upon my soul in their full majesty, and have put to flight my narrow theories and metaphysical dogmas. Love God and keep his commandments. Then shall we always be friends. Honorable sirs, the day is drawing speedily to a close, and other duties demand my attention, so that our interview must terminate; but feel free to call upon me at any time that you may desire so to do. Farewell! May God be with you and ever guide you in the spiritual war upon which you have entered under the leadership of his beloved Son!"

CONCLUSION.

My God, I love thee—not because
I hope for heaven thereby :
Nor yet because, if I love not,
I must forever die.

But, O my Jesus, thou didst me
Upon the cross embrace ;
For me didst bear the nails and spear,
And manifold disgrace,
And griefs and torments numberless,
And sweat of agony,
E'en death itself ;—and all for me,
Who was thine enemy !

Then why, O blessèd Jesus Christ,
Should I not love thee well ?
Not for the hope of winning heaven,
Nor of escaping hell ;
Not with the hope of gaining aught,
Not seeking a reward ;
But as thyself hast lovèd me,
O ever-loving Lord !

E'en so I love thee, and will love,
And in thy praise will sing ;
Solely because thou art my God,
And my eternal King.

—A translation of a Latin hymn, written by Saint Francis Xavier, apostle to Japan, 1550 A.D.

MANY years have elapsed since the closing scenes in the last chapter. Momentous changes have taken place in the Empire of the Rising Sun. Feudalism has disappeared from the face of the land, and the Emperor has granted a constitutional form of government to the people. A complete system of telegraphic wires stretches all over the country. The steamboat and the railway have revolutionized methods of travel. Newspapers circulate freely, and a most efficient postal system makes it easy to communicate with the remotest provinces. Schools and colleges of the highest grade have been established in the great centres of population, and general intelligence and learning are being scattered broadcast throughout the land.

Not less marked have been the changes in the religious features of the country. Buddhism has been disestablished as the state religion of the realm, and has been contemptuously set aside as having been "weighed in the balance and found wanting," and its stagnated life is slowly ebbing away, notwithstanding the frantic efforts of the priests to assimilate Christianity and to spawn it on the country as a modified Buddhism. During all these years the religion of Christ has advanced with steady strides to conquest after conquest, until its converts now cover the empire, and are to be numbered by the thousands. It is not only tolerated by the Japanese government, but it is directly and indirectly encouraged in many ways. One of its most eloquent and able advocates is Tomokichi, the son of Nakashima.

Shortly after the interview set forth in the last chapter, Mr. Yamada and his entire household made public profession of Christianity by receiving baptism at the hands of Mr. Plympton, and from that time onward he became a most zealous and valuable supporter of Christianity. The path upon which he had entered, however, was by no means one of roses. He had to face coldness and derision on all sides. But he persisted in his course, and in a few years saw many of those who had derided his action come forth and acknowledge the saving and elevating power of Christ's teachings. He grew daily in favor with his government, who gladly availed themselves of his adroit ability and loyal faithfulness by promoting him to positions of great responsibility and trust.

Through his influence Tomokichi and Kunisaburo were sent abroad, and were educated in one of the great universities of the United States. Tomokichi then graduated from a theological seminary, while his brother went through a thorough course of medicine and surgery in New York City. Returning to Japan, they took charge of a school of Christian morality that had been founded by Mr. Yamada during their absence. Here they settled down to lives of great usefulness. Doctor K. Yamada (née Nakashima) organized a dispensary and a hospital, and became greatly celebrated for his medical and surgical skill ; and his name spread into foreign lands as being the author of a famous treatise on the diseases peculiar to the Japanese people. The Rev. T. Nakashima became, as before intimated, an eloquent and powerful expounder of Christian doctrines. His sermons were eagerly listened to by multitudes of his fellow-countrymen. He received calls to preach and to lecture in all parts of the empire, and his sermons were put into print and were eagerly read by the people everywhere. As to our friend Konishi, my report is equally flattering. He was rapidly promoted from one post of honor to another until he was finally sent abroad to represent his country in an important diplomatic position, where he now resides with his family.

The speeding years are now leaving deep imprints upon the brow of old Mr. Yamada, but he heeds them not, although he begins to notice that his eyes are not as clear nor is his hand as firm as in the days of yore, when he roamed the mountain fastnesses of Yamato and Shinshiu. The greatest delight of his old age is to see his countrymen advancing in all that pertains to elevation of character and to intellectual and material development. It is the delight of his heart to aid the deserving and to encourage the despondent. Thus loved by his neighbors and revered by his friends, he is peacefully and joyfully approaching that spiritual kingdom for which he has so long been preparing his soul. Like a tale that is told, like a dream that has flown, the shadows of the past have faded from our view ; and, as the shades of the sweet islands of the sea float away from our gaze, we bid a long farewell to the scenes of Old Japan.

www.ingramcontent.com/pod-product-compliance
Lightning Source LLC
Chambersburg PA
CBHW022028120726
47901CB00006BA/1509